DEVOURING THE DEAD

RUSS WATTS

PART ONE

GROWTH

CHAPTER ONE

Andrew James Collins had gone through his regular Monday morning procedure like every other week: up at six, teeth brushed, face washed, and out the door by six fifteen for a run. It was getting harder to leave his sleeping wife, Grace, when he got up. All he really wanted to do was snuggle down under the covers with her. With a baby on the way, she had had to give up the running and he was sad she couldn't come with him anymore. He was looking forward to being a father for the first time though. These early morning runs gave him the chance to think about the future. He forced himself out of bed nearly every morning, the upcoming marathon was his prime motivator. This one would be his third and he wanted to improve on last years' time.

He kissed his wife goodbye and crept out of the bedroom discreetly. Andy pulled on his trainers and did his normal warm-up downstairs in the front room, doing some basic stretching. He left the house quietly and took off down the street. It was overcast and threatening to rain, so he planned to make today's run a quick one and cut through the park. He passed through the streets, listening to the world waking up around him. The odd car and delivery truck passed him by and occasionally he would run past someone on the path clutching a newspaper or a carton of milk.

He ran through Jamaica Street quickly, down another quiet residential road, until he reached Stepney Green Park. He knew he could run around it this morning, double-back on himself, and that way hopefully beat the weather. If he was doubly lucky, he could get back in time for a cuddle with Grace before he had to get ready for work in the city.

As he jogged through the park, he enjoyed the smell of the grass and the trees. His breath fogged out in front of him in the crisp air and he ran past a park bench where an old man was sleeping, covered in soggy newspapers. There was another jogger on the far side of the park, but otherwise it was deserted. The sky overhead was darkening ominously and he increased his pace.

A boom of thunder rolled out above the trees and he felt a large raindrop break on his head. The thunder faded away and Andy followed the curve of the path through the park and out into the open. If the raindrops became a downpour, there would be little shelter. There was a crack and a flash and Andy thought it was lightning, but the ground abruptly exploded in front of him. Grass, mud, and dirt flew up into the electrified air.

He went sprawling, landing on the dewy grass. Clumps of sodden earth landed on him and he tasted blood in his mouth. He got to his feet and waved his hands in front of his face, trying to waft away the cloying dirt in the air. More thick droplets of rain began falling. Surely, the lightning hadn't struck the ground; there was no conduit. Andy could see nothing for it to strike.

As the air cleared, he saw a hole in the ground ahead, about six feet in diameter. It was circular and deep, and Andy's first thought was that a bomb had gone off. Why would a terrorist detonate a bomb in the middle of an empty park in the morning?

Carefully, Andy walked toward the hole. There was no burning smell, no smoke, and he began to think perhaps it wasn't a bomb. It just didn't make sense.

He scanned around the park but the other jogger had disappeared, and the homeless man was still on the bench sound asleep. Evidently, the noise and the light hadn't been enough to shake off the old man's hangover. Andy couldn't see anyone else around; there were no prying eyes or hidden cameras on the trees, and no sirens or SWAT team sprinting toward him. He took one more step toward the hole and stopped.

A strange, moth-like creature flew up into the air and hovered about ten feet off the ground. If that's a moth, he thought, it's the biggest bloody moth I've ever seen. The body of the creature was the size of a rugby ball and its brown leathery wings stretched out about six feet from tip to tip. Two antennae were sticking out of its head, waving around like divining rods. They were covered in a light fur that appeared oily; the raindrops were splashing off the creature and onto the ground, leaving the flying beast dry.

Andy looked at it with amazement. The creature had no eyes or mouth that he could see; it was like a massive moth with no face. It fluttered its wings slowly and secreted a dark liquid from its rear, a dark gooey substance that dribbled down its belly before dripping onto the earth below. The creature still hovered in the air with only its wing flapping and its antennae wiggling around. Andy took a few paces away and the creature started to follow him. Its wings flapped slowly and Andy was amazed it could remain air-born. He tried to think if he had seen anything like this anywhere before; he'd seen bats and bizarre creatures that lived in remote jungle caves on documentaries, but nothing like this, nothing in a central London park.

He took another few steps and the strange creature followed him again, this time coming closer. He wasn't sure if it was the developing rainstorm, but the air seemed alive, as if the very atoms were crackling.

Thinking he must tell Grace about the weird flying animal, he watched as the flying beast rose higher into the air. Relieved that it was leaving, Andy heard a low humming noise. Looking closer at the moth-like creature, he realised it was coming from the animal. Its body was vibrating, its wings suddenly flapping furiously, and its whole body shuddering. Andy stepped back, alarmed, and the antennae suddenly went stiff, pointing directly at him. He turned and ran as the creature swooped.

He heard the wings beating behind his head, as he ran on the soft and slippery ground. Panicking, he turned and the creature was right in front of his face. Its wings wrapped themselves around his head and the rigid antenna dug themselves into his eyes. Andy screamed as the stinking creature's body enveloped his face, muffling his shouts for help, and covering his bleeding eyes.

Andy sank to the floor, blinded as the antennae probed further into his head, reaching into his brain. Unable to breathe, Andy pulled frantically at the creature, but his fingers could not find a hold and the more he pulled, the more the creature dug in. His fingers slipped uselessly off the creature's furry body. Andy's lungs filled with blood and his heart beat furiously. Aware he was dying, Andy tried with one last attempt, one final adrenalin-fuelled charge, to rip the creature from his head.

The animal's body quivered and with a tremendous thrust, it ejaculated a brown thick liquid into Andy. Its antennae were used for both sensing prey, and delivering its fatal poison. Andy's body pulsed, soiled itself, and lay still as the creature continued trembling, its sticky seed flowing into Andy's brain.

Finally, it was spent and the creature unwrapped itself from him. With its job done, the creature used its last ounce of energy to fly up into the nearest tree where it curled up in the concealing branches to die. The animal knew it had a short life-span, but was content it had fulfilled its purpose. It had little energy left and would probably wait here for a while until it slipped into sleep; unless something else came along to draw its attention.

The storm grew stronger and the rain fell on Andy's dead body, the water pooling in his empty eye sockets. Dark brown droplets of liquid oozed from his ears, nose, and mouth, mingling with blood before trickling down onto the wet ground. Blisters appeared on his face and painful red boils erupted on his neck that popped like fresh kernels of corn in a microwave.

A young woman, another jogger, entered the park a moment later and saw Andy lying on the floor ahead of her. She raced over to him, but she knew that he was clearly dead. Assuming he had suffered a heart attack, she didn't touch his body, but left him alone and called for an ambulance, the police, and then finally her boyfriend to tell him of the excitement. In all the confusion and drama, she didn't notice the unnatural hole in the ground. She was so busy tweeting about the dead jogger in the park that she failed to notice when the ambulance men took Andy away, and a strange, furry, creature with huge wings flew up into the air above her.

* * * *

The bus journey to work changed little, no matter where you were headed, thought Tom. He looked around the bus at the coughing lady, the stinking old man with rolls of newspapers under his arms, the obnoxious school children playing obnoxious music from their obnoxious phones, and the atypical surly driver. Tom tried shuffling further to the window, away from the fat woman next to him whose blubbery rolls of fat were threatening to engulf him and his bag. He cursed her in his head and focused on the street outside, raindrops spilling down the glass and obscuring his vision. He used to get off here, go into college, grab a coffee, chat to a couple of guys on his course, pretend to be interested in what his boring tutor was lecturing him about, shoot home as quickly as possible to avoid doing any real work, and get straight back to doing nothing.

There was no escaping it though - those cushy days were over. One week. His parents had given him one week's grace between leaving college and forcing him to get a job. So here he was, squashed up on a bus that smelt of piss and chips, headed to what was probably going to be a very boring day at a new job. His father had a word with a friend, and got him in 'Fiscal Industries.' Even the company's name sounded boring. Apparently, it was a call centre and he didn't know what he'd be selling. Thanks dad, thought Tom.

He yawned and his breath fogged up the glass. The fat lady got up as the bus stopped, and Tom was grateful he wouldn't have to squeeze past her when he got off at the next stop. The streets were full of people, scurrying through the rain to work. His father had told him he was wasting his time taking media studies at college. Certainly Tom couldn't see how he was going to use his knowledge in a call centre, selling foot-rot pills to old folks for seven quid an hour.

He'd rarely been to this area of the city, but then he'd seldom had cause to. Tom preferred to stay near home or college; there were enough pubs not to need to go into the city. Here, executives, rushing from one meeting to the next, populated it. Why would he want to mix with people he had nothing in common with? Abundant skyscrapers scratched the skyline whilst at ground level, the rain pelted down on grey concrete and black suits.

Tom finally spied the building he had to get to, and pushed the button to get off. He tried not to breathe in as he passed the old man with the newspapers. He slung his satchel over his shoulder, and stepped off the bus into the rain as it pulled up by the side of the road.

"Watch out, idiot," said a nondescript man bumping past him, trying to dodge the raindrops as he rushed to his office. Tom shrugged and looked at his watch: nine a.m. He looked around at where he would be working as the bus pulled away. He stood under the bus shelter, sheltered from the rain, marvelling at the skyscraper in front of him. He tried counting the floors, but could only get up to twelve before the misty rain hid the rest. We used to build churches, he thought, now we have giant, glass, monoliths to worship, and money. C'est la vie.

Tom checked the road and ran across to the entrance. He was struck by how much glass there was: the doors, the walls, and even the tables. Hope they've at least got proper walls in the toilets, he thought, as he slipped unobtrusively through the large sliding doors. The interior of the foyer was huge: marble columns sprouted from a smooth, slippery marble floor, and vast chandeliers hung from the ceiling. Men and women bustled past him, to and fro, ignoring him; Tom felt invisible. He approached the reception desk.

"Good morning," said the beautiful young girl behind the glass desk. Tom couldn't help but notice that her complexion was perfect, and her hands were perfectly manicured. Through the glass desk, he also noticed her long legs. Maybe it wouldn't be so bad working here.

"Hi, I'm Tom, Tom Goode. I'm here to start work today at Fiscal Industries," he said, smiling, while reading her nametag: Jessica.

"Certainly, sir, please take a seat, I'll get someone to come and fetch you," said Jessica. She gave him a smile and picked up the phone.

"Thanks," Tom said. "So, Jessica, what's it like working here? You like it?"

She ignored him and proceeded to ask someone to come down to get him.

"Seats are over there, sir," she said, ignoring his gaze, and spinning her chair around to talk to her colleague.

"Pleased to meet you, too," he muttered, walking away to the black leather sofas. He sat down and marvelled again at the building. The entrance alone was bigger than his entire flat, and the whole place was spotless. Men and women sped past him to the lifts at the far end, already at work on their mobiles. Suddenly Tom felt very out of place. He straightened his tie and looked down at his shoes; he hadn't even polished them this morning. He surreptitiously licked one finger and bent down to rub the scuff marks and dirt off. As he did so, his phone vibrated and he took it out.

"Hi, Mum, I can't really talk, I just got here," he said glancing around and talking quietly. He bet none of the suits filing past him talked to their mothers in the morning.

"You're there already? Oh God, Tom, just leave, come home quick, come now," said his mother rapidly. She spoke without pause, without hesitation. Tom frowned. His mother was not the nervous type or one to worry unduly. Plus, his parents lived miles away, on the edge of the city. It would take him hours to get home.

"What's wrong, Mum?" he asked. "I just got here, I don't think I should leave before I've even..."

"Shut up, Tom, just leave now, something's happened... city... you..."

"Mum? Hello? Mum?" Tom looked at his phone. The line was dead. He tried calling her back, but he just got an engaged tone. Surely if something was wrong, then everyone would know about it? Queues of people were still going past him into the building and outside, it appeared normal. He could see buses and taxis driving past, trees blowing in the storm, and bits of rubbish swirling down the drain. Hundreds of people were spilling out of the tube station. Surely, his mother was mistaken?

"Hi, Tom Goode? I'm Jillian, from Fiscal Industries. Welcome," said the woman standing beside him. She stared at him, holding out her hand.

"Oh, hi, yes, I'm Tom," he said shaking her hand. He stuffed his phone back into his satchel and got up.

"Great, follow me please, I'll take you up. We're on sixteen. Best views across the city - when it's not raining," said Jillian, winking at him.

Tom smiled back and followed her. He would call his mother later at lunch time; she was probably worried about nothing. He was already anxious about his first day at work and an odd phone call from his mother was not helping settle his nerves. He couldn't help but think that today was not going according to plan; the receptionist had been hot, but was a bit of a bitch quite frankly, and then being told to leave the city? He couldn't very well ask his new boss if he could just go and call his mummy, could he?

He followed Jillian to the lift, where she swiped a card outside the door and took him in. She stood facing the doors with Tom behind her, as they rode up with two suits to his right. He looked her up and down; she was probably thirty something, married with kids, no doubt, slim, smartly dressed. She seemed nice enough. Perhaps he was worried about nothing. He would spend the day in a nice warm office, meet some new people, and go home a little bit richer than when he started. Sadly for Tom, he was wrong; he would never go home again.

* * * *

Sally ran so hard; she thought her lungs were going to burst. As a trained nurse, she knew that was not possible, not literally, but she had seen other things today that she knew were not possible; not in the world she lived in, and yet she had seen them. The unimaginable horrors she had seen would not be shaken from her; she forced herself to forget and think about home. She had to get home. Her son would need picking up from school soon. She *had* to get out of here. Her son needed her.

Sally kicked off her shoes as she ran and left them behind. Her bare feet hurt on the road, but she could run faster without her shoes slipping in the rain. She glanced over her shoulder; they were still coming.

When they had brought the body in, they hadn't known the true issue they were dealing with. A male had been found in Stepney Green Park, apparently attacked, the victim of a mugging, and left for dead. First reports were that he had suffered a heart attack, but he had suffered facial wounds consistent with a beating. Whoever had called it in, had been a poor judge, as they had told them that the man was dead. When he arrived at the hospital, he was very much alive. They had to restrain him as he lashed out whenever they tried to help him.

They had taken him straight to ER and worked on him, but he died shortly after. They thought it was a simple mugging gone wrong, although gouging someone's eyes out for twenty quid was unusual. The police went to inform his next of kin, while they, Doctor Collins and Nurse Tina, noted the time of death and began tidying up. The man had fought for his life; he had regained consciousness very briefly before the end, spluttering something about the dark before passing out. His body had been wracked with convulsions and he had vomited blood everywhere. From the state he was in, she had wondered if it really was a simple mugging gone wrong; now she knew better.

As she cleaned the blood off the floor, she heard Tina cry out. Sally had looked up to find the deceased jogger sitting up on the hospital bed, and biting Tina's arm. As Tina tried to push him off, the man bit her harder, ripping skin and tissue away. As the blood poured over Tina's uniform, Doctor Collins tried to push the man back down. Sally could see the Doctor was confused. He had been declared dead two minutes ago, and there was no way they had got it wrong. Sally had to admit she had frozen. She had been trained to deal with angry patients, dangerous ones, and people with mental problems or on drugs; but a dead man coming back to life?

By the time she sounded the alarm, it was too late. Doctor Collins was dead and Tina lay dying. The deceased ran out into the corridor, oblivious to Sally, and she could still hear the echoing screams from the corridor now. After that, it was total mayhem. People were been running all over the place. She heard the police firing shots, something she never dreamed would happen in her hospital, ever.

Venturing out into the corridor, she saw bodies everywhere, people bleeding all over the floor, bloody hand prints on the wall, and a trail of blood and vomit indicating where the deceased man had gone. Doctor Collins rushed out of the emergency room behind her and grabbed her. Luckily, he slipped in a pool of blood and crashed into a gurney. Sally had frozen once again, incredulous that the Doctor could be back on his feet. She had seen his throat being ripped out only minutes earlier. She saw other people in the hospital too, patients she had treated earlier, running around, biting, and clawing at anyone moving. An old wheelchair bound woman, Edith Smyth, crippled with Parkinsons, was holding a young boy up against the wall, sucking at his ragged neck like a vampire. As a doctor ran past, Sally watched Edith drop the boy and run after the doctor. Tina sprung out of the ER, too, blazing past Sally and knocking her over as she ran toward the dying boy on the floor. At that point, Sally ran and didn't look back.

She managed to get out of the hospital with a few others. There was utter chaos and confusion in the entrance as she fled, ignoring her training, and the cries for help. Outside, it was raining and she ran straight across the road, headed for the tube station. She called her sister, Kathleen, and told her what was going on as she waited to get into the station. A crowd of people blocked the entrance though, so she hadn't been able to get in and she knew better than to wait any longer; in seconds, they would be everywhere. She heard the shouts and screams close behind her, and ignored them. If she ran down the embankment, she might make the next tube stop. She prayed it was still running. Dropping her phone while she ran, she left the mob at the station.

Sally ran across the road, dodging taxis, buses, and reached the steps to the river. Fifteen or so wet concrete steps faced her, the hospital was behind her, and her future was in front of her. Looking down, she saw a couple holding hands beneath a large umbrella. They looked up at her and the woman smiled. Sally paused.

"Run. Run! Get away from here as fast as you can!" Sally screamed at them from the top of the steps, and they looked at her, clearly thinking she was mad. It wasn't just the bizarre command to run, but she had bare feet and was drenched. The rain had mixed with the blood soaked shirt she wore and bright crimson drips of water trickled down her arms and fingers.

"Are you all right?" said the man taking a step toward her.

"Brian, be careful," said the young woman.

"It's okay, Lyn," he said. There were sounds of cars sliding and screeching to a halt, horns blaring, and glass shattering from behind the strange woman on the bridge.

"Please," said Sally sniffing, taking a step forward, and trying not to breakdown and cry. She couldn't, not yet; her son would need fetching from school. As the rain splashed her face, she realised she couldn't leave these poor people standing here. It wasn't fair to do that to them. How many people at the hospital had she abandoned: patients, colleagues, and friends? How many were dead, how many alive? "Please trust me and just run."

A figure appeared behind Sally and grabbed her, sending them both flying down the steps and crashing at the couple's feet. The woman screamed as Sally landed on her head, breaking her neck instantly. The man who grabbed her, rolled on top of Sally and his teeth latched onto her cheek, ripping it off. He tore at Sally's face, biting and chewing her supple flesh. Sitting on top of Sally's body, the attacker chewed her skin as blood oozed from his mouth. Lyn screamed. Brian stood stock still, in shock, ignorant to his girlfriend's screaming. The man who killed Sally, stood up and pounced.

Lyn's screaming stopped as they fought; the young woman tried to fend him off, but he was too strong. He fought with her and they inadvertently found themselves by the edge of the Thames. Lyn kicked and punched him, but to no avail. Eventually, she lost her balance and they both fell over the side and into the water.

"Lyn?" whispered Brian. His brain could not process what his eyes were telling him.

"Lyn? Honey?" He slowly approached the river bank and looked over the side. His wife was floating away downstream, face down, in the brown, choppy, water. Her overcoat was heavy and dragging her down into the sludge at the river's edge. The man who had attacked her was stuck in the sludge too, trying to drag himself up the bank and out. The man looked up at Brian and snarled.

Brian dropped the umbrella and fell to his knees. He had to call the police. He had to do something. Lyn was...she had been there a second ago. What had happened? There was no time to do anything though; he had been too slow.

Sally stretched her limbs and crawled to her knees, her crooked neck sloping to the left, and her bloodied face was twisted cruelly. Her eyes locked onto Brian as he sat in the gutter, rainwater puddling around him as he stared at Lyn floating away. Sally crawled over to him on hands and knees. She did not feel the cold concrete beneath her, or hear the vehicles crashing on the bridge above, and she would never reach her son. Brian turned around just in time to see Sally's dead eyes and sharp teeth bearing down on him. It was the last thing Brian saw.

CHAPTER TWO

The tower's security officer, Ranjit, watched closely on the monitor as hundreds of people poured into his building. It wasn't literally his building, of course, but he felt like it was his. He had been in charge of security here for several years now and knew every inch of the building. He felt safest here in his den, or the 'crib,' as the guys called it; this was where the action was.

He reclined back on his chair and stared at the bank of monitors in front of him. There were cameras all over the building, and most of the people who worked here, didn't know about them and never would. He found the mornings amusing. Hundreds of men and women filed past each other through the big sliding doors, yet hardly anyone spoke to one another. He had cameras trained inside and outside the foyer, in the lifts, the stairwells, the basement, and the bathrooms; in fact every single room on every single floor. About seven years ago, they had tried to tell him it was an invasion of privacy; that you couldn't possibly need to see everything, and cameras were unnecessary. He soon explained that if they wanted to be blown up by a terrorist or brought down by a conman defrauding them out of millions, well, yeah, sure, take out all the cameras. Then they could see how long they would last when people knew no one was watching, and they had free reign. He pointed out how many terrorist attacks could have been stopped if the perpetrators had been monitored effectively. That shut them up, and since then, he had been in no doubt as to who was really in charge.

Ranjit watched as a young man approached Jessica at the front desk. He had seen it before: the young man would try to start a conversation, and she would blow them off. She pretended she was above everyone else, as if somehow by being born beautiful, made her better than they were. He knew differently; he watched her screw a random woman up on twelve in the bathroom after last year's Christmas party. They had seen each other for a while, but then Jessica must've broken it off. He watched the woman cry in the bathroom before she left for the day, and she had never come back. He tried to find Jessica playing around again, but he hadn't caught her; yet.

A team of ten worked for him and did the rounds, checked the locks, worked the nightshift for him, and basically did all the shit that he didn't want to do. Here, in the crib, he was in charge. He stuffed another doughnut into his mouth, sucking on it, relishing in the sweet sugar before he swallowed the last dry crumbs. His gut hung over his trousers so much it was a struggle to reach his desk anymore. He leant forward slowly and caught a reflection of himself in one of the screens. A fat face with three chins looked back at him. He rubbed his bristly chin. I should probably shave, he thought, but does it really matter? He picked up the coffee his second-in-command, Stu, had brought him, and sipped it. It was still burning hot and he put it down quickly.

There it was, just as he predicted; the young man had left, idling off to the sofa, rejected. Jessica was talking to her colleague. Ranjit zoomed in, unable to remember who was working the morning shift with Jessica today. Oh yes, Brie. She was more to Ranjit's taste: dark smooth skin and silky black hair. He had not seen much of her, sadly, despite tracking her every movement. She turned up to work, left, and did nothing in between. If only he could put a camera in her panties and follow her all the way home. There was no way she was a dyke, too.

He watched as Jessica laughed and put her hand on Brie's bare knee. Brie put her hand on Jessica's, too, and it lingered there a moment longer than it should, if it had been merely a friendly gesture.

"Well, fuck me," said Ranjit, and he belched out a sweet, sugary burp. He zoomed the camera right in on Jessica's face. Her eyes sparkled and he knew it; they were at it. Damn dykes. He didn't approve of dykes, gays, or whatever you were supposed to call them these days. As far as he was concerned, they were deviants. He despised most of the people in this building in fact, regardless of whether they were straight or not.

Christmas parties were the worst. They really showed off the worst of humanity then; such pathetic, sordid, disgusting behaviour. He was guaranteed a show though. Last year he had seen five blow jobs, three quick fucks in the disabled toilets, and in the stairwell where they thought no one was watching, Mr White from ten, and Mr Davis from nine, screwed each other silly. Ranjit had turned off at that point: there was a limit.

He leant back in the chair and turned to floor sixteen. That was his favourite floor. It was a call centre for Fiscal Industries who owned the building, full of young people, slutty girls who wore short skirts and tiny tops. In the summer, he kept the air conditioning down so they would keep stripped off. Ranjit hated winter.

He tapped the screen; there was the blonde who always started early. He called her Blondey for no other reason than he couldn't think of anything more suitable. She stood up, and threw her headset onto the floor like a spoilt brat. She wore a white blouse and black skirt that showed off her long legs. He bet Stu twenty pounds that she would bang someone in the toilets within a week of starting: Ranjit had gone home twenty pounds richer on Blondey's third day.

There was the boss, Jillian something, and she always came in early to work, although Ranjit knew she didn't actually do any work in the mornings. She spent hours poring over dating websites. One of the rewards of management was access to the internet, and she certainly used it. He watched her scour numerous websites for a date, cyber or real, so he guessed she was single. She didn't wear a wedding ring either. Ranjit touched himself as he saw Brie spin around in her chair, inadvertently flashing her legs at him.

Up on nine, Mr Davis was setting himself up at his desk for the day; Ranjit wondered if his wife knew he was actually queer. He wondered if Mr Davis knew. On the second floor was the café. It stretched three quarters of the way around the building, glass walls looking out over the plaza. On one side, it had a terrace, where in the summer, the smokers congregated amongst the miniature trees and pot plants. Not much happened there; just boring office meetings mostly. Two summers ago, someone had choked on a chicken bone and died right there on the floor. They died quickly, their body twitching whilst the poor saps stood around him waiting for an ambulance, not knowing what to do. He had watched reruns of that one for weeks before he'd bored of it.

A cursory glance at the monitors would seem boring to the untrained eye: floor after floor of suits, paperwork, computers, filing cabinets, and phone calls. Just women and men making money, more women and men losing more money. But to Ranjit, this was just the surface. He could train a camera anywhere. He could see the email they were writing, the zero's on the cheque they were writing, even how big a dump they took after lunch.

Ranjit watched the foyer thin out, as most of the workers had started for the day. He would have to get Ahmed to mop the floor. They brought in so much rainwater that the marble floor would be slippery, and he didn't want to have to deal with any ignorant idiots turning their ankles over on it. The paperwork involved with accidents at work was horrendous, and that would be a day wasted.

He noticed Jillian walk out of the lift and over to the sofa, offering her hand to the new boy. So, he must be going up to sixteen; lucky boy. If he were extra lucky, they would put him next to Blondey. If he were unlucky, he'd be sat next to the nerd in the corner, who picked his nose all day, and when he thought no one was looking, wiped the resulting snot balls under his desk. Ranjit picked another doughnut out of the box and sat back, watching his little world turn in black and white.

* * * *

Amber tried to stifle a yawn but failed. Her cherry red lips parted and a huge yawn erupted from her mouth. She rubbed her eyes, sighed, and readjusted her headset. The cursor on her computer screen blinked at her with monotonous regularity. She hated the early shift. Sure, she got to leave early, but was it worth getting up at six in the morning? The cold walk to the train station was not inspiring, even in the summer: soggy streets crowded with traffic, dirty air filled with pollution, and annoying losers who had to get up like her to go to work far too early. In winter, it just seemed worse.

Every morning was the same: she was logged in by seven, yet the first two hours of the day were spent staring at a blank screen and listening to nothing but silence in her earpiece. True, she was getting paid to do nothing, but it wasn't much of a life. It was even more boring than the shop she had worked in before. She couldn't even use the internet now. They had blocked it for 'security reasons' they said. Everyone knew it was because the job was so mundane, that if they had access to the internet, then everyone would be reading the latest sports / gossip / news, or more likely, looking at porn, instead of working.

At the recruitment agency, they told her that Fiscal Industries was one of the top something-or-other places to work in the country; that it was a dynamic, vibrant, modern workplace, offering a high quality blah blah blah. She'd seen the salary on offer and tuned out after that. What they should've told her, was that in return for a decent wage, you've got to sit staring at a computer, aware that you're stuck in a dead end job, and bored off your tits for most of the day. She'd still have taken the job.

Amber yawned again and looked around the office. It was a typical Tuesday. The boss, Jillian North, was sat in her office behind the safety of her oak desk, the frosted glass walls keeping a safe distance from her and the office floor. In there, she couldn't hear the insults and names they called her. Amber could see her hunched over her desk, probably analysing figures and statistics so she would have something useful, yet pointless, to say at the morning meeting.

A dozen cubicles over from her sat Freddy, one of the few people in the office she could bare to talk to. He was about her age, but she had no interest in him beyond work. He was lanky, spotty, and a complete nerd. He was more inclined to read books, than chat up a girl. They both started on the same day and Amber suspected at first that he might fancy her: most men did.

He had told her though that this was just a stepping stone; that he wanted to get into the 'world of finance,' as he kept calling it, make his millions and retire. The fact that he had left school at sixteen and this was his first job, didn't seem to faze him. He was very laid back which Amber found sweet, although ridiculous. She intended to get into the 'world of finance' too, but she had no intention of working her way up the corporate ladder. She was far too good looking for hard work. Hell, she would find a rich director or executive type, get married, and be set up for life. She knew she was good looking and good at fucking; it was only a matter of time now before she found Mr Right.

Amber was slim and athletic, thanks to daily trips to the gym, and a high metabolism, thanks to her grandmother. Sitting at this desk for the last six months though, was starting to have an effect. She had noticed a few more pounds here and there, a slightly darker shade under the eyes, and a lethargic approach that was beginning to intrude her trips to the gym. These mornings were killing her; she had to talk to Jillian and get back onto the late shift, where she could get a good lie in and then party straight after work. She wasn't going to meet the right man sat here reading magazines and getting fat.

The office was empty apart from Freddy, Amber, and Jillian. Any minute now, thought Amber, glancing at the huge clock on the wall above her, and a hundred people would be walking in. A hundred computers would switch into life and the day would begin in earnest. It was better to have company than be sat here alone, but in truth, she couldn't stand half of them and the other half she didn't know.

In Amber's pod, there was just herself, Brad, Jenny, and Rob. Jenny was a middle aged, fat cow, who everyone ignored, which was fine because Jenny ignored them. They knew little about her except she was most likely single. Her desk was cluttered with cats: her mouse mat was in the shape of a cat, her screensaver was an adorable kitten dressed in a little kitty-jumper, and even her mug had printed on it, 'I heart cats.' God, what a failure of a human being, Amber thought.

Rob was slightly older than Amber, and overtly gay. He told Amber every Monday what he'd done at the weekend, and who with, in excruciating detail. He was funny she had to admit. Shame he was leaving. Apparently, some new guy was starting today to replace him; fresh meat. Amber kept her fingers crossed he was good looking.

Rob's last day was coming up this Friday. He was going off to work in Uganda or something with a volunteer group. She couldn't understand why anyone would want to do anything you didn't get paid for, but at least Rob's leaving was a good excuse to go out Friday night. Amber was already planning on wearing a revealing red dress which showed off everything she wanted too, and then some, which led her to thinking about Brad: delicious, dreamy, Brad.

He had only been with the company a few weeks, but Amber was keen to get closer to him; much closer. He was American and spoke with a soft, southern accent. He was on a gap year and a self-proclaimed player. He told her that he liked being single; he was far too young to settle down, so he was over here exploring the rest of the world. First stop, London, and move on from there. She got the impression his parents were rich; she knew they paid the rent for him so he could work and save for himself to travel. Money - tick. Good looks - tick. He had to be worth a screw at least. Amber knew he had been checking her out and if he didn't take advantage of her soon, she was liable to drag him into the rec' room and...

Amber's headset beeped and rudely interrupted her crude daydreams. She prepared herself for the usual 'Hey, I need my money now, what the hell are you guys doing?' type of call which was the norm for the morning. It was often this time of day when some of their clients tried to withdraw cash on the way to work, and realised they didn't have as much as they thought. As if it was Fiscal Industries fault for them not having enough money.

"Get out, get out, get out," shouted a man's voice down the phone. Amber jumped. The man's tone was urgent and he sounded almost frantic. She guessed that he must be running too, as he was breathing heavily, yet in short sharp bursts.

"Sorry, sir, what is...?" Amber had to rip the headset off as the man let out a deafening scream at her. She could not make out any words, just a guttural cry, which stopped when the line went dead a moment later.

"Jesus Christ, freak," she said ruffled. She stood up when he had screamed at her, as if she physically needed to step away from her desk. She threw her headset to the floor, distancing herself from the phone call as much as possible.

"You all right, Amber?" said Freddy from across the room.

"Yeah, I'm all right, mate, just some weirdo. You get them now and again, eh?" she said, sitting back down. Freddy grunted and sat down, returning to his magazine, 'Economic Times.'

Amber scooped up her headset and reluctantly switched her phone back on, as the first dribble of workers came in; the rows of computers filled up and the noise increased as the office drones chatted amongst themselves. Amber shook her head.

"Fucking dick. If that was a joke that was *not* funny." Amber curled her blonde hair behind her ears and looked out of the window. She could not see far. Thick raindrops splattered against the window, hiding the foggy ground below. Amber shivered. The noise in the office was growing louder as squeaky chairs filled up with ample backsides: twenty, thirty, forty people. Idle chitchat about the rain intermingled with discussions about how the day would pan out: who would get the most investment, who would lose the most, and who would be first to tell Jillian to piss off. Within an hour, there would be exactly one hundred and seven people on floor sixteen. By the end of the day, exactly eighty nine of them would be dead.

CHAPTER THREE

Caterina was the first one to notice anything. Well, actually, Kyle McCarthy was, but he ignored the seventeen missed calls on his mobile as he was focussed on his targets for the day. Night-time was for playing, daytime was for working, that was Kyle's motto. If Kyle had listened to any of his voicemails, he could have taken action and saved the lives of most of his colleagues, as well as himself. As he didn't, he and his workmates would be very dead, very soon. Well, dead-ish.

The morning passed as it usually did, with one majorly mind-numbing meeting, cups of tea, and several trips to the toilet. Caterina idly rubbed her belly, waiting for the next call, deciding if she should choose her baby's name now, or wait until she was born. She had found out it was going to be a girl and was currently trying to choose between Kirsten and Kristen.

A few minutes ago, she had been introduced to Tom, who was replacing Rob. She politely said hello, not really interested until she actually looked up at him and realised he was quite handsome. When Jillian led him away, Caterina got her phone out and was texting a friend about the new hot guy at work: Tom. After the baby was born, she would love to jump his bones, she told her friend, Eva. He's got a cute face and nice hair. Usually, Eva texted straight back, but Caterina had been left waiting a whole nine minutes before she got a reply, which irked her. She had contemplated going to the toilet again, but Jillian would probably notice if she had her third break of the day before nine thirty: bitch.

Eva had finally answered and said they had been evacuated and she was going home. Why, that's not fair, texted Caterina. Don't know why, texted Eva, something heavy going on, police everywhere, been told to go straight home. Wish I could go home, this place is shit, texted back Caterina.

Her friend only worked in the office five minutes down the road. If Eva's office was being evacuated, then surely Caterina's had to be, too? She hatched a plan. If you wait for me, I'll come with you - I'll just tell the Queen B I'm not feeling well, she won't say anything, she's too scared, wait for me, yeah? texted Caterina. Another tiresome five minutes passed before she got a reply.

No.

That was all it said. Just one word. Caterina knew Eva could be a bit sharp sometimes, but that was definitely no way to treat a friend, especially a pregnant friend. No need to be so blunt - stop being a bitch and wait for me, she texted back. Caterina got no reply. Of course, she didn't know that Eva was now shuffling around the city with no arms, no heartbeat, and utterly incapable of using a phone, let alone comprehending what one was.

Sighing with exasperation, Caterina got up, flicked her phone off, and went to find Jillian, who was in her office with Tom, going over health and safety rules. Caterina approached the office, knocked lightly, and walked in.

"Caterina, can this wait? I'm just in the middle of something with Tom," said Jillian offering her a fake smile, looking at the fat lump in her doorway. If she was fat now, Lord help her when she was heavily pregnant. Jillian had to fight the urge to punch Caterina in the face; she was the most selfish person she had the misfortune to work with.

"No, it can't wait. I'm sick. I need to go," said Caterina bluntly. She made no effort to pretend to be sick, but stood in the doorway with her hands on her considerable hips. Tom raised his eyebrows but said nothing. 'Don't make waves on your first day,' his father had taught him. It was one of the rare pieces of good advice he had actually been given by his father.

"Sorry, Tom" said Jillian. "What's wrong, Cat'?" Jillian knew that Caterina wasn't sick and was using her pregnancy to get out of work. It was a game they played more and more frequently of late.

"Baby stuff innit." Caterina stood her ground, not moving from the doorway, not breaking eye contact with Jillian, and not prepared to lose the game this time. She knew that she would win; Jillian had the backbone of a jellyfish.

"Fine," said Jillian, "just let me know later if you're not going to be in tomorrow, please."

Caterina flashed Jillian a sickly smile and walked away.

"Baby stuff, eh?" said Tom breaking the silence.

"Yeah, she's about four months gone. Look, Tom, some advice." Jillian sat back in her chair. "I shouldn't say this, but I know your father, so I think I can trust you. If you want to get on here and make something of yourself, you can, but don't mix with the likes of her. She'll just bring you down. There are some good eggs out there on the floor, but...well, mostly, they're rotten."

Tom was surprised at her honesty. He wasn't so surprised that she knew his father. Tom knew he had pulled some strings to get him in.

"Well, yeah, I'm just here to get on with the job really," said Tom, not even knowing what the job was.

"Right, well let's get this finished and then we'll get you out on the floor." Jillian shuffled in her seat and pointed back to the computer. A series of short raps came from the door and Jillian sighed.

"Caterina, I'm busy, I told you..."

"Sorry, Jillian, it's me." Tom saw an old man's face appear through the door and wondered who else was suffering from a case of skive-itus.

"Morning, Jackson, sorry, what can I help you with?" said Jillian.

Jackson Miller was the company's longest standing employee. He had been here before Jillian had started and had seen a lot of people come and go in his time. He was unofficially second in command. Jillian wasn't permitted to employ any supervisors, but could rely on Jackson to keep things in order when she wasn't around. So she knew he wouldn't come and see her unless it was important.

"Sorry Jill, it's just that Caterina's causing a bit of trouble. She said she was going home because there's some problems outside. She heard it from some friend apparently." Jackson stopped, seemingly unable to decide how to continue.

"And?" said Jill. Today, evidently, was not going to be a simple one. She rifled her fingers through a wave of dark hair.

"Well, that got everyone checking their phones and it sounds like she's telling the truth. Kyle said his brother's been calling him and left a dozen messages telling him to leave the office - that it's not safe here. Benzo's on the phone to his father as we speak."

"Oh, for crying out loud," said Jillian standing up. "If there was a problem in the city, security would tell me and I would deal with it. They're a bunch of kids, Jackson, you know what they're like." She walked over to Jackson ignoring Tom.

"Well, yes, I do know. Cindy and Parker are gossiping like there's no tomorrow and I can't shut them up. I'm worried half the office are about to walk out."

Jillian ushered Jackson out of her office and followed him, leaving Tom sitting in an empty room. He wondered if he should sit and wait or see what the deal was. He decided sitting in an empty room didn't show much initiative, so he followed Jillian out onto the floor. He headed to where a large crowd had gathered. They were clustered around one man's desk. Tom could hear Jillian barking instructions out to sit down and monitor the phones, but nobody seemed to be taking any notice.

"Quiet!" shouted a man sat at the desk where everyone had crowded around. The man was dressed in a smart suit and had a telephone pressed to his ear, his finger stuck in the other.

"What's happening, Benzo?" said a female voice from the back of the group. The speaker was hidden from Tom's view. Benzo just flapped his hand in the air signalling them to be quiet.

"Why do they call him Benzo?" Tom whispered to Jackson.

"His real name is Marin Rakeen de Lakehal Benzema."

"Oh, right," said Tom nodding. Jackson just winked at Tom knowingly.

"All right, everyone," said Jillian, "let's see what he can find out. Please sit down and be quiet."

The office fell into a hush. A minute passed and Benzo said nothing. Then he slammed down the phone and stood up sending his chair wheeling back into Jackson's shins.

"I'm leaving, Jill, and I suggest we all do the same." There was a flurry of people standing up and gathering up coats and bags.

"All right, all right, hold on everyone. What did your father tell you, Benzo?" Jill stood next to him, her arms folded. The crowded office stopped again and Tom felt very self-conscious in the quiet room; as if it were him expected to make a speech. Benzo spoke slowly and clearly.

"I couldn't get hold of my father. I got the pass off and they only do that when it's important. Eventually, they put me through to the DCI. He knows me. He said...he said, there's been an incident at St Thomas', a bad one. He said there was some sort of infection spreading and quickly. He told me we should either stay where we are and lock the doors, or better yet, get home fast. He said it was coming this way. Then he got cut off, or hung up, I'm not sure."

"Fuck this, Jill, I'm outta here," said Rob. "Can you hear that?" He pointed to the far end of the office, toward the exit door. The sounds of hundreds of people running down the emergency exit stairs reverberated around the room. Nobody had even noticed it before.

"Hang on, everyone, I'm going to check with security," said Jill, but it was useless. The panic had started and people began leaving. Rob marched out first, his leather jacket flying behind him, swiftly followed by Benzo.

"Wait, you can't leave, there's work to do. Stay here where it's safe. Come on, what are you doing?" Jill tried to reason with them and a few listened, but most ignored her. They were used to ignoring her pathetic orders and now that their lives might be in jeopardy, they were intent on ignoring her even more.

Against the tide, Caterina resurfaced. Back in the office, she headed straight for Jillian's office. "Jill, the lift's broken, I've been waiting for ages and it ain't coming." She saw everyone leaving and suddenly realised that Eva might be in serious trouble: so might she.

"Is this a fire drill, or for real?" asked Caterina as Kyle bundled himself past her to the stairs.

"I don't know, Caterina. Look, the lift's probably been deactivated; it seems there is an...*event* taking place in the city. I recommend you sit down and wait here. It's safer in here than outside right now, until I know what exactly is going on." Jill ran her hands through her hair. Jackson wheeled a chair up to Caterina and paused beside her.

For once, Caterina didn't answer back. She meekly sat down on the chair as the final person to leave the office rushed out, banging the door shut behind them. Jackson rested a hand on Caterina's shoulder. She could see the concern on his face and decided it best to stay here, for the time being at least. The thundering noise of thousands of scuffing shoes and heels faded, and Jill looked around the office.

"Right, well, I appreciate everyone staying who has," she said, her voice wavering, faltering with nerves. "I'm going to my office now to speak to security, to find out what is *really* happening. If you need anything, come and see me, but otherwise, I suggest you head to the rec' room and wait there. I'll fill you in as soon as I can. Jackson, can you please do a roll call and see who we have left? I need to fill in the report for health and safety on this and know who's left."

With that, Jill walked back to her office, consciously keeping her head up, and back straight. She switched the phones to emergency override, so that the call centre was effectively shut down and any callers would just hear the pre-recorded message about the centre having been evacuated. This way, she wouldn't have to deal with a million complaints tomorrow about clients not being able to get through. She was surprised that she hadn't been made aware of any issue in the plaza, or the city, and wondered if it was a hoax. She dialled security's number.

Everyone who had stayed, silently made their way to the rec' room and Jackson wrote down a list of names of everybody there. He counted eighteen names on the list, including himself, and amongst them, were some colleagues he could almost call friends: Jill, Caterina, Freddy, Jenny, Cindy, Amber, and Parker. Some of them, such as Brad, he could not, and would not, call friends. He wished he had a hundred and seven names on the list today though. Jackson had a bad feeling about this.

* * * *

DI Benzema jumped out of the squad car as it screeched to a halt on Waterloo Bridge. The driver jumped out.

"Move it, constable!" the DI shouted.

The squad car driver followed the DI out onto the bridge in the rain. People were running amok, and he was confronted with so many people he didn't know where to turn; some were clearly injured and bleeding. The constable did not heed his superior's advice and 'move it' quick enough though. An old woman in a sodden medicinal gown grabbed him and sunk her teeth into his neck. The policeman's blood drizzled down the old woman's lips and they sank to the ground together, where another patient, an old man, joined them, ripping the constable's face off.

As much as he wanted to, DI Benzema knew he could not stop and help. He ran toward the hospital defying his natural instincts. People lay dead or dying in front of him: on the road, the pavement, and the grassy knoll in front of the hospital. He saw fighting outside the tube station that had developed into a brawl involving at least fifty people. As he ran, he dodged anyone that reached for him or called out for help. He had strict instructions to get to the hospital; he had to find Doctor Garner. As the DI ran through the shattered doors of the hospital, he heard the whirring blades of the helicopter approaching above. He had to hurry.

Inside the hospital entrance, he skidded to a halt. The receptionist lay over the front desk, her innards pooled around her. The floor was awash with blood and it was eerily silent compared to the cacophony outside. He saw the sign for Intensive Care and ran. They had received a phone call from Doctor Garner that the patient had shown up here about two hours ago. Doctor Garner had told them that he was holed up in Intensive Care with vital information; the only way to stop the infection spreading.

DI Benzema ran through the corridors past empty beds and bodies. Sickly green walls were splashed with bright red blood and occasionally he slipped; pools of blood had been left to collect unattended on the tiled floor. The Doctor's call had apparently been taken very seriously. The DI had heard that orders had come from a very high ministerial level and that the Doctor was to be extracted immediately. Benzema knew that was code; the information was to be extracted and the Doctor was just a bonus. The army was flying in to take him out - they just needed someone on ground level to get the doctor up to the roof. DI Benzema knew the area better than anyone on the beat. He had grown up here and lived and worked in the area his whole life. In this very hospital, about three floors above where he was now, his own son had been born.

They had not wanted to attract too much attention and lose Doctor Garner, so had decided to send DI Benzema in alone at first. There was little time to assemble a taskforce anyway; the situation was spinning rapidly out of control and the Doctor was a priority. Emergency services were stretched beyond the breaking point already across the city. The DI heard more sirens outside and hoped his backup was coming. Reaching Intensive Care, he stopped and called out.

"Doctor Garner? Are you here? It's the police, I've come to help!" With the adrenalin pumping through his body, he had to force himself to stop running and just listen. He wanted to explore the hospital, throw open every door, and find the Doctor quickly. He didn't know how long he had before his location would be compromised.

Suddenly, there was a clatter of footsteps running toward him from behind a set of double doors and DI Benzema braced. He gritted his teeth and subconsciously balled up his fists.

"Thank God, you've got to get me out of here!" said Doctor Garner, running through the doors. He had a dishevelled appearance and his eyes looked about wildly all the time. His white coat flapped around his tall frame, making his entrance all the more dramatic.

"Doctor Garner?" said DI Benzema relaxing slightly.

"Yes, yes. You're the cavalry I take it?"

"DI Benzema, at your service. Are you ready, Doctor? We have to get you to the roof right now, there's a chopper waiting for you. Is there anyone else here?" The DI took hold of the Doctor's arm.

"No, I'm afraid everyone is gone; metaphorically and literally, if you get my drift. I'm the only one left. I've got the information though, don't worry." Doctor Garner patted his pocket proudly.

"We can probably take the lift; it goes right to the roof. It should still be working," said the Doctor.

Brief introductions over, the DI and the Doctor ran to the lift and waited impatiently for it to appear. The sirens and screaming outside had not abated; the sound of death was very close. As the lift arrived, the doors opened and a hospital orderly, slumped against the doors, fell out.

"Good Lord. The poor fellow's neck is broken," said Doctor Garner. As they stepped over the body and into the lift, the dead orderly sat up and grabbed Doctor Garner's leg. He bit clean through the Doctor's trousers, breaking the skin, and ripping out a chunk of the good Doctor's leg. The orderly noisily chewed the bloody tissue and muscle as the Doctor cried out in agony and collapsed into the lift.

"Shit!" DI Benzema pulled out his hastily approved firearm and put three bullets in the orderly's head. The dead orderly fell backward and the Doctor's blood trickled from his mouth. DI Benzema didn't know if the orderly was likely to get up again, but took no chances, and kicked the body out of the lift. He pushed the button to take them to the roof.

"What can I do, Doc?" DI Benzema bent over as the Doctor tore a piece of material off his gown and wrapped it around his bleeding leg.

"Call me Robert, for starters. Not much else I'm afraid. Just get me out of here." Doctor Robert Garner winced as he applied pressure to the wound on his leg, trying to stop the bleeding. "Shit that hurts. Just get me to the roof. I need to..."

Doctor Garner drew in a quick breath and grimaced with pain. The infection was spreading rapidly through his bloodstream, coursing through his nervous system. His leg went into spasms and the Doctor had to concentrate just to retain consciousness. He watched the numbers on the wall light up: three, four, five, six...finally they reached the roof.

"I'm Harry, okay? I'm going to get you out of here. Just try to take it easy, you'll be out of here in a minute." DI Benzema stood up as the lift doors opened out directly onto the roof. Gusts of rain blew in and an armed soldier was stood right outside, his weapon pointed straight into the lift.

"Thought you had taken the scenic route. I presume this is Doctor Garner?"

"Yes, but he's hurt, so..." The DI stood aside as two burly soldiers, ignoring the gale bellowing across the rooftop, picked the pale Doctor up and carried him to the helicopter.

"Don't suppose you know what's going on?" said the DI to the armed soldier. He stood in the doorway, forcing the lift doors to stay open.

"No idea. 'National Security' or some such bollocks." The soldier turned immediately and ran after his colleagues. No sooner had they all gotten into the helicopter, than they were up in the air, the pilot steering them expertly and safely off the roof. As he stared up into the sky, DI Benzema wondered what the hell he was going to do now.

* * * *

"This is stupid, why should we sit here all day not knowing what's going on?" said Parker. It had been an hour since Jillian had burrowed down into her office to find out what was happening.

"Look, if we go down to the second floor, we can get out on the terrace and have a look see. Not to mention a quick fag. I'm not waiting anymore, this is a waste of time. She can't make us stay here. I'm going now," he said and got off the sofa from next to Tom.

"Take your umbrella, mate," said Freddy. The rain was lashing at the windows and only seemed to be growing in intensity.

"If Jillian wants to know where I am," Parker said, putting his jacket on and checking the pockets for cigarettes, "then you can bloody well tell her. I'll be back soon."

Tom watched as Parker strode across the office and left. He seemed calm, despite the situation. Desperate for a cigarette, but level headed. Tom reasoned that if there was an outdoor area on the second floor, it would be a good idea to check from there: safe enough to see down without getting into any danger. The rec' room had been awash with ideas about what was going on and with no information coming from their esteemed leader, Jill, a hundred possibilities had been mooted. Amber thought it was a lot of fuss over nothing and that they'd all be home by tea time; Jackson and Freddy agreed that it was probably a dirty bomb let off by one of the Arab factions. Brad suggested it was an alien invasion and Jenny was worried the government had created a superbug that was making its unstoppable way around the world, turning everyone into bloodthirsty zombies.

"Hold up, I'll come, too," shouted Cindy. She ran out and Tom watched as the woman grabbed a shiny red raincoat on her way. He got up and went to the water cooler to refill his cup, leaving the rest of the group to continue their gossiping. A man, Brad, was there by the water cooler, as if waiting for him.

"That's Cindy," said Brad to Tom. "Don't worry, I don't expect you to remember everyone's names. Cindy has a major crush on Parker, but she's wasting her time."

"Brad, isn't it?" said Tom smiling, shaking hands. "Tom Goode."

"You're sure having an interesting first day, buddy," said Brad, shaking Tom's hand.

"True, true," said Tom watching the cool water fill up his glass. Brad had piercing blue eyes and a firm shake. Tom hadn't noticed before, but Brad had quite an imposing presence. He was tall, tanned, and toned; the typical blue-eyed American boy-next-door.

"So you think Parker will find much down there?" asked Tom.

"No idea," shrugged Brad. "But Cindy will suck his prick off given half the chance." Brad laughed at his own crude joke and Tom, not wanting to appear rude, faked a laugh back.

"Say, I'll give you a head's up on everyone. Forget the cowards who ran, you'll probably never see them again anyway." It was Tom's turn to shrug; Brad had an unusual sense of humour.

"That's Freddy – super nerd, but super intelligent. Next to him you got Jackson; he's pretty cool. He knows everything about everything, which is useful at times, but he can get annoying. Over there, you see the redhead? That's Jenny. She keeps herself to herself and loves cats. A little too much if you ask me. Those other fat chicks next to her? I have no idea what their names are."

Tom nodded his head in acknowledgement as Brad listed the names of the remainder of the staff who were in the rec' room. When he didn't know their names, he just used nicknames: Big-tits, Pimple-face, and one short, stocky, fellow, who Brad named Elma Fudd. Tom forgot many of the names straight away.

"And, finally, you see the blonde by the window over there looking at her reflection? That's Amber. Loves herself, but with her tits, why not? I fully intend to fuck the *hell* out of her by the weekend, so hands off, buddy. You can get yours later."

Brad nudged Tom and winked, letting out a small laugh. Tom wasn't sure how much of a joke this was supposed to be and just nodded in agreement. It was certainly proving to be an unforgettable first day.

* * * *

"Wait up!" called Cindy, skipping down the stairwell after Parker. She caught up with him two floors down.

"Cindy, you shouldn't be here. We don't know if it's safe," said Parker. He had volunteered to go downstairs hoping for some solitude and a cigarette in peace. With the storm going on outside, he wasn't sure if they would be able to see anything of use anyway.

"You'll protect me though, eh, Parker?" Cindy beamed and winked at him, wrapping her red raincoat around her. The stairwell was cold. Parker couldn't help but smile. Cindy looked like a child, her gleeful manner only outshone by her ridiculously brightly coloured coat. He knew she fancied him and they got on well, but he saw her more as a sister.

"Okay, come on then," he said giving her an over-the-top wink back. Parker began down the stairs with Cindy following. All the way down, she chatted to him: about the rain, the exciting stuff they were going to see outside, and what she was planning on buying at the weekend at the flea market. She bounded after him happily, forgetting the day's troubles. Parker let her chatter away, unable to interrupt, thinking mostly of the cigarettes waiting in his pocket.

As they entered the second floor, the sound of the howling wind became stronger. Parker was surprised to see what a mess the café was in; chairs and tables overturned, trays and rubbish strewn around the floor and food left abandoned and uneaten. It was like the Mary Celeste, he thought. He walked into the centre of the room and called out.

"Hello? Anyone here?"

Only the wind and the rain answered him.

"Look at the storm, Parker, it's so loud and...so thick!" said Cindy. The wind was slamming huge drops of rain against the windows. The sky, although it was still morning, was nearly black. Cindy peered through the glass. "I can't see a thing," she whispered.

"Come on," said Parker, "let's go out onto the terrace and see if we can see any better." He took a cigarette out and pushed it into his mouth. Zipping his jacket up to his chin, he took Cindy's hand.

"Don't want you getting blown away," he muttered. He was genuinely worried that a single gust would be enough to send her over the edge and onto the street below. It wasn't easy replacing sisters. Cindy took his warm hand and her heart beat a little faster.

"Thanks," she said timidly, and pulled her hood over her head so only her face was showing, peeking out like a rabbit from its warren.

Parker pushed open the door and it crashed back against the outside brick wall, the door handle ripped from his hands. His cigarette flew out of his mouth and he resigned to having to wait a bit longer for his nicotine fix.

They stepped over the door lip and out onto the terrace. In one corner, was a pile of shrubs and ornamental trees that the storm had uprooted and smashed into one green, flapping blob. The flat roof was wet and slippery and Parker gripped Cindy's hand tighter. Slowly, step by step, they walked through the drenching rain and puddles, their heads bowed, until they reached the wall and could look over the side.

Thirty feet below them was a pile of bodies, at least fifty deep. Clothing blew around in the whirling wind, but Parker could see the dead faces below. On the road, and in the square in front of them, scores of people were running around. Fighting against the storm, some slipped and fell, only for someone else to jump on top of them. It was too far to see clearly what was going on, but Parker knew something terrible was happening. What was this madness?

"Look," said Cindy. She clung onto Parker and pointed. An army truck was coming down the road and mowing down anyone who got in its way. Soldiers were firing from it and as far as Parker could tell, they were shooting aimlessly. Another truck appeared behind it and then another. The trucks slid to a halt in the middle of the plaza and the soldiers dispersed, shooting at random. Some of the people running around actually ran toward the soldiers. Parker later swore he saw people getting shot, but they carried on running. Given that was not humanly possible, most of the others believed that Parker had lost the plot.

Some of the soldiers down below in the plaza were overcome and Parker lost sight of them. Crazy people of all shapes and sizes ran around as if 'The Anarchy Party' had been voted into power. Across the square, he lost track of the numbers of soldiers he saw. Fire fights and fist fights exploded beneath the rain clouds. For every person that was knocked down, another stood up. It seemed that the soldiers were being outnumbered. Parker couldn't understand why so many people were fighting them; surely they should welcome the army? They were on the same side weren't they?

Suddenly, the brickwork beneath them exploded in a cloud of dust and Parker heard the bullets ripping into the wall. He dived back, pulling Cindy with him and they fell in a heap together, bullets pinging off the wall above them.

"Are you all right?" shouted Parker above the wind and the gunfire. Cindy did not answer. He rolled over in a deep puddle and pulled her to him. Parker shoved her hood back and saw where a bullet had entered her left eye. Cindy lay still. Her right eye was staring up at the heavens, unflinching, as the rain fell on her innocent face.

"Cindy?"

Parker scrambled to his feet and dragged her back inside the café. Once inside, he pulled the door shut and knelt over her on the cold damp floor.

"No, no, no, no." Parker looked at Cindy laid out on the café floor, water pooling out beneath her. He pushed her hood back and gently laid her head down. The bullet had passed straight through her, killing her instantly. Blood was still seeping from the back of her head, congealing in the fur-lined hood.

"Oh, my God," said Parker quietly. He had worked with Cindy for months. Only last week they had gone for a drink after work. He had been drinking coffee with her just one hour ago. How could she be dead? He was too stunned to cry. Parker sat back on the tiles and the sound of the gunfire outside diminished. The bodies; there were so many bodies out there. From their clothes, he knew they were city workers. Probably some from this building: from his own office.

Parker crept away from Cindy and rested his head against the cool interior wall. He fished a cigarette out from his pocket, lit it, and inhaled. Would the fire alarms work anymore? Parker didn't care. How could he go back up and tell the others what had happened and what he'd seen? How could he tell them he had let Cindy get killed like this? Parker wrestled with his thoughts as the exit door at the opposite end of the café very slowly pushed open.

CHAPTER FOUR

Christina Spinnamaker was sat alone up on the twenty fifth floor, wondering how it had come to this. She had implored her staff to stay, practically begged them, yet not one of them had. Some of them had come up with plausible reasons: I need to get to my wife / children / parents. Some of them had not bothered disguising the truth; no. No excuses, just a simple no. At first, she couldn't blame them for wanting to leave and had been tempted herself. Surely the reports had been exaggerated? Some sort of outbreak at St Thomas hospital was spreading and the infection was instantaneous. Go home. Stay indoors. A typical overreaction, she had no doubt, from on overreacting government. Always reacting, never acting.

But then the infection had reached the city. St Thomas hospital was a couple of miles away, but they had been told by security to stay indoors. There was no time to get home; just stay in the office, lock the doors, and wait for the all clear. It was then she began to wonder if the situation was as grave as they were being told. She was the only one in the office with internet access and she had tried all the news sites for information. Strangely there was nothing: the BBC, CNN, and all the independent sites were full of salacious scandal, but nothing of their current plight. Was it just a hoax?

Some of the staff had gotten jittery early on, saying they had received texts and calls from partners and family members, urging them to get home. It seemed word was spreading fast, yet officially, there was no news. She had tried calling security back, but just got the standard voicemail that they were busy and couldn't answer the phone. One of her junior clerks, Edward, had volunteered to go down a floor and ask the lawyers on twenty four if they knew anything. She let him go and gave everyone else menial jobs to do; keep them busy, keep their minds occupied, she told herself, and they will respond to your authority. Her authority had lasted all of ten seconds, once Edward had come back.

He had run in shouting that they were all leaving, that all of the lawyers were running down the stairwell, going home, and getting out of the city. Edward told them he had spoken to one of his friends, a trainee barrister, Nigel.

"Haven't you heard?" said Nigel, as he put his coat on.

"We haven't heard shit. What's going on?" Edward was holding onto his friend's arm tightly. Edward feared Nigel would be gone down the stairs before he had got any answers at all.

"The dead? The sick? At St Thomas.' Christ it's unbelievable. You've got to get home mate. Come with me if you like. I'm off. Kathleen's at home waiting for me."

Nigel paced toward the exit, shaking a sweating Edward off.

"I can't. I mean, I just have to run upstairs and tell the others. But what do you mean - the *dead*? What happened at the hospital? There's fuck all on the news."

Nigel paused by the exit holding the door open. Everyone else on the floor had left; it was now just him and Edward.

"You won't find anything on the web, so don't bother looking. They're going to cover it up. Kathleen's sister, Sally, you remember we met her last week? Well she's a nurse at St Thomas'. Kathleen told me Sally got out in the nick of time before they got cut off. They took someone in who was sick, injured, and covered in mould and fungus and all sorts of shit apparently. Kathleen reckons it's some sort of government science project gone wrong.

"Anyway, Sally said the man died, right. They were clearing up and two minutes later, the man was on his feet! This bloke had boils all over his body, his skin was falling off him and...fuck."

"What?" said Edward trembling. He remembered Sally. She was a nice girl. Then he thought of his own wife. Would she be at home, too, waiting for him? She hadn't answered his calls. Nigel carried on.

"Sally said this dead man just started attacking the doctors and nurses. Like a wild beast. One minute he's laid on a slab, next he's up running around biting people. Sally said she saw the doctor go down in front of her with his throat ripped out. She watched him die and next minute he was up and about, too, running around like a madman. She said he ran into the corridor and killed the first person he saw, just beat them to death, and then moved onto the next poor sod. It spread; every dead person getting up and killing. And so on. You see?"

"Nigel, this is crazy. You can't be serious? You're having me on, right?" Edward had turned pale and Nigel was itching to get going. Footsteps were echoing up the stairwell from the hundreds of people leaving below them.

"I'm deadly serious, mate. Kathleen said Sally made it out of the hospital but the infection, whatever it is, was spreading and fast. She was running down to the tube and could see people pouring out of the hospital behind her. But they weren't running away - they were running toward her. They were dead, but they were coming for her. Sally was trying to get to the station entrance and told Kathleen the gates were being shut. There was a big crowd and she didn't know what to do. Was going to run for it I think. Then she got cut off. Kath called her back, but got no answer. We're just hoping she made it. Kath's worried sick."

"Fucking hell." Edward put his hands in his pockets. He looked at Nigel, a friend he had known for years, in wonder. "And that's what this is about? The infection is heading this way?" he asked.

"It's not the infection you've got to watch out for, mate," said Nigel, "it's the dead. If they don't infect you, they'll kill you. Either way, I'm getting out of here. Now you coming with me or staying?" Nigel took a step back into the stairwell.

"No, no, I'm going to tell the others upstairs. Then I'll get off home. I'll see you later, mate. Take care, eh?" Nigel nodded and ran off into the stairwell, his feet clattering loudly on the bare steps. Edward did not see Nigel again.

When Edward had relayed the story to his co-workers, there was nothing Christina could do to hold them back. It was chaos: everyone grabbed their coats and bags and could not get out of there fast enough.

"Wait. Security told me we should stay put. It's not safe out there you know." Christina had tried in vain to make them stay, but they were too panicked now.

"Come on, hurry up," Edward had shouted, encouraging his workmates to follow him. One by one they had fled, leaving Christina alone, wringing her hands. She had tried to stop them. Maybe they would be all right? They were probably all at home now, laughing and toasting their success in escaping, whilst she was stuck in the office. Maybe she was wrong and Edward had been right?

Edward had not been right. When they had got downstairs, many of them already flushed and out of breath by charging down so many flights of steps, they had run onto the wet streets to be greeted by hell. Through the rain, people were running everywhere. They heard screams, sirens, metal scraping on metal as cars collided and the tremendous thunder of hundreds upon hundreds of feet pounding the roads, running in all directions.

As soon as they were out of the building, Christina's staff scattered. Edward followed three of his colleagues toward the tube station only to find it closed. There were scores of people climbing over the barriers and running down the tracks past a stationary train. As he followed them past a ransacked coffee shop, banknotes fluttering in the wind, he heard a terrifying roar from the tunnel ahead. From the darkness came a wave of people, running back to the station.

"Stop! Please, stop!" He heard people call out, but it was futile. Up ahead in the tunnel the dead were coming. Masses of people were still trying to get into the tunnel to escape the streets, only to meet a wave of people, dead and alive, coming back. In the confusion, scores of people were crushed in the icy blackness of the tube tunnel.

Edward saw the dead rushing through the crowd; biting, tearing, and ripping at anything that moved. Those who had been crushed by the stampede lay still. Those poor souls killed by the dead, or those mortally wounded, soon sprang back up and feasted upon the dead, or chased after the living. Edward retraced his steps and clambered carefully up onto the roof of the coffee shop, as those around him charged around in a mad panic.

One by one they fled, or were struck down by the dead. Edward pressed himself against the small roof of the shop and clamped his mouth firmly shut. He put his hands over his ears to block out the sounds of the living being torn apart; their awful screams made him dizzy. He could almost feel his own mind shattering. He cried as he waited there for it to stop, wishing he were with his wife.

Finally, the screams subsided, but the dead did not disperse. They stayed, feasting on the juicy, warm flesh that had been unable to rise again. Some ran into the carnage of the streets. Some stayed in the station. They could smell life. They could smell Edward. They would not rest until he was found and devoured.

* * * *

Christina stared out of the huge window, wondering if Edward had made it home. They had left hours ago. She had tried the phones but they were all dead. The internet told her nothing. It was as if the internet was dead too; there had been no news stories of any kind since nine this morning. Since a very brief call from someone called, Ranjit, this morning, she had rung security back every hour but had received no reply.

She tried looking down at the ground to see what was going on, but it was pointless. The storm had not let up and the rainy mist obscured any vision of the ground below. It was impossible to hear anything either. The silence of the office and the quiet ticking of the clock were both irritating and stultifying.

Christina walked over to the lifts and tried the buttons, but they were still not working. Presumably in an emergency, they shut off until someone turned the power back on again. She walked over to the exit door and poked her head around it into the empty stairwell. It was bizarrely quiet.

"Hello?" she said, her voice echoing back to her. There was not a thing to be heard. She did not like the idea of being trapped in here and went back to the office to grab a litter bin. She opened the exit to the stairwell once more and wedged the bin in the doorway so it would not shut on her. If the door got locked, she would be stuck in here forever. What if the police or the fire brigade came, couldn't get in, and left her behind? She felt much better knowing there was an exit for her.

Christina walked back through her office slowly. It was so strange to be here in daylight. It was doubly strange for it to be so empty. She had bought top of the range computers and the best workstations money could buy. She rented this floor from Fiscal

Industries, because, quite simply, it had the best 'pulling power.' She could have gone elsewhere and saved a stack of money. But you reaped what you sowed and up here, on the top floor, she reaped a lot.

The main meeting room had views over the city and on a clear day, you could see to St Pauls. She sat down in the reclining leather chair she had bought herself and wished today was a clear day. All she could see now was a dirty great cloud chucking water all over her precious office windows.

She had tried to bond with her staff, but the truth was, she wasn't very good at that kind of stuff. They got on fine and there was no disharmony in the office, but she knew they didn't like her. Just look how quickly they had bolted today. Given the opportunity to risk it outside or stay in a safe place with her, they had chosen to go. She could have gone too, but...where would she go? Home?

Home was comfortable, but to be honest, she thought, I am home. Christina closed her eyes and snuggled into her black leather chair. The scrunching sound of the leather was soothing. It was another extravagance she didn't need, but had felt compelled to buy when she'd seen it. She had two houses: one in Surrey, one in France. She had two cars: a Jag' and a BMW. She had two holidays every year; that was all she permitted herself, even though she knew full well she could take a year off and her bank manager wouldn't even flinch. She was satisfied with her lot. It had taken years of hard work, but she had made it. The houses, the cars, the incredible amount of zeros on her bank balance. But there was something niggling at the back of her mind.

The sight of her staff running out the door today came back into her mind, unsettling her. Just like her husband, they had run at the first sign of trouble. Her husband had left her years ago, just as her business was taking off. She had told him that she was starting to bring in some real money now, but apparently, that was not enough. He wanted *her*, he said, not a pot of gold. Idiot. She was better off without him. If he was still around, she'd have had to give him half of everything and sharing was not a natural part of her make up.

Christina felt awkward. Her favourite chair no longer seemed so comfortable and she stood up. Sitting around waiting to be rescued was boring. She went to touch her wedding ring and realised she hadn't worn it in years. Come on, Christina, she thought, keep it together. She went back to her desk and pulled out a report she had been meaning to read. The hours dripped by slowly and she was unaware of the time passing. She finished the report and played with some numbers on her computer, making a note to have a word with Janet tomorrow about the Collin's file, and the lack of increase in funds they were seeing; or not seeing.

It dawned on her then that Janet might not be in tomorrow. And then she realised that actually none of her staff might appear tomorrow: Edward, Kate, Morris, even Phil, the hunky man who cleaned and watered the plants once a week. What if they didn't come back? What if they couldn't? What if there was a serious problem out there in the city and she was stuck up here alone? Christina felt very alone and goose bumps tickled themselves down her arms.

Glancing at the clock, she saw it was nearly five p.m. She tried her mobile again, but there was no signal.

"Damn it, what is this, the fucking eighties? What the fuck is going on?" Christina angrily threw her mobile across the room and it shattered as it exploded against the Formica wall. She picked up her stapler and did the same. Her mouse and a cat's cradle swiftly followed, piling themselves on top of the broken phone.

"What the fuck is going on?" she said again, as she began sobbing into her hands. Her shoulders shook as she slumped over her desk feeling desperately alone and afraid.

* * * *

The remainder of the day was boring for some, and a bit of a blur for others. Parker had reappeared with Benzo and a strange woman, and he told them what he'd seen: the bodies, the soldiers, the insane fighting. He told them what had happened to Cindy. Nobody blamed him, of course, but he felt guilty. Parker went and sat at his desk, his head resting on his folded arms.

"I should talk to him," said Jenny.

"I think you should leave it for now," said Jackson. "The lad just needs some space to deal with it. If he wants to talk later, so be it. For now, let him be."

Jillian told everyone to stay on the floor and she would keep trying to contact security whilst Benzo told them why he hadn't been able to get home.

"God damn security, that's what happened!" he said, furious. Bar Jill and Parker, he was sat in the rec' room with everyone else sat around listening intently.

"When I got to the foyer, I think I was pretty much the last one there. Most other floors had already evacuated. People were just pushing and shoving and practically climbing over each other to get out. Jessica here," he said, nodding to the girl sat beside him, "got knocked down and I stopped to help her."

"It was unbelievable," said Jessica. Dark stains on her cheeks and around her eyes gave away that she had been crying. Her legs were bare and she had cuts and scrapes on her knees. For the first time, Freddy started paying attention to what a girl was actually saying and put his magazine down. A few in the group recognised her as the building receptionist, but most just filed past her every day without a glance. Tom recognised her instantly.

"I was with Brie, my colleague, and we were ushering the last people out when some tosser pushed me over. Benzo helped me up, but then we heard one of the security guards saying they were shutting the doors. I think it was Colm, but I couldn't see clearly. He hopped through the doors, smashed his radio on the ground and that was it. The doors slid shut and I saw him and Brie running away and all these people outside...I don't know what happened really. It looked like they were fighting with each other."

"Jessica and I went to her desk to try to call security and get them to open the doors, but there was no answer. We stayed a while, ringing anyone we could, but the phones must be dead. We couldn't find anyone," said Benzo.

"I guess they all got out and left you behind?" said Jackson.

"No, they couldn't have," said Jessica. "You can only lockdown the building from the inside, which means there has to be someone from security left here. My guess is it's Ranjit."

"Who's he?" asked Tom.

"I've met him a couple of times. He's a fat freak. He just sits in the security office all day perving over us. He thinks we don't know but we do. You never see him on the rounds, coz he's too lazy. He'll be there now, I bet." She looked up around the room at the ceiling, looking for cameras. "He's probably watching us right now."

There was murmuring and chatter around the room.

"Well, let him. He's as stuck in here as the rest of us. If he won't answer the phone or open the doors, there's not much we can do," said Freddy.

"This is nuts," said Jackson. "The very protocols and fail-safes they put in place to help us in a time of crisis like this, are trapping us here. We'd be a damn sight better off without them if you ask me. Bloody security are a law unto themselves. I'm going to see Jill." Jackson stormed out.

"How did you find Parker?" said Tom breaking the silence.

"As we couldn't get out or reach anyone, we decided to head back up here. Jessica wanted to grab a first aid kit so we stopped on the second floor café. Parker was..." Benzo stopped and looked downcast.

"Is Cindy still down there?" said Tom. He took a step forward from the crowd around Benzo so he could see him clearly. It didn't seem right trying to hold a conversation when they couldn't see each other.

"Yeah, we covered her with a blanket we found in the kitchen. Didn't know what else to do really, you know? Parker didn't say much. He just came up here with us. We only heard the shooting from the stairwell. We know as much as you do."

Tom sighed. "When we get out of here, we should take Cindy with us if we can. At the very least, put her someplace safe. We can't let the government cover this up. When the streets are back under control, we have to let everyone know what's happened here today."

There was more murmuring amongst the group. Brad stayed at the back listening and watching, especially the attractive new girl, Jessica.

"From what I saw, it's going to take a while to get anything out there under control," said Parker from the doorway. The room hushed as he walked in toward the water cooler.

"Make yourselves comfortable, because we're not going anywhere," he said. They watched as Parker poured himself a glass of water, then he left as quietly as he had come in.

And so the group dispersed into smaller groups. Some stayed in the rec' room where they could play cards, make cups of tea, and chat about anything but what was happening outside. Tom, Caterina, Brad, and Amber went to one corner of the office to discuss what was happening whilst Jackson and Freddy went to another. Their mini society was already fracturing.

Jillian stayed in her office. She could hear clearly through the wall what was being said next door in the rec' room. She knew her task was fruitless. They had had a seminar a few months back on what would happen if the city was targeted. If terrorists planted a bomb in one of the buildings there would be an emergency evacuation if time permitted, then lockdown. So far it had gone according to plan, except for one thing: communication.

Jillian was supposed to be notified when any terrorist incident occurred immediately. She should have had phone calls, emails, constant updates from one of the security guards. Instead, there had been a blanket of silence.

The lifts had been shut down, the doors to the building locked, and the phones cut off. All mobiles signals would be cut off in case the bomb was to be detonated by radio signal. She tried the internet, but still had no access. It seemed they had cut that off too. They were effectively in a panic room; two hundred feet high with no way in for the terrorists, or whoever they were. Jill knew though, that meant there was no way out either.

CHAPTER FIVE

"Of course it's a cover up," said Parker. "Governments have been trying to cover crap up for years. Twenty years from now, we'll probably be reading about Zombie-gate."

Brad and Tom couldn't help but laugh. Parker walked away. He didn't have the energy to get into another fight. He wasn't ready to joke about it either.

They had eaten lunch a couple of hours ago and were trying to stave off boredom. Nobody dared to go downstairs again and were just hoping the phones would start ringing and they would be given the all clear.

"What does he mean 'Zombie-gate'?" said Amber frowning. She looked at Tom and Brad sniggering. "I don't get it."

"Oh, read a book for fuck's sake," said Jenny scornfully.

"A book?" said Amber. The laughter increased.

"Seriously?" Tom looked at her, incredulous, and let out a long sigh. "Sheesh, I didn't realise I was that old."

"Let me enlighten you, darling," said Jenny, leaning forward over the desk. "When you were just a twinkle in the milkman's eye, we used to read books: great wads of paper, bound together with words on. This was before the Kindle was invented. Let me guess, you've probably got one of those Express things at home, right? Like a sheet of paper but with lots of novels in it? Shakespeare? Dickens? Heard of them?"

"Oh, all right, yeah I got one of them. Never heard of Shakespeare or whatshisname. I don't like reading much. I've heard of them books you're talking about. Sounds, well old, like something my dad would like." The group chortled and Amber went red.

"Oh, whatever, you don't have to be so stuck up about it, just because I'm younger than you." She stood up and looked at Brad. "I'm going to the tenth floor, I hear they've got a bigger rec' room there with much stronger stuff than just cups of bloody tea. I need a change of scenery. Anyone coming?"

Nobody answered her because nobody wanted to go with her. They were comfortable enough here, waiting for news from Jill. Amber's company, whilst physically attractive, could be testing. As she turned and walked away, Brad stood up and followed her.

"Back soon, folks, I'll just make sure she's okay," he said swaggering off.

"I'll bet he does," said Jenny quietly, exchanging looks with Jackson.

Out by the exit to the stairwell, Brad caught up with Amber, as she had hoped, and he put a hand on her shoulder. The chatter of the group had started again and was distant.

"Hey, babe, you all right?" he asked her.

Amber looked up at Brad and fluttered her eyelashes. She leant closer to him. "Yeah, sorry, I just need a break. It's hard enough working with them. Don't ask me to spend the night with them too."

Brad drew her close and they pressed against each other. He could feel her pert breasts pressing against his chest and she put her arms around his waist. She looked up and he leaned in to kiss her. A faint bang startled them as someone in the rec' room went to the toilet, the door banging shut behind them.

"Come on, let's go to the café and see what's going on outside. It might be clear now," said Amber tugging Brad along into the stairwell.

"Actually, I have a better idea," said Brad stopping. "Let's go upstairs. I think everyone else has left, so let's explore a little. When else do you get an opportunity like this?" He flashed his teeth and Amber melted.

"Okay, I'm game." Amber pushed her blonde hair behind her ears and walked on ahead of Brad up the stairs, so he could follow her slim legs all the way. One floor up and they found the door was locked. On the next floor, Amber pushed the door open and walked in. It was a reception area carpeted with lush green plants decorating every corner.

"Hello? Anyone here?" She giggled as Brad took her hand and he led her through another door into an office. It looked much the same as theirs except with less cubicles and more space. The silence was bizarre. To be stood in such a huge room without the normal chatter and hum of life, was a little unnerving.

"This way," said Brad, and Amber duly followed him, holding his hand firmly. He found his way into a large lounge area with soft recliners, drink machines, a sink, and two long, brown, sofas. Amber walked over to the window and pushed her face up against the glass.

"I can't see anything. It's so gloomy out there," she said. She felt Brad's arms slip around her and he nuzzled her neck. She sighed and closed her eyes, letting his hands ride up inside her top to squeeze her breasts through her silky bra.

"Oh, Brad," she murmured as she let him take off her bra. He stepped back and in the dim light, she turned around to face him, pulling her top off so he could see her small but pert breasts, her pink nipples standing out in the unlit room. She licked her lips and knelt down before him unzipping his trousers. She pulled his pants down and took his erection out. Brad looked at the reflection before him in the large window. He smiled at himself and watched Amber's blonde head bob up and down as she sucked eagerly on his hard cock, his hands resting on her bare shoulders.

Ranjit leant back and unzipped his trousers, focusing the camera on Blondey. After all the stress and shit he had dealt with today, he could do with some entertainment.

* * * *

Christina wiped her nose and got up. Ten minutes of crying and she was through. Her staff would have egg on their faces when they came back to work tomorrow. She wandered aimlessly through her office looking for a distraction. She eventually found herself back in the boardroom. The storm was dying down and her eyes ached. She rubbed her puffy, red eyes, and looked east. Through two skyscrapers opposite, a small gap gave her a glimpse of the airport. Occasionally, she would take a break in here on her own, and watch the planes taking off and landing. She didn't like to visit the kitchen often. Invariably, the staff would leave as soon as she came in and eventually she stopped bothering. Today was so quiet though, she felt like she needed to see those planes, to know there was still life out there somewhere.

The clouds obscured any clear sight of the airport but she noticed it was unusually quiet. There were no planes in the sky and no movement on the ground. Even the runways were quiet and dull. The usual twinkling landing lights were all off. She had never seen it so empty before.

Christina wondered if perhaps the situation was more serious than she had given credence to before. From the boardroom, she dialled security, but there was no answer again. She went to the lifts but there was no response. She hit the call button repeatedly but it brought nothing up to rescue her. She went back to the boardroom and sat casually on the table, its smooth mahogany finish cool against her legs.

"I'm not walking down twenty five sodding flights of stairs," she said aloud. In this room, she was used to an answer when she spoke: mostly yes's, rarely a no. Now her voice was unaccompanied by anything but the sound of her own beating heart. Well, that's something, she thought.

Her stomach grumbled. The evening was drawing in and she began to wonder if she was going to have to stay the night. It was that or walk down to the ground and see what was happening. Maybe Edward and the others would be down there waiting for her, ready to have a good laugh.

"Suppose I'd better go," she said to herself. Sitting there quietly, procrastinating as the weak rain pitter-pattered against the window, she began to hear another noise: a beating, thumping sound, at first faint, but increasing in volume by the second.

Christina slid off the table and stood by the full length windows looking out over the grey world. It didn't occur to her to look down. She had trained herself over the years not to do that anymore: the height was disconcerting. If she had looked down though, she would've seen the city as it had become in the last twelve hours: the dead, the fires, the burning trucks and the shambling corpses. She would've grasped the severity of her situation at last.

Suddenly, the noise increased sharply and an army helicopter appeared, its rotor blades spinning rapidly. Unknown to her, it was the same one that had ferried Doctor Garner away earlier in the day. It had gone back to St Thomas hospital at his bequest, before he died, to retrieve some key information: a body. He had described it and the soldiers had managed to find it where he said it would be. They were transporting it now back to a secret location.

The khaki green helicopter was huge. She had never seen one so close before and it was now only about fifty feet away. It was headed in the direction of the airport when, without warning, it veered off to the left. Christina watched as the overhead blades came within inches of striking the tower opposite her. She looked on as the helicopter momentarily hovered, righting itself, before lurching again to one side. It was caught in a spin and the metal beast came straight toward her. Christina screamed and froze.

It stopped just in time, inches away from crashing straight through the boardroom windows making mincemeat out of her. She clearly saw the pilot who was struggling with the controls. Two men appeared to be fighting, knocking and pushing him, when suddenly they were upon him. The pilot's mouth shouted unheard obscenities and then the helicopter swung round and plummeted down.

Christina watched it disappear from view and she fell to the floor, her shaking hands grateful to be able to clutch the firm flooring. She rested her clammy forehead against the cool glass. It was unreal. Moments later, the building shook as a fireball billowed up from below.

"Oh God," she said, "what's happening?" Never had Christina felt more alone.

* * * *

Thirty minutes earlier and with no information from Jill, Jackson decided they ought to try downstairs again and see if they could get out, or at least figure out what was going on. He talked to Freddy and Benzo who agreed with him, and they talked to Tom and Brad. Between them, they decided they had to risk it. There was no way Parker was going back down, so Brad decided to go with Tom. Sitting up on the sixteenth floor was getting them nowhere; people were starting to get hungry and whilst there was food in the kitchen, none of them liked the idea of sleeping at the office.

"So, buddy, you good to go?" said Brad.

"Yep, sure. We should stick together. Safety in numbers and all that." Tom thought it was a good idea to check downstairs too. He still felt a bit like an outsider, being the new guy, but he wanted to get involved. He didn't feel much like sitting around anyway; he wanted to do something useful. Brad seemed pretty dependable. Being able to hold a civil conversation was something that seemed to elude a lot of people these days, so Tom was thankful of his company.

"Let's get this done, then." Brad strode off to the stairwell and Tom followed. As the door swung shut behind them, the office was again thrust into silence.

On the way down, they didn't speak. The stairs were illuminated by the emergency lighting; a strange orange light that only heightened Tom's feeling of wariness. They descended the stairs and on each floor Brad tested the exits. Every door was unlocked; some swung open easily, some seemed to get stuck as if there was something lodged behind them. They didn't venture any further than the doors, as there seemed no point at this stage. Upon reaching the ground floor, Brad stopped, resting his hand on the last door handle.

"What's up?" said Tom.

"You ready for this?" asked Brad. "We don't know what's on the other side of that door, buddy. Could be nothing, could be a whole heap of trouble. You okay with that?"

"I'm ready," said Tom. He had to stop himself from smirking. In the office, he could tell that Brad was playing the hero; flexing his muscles both literally and metaphorically, but there was no need to do it down here. It was just the two of them and Brad was not Tom's type: wrong sex for starters. Tom could tell that Brad was used to being in control and having his own way. Brad wasn't really asking Tom if he was ready for trouble - he was asking him if he was a coward or a fighter. Brad just wanted to let Tom know who the boss was.

"Go ahead, Brad, I've got your back," said Tom, lowering his head submissively, but keeping his senses alert. Brad opened the door slowly and looked out. The lobby appeared empty. He pushed the door open further and took a step out. It was cold and dark. There were no lights on in the foyer aside from the emergency exit signs above the doors. The front desk was empty. Brad motioned for Tom to follow and he let the door swing behind him. Suddenly, he realised if it latched shut, they might not be able to get back in again and he grabbed the handle. Tom took his tie off and shoved it between the door and the frame, propping it open.

"Can you see anything?" Tom whispered to Brad who was creeping forward.

"No, it's too dark outside. Look, the rain's nearly stopped. I'm going to try the front door, see if it's open yet." Brad crept toward the huge glass doors and when he reached them he pulled on the handle, but they wouldn't budge. He shook them harder, but they didn't move an inch.

"This is weird," said Brad as Tom came up beside him.

"Is it? From what Jessica told us earlier, I'm not surprised," said Tom.

"You know how much money Fiscal Industries makes per year? More than you can count to, buddy. And they don't do it by working nine to five and going home for a fish supper. This place crunches numbers twenty four hours a day. For them to be closed up this long, means whatever is going on out there is heavy shit. I don't like this."

Tom and Brad cupped their faces against the glass and strained their eyes, trying to penetrate the darkness. The street lights were out and all they could see was the night. The roads were empty, bar a couple of taxis, which were clearly empty. The taxi's doors were open though, which was unusual. Brad took a step back from the door and began waving his hands over his head.

"Hey, anyone there? Hey! Can you hear us?" Brad called out and was looking up at a camera he had noticed above the doorway. There was a small red blinking light on it indicating it still had power. Brad lowered his arms.

"The camera's still on, but I don't think anyone's home. Maybe Jessie had it wrong."

"So what now? You heard what Parker saw happening earlier. Something's going on. Where is everyone now?" said Tom puzzled. "How come there are no lights on out there? Even the street lights are off. I think we're gonna have to stay put tonight and try and leave tomorrow. I don't think we're going anywhere tonight."

"Well, there's no way we're going out the front door. These doors aren't made of ordinary glass. They're built to withstand bullets and all sorts of shit. Money can buy you pretty good security. I guess we..." Brad stopped and held up a hand.

"Listen," he whispered. Tom froze. He had heard it too. There was a scuffling sound outside. They looked but couldn't see where the noise was coming from. Brad pushed his nose against the glass, peering intently through to the outside world.

He jumped back suddenly when a dog appeared out of the gloom and ran up to the door. Tom couldn't help but laugh. Tough guy spooked by a dog. Brad whirled around.

"You think that's funny, buddy? Take a closer look," said Brad angrily, stepping back from the door slowly, not taking his eyes off the dog.

Tom approached the door and looked at the dog. He wasn't too familiar with dogs, but it was a Golden Labrador of some type. There was something odd though. The dog's coat was matted with blood and it wasn't barking or making any sound. The dog opened its mouth and tried to bite the glass. Its teeth clacked annoyingly on the door. Tom's brow furrowed with concern. The dog's eyes were pure black and Tom bent down to look closer. The dog's throat had been ripped out; there was no way it could be alive. It began pawing at the glass, its mouth salivating and leaving slimy trails over the pane. Tom stood up and backed away.

"What the hell is it? I mean, it can't be, it's..." Tom refused to believe what he was seeing.

"It's dead, buddy," said Brad. Tom stood beside him marvelling at the dead dog that was trying to get in. He might not know much about dogs, but he knew that dead dogs should stay that way.

Suddenly, a figure appeared behind it. A young woman in a blue skirt, naked from the waist up with dirty blonde hair flying wildly about her face, ran up to the glass doors quickly and began pounding on them with her fists. Brad and Tom both jumped back, shocked.

The woman said nothing and ignored the dog who reciprocated. She began trying to bite at the glass door too. Her naked body was pressed up against the glass, but Brad and Tom felt repulsed.

"Look at her," said Tom quietly. "Look at her face."

He felt sick. Brad saw the cuts on her face and the deep gashes across her cheeks. Above her right ear, her head had been torn open, her scalp removed, exposing her brain. Her eye sockets were empty and blood seeped from them. The woman continued to throw herself against the glass, the bangs ringing around the large foyer.

"So it's true. Shit. When Parker started talking about zombies this afternoon, I figured he had lost the plot. What with Cindy dying and all the rumours, I mean... that is some bullshit right there." Brad and Tom took another step back.

"Bulletproof you said, right?" asked Tom, taking another step back. The woman continued pounding the glass doors.

"Yeah," said Brad biting his lip. His bravado was disappearing fast.

"Reckon it's enough to hold fifty of those things back? A hundred?" asked Tom.

Brad shrugged. "Come on, Tom, let's just get back upstairs." He turned away just as another two figures emerged from the blackness outside and joined the dog and the woman; one, an older man, grey suit hanging loosely over his slim frame, shuffled up to the glass and stared. The man's skin was pale and he raised his arms. His hands were missing and he pressed bloody stumps against the glass doors, smearing bright red blood everywhere. All the while, his eyes stared into the foyer at Tom and Brad.

The other figure, another man but slightly younger, was uttering short grunts. He crawled up to the glass and sat in front of it, hammering on the vibrating glass doors. To Tom, he looked fairly normal, but the man's spine was broken from where a fleeing taxi driver had run him over. The man's legs were mangled beyond use. When he opened his mouth, Tom could see the man had no tongue. He didn't want to think what had happened.

Tom and Brad left the foyer. The thumping sounds of the dead pummelling the glass doors echoed through the building's empty corridors. The dog and the four zombies were rapidly joined by more. Tom and Brad headed back up the stairwell to tell the others what they had witnessed. The exit door in the foyer slowly swung shut behind them, stopping when it reached Tom's discarded tie. Their footsteps echoed down the stairwell and through the crack in the door, joining the dead, leaving the faintest gap between them.

* * * *

"Hey!" Benzo was stood in the doorway to the second floor. Tom and Brad followed him through, and into the cafe.

"What are you doing here?" Brad asked him.

"Parker wanted to come down. We didn't think it was a good idea coming on his own, so I came with him. He was thinking about what you said earlier, Tom, about taking care of Cindy? He's putting her in the cold store."

Tom didn't know what to say. It was logical if a little odd, but these were odd times.

"Solid, buddy, solid," said Brad. Parker walked out of the kitchen and approached them.

"What did you see?" he said calmly, wiping his hands on his trousers.

"A shit-storm of shit," said Brad picking up a coke from a table. He chugged it down.

"Or in other words," said Tom, "the doors are locked; which is probably a good thing. Right now, there are bunches of dead people trying to get in. Whatever this infection is that your dad told you about, Benzo, it's fucked up."

"Dead people? Come on, man," Benzo looked sceptically at Tom. Parker silently nodded.

"If you don't mind getting wet, take a look." Tom walked over to the café's terrace door and the others followed him. They filed out onto the flat roof, noticing the broken brickwork that the bullets had torn through, killing Cindy. Tom led them to the other side that he guessed would look down over the front doors.

"Holy fucking shit," said Benzo slowly. Below them a crowd of zombies had gathered, stretching right into the square. The numbers were incomprehensible; on all sides of the plaza were skyscrapers, illuminated only by the weakening sun behind the rain clouds. A few windows were lit up but most of them were dark. Thousands and thousands of zombies jostled and shoved, trying to get into the buildings. They had succeeded in getting into the stock exchange; Tom could see zombies on the roof and on the ground, milling in and out of the building as if going about their daily business.

More poured out of the tube station and from across the bridge, mindless killing creatures swirling around the city deliriously. They battered at doors, windows, walls: anything that was between them and the living.

"Why?" said Parker. "What kind of infection does this?"

"Alien," said Brad matter-of-factly. "Told you so, didn't I. Never thought I'd see it in my day though."

Parker snorted. "Alien my arse," he said under his breath.

"My dad said it would come eventually," said Benzo, "The breakdown of society, authority, laws & moral values. It's not like he was fucking depressed or anything, but when a cop got killed last month he was...well. Look at it." He could barely believe what he was seeing. "The streets are basically full of dead bodies. You see any sign of order out there? Respect for the living. Hell no. All I see is death."

"I guess the streets aren't paved with gold anymore, eh, buddy?" said Brad. Nobody appreciated his wisecrack and they ignored him. The air was cold and the depths of night were not far away.

"You know what?" said Tom, "we brought this on ourselves. These things, these zombies or whatever...they're not going to the cinema or the shops. They don't seem to have any reasoning and they're not hanging out at home in front of the box. They might have died here, but they haven't gone home have they. No, they're going to where you spend ninety per cent of your daily adult life: work. What does that say about how we live our lives and where our priorities are? Hmm? I can't see them leaving anytime soon if I'm right. God, I hope I'm not right."

They were quiet. Parker thought that this new guy knew how to cut to the chase. He hadn't spoken to him much yet, but he actually looked normal. He wore a dark grey suit, was of average height and had short cropped hair. He didn't walk with a limp, tell you about how he had found the path of Jesus, or crack jokes about midgets. It was almost unusual to come across someone these days that you could class as 'normal.'

"What's that?" said Tom. He leant on the wall and tried to concentrate on the strange droning noise above the grunting and groaning of the zombies. The odd noise intensified and it seemed to be coming from above them. Shielding his eyes from the rain, he squinted up and saw a helicopter.

"Is that a bloody Chinook?" said Benzo. "What the hell?"

"Look out!" Tom shouted as he realised the helicopter was spinning out of control and heading straight for them.

CHAPTER SIX

At the last moment when Tom thought he was history, just another zombie-in-waiting, the helicopter flung itself across the roof and smashed into the Akuma Insurance building opposite. It hurtled into the second and third floors, the aviation fuel exploding as the helicopter churned a destructive path through the building, tearing into anything in its way. Brad was the first to pick himself up off the wet roof and look around.

There was a huge hole where the helicopter had entered the building. Streams of fire ran out of it and with the rain petering out, the fuel was burning well, setting the building and its contents alight. Parker marvelled as black smoke billowed out of the side of the building. On the street below, the zombies were not put off and soon found a crack in the wall caused by the explosion. With the building now exposed, they ran into it, seeking out the living.

"Come on, guys, let's move," said Tom. They went back into the dry café.

"Man, I thought we were toast," said Brad sitting down at the nearest table.

"I can't believe this," said Benzo. He looked pale and was trying not to vomit.

"I have no explanation for what the fuck we deserved to get involved in this shit-storm," said Brad, "but we gotta roll with it. There are people out there dead and dying. We can survive in here if we play this right." They nodded in unison, agreeing with him.

"Well, it seems we'll be spending the night." Parker broke the sombre mood, shaking himself like a dog, sending droplets of water flying. "We should take some food and water back up with us."

"True. Who knows how long we're going to be stuck in here," said Benzo scooping up a bottle of water. They quickly rifled through the cupboards, grabbing ready-made sandwiches and crisps, cans of coke and bottles of water.

"What was that with the helicopter?" said Tom as they walked up the stairs together, back to the sixteenth floor.

"You know those things weigh about ten tonnes," said Benzo. "We'd be goners if it had come down on us."

"I would say that was the last ditch attempt by the government to control this. And failing miserably, of course," said Parker. "All those soldiers and trucks I saw earlier? Where are they now? If there's one place in the country that the government would need to protect, surely it's right here. And they failed."

"How do you mean, buddy?" said Brad, "The failure part, well that's obvious. But there are no residential areas here, no schools and no power plants. I would say their resources are spread trying to save the rest of the city. Who cares about us, really?"

"A lot of people actually, and a lot of politicians, too. Parker's right. This area, these people that work here, they're important; they're not doctors or teachers, but they've got the one thing everyone wants: money," said Tom, "Makes the world go round, right?"

"There's something else, too," said Benzo. "This is one of the most valuable and important places in the city, or even the country. Think how much this land alone is worth, plus the buildings on it. Yet, they haven't been able to protect it."

"And?" said Parker swinging his bag full of drinks over to the other shoulder.

"And what does that tell you about the rest of the country? The rest of it that's *not* so valuable? What state is that in now?" said Benzo.

"Fucked up I'd say," retorted Brad. A nervous laughter filled the void of the stairwell. They walked on in silence, occasionally stopping for a quick break to catch their breath.

Tom thought on what they'd said. He was also worried about downstairs. Those doors in the foyer may be bullet proof, but if enough of those things were pressed up against them, would their sheer weight be enough to break through?

Back on the sixteenth floor, they told Jill and the others of the zombies, the dead, and what it was like outside.

"We saw the chopper go down," said Jackson.

"Yeah, we were worried about you," said Jessica looking at Tom. She took a large bag of sandwiches from him and they continued talking. They all agreed they would have to sleep in the office tonight. There were some dissenting voices, but when it was pointed out that there was no way out of the building, quite literally, they soon quietened down. They made plans to spread out coats and cushions, whatever they could find to make themselves comfortable.

Jenny and a girl named Chloe, helped dish out the food. There was plenty to go round and Benzo had found a huge box of chocolate cookies in the café for which everyone was grateful. As the night drew darker, the office was illuminated by the computer screens. They switched the overhead lights off and the room was full of dancing images from computer screens: kittens, coloured balls, palm trees, and even a flying Jesus. There were a few tears when people realised they weren't going home for the night: wives and husbands, girlfriends and boyfriends would be at home, alone, wondering where they were. With no internet and no phones, they had no way of reaching them. Tom didn't say what he was thinking; that there might not even be anyone left to reach.

Jill retreated further into her shell. She felt awkward in the office now. They didn't listen to her. She felt she had to remain aloof, to keep the chain of command, but now when it was needed most, she backed away from it. On a regular working day, if there was trouble, she could send them all an email. If a client was complaining, she could take the call in her office and deal with it. Now she was stuck in the office with seventeen staff members and nowhere to hide: her office was her only refuge.

Whilst the others talked and chatted until they fell asleep, Jill stayed in her office, watching and listening to them. She thought about Cindy down on the second floor, shoved into a meat locker with a bullet in her brain. She thought about her fish at home and who would feed them. She thought about her own life; how pathetic it was. She should be feeling free, taking command of the situation. But she was sleeping in a cramped office, eating a cheese sandwich with nothing but a crappy photocopier for company. Even her fish probably wouldn't notice she wasn't at home. Would her staff even notice if she wasn't there?

* * * *

He flicked the camera off, disgusted. At first, he had been fascinated, even a little excited, but now - nothing but disgust and hatred. Ranjit picked up the phone again and tried dialling home. His wife should be home by now, so why wasn't she answering? God help her if she had been caught up in this. He opened his wallet so he could see her face again and there she was. Keti, his wife of seventeen years was holding his daughter, Vachya. It was his favourite picture of them. His daughter had died of cot death not long after they had taken her home.

It wasn't much longer after that when his wife had become distant. He loved her, and he thought she probably still loved him; but there was something between them now. She hadn't wanted to try again.

"Keti, Keti, where are you?" he whispered. She was so beautiful. Compared to the people in this building, she was an angel. He wished he could see her again, but he was starting to doubt it was possible. Ranjit turned to the camera over the front door; they were still there.

He had to lock the front doors and then lockdown the entire building. He tried calling each floor, to evacuate, but it happened so fast that he hadn't been able to reach everyone. His team had gone to the building perimeter to turn back the attackers, leaving him to deal with the internal issues. One by one his team failed to respond on their radios. One by one they had fallen. Watching the riots outside, Ranjit knew what was happening. His team was either being overrun, or were fleeing. He had seen Colm throw his radio on the floor just before he'd locked the front doors and run for the tube station. Ranjit had not seen him again, the coward.

He yawned and knew there was no choice; he was going to be spending the night here in this room. Thankfully, he had the foresight to furnish it with a vending machine a few years back so he wouldn't go hungry or thirsty. He pulled open another can of lemonade. He wouldn't be bored either. He would miss his wife, but there were fourteen monitors surrounding him and over sixty cameras throughout the building.

There was no way he could go home or open the doors now. Since the explosion earlier in the evening, the dead outside had only increased in number. The police call he received earlier hadn't told him any specifics, but he had seen enough to know this was not something they could handle. He had seen people out on the street being attacked, bitten, and killed; moments later they got up and attacked someone else. He watched it over and over and over.

The cameras told him everything he needed to know, for now. Outside was a war zone; there weren't hundreds of people outside, there were thousands. And they weren't people anymore. He didn't know what you would call them, but people who died and then got up again to kill were not normal. It wasn't a white man's disease either. Ranjit's team consisted of British, Asian, and Americans, and the crowd banging on the building's front door was a mixture of men and women, black and white, Chinese, European, and even some animals; a couple of dogs were trying to hack their way through the glass unsuccessfully. Occasionally, a bird or a bat would fly straight into the glass doors. It would thump against it and drop down to the ground, dead. Then its wings would stir, it would fly up into the sky again and minutes later, repeat the process.

Ranjit shuddered. He could live on chocolate bars and fizzy drinks only so long. He missed his wife's cooking. She was probably at home now putting his uneaten korma in the fridge. Why hadn't she tried to call him earlier? The phone lines just made clicking noises now. He couldn't get through to anybody, not even the police. He needed to piss and he banged his fist on the desk in frustration, making all fourteen monitors shake.

The toilet was in the adjacent locker room, which was off limits. He locked the internal door when Stu had come back in, the only member of his team not to desert him. It turned out; someone had bitten Stu, so he came back in for first aid. Before Ranjit could haul himself from his chair, he watched on the monitor as Stu collapsed. What if he had been infected like the others? Ranjit locked the doors and true enough, moments later, Stu had gotten up. But he was not Stu anymore.

Ranjit wished the monitors had sound. The constant banging coming from the door to the locker room was annoying. How was he going to get any sleep with this racket going on? He looked at monitor five - Stu was still throwing himself against the door trying to get into Ranjit's control centre. His face was covered in boils and he had not spoken a word in the last twelve hours. Ranjit tried to talk to him through the door, but it was useless. He could see from the camera clearly that Stu was dead. Somehow he was still moving around. How would he get out of here and back to Keti now? Perhaps Stu would get bored and give up. Ranjit knew that was unlikely; he hadn't given up in the last twelve hours and showed no sign of tiring.

Ranjit yawned again and leant back on his chair. There was not much going on. Most floors were empty. There was a couple still on ten, one woman on twenty five, and a man that Ranjit recognised as one of the cleaners, on thirteen, but mostly the survivors were just on sixteen. He had to turn the camera off from eighteen; what was going on there was far worse than anything he had seen before.

Ranjit wondered how floor sixteen was managing. He moved the camera around but they all appeared to be sleeping now. There was the new boy on the sofa, Jill sleeping on her own in her office, and Parker curled up in a corner by the fire escape. Ranjit hadn't seen Cindy die, but he had seen how cut up Parker was about it and felt sorry for the boy. They weren't all bad.

There she was. Ranjit found who he was looking for lying next to Parker. The dyke receptionist, Jessica, was sound asleep only feet away from Parker. Did she swing both ways? Ranjit tried to think if he had ever seen her with a man, but couldn't think of any time. He winced as a sharp pain flashed through his groin. He really needed to piss.

The locker room door vibrated as Stu threw himself against it and Ranjit wheeled his chair back trying to not listen. He plucked an empty water bottle out of the bin and unzipped his trousers. As he sat in his chair, pissing into the bottle, the acrid stench of urine drifting up to his nostrils, he turned back to the monitors. The building was surrounded. More than that, the cameras showed that the whole plaza was surrounded. Dead corpses desperate to get in and a lifeless city: no street lights, no traffic, and no city workers going home late from the pub. Ranjit wondered again how he was going to get home to Keti, whilst the banging noise from his dead colleague, Stu, just increased.

* * * *

Around eleven, when most of the office was asleep, Jenny suddenly sat bolt upright. She looked over at Jackson who was reading a paperback and nudged him.

"Hey, Jackson, have you seen Amber?" she said quietly.

Jackson cleared his throat and thought for a minute.

"Not for a while, come to think of it. Why don't you ask Brad, he went off with her earlier didn't he?" Jackson yawned and lay back down, resuming his book.

Jenny rolled over and pulled her ample frame up using a desk to hold onto. Treading carefully between sleeping bodies, she went over to Brad who was chatting to Parker quietly.

"Brad, have you seen Amber? She's not here and I'm worried. You were with her this afternoon weren't you?" Jenny hated talking to him. She knew he despised her, called her names behind her back, and on more than one occasion, to her face.

"Yeah, we did some exploring this afternoon. I left her on ten. She was going through the drinks cabinet we found. I wanted to come back and help the group, so I left her there. I wouldn't worry, she's probably sleeping it off." His blue eyes stared at her and Jenny, unable to hold his gaze, looked down at the floor.

"Okay, well if you're sure? You don't think we should go look for her?"

"Go back to sleep, Jenny," Brad said.

She nodded timidly and went back to her space on the floor close to Jackson. She lay down and tried to relax.

"Fat fuck," muttered Brad watching her leave.

Parker sighed. "I'm going to try to get some shut eye." He rolled over and faced the window.

Brad stayed up a while looking outside into the night. The tower opposite was still burning. Nobody had come to investigate the explosion; only more zombies. No fire engine had come to put the flames out. The building was burning away merrily, spreading exponentially, lighting up the night sky.

Brad lay down to sleep but couldn't. He felt restless. He didn't like sleeping in such close proximity to other people. Fucking was one thing, actually *sleeping* was very different. He could hear them snoring, their breathing, people turning over and rustling their coats. He lay there a while, but eventually, he got up and looked at his watch. It was approaching midnight. He trod softly through the office and out into the hall, careful not to disturb anyone, and let out a sigh of relief.

Free again, away from the snivelling cowards, the pathetic scum who were looking up to him for answers and help. A couple of the guys were all right: Tom and Benzo. Beyond that, he wouldn't put his life in any of their hands. Even Parker had fucked up with Cindy.

Brad slipped out into the stairwell and began walking upstairs, back to the eighteenth floor. For the first time that day, Brad thought about his father back home in Dallas. He wondered if the news had reported what was happening here in London. Surely, with twenty four hour news channels, it would be all over the world by now? The UN was probably passing a decree at this very moment to send in rescue teams and the relevant charities would be ringing their bells.

Brad didn't doubt that his father would come and get him. Tomorrow, or the next day, and he would be out of here sipping a cold beer on his father's private jet, back to Dallas away from this shitty weather and shitty country. He was the heir to the family throne, there was no way his father would leave him stranded here. It didn't occur to Brad that what was happening in London might not be an isolated incident. His thoughts of Dallas included sunshine, parties, and bars. He didn't think how many people in Dallas might be infected right now, marauding through the city, breaking into his father's citadel, killing, maiming, destroying, and eating his father alive. Brad thought only of himself and how he was going to survive; that, and the fun he was having with Amber.

* * * *

Chloe was curled up asleep in the corner of the office, a thick A4 file doubling up as a pillow and a bundle of photocopier paper reinvented as a blanket. Above her, Tom read a motivational poster on the wall:

FIGHT for your customer,
FIGHT for your career,
FIGHT to work for the best -
Fiscal **I**ndustries, **G**oing **H**igher **T**ogether!

As corporate mottos go, thought Tom, it was definitely one of the more aggressive he had seen. There were no birds on trees or laughing children playing on the beach. The backdrop was a computer morphing into a man, punching another smaller looking computer to the floor. Clearly, Fiscal Industries was not short on confidence; this was a place for go-getters and money-men.

"That's the way it is," said Jessica, interrupting his thoughts. Startled, Tom turned around to find her stood behind him.

"Sorry, I thought everyone was asleep," said Tom. "I hope I didn't wake you, I couldn't sleep. Too much stuff flying round my brain."

"No, that's all right, I'm a light sleeper." Jessica swept her hair back over her ears in the dim light.

Tom looked over her shoulder at the clock on the wall. It was barely three a.m. "Sorry. That's how what is?" he said. She turned and he followed her back to the kitchen, leaving everyone else sleeping. In the kitchen they were alone.

"I just meant, you know, how it is here. So corporate and...*hard*, I guess is the right word." She covered her mouth as she yawned and Tom had to admit it, even at three a.m., even in these circumstances, she looked beautiful.

"How long have you worked here?" he asked.

"A few years. It's all right, I've had worse jobs. I'm pleased I'm not doing the hard graft like most of the suckers here. There are a few good people working here, but mostly, they're here for the money."

"I suppose you've met most of them working down in reception?"

"So you remember me then?" she said stifling another yawn.

"Yeah," Tom said, pleased the dull lighting hid his blushing cheeks. He held out his hand and she took it.

"Jessica. But you already know that." She shook his hand and smiled. Her hand was cold.

"You think we'll get out of here tomorrow?" she asked him. "I'm worried about my mum. She'll be going crazy not knowing where I am."

"I don't know," said Tom truthfully. "It's pretty weird out there. I'm going to suggest to some of the others that we do some scouting around. The front foyer is a dead end, quite literally. I was thinking maybe there's a fire exit or a back door or something? And if not, then we're going to need a lot more sandwiches."

"Mm, well, I'm sure it'll all be sorted by morning," whispered Jessica. She shivered. "Well, I need some rest. I'm going to try to sleep. Good night, Tom."

She gave Tom a hug and he embraced her slim body. He could smell her sweet perfume and brushed his cheek against her lush brown hair. He could feel how cold she was and as they parted, he took off his jacket.

"Here, take this, I think you need it more than me."

"Oh, well thanks, if you're sure. I'll give it back to you tomorrow." Tom stayed in the kitchen as she left. Jessica resumed her position on the floor near Parker.

"You're an idiot," he said to himself, and Tom sat down on the sofa. He closed his eyes and wondered what his parents were doing now. Were they safe at home? His mother had phoned him earlier so hopefully that meant she was. His dad was a workaholic, so he may well be stuck in his office too. Tom hoped his mum would be okay at home alone. His drowsy mind thought of Jessica, of his new colleagues and friends, of the helicopter crash, of the dead, and of how they were going to escape tomorrow.

By the time the office door swung open again a couple of hours later, he was fast asleep. Neither he nor anyone else on the floor heard Brad come back in.

CHAPTER SEVEN

Brad looked down at Amber, standing over her. Her bloodshot eyes stared back at him, dried lines of salty tears lining her cheeks. Hew swollen tongue hung limply from her mouth, her red lipstick smeared around her lips. He sighed. He hadn't intended to kill her. Not here, not at work. He had just got caught up in the moment. He looked again at her eyes bulging from their sockets unnaturally like a cartoon character. Her throat was red and he could still make out the purple traces of his fingers where he had throttled her after they had fucked. Even now, she looked like a whore to him.

Amber's body lay on the sofa where he'd left it. One arm had fallen down and her fingers brushed the carpet. Her legs were still splayed apart, her vagina cold but moist. He contemplated fucking her again now, whilst he still could, but wasn't sure if it was a good idea now that he was here. He had no qualms about going back for seconds when he was through with them, but he didn't want to get caught at work. If only he could be at home in private with Amber.

Brad walked to the window, naked. He had fully intended to take her home on Friday night after the party and do the slut there, but she was so damn arrogant, so persistent, that he hadn't been able to wait. Maybe it was for the best. He hated the cleaning up afterwards when he did them at home. The blood splatter, the hair, the laborious task of chopping them up and dragging them out to the back yard to burn them. A dead body was surprisingly heavy. Still, he supposed he was comfortable there and had his routine. He would shower, dress, and put on some soothing music; Handel was his favourite. Then he got down to the dirty work of chopping them up. Burn them. Bury the charred remnants. When they were gone, he would shower again and wash the scum and the filth off. What was he going to do here? There was nowhere to dispose of her and he wasn't stupid enough just to stuff her in a cupboard and hope no one would notice. That was how you got caught.

No, he had to be careful with this one. With all the trouble outside, nobody would notice she was gone for a while. In fact, with what was going on out there, this was probably a good opportunity. Brad smiled and turned away from the night sky. He could just throw her out, find a window that opened, or if he really had to, just drag her up to the roof and throw her off. Down on the streets she would be just another dead body; another piece of trash to clean up.

He glanced over at the clock and realised it was getting late. He should get back to the group before they noticed he was missing. They would be cowering under their desks by now, waiting for help that probably wasn't coming and singing kum-by-yah.

Brad chuckled and looked at Amber. Shame she had such a mouth on her. She had a good body too. He'd put her mouth to good use, but he knew she wouldn't be able to keep it closed later. He could've strung her along all night at home and really taught her a few tricks. He found himself growing hard again and walked over to the sofa.

He listened; it was deathly quiet. There was nobody on this floor and no one was coming looking for them. He crawled over Amber and knelt between her lifeless legs, pulling her closer as his penis grew harder. Why shouldn't he have some fun with her? He could get rid of the slut later. He pushed himself inside and began fucking her cold corpse. For Amber, the night was still young.

Ranjit flicked the monitor off, horrified and terrified in equal measure.

* * * *

Jillian tried to get things organised whilst they waited to hear news from downstairs yesterday. After Tom and Brad left, she checked the internet again, but there was nothing. She couldn't even get access to any websites; her computer kept flashing up the same old message: 'Access Denied.' Given how important she was, there had to be some mistake.

She called her friends, what few she had, her parents, even her ex-husband, but all she got was dead ends, answer machines and phones ringing out. She repeatedly kept trying security, but was repeatedly pushed away by an engaged tone. The evening had been the same and when she'd woken up early this morning, there was still nothing. The phone lines were completely dead now and her mobile could not get any reception no matter where she waved her phone around.

Jill gingerly got up and stretched. Her office floor had not been the most comfortable of places to spend the night. Her watch told her it was nearly seven. She was going to have to make some decisions today, as they couldn't stay here indefinitely. She stepped out on the office floor and was instantly reminded of the images she had seen of a refugee camp. Bodies lay everywhere. She could hear chattering from the kitchen and the kettle boiling, so she knew others were awake, too.

She decided she would have to send one of her agents down to security to see if they could get any information and find out when the doors would be opened. Someone else would have to go back down to the terrace café and see what the streets looked like. Someone else would have to go to the café kitchen and get more supplies. She, of course, would stay here and supervise.

Some of her staff, who had already woken, gathered together in the rec' room and were making cups of fresh tea and coffee.

"Morning, Jill," said Jackson, handing her a cup as she walked in.

"Jackson." She took it and drank eagerly. She counted nine people in the little kitchen. The others must still be sleeping. She opened her mouth to announce the plans for the day when Caterina walked in.

"Jill, you've got to sort this out, the toilet's blocked innit." Caterina stood looking at Jill, her hands on her ample hips, as was her favourite pouting pose, purposefully letting her pregnant belly stick out.

"I'll see what I can do, Caterina, but I doubt maintenance is in today." Jill turned to Jackson and he smiled sympathetically. Caterina grumbled and walked out cursing under her breath.

"That's not all, Jill," said Chloe. "I tried the shower this morning and it's not working."

"Chloe, that shower is only for executives, you know that, you shouldn't be in there."

"Yeah, well I doubt the executives will be in today either, Jill," said Chloe raising her eyebrows. Brad chuckled. He had never spoken to pimple-face before, but she had spirit. Most people didn't answer back to Jill like that, not when you were replaceable.

"I'm hungry, what's to eat?" said Parker as he and Jessica walked in. He had dark bags under his eyes and Jessica followed him in like a zombie, dragging her bare feet across the floor.

"Man it stinks in here," said Benzo. He was eating a limp lettuce sandwich and walked in to sit beside Brad.

"Yeah, well don't go expecting a shower anytime soon," said Chloe. Brad caught her eye and smiled. She nervously smiled back.

The office was suddenly full of talk: what there was to eat, when they would be leaving, and why nothing seemed to be getting done. Jill kept quiet, listening to everyone, until she could take no more.

"All right, just shut up - the lot of you!" She ensured that anyone who wasn't awake was now. The office hushed immediately. Jessica and Parker looked at each other and Jessica had to put her hand over her mouth to stop from laughing out loud.

"For Christ sake, I've got a plan on how to deal with all of this, just settle down and let me get on with it," said Jill.

"You going to send us an email?" said Freddy.

Jessica could contain herself no more and laughed, her giggle bouncing around the room as others joined in. The laughter increased as Freddy's guffawing boomed around the office.

"Freddy, what do you...everyone just be quiet, I can't think...please, this is not helping...I can't...please." Jill felt the walls closing in around her. She felt dizzy and Jackson took her arm.

"That's enough everyone," he said, "getting at Jill isn't helping, and it's not her fault we're in this mess." The room quietened down as he spoke, his voice both authoritative and soothing. "We're going to sit down and work this out together."

"I am so frigging tired," said Parker. "I need a cigarette."

"Guys, you need to see this." Tom stood in the doorway to the rec' room. Jackson could see Tom was shaken. Everyone looked a little off this morning, but Tom looked like he had seen a ghost.

Tom left the room and walked across the office to the tall windows on the far side. Everyone followed him.

"Look."

Tom pointed to the Akuma Insurance tower opposite them. It was a few stories taller than the Fiscal Industries building. The storm had well and truly gone, replaced by early morning sunshine that sparkled off the glass structures around the plaza. The rain had left the windows sparklingly clean.

The Insurance tower was burning fiercely, alight from the ground floor up to about the eighteenth. Incredible amounts of black smoke billowed from it, circling up high into the sky where it faded to grey and dissipated.

"Oh my God," said Jenny. She took Caterina's hand.

"How is it still burning?" said Jessica.

"No one to put the fire out," surmised Parker.

"Fuck the fire," said Benzo, "look up there." He pointed up and a few floors above them, a window had been smashed open. A lone man was leaning out. He seemed to be gulping, as if trying to swallow the fresh air. He had a white shirt on and a tie hanging loosely around his collar. On the floor above, they saw another open window and a cluster of people, men and women. They appeared to be trying to talk to one another when suddenly the lone man was grabbed and hauled back into the building.

"Where is he, what's happening?" said Jessica.

"I think..." began Tom, but there was no need to answer. The lone man reappeared at the window holding onto someone else. It was impossible to tell if the other figure was a man or a woman. All they could make out, was that this figure had a strong hold on the other man. It appeared to be biting him and blood was pouring down the man's creased white shirt. The two struggled with each other in the window frame. A moment later and they stumbled out through the open window.

Tom and the rest of floor sixteen watched in horror as the two figures fell, still holding onto one another, through the smoke and the fire to the ground below. There were audible gasps in the room and shrieks from Jenny and Jill. The others recoiled, unable to watch. Chloe started crying and Brad put his arm around her.

The two figures hurtled down until they reached the ground and Tom watched them explode, blood shooting out in all directions. It was like watching a large fly being swatted against a window, blood and innards spewing out in a thick sticky mess.

He slowly looked up past the open window to the floor above. Now there was just one woman stood there. The others had disappeared behind her. Her eyes were closed and she was clutching her arms to her chest. She took a step forward, raising her foot over the window's edge, out into the open air.

"Oh no." Tom shook his head slowly and put his hands over his mouth. The woman took another step and exited the building the only way she could, on her own terms. She flew rapidly through the air. Her face was calm and emotionless as she disappeared into the smoke and then reappeared further down. She landed close to the other man, her bright red blood splashing out over the pale concrete. Around the fresh bodies swarmed hundreds of zombies. The streets below were full of them. It was hard to see any of the street or plaza at all, so full was it of the dead.

"Screw this," said Parker. He threw up into a bin and walked away, unable to watch any more. Others began to join him, knowing what was going to happen, but unwilling to watch. Tom stared as another figure, another woman in a white blouse, whistled past his eyes. She was screaming and screaming until she hit the side of the building and bounced off. Then the screaming abruptly stopped. Tom sank down to the floor. He put his hand in front of his mouth and told himself to get a grip. He tried to tell his hand to stop trembling, but it wouldn't. He told his stomach to hold onto its contents, but they refused to obey and he threw up in the nearest waste basket that he could reach.

"Fuck this, what are we gonna do? We've got to get out of here!" Freddy was pacing up and down anxiously.

"Like that? No fucking way," said Brad. The office was now full of crying and sobbing. Nobody said anything for a few minutes as they digested what was happening mere feet away. Everyone was facing the floor or into the office. Not a soul could bear to look out the window for fear of what they might see. The same thoughts reverberated through everyone's minds. How long would it be before it was their turn? Would they jump too?

"We should wait it out," said Jackson, eventually breaking the silence. "Those things down there can't last forever. Our building is secure and safe. Sooner or later the government will have to act. They'll send someone. They can't just leave us." He was sat leaning back against the wall by the water cooler. He looked like he had aged ten years overnight, thought Jenny.

"I agree," said Brad. Tom was surprised to hear Brad siding with Jackson. He had assumed Brad would want out of here as quickly as possible.

"Look, there are twenty five floors in this damn building. That means about twenty five kitchens and the café on the second floor. I'd say about half of them at least would be well stocked, so there's food and water here. We just have to get organised. We can search the floors carefully and regroup back here. If we stay here, we'll be safe."

"Exactly," said Jill. Her face lit up. Finally someone was seeing sense. "We can go without our luxuries for a couple of days. We can survive this. Those things can't get at us here."

"But my wife..."

"My parents won't..."

"I need to get home to..."

Jill was met by a chorus of disagreeing voices. She stood up and rubbed her tired eyes.

Caterina walked back to the window and looked down to the ground below. "There's so many of 'em."

"I think we should leave," said Tom. "We're only as safe in here for as long as we think we are. We need to find a way out."

"Seems to me we're in a bit of a quandary. The only way we're going to sort this, is with more information," said Jackson. "I can see logic with both sides of the argument."

Brad rolled his eyes and arched his back. His neck cracked as he limbered up. He had not had much sleep in the night.

"We need to make sure we're secure here, but we also need to come up with an escape plan, 'cause I sure don't see any sign of help coming," said Jackson. "I can organise things and I'm happy to co-ordinate everything, I suggest we..."

"Hey, Jackson, chill buddy. This ain't World War Two and you're not in charge. This is a democracy," said Brad.

"Listen, son, I'm just suggesting that I have more experience than you, so it makes sense to..." said Jackson. He pulled himself up off the floor using the water cooler as a hand rail.

"Oh, fuck off, Jackson," said Brad walking towards him. "If there was a crown of thorns here, you'd be parading around in it. You're such a fucking martyr. You can't save everyone, buddy."

"All right, come on guys, knock it off, we're all stressed out," said Tom.

"Yeah," said Benzo, taking hold of Brad's arm, "let's just chill and figure this out." Brad and Jackson stared at each other while the room watched. There was no sound, but the ticking of the clock on the wall. Finally Jackson held up his hands.

"Whatever, let's just get this sorted. I'm tired." He slumped back against the wall.

"Tom, buddy, why don't you go downstairs, see if you can find anything from security," said Brad taking Chloe's hand. She looked up at him, surprised. "See if there's another door somewhere that might be clear? A fire exit or something, you never know. Until we find anything better, we'd better get prepared. Let's pair up, search this building floor by floor, and bring any food and drink we can back here."

"I'll come with you, mate," said Freddy to Tom. "Getting out of here is my priority. This place is just a fucking tomb."

"Okay, nut up people, find a partner and get looking," said Brad. "Jill, make yourself useful for once and draw up a list for us. One pair to search two floors each just about covers it. We should get this done by lunchtime. I'll start with Chloe and cover seventeen and eighteen."

Brad walked off pulling Chloe behind him, straight out into the stairwell. Jill said nothing, but grabbed a sheet of paper and drew up a list. At no point did she even attempt to handle the shift in power now developing. Brad's condescending words sailed clean over her head. Once all the floors had been covered, she handed the list out so everyone knew where to head.

"I'll stay here and tidy up," she said. "Caterina, in your condition, I think you'd better stay here too. Maybe you can sort out the kitchen, please? It's bit of a mess."

Caterina huffed and then shuffled off to clean the kitchen, secretly glad she didn't have to wander the building. Despite what had happened in the other tower, she felt safe here. Who knew what was on the other floors. There could be more of those people: the infected and the dead.

Jackson wandered off with a man named Troy. He was a quiet man, subservient, and went along with any suggestion the group offered.

With Caterina in the kitchen and the others off searching the building, it wasn't long before Jill was alone. She wheeled the television in from the meeting room and turned it on. Not surprisingly, there was nothing on. There was no emergency broadcast signal, no news, and nothing but snow on all the channels. She looked around the office. How long would they have to stay here? She returned to her office and thought about the women who had jumped. God help them all if it came to that. She couldn't imagine the terror they must have felt stepping out of the building. Taking one's own life was the ultimate decision. Perhaps it was better to die now, than suffer for eternity.

* * * *

Christina had spent the night in the boardroom, lying under the huge desk. She had drawn the blinds, blotting out the night, but she couldn't bring herself to leave. After the helicopter had crashed, she was scared. She was scared to leave, but scared to stay. She had fixed something to eat in the kitchen, but hadn't really had much of an appetite. The night had been restless, her thoughts and dreams random and obscure. In one, Edward had come back, but he had walked in to Christina's office and just kissed her, then left without saying a word. In another, she was lying on the beach in the south of France where she had gone last year, except the beach was empty. All the tourists had gone and she was lying peacefully on the beach as the ocean lapped at her feet. A cloud suddenly blocked out the sun and when she opened her eyes, a helicopter was plummeting down to her.

Christina drew back the blinds and was shocked. The building opposite was burning from top to bottom. She knew people who worked for Akuma and was worried.

"How on earth...?" She looked from side to side but the other buildings were the same as yesterday. It seemed quiet. The sun was shining. She tried to see the airport, but the smoke blocked her view. She realised that the helicopter had crashed into the building last night. Shouldn't the fire brigade have come by now to put it out? Where were the police? Christina looked down at the ground. There were thousands and thousands of people filling the streets. Was there some kind of demonstration or protest march going on? She had seen a few lately, especially around the city, but normally, the hippies were quietly and quickly moved on. This was something else.

She picked up the phone but it was dead. She went back into the office and tried calling security from her desk, but there was no answer. All the outside lines were down. She tried email, but she hadn't had any since yesterday morning. She tried the internet but could not get access.

"This is ridiculous." Christina could feel her anger rising again as she picked up her black suit jacket and went to the stairwell. She was just going to have to go downstairs and face the problem head on. Christina started the long journey down.

* * * *

"Oh, Brad, I just don't know what to do," said Chloe, rummaging through the kitchen cupboards on the eighteenth floor. "I mean, is it that bad out there? Really? I want to go home, but..."

"Hey, buddy, yes it *is* that bad out there. You find anything useful?" Brad had a plastic bag over his shoulder full of packets of biscuits.

"No, not really, whoever worked on this floor was well stingy." She slammed the cupboard shut. "All I could find was this bloody packet of mints."

Brad looked at her holding up a thin tube of mint sweets. She wasn't the most attractive of girls, but she had a good figure.

"You know it's funny we work in the same office and yet, I don't think we've ever spoken to each other. How old are you, Chloe?"

"Twenty one." Brad just looked at her and nodded. Chloe had looked at Brad many times, particularly at those crystal blue eyes, but had never been brave enough to speak to him before.

"How old are you?" she said, unsure of herself, putting the mints back down on the desk.

"Older than you. And old enough." Brad put the plastic bag down and walked out of the kitchen area. He gave her a big grin. "Come on."

Brad went to the lounge area where there were some big sofas and he sat down. Chloe followed him and sat down next to him. She pulled her short skirt down as she sat and clasped her hands on her bare knees.

"We should keep looking for stuff, you know," she said nervously, looking ahead into the vacant office.

"Yeah, we will. I just want to make sure you're okay," he replied. He put his hand on hers.

"I'm okay, I suppose. I'm a bit worried but..."

"I hope we make it out of this," he said, removing his hand and reclining in the sofa. The room faced away from the burning building, so the sunshine was beaming straight into the room and Chloe's legs were already getting warm.

"Do you think we will?" Chloe turned to look at Brad. The sunlight was making his eyes seem even bluer than usual, and he looked at her tenderly. He just nodded and took her hand again. He leant forward and kissed her gently on the lips.

"Chloe, you're so amazing." Brad was well practised at this and found it hard not to laugh. It was so easy. He knew he was a killer, but he was not a rapist; they always wanted him.

"Oh, Brad," she murmured, and she held him close, kissing his neck as he caressed her. He unzipped his jeans and pushed her head down. Inexperienced and unable to resist, Chloe bent over and took Brad in her mouth.

"Gentle, Chloe. Slower."

She sucked on his hardness, amazed that he should like her so much. He was going to take care of her. Maybe he would tell everyone he was her boyfriend and then she would have him all to herself. His hands were forcing her head down so hard that she was struggling to breathe though, and Chloe stopped.

"Sorry, I just had to..."

"It's all right, babe," Brad said standing up. He pulled his shirt off over his head exposing his flat stomach. He let his jeans drop to the floor. "Take your clothes off."

Chloe was shaking like the last leaf on the tree in autumn, but undid the buttons on her blouse and cast it aside. She reached around her back and took off her black bra, draping it over the sofa. He admired her full breasts and she reached out to take him in her mouth again. He stopped her.

"And the rest," he said.

"What if someone comes?" Chloe said looking around, looking mischievously up at Brad, dreamy Brad.

"I'm hoping someone does, if you know what I mean?" Brad winked, took hold of her hands and pulled her up. She stood before him and they kissed. Chloe longed to feel more of Brad as he licked his way down her chest, between her breasts and over her nipples to her belly. She let him unfasten her skirt and it slid to the floor. Closing her eyes, she felt Brad pull her panties down and she moved her feet apart so he could find her. She moaned as he caressed her and used his tongue to pleasure her.

"Oh, Brad." When Chloe was close to orgasm, he suddenly stood up and kissed her again. She could feel his proud erection against her thigh. He pushed her onto the sofa and she fell over the arm. Knowing Brad was behind her, she spread her legs and she felt his hands on her waist. He instantly thrust himself inside her and began fucking her. At first, he went slowly and she enjoyed it; it was only the second time she had gone all the way with a man. As Brad continued though, he got more forceful and he began to hurt her.

"Brad, I..."

"Shut up." Brad moved his hands up her body and crudely grabbed her tits, crushing them with his exploring fingers. He felt her try to pull away and grabbed her closer, fucking her harder and forcing her down into the sofa so she couldn't get away.

"Brad, don't..." Chloe didn't have the strength to throw him off and knew it. She closed her eyes and thought of home as he fucked her, wishing it to be over. All thoughts of mutual orgasms were gone and she wanted it to stop. Brad didn't care about her or he wouldn't be hurting her like this. She tried to get up again but felt his hand push down on her neck, pushing her face into the crease of the cushion. Worried that if he pushed her down any further she wouldn't be able to breathe, she stopped fighting him and let him fuck her.

It seemed to take a long time before he came. After he had, he collapsed on top of her and she felt his warm sweaty body on her back before he rolled off.

"Buddy, that was just what I needed," he said as he sat beside her. She slunk back onto the sofa and sat beside him, not touching him. She brought her knees up to her chin and closed her eyes.

"What's wrong with you?" he said. She had crossed her arms in front of her and was facing away from him. She wanted to get dressed, but was worried what he might do if she tried to leave.

"Brad, I told you to stop and..."

"And what? You wanted me to fuck you. Someone's got to teach you the ways of the world, girlie. Stay there, I'm not done with you yet." Brad laughed and got off the sofa picking his clothes up.

"Whatever. I'm going to see Jill." Chloe bent down to pick her clothes up and felt Brad's hands on her neck.

"Ow, stop it. That hurts."

"Fucking hell, you whores are all the same. Get up." Brad forced Chloe up and grabbed her arm, twisting it behind her back. He marched her over to a wall.

"You sure you don't want me to fuck you again? Are you absolutely, positively sure?" Brad stared into her eyes. Suddenly, his blue eyes didn't seem so charming. His face was set like stone and Chloe was anxious to leave.

"Yes. Please, Brad, let me go, you're hurting me." Chloe was now more scared of what was happening inside the building than outside.

"Well that's a shame, Chloe. I know I'm a good fuck and you weren't so bad. That's a real shame. You know what happened to the last cunt who fucked me, then tried to fuck me over?"

Brad pulled a handle on the wall behind Chloe and a door flung open. Nestled between a row of hanging coats was Amber. She had been propped up against the back wall and her bulging dead eyes stared back at Chloe. She was naked and covered in cuts and bruises. Her twisted legs had turned a horrible shade of purple and her face was locked in an expression of shock. Brad let go of Chloe's arm and she spun around. Brad looked at Chloe's face, so young and full of fear.

"What did you...?" Brad grabbed Chloe's throat with both hands and squeezed. Her weak arms were no match for his and she clung to his forearms until the end. It only took about thirty seconds before her body went limp. He kept squeezing, to make sure. When she could no longer support her own body weight, he took her dead body and dragged it back to the sofa.

"I told you I wasn't done with you yet, bitch." He threw Chloe back over the sofa, putting a pillow under her stomach, raising her backside into the air. He aroused himself, ready to fuck her again. Unlike Amber, she was still warm to the touch.

"Enjoy the show, babe," he said to Amber. Her limp face did not answer and her dead eyes were incapable of witnessing the violent abuse that Brad inflicted on Chloe's dead body. Her fingers did twitch though as the infection began to trickle through her lifeless body, the infected rat that had bitten her long since gone to find another source of food.

CHAPTER EIGHT

"Philip, come on, we can't."

Philip looked at his wife with mock disdain. "I think we can and we shall and we will." He poured the red wine into the wine glasses that were still dirty from the night before, picked them up, and walked back around to the plump leather chairs where they were sat. He handed his wife a glass.

"So what shall we do today, Kate?" He raised his glass to toast her and his face fell when she refused to raise hers.

"I'm serious, Philip, we can't muck around forever." Kate put her wine down on the glass table and put one hand to her temple. "Besides, I've got a headache."

"Ah-ha, I knew it! You're just a lightweight." Philip took a sip of wine and embraced the burn. They had spent all last night drinking, before succumbing to sleep on the very same chairs where they were now. They wore the same clothes as yesterday, the same clothes they had slept in. What choice did they have?

"Darling, I'm just going to remind you of one thing," said Philip.

"What's that?" said Kate. She curled up into the black leather and willed her headache to go away.

"You're right, we can't muck around forever. We also can't fuck around forever. In fact, I would say we can't do a lot of anything forever." Philip laughed at his own joke.

Kate looked at her husband, unsure if he was actually trying to prove a point, or if he was just drunk. She reached for the wine and took a sip.

"Do you remember what we did yesterday? After everyone ran? We came here, to the bar. It was your idea. I distinctly remember you saying, 'Screw them all, let's go to the bar and get shit-faced.' Yay or nay?" Philip felt the flush of red wine in his throat and suppressed a burp.

"Something like that," Kate said. She had said it impulsively and regretted it now. She had never had as much stamina as her husband for drink. They had met in a wine bar twelve months ago, been married six months ago, and drunk through pretty much the whole thing since. Any thoughts of having children she had given up on a long time ago. Even if they'd decided to have kids, Philip spent so much time drinking that they rarely made love anymore, so it would be a long time coming.

"Well, I thought it was a good idea." Philip got up and walked over to the window. Ten floors below him was the plaza.

"They're still there, those things. Those bloody infected *things*. Christ, what a disgrace. I tell you, Kate, coming here was the best bloody idea you've ever had. Apart from marrying me, of course." He continued staring at the streets below.

"Philip, don't you think we should try to do something today?"

"Like what? Fight back like the army did? You saw how that turned out yesterday." Philip turned around and looked around the bar. It had been set up as a place to wine and dine clients. The office on the other side of the floor was completely separate from this area. If you didn't know better, you would think you were in a fine dining restaurant in the city.

"Look at this place, Kate. It's perfect. We've got enough food and booze to last us ages. I'm not going to try and fight off a thousand of those bloody...chavs downstairs, when I can wait up here for someone else to sort the damn mess out. This is Armani you know," he said pointing at the suit he wore.

"Like who, Philip? Who is going to sort this? You just said so yourself, the army crashed and burned, much like the Akuma Insurance people." Kate looked wistfully out at the burning building opposite. It was starting to burn itself out. The flames were subsiding although the black plumes of smoke still ascended from the building's orifices.

"Look, I don't know, the government will sort something out.

The Tories can't fuck this one up. If they lose the city, its game over. No, they'll do something. I'm not pussying out like the chasers over at Akuma."

Kate physically cringed. She hated it when Philip referred to them as chasers. Anyone who worked in the Insurance building was one, he said, just another grease-ball climbing the slippery pole, chasing the money. Anyone like that ended up working in the Akuma building. He seemed to think that what he did was somehow superior to them, as if he wasn't chasing after money day and night himself.

"Have some respect, Philip. You think they would've jumped if there was any other way out?"

He shrugged his shoulders. "So what then? You can take the fire escape if you like, but I don't think you'll get far. No, you're better off waiting it out up here with me." Philip walked back around the bar and found a packet of peanuts. He threw one over to Kate. "Breakfast?"

"Shush, hang on, I hear something," she said tossing the peanuts away.

"Oh come on, darling, I..."

"Shush!" Kate stood up and glared at him. It was not a face he was used to and he shut up. Maybe she had heard something; they listened and then he heard it too: footsteps.

Philip picked up an empty wine bottle and held it by the neck over his shoulder, ready to strike.

"It's coming from the stairwell. Maybe it's help?" said Kate, cheering up as she walked over to the door.

"Maybe," said Philip warily. Kate pushed open the door and disappeared. Philip heard talking and waited. His wife did not come back and he counted the seconds.

"Kate?" He went over to the door and raised the wine bottle higher. The door abruptly opened and Kate came through followed by two figures.

"Philip, we're not as alone as we thought. This is Benzo and Michelle. They're from floor sixteen."

Philip dropped the bottle to the floor, embarrassed, and shook their hands.

* * * *

83

Jenny had managed to swap with Benzo, grateful that she wouldn't have to go far. He had agreed to swap with her and now she only had to do floors thirteen to fifteen with Dina. Both were larger ladies and stairs were alien to them. It had taken them an hour to go through floors fifteen and fourteen, coming up with surprisingly little. There were fridges on both, and they'd grabbed a loaf of bread and a tub of butter encrusted with sticky jam residue. Other than that, they had turned up nothing of value. They were just carbon copy floors of their own: endless rows of computers and telephones, square desks and shiny screens.

"I'm worried about Amber," said Jenny to Dina as they approached the thirteenth floor.

"Who's that?" said Dina.

"Blonde girl, really pretty. Sits next to Brad?"

"Oh, yeah." Dina was not much of a conversationalist - which was not ideal, considering she worked in a call centre. Jenny didn't care much for her to be honest; she was a cat person and Dina was a dog person. There was never going to be any love lost between them. Dina was an institution at Fiscal. She had worked there almost thirty years, starting a year after Jackson, and her bob of white hair was as familiar as anything in the office. She had seen many blonde bimbos come and go over the years.

"I haven't seen her today, have you? I hope she's all right." Jenny coughed and pushed open the door to floor thirteen, leaving the cold stairwell behind.

"She'll be fine," said Dina. "I'm more worried about what's in here. It's a bit spooky."

Jenny looked at her frowning. "Why?"

"Floor thirteen isn't it. It's unnatural." Jenny wasn't the only one who found Dina odd. Apart from an overzealous passion for dogs, her other passion was God. Jenny knew she went to church religiously, never missing a service. Her husband had died many years ago and since then, there had been only one other man in her life: Jesus.

On the desks at work, Jill allowed them one photo. Jenny had a picture of her cats. Rob had a picture of David Beckham. Parker had a picture of Victoria Beckham, and Amber a picture of her parents. Dina had a picture of Jesus on the cross: now that was just weird.

"Let's just find the kitchen and get out of here. This is the last one and then we can get back upstairs," said Jenny, not wanting to draw her colleague any further on why floor thirteen should be unnatural. She knew it was likely to lead to a cross-examination of Jenny's moral and religious beliefs and she really couldn't be bothered with it all right now.

They found the kitchen and began examining the draws and cupboards. Jenny found a packet of mint chocolate biscuits and popped one in her mouth. It was only fair: she'd been up and down those stairs for the last hour.

Dina found a bag of salad in the fridge that had turned soggy. Jenny found a packet of cheap Japanese noodles and decided to take them back with her upstairs. Dina found some crisp light wafers and put them back. You can't eat cardboard, she muttered to herself.

"What are you doing?" A man appeared in the kitchen doorway, his booming voice startling the two women. Jenny shrieked and dropped the biscuits on the floor, whilst Dina grabbed a fork, the nearest thing to hand, and brandished it in front of her.

"Who are you people?" the man demanded again. Jenny looked him up and down. The man held a long mop above his head. He was dark and swarthy, but he wasn't dressed like the others. His clothes were dirty and he seemed to be wearing an overall of some sort. With her pounding heart slowly calming down, she managed to speak.

"We're from floor sixteen. We were just looking for some food. I'm Jenny and this is Dina."

Nobody moved and three sets of eyes glanced around from one to the other until the man laughed.

"Sorry, you can put the fork down, darling, you just spooked me," he said. The man took a step into the kitchen and the women relaxed. He put the mop down, leaning it against the kitchen counter.

"I'm Reggie. So you're from sixteen, eh? Are there many people left there?"

"Yes, well, no. There's a few of us," said Jenny as Dina put the fork back on the counter. She just smiled at Reggie. In her world, she didn't mix with such people. Nobody like this man attended her church group and she was quite happy about that.

"Well, I'm pleased to hear I'm not the last man on the planet," Reggie said laughing. "Look, I'm sorry for jumping out at you, but I thought I was alone and I think you made me jump as much as I did you. Um, there's not much food here I'm afraid. I was going to go downstairs to the café to see if I could find something actually. Do you want to come with me?"

"Thanks, but actually we've already sent someone down there," said Jenny. Despite her initial shock, Reggie seemed a nice man. "So who are you exactly? I mean, no offence, but you don't really look like you work here."

"Coz I'm black?" he said. Reggie crossed his arms and frowned at her.

"Oh, no, oh goodness now, I mean, sorry, no not that..." stuttered Jenny. Dina looked down at her feet.

"Ha ha, I'm just messing with you! Ha!" Reggie's laugh bellowed out and Jenny began to laugh too, relieved.

"I know, it's my overall. I'm the janitor. I fix the lights, the wiring, just bits and bobs, you know."

"Well, Reggie, if you want to come back up to sixteen with us, we're gathering there and hopefully the others have had a bit more luck like finding some food." Jenny held up a wilting, squashed loaf of bread.

"Thanks, don't mind if I do. Been awful lonely here this last day." He looked sad and Jenny touched his arm as she passed him by. Reggie plodded after Jenny to the stairwell and Dina picked up the fork before following: just in case, she thought.

* * * *

Brad stuffed Chloe into the closet next to Amber, promising himself that he would get rid of them soon. He knew it was risky leaving them around, but really, who was going to come snooping through broom cupboards and coat cupboards now? Tonight, he thought. Tonight he would sneak back up here, jimmy open a window, and dump them. Okay, he might have a little fun first, and then dump them. Who knew how long it would be before he got another chance. They could be stuck here for a long time.

He closed the door and the sunlight disappeared from Chloe's and Amber's faces. He rustled briefly through the kitchen and found some yoghurt. That'll do, he thought, and slung the six-pack into the plastic bag with the biscuits he'd found earlier.

Before he left, he checked around one more time. He had scooped up Chloe's clothes and buried them in a desk drawer. There was no evidence of a struggle and no sign that anyone had even been here. He hadn't gotten this far by being messy. Brad re-entered the stairwell and heard the faint clip-clopping footsteps of his colleagues, searching up and down for food and water: idiots. He knew they wouldn't find much. His suggestion of searching the building had just been a ruse to get some alone time. They'd get all the food they needed from the café.

Brad turned up the stairs and came face to face with Parker.

"Oh, hey, buddy, what did you find? Anything good?" asked Brad.

"Yeah, we got a decent bag full of sandwiches here. It'll do for now. You?"

"Hi, Brad!" chirruped Jessica from behind Parker.

"Nothing, just this." Brad showed Parker the bag of food, ignoring Jessica.

"Well we can help you, mate. You were checking eighteen weren't you?" Parker said taking a step down toward the door.

"Yeah, no, thanks, buddy, but I've got it covered." Brad stood in the doorway. "We searched everywhere, there's nothing left, trust me."

"All right, your call. Hey, where's Chloe?"

Brad forced himself to smile. "She went on ahead of me back to sixteen. Said she needed the ladies."

"I'll go find her," said Jessica pushing past them, down the stairs. From behind Jessica another figure appeared and Brad frowned.

"Who's this, Parker?"

"Oh, shit, sorry, forgot to do the intro's. Brad, this is Christina." He stepped aside and Brad saw a woman in a dark business suit step out, offering her hand. She looked tired but trim. She was what, forty, forty five? Brad flashed her his best blue-eyed smile.

"Morning, ma'am," he said briskly shaking her hand. He tried not to let the surprise show when she grasped his hand back and shook it vigorously. No limp fish here, no sir.

"Brad." She said his name in a monotone voice; as if she was seeing him but not all there. He let go of her hand.

"She all right, buddy?" asked Brad as they continued together downstairs back to sixteen.

"Yeah, I think so. We found her on the top floor. Her office was a mess and I don't think she's eaten much in the last twenty four hours." Parker looked over his shoulder at Christina. She was holding onto the bannister, looking down at her feet, not paying any attention to the two men in front of her.

"Another mouth to feed, huh? Hope Benzo got something tasty from the cafe, buddy." Brad walked on ahead and Parker sighed. Sometimes Brad could be a real dick.

"Come on, Christina," said Parker. He took her hand and guided her down the steps toward floor sixteen.

* * * *

Jackson walked back into the office on floor sixteen and saw everybody was sat around in the centre of the office. Some were on chairs, others just lying across the floor or draped over bags. It was like they were at home now, all pretensions of office etiquette long gone. He and Troy had not turned up much of use. Troy retreated to a corner of the room on his own, leaving Jackson alone. They had hardly talked the whole time they were searching. Jackson went into the kitchen to see what they had managed to amass so far. There was a reasonable selection and it would probably last them another day. But then what, he thought.

He ran his hands under the tap and splashed water over his face. What on earth would his wife be thinking now? Poor Mary; she wasn't used to being on her own. Jackson tried to send his thoughts through the air to his beloved wife: lock yourself in and don't try to come looking for me. I'll be home soon as I can, honey. Just stay safe, please, stay safe.

He used a paper towel to dry himself and went back into the office. Now, he looked again and noticed some new faces. So they had found more than just food and drink. There was a couple, looking very tired, sat on a couple of chairs. Then there was an older woman in a suit and a man in overalls. Twenty five floors and that's it? There must've been over two thousand people working in this building and they were all that was left? He couldn't see Jill; she must still be hiding in her office. Jackson sat down and listened to the conversation going on.

"The foyer was scary, I tell you," said Tom. He was holding court whilst the others sat around him. It was as if he was telling a story around the campfire, thought Jackson.

"There's certainly no way out through the front door. They're packed right up against the door and the walls. It's like being an animal at the zoo. They're just staring in at us; watching us watching them. When Freddy and I moved, they moved with us. They were biting and scratching and kicking, thousands of them, fighting to get in, to get to us. They obviously know we're in here."

"Or there's nowhere else they want to go," said Parker absently.

"Maybe they want do the filing," said Brad. Nobody laughed. Jackson fought the urge to wipe the smirk from Brad's face.

"I hate to say it, but there's nobody alive out there," said Tom. "Not in the plaza at least."

"Figured as much," said Reggie sucking his teeth. "I ain't seen much of the world with these eyes, but I know death when I see it."

"Anyway," said Tom as he went on, "Freddy and I tried the reception phones but they're all dead, just like ours. So we decided to try and find security, see if we could find their office or something. There was a door behind reception so we did some exploring. There are lots of smaller rooms down there, probably for building management or admin' or something. We almost got lost down there, it's like a rabbit warren. Behind one, there was an almighty thumping, like something was trapped in there."

"Or someone," said Caterina.

"Well, we tried opening the door but it was locked. We asked if there was anyone in there but nobody answered. The banging went on and on, and in the end, we gave up. At least if it's locked, whatever is in there can't get out."

"So how did Freddy get hurt?" said Jenny. Jackson looked around the group and noticed that Freddy wasn't there. His stomach turned over.

"Well, we found a room that led to another stairwell, separate from the one we've been using. We went down and at the bottom, another door led into an underground car park. It was dark, really dark. We called out, but it was empty. Nobody answered us. There are a couple of cars down there but otherwise it's empty. Well, sort of.

"We were about to leave when Freddy shouted something, which I won't repeat, but it involved a lot of words starting with f and s. I turned around and he was dancing up and down on the spot like a bloody madman. He kicked his legs around and a rat flew out of his trouser leg."

"Jesus, a rat? Ugh." Kate sunk deeper into Philip's arms.

"The rat flew back against the wall, then it just got up and ran straight back at Freddy. He managed to kick it away and it came back again."

"Are you sure it was a rat?" said Parker. "They don't usually attack humans and if they're cornered like that, they would probably run the other way, not keep attacking."

"Well, this rat obviously likes to be different," said Tom. "Freddy stomped on it until it finally stopped moving. I tried shooing it away but I had nothing to help with. We were stupid. We should have gone prepared and taken a weapon, a knife or something."

"It wasn't your fault, Tom," said Parker. He thought about Cindy lying in the meat locker downstairs.

"Well, the bastard's bitten Freddy badly. His leg has got some nasty bites on it. He's in the bathroom now trying to wash the wounds. We found a first aid kit and there was some kind of cream in it."

"I think I'll go make sure he's okay," said Jackson, leaving the room.

"And that's it really," said Tom. "All in all, it was a waste of time. Freddy got a nasty bite and we came up with nothing. We couldn't find any other door out of here. No rear exit and no door to the outside that wasn't locked or blocked by a thousand zombies."

"Zombies?" whispered Philip to Kate. "I'd like some of what this lot have been smoking." Kate shushed her husband, fed up of him never taking anything seriously.

"I don't agree, buddy," said Brad. "That car park you found underground. I didn't even know about that. Who did, right? It must be for the top dogs. I don't know where it leads, but if the cars got in, there's a way out. That could be our way out of here."

"That's true; we should go now while we can!" A woman stood up. Tom had not spoken to her before. She was new.

"Even *I* couldn't get a space there, but I know of it. Of course, I'm so stupid! There's a tunnel that runs right under the river and it comes out near the Onevision conference centre." The small group of faces looked blankly back at Christina.

"Well, anyway, I can show you, it's really close. The tunnel will be deserted. We *could* get out that way." Christina felt a weight lift from her shoulders. She would be back home again soon and back to her normal life. She had enough of this building, of this life, and what it had made her become.

"Whoa there, hold on everyone," said Parker. "It's a plan, but right now that's all it is. Freddy and Tom went down there and came back with a rat bite. If we all go down there gung ho, who knows what we could find or what we could come back with. It could be far worse than a rat bite if we're not careful.

"We need to find torches, get prepared, and think this through. What if we get through the pitch black tunnel somehow to the other side? Then what? And what if we find a thousand more of those zombie things waiting for us? What if we walk right into the infection?"

"He's right," said Benzo. "Look, there's a pile of food in the kitchen. I say we eat, drink, and think. In that order. There's no hurry as far as I can tell. We're not going anywhere and neither are those things outside."

There were murmurs of agreement from the group, but they were excited. There was something they could latch onto now; it was only an idea, but it was something. There *might* be a way out.

People started leaving the office to get food, drifting into the kitchen. Tom saw Jill turn away from her office door and shut it behind her. She was withdrawing more and more into herself and cutting herself off from the others. He told himself he would try to talk to her again later.

Tom didn't feel as hungry as the others, he just wanted to see how Freddy was doing. He went to the bathroom to find Jackson. As he entered the stalls, Tom was shocked. Freddy looked up at him and Tom felt like he was looking at a dead man. Freddy was not just pale, but practically white. The bright lighting only heightened Freddy's deathly looking face.

"Help me," said Jackson as Freddy collapsed. They caught him and lowered him carefully to the bathroom floor.

"What the hell is going on?" said Tom. "A rat bite can't do this, surely?"

"That's what I thought. Look at his leg," said Jackson. Tom peeled back Freddy's jeans and rolled them up exposing his shins. He couldn't even see where the rat had bitten him anymore. Freddy's skin was mottled with green and blue bruises and blisters ran all the way up his leg. Freddy's neck was clammy and there was a faint white furry growth stretching around his neck and chin, almost like mould. Tom felt Freddy's forehead; it was ice cold.

"We've got to get him out of here," said Jackson. "He's infected."

CHAPTER NINE

Tom dangled his legs over the roof edge not looking down, but across the city. From up here he was level, or above, most of the other buildings in the vicinity. The Akuma Insurance building was now just a smouldering wreck. He counted six other flat roofs that he could see, all empty. He thought he might see others up here, perhaps people waving for help or painted signs declaring they were trapped or needed help. All he saw were grey squares of concrete, rusting unused fire escapes, and ventilation shafts.

The windows of the office blocks were more interesting. The closest building to him that was still intact, was a grey monolithic structure dedicated to easy loans with stupendous repayment options. Its huge structure reached high up above Tom, looming over him and casting half the roof into shadow. Its fifty nine floors dwarfed the meagre twenty five of the Fiscal Industries' building. Most of the people inside were no different to him, not really. They were just trying to make a living; to get by. Well, thought Tom, they're all dead now.

Every window in the building was blown out. Fire had engulfed it from the ground floor to the top, or at least as far as Tom could see. It still burned fiercely on some floors, others were gutted, and he could see smouldering traces of the building's past life: telephones and chairs reduced to ashes, black computer terminals that had melted into the floor, crisp flakes of paper swirling around in the acrid smoke, out into the air outside where it cascaded gently down to the ground. Tom looked at the floor directly opposite him as something moved inside. It was probably something falling off a desk, blown by the wind. He focused on the room and saw it again. There was a figure moving and walking around.

"Hey! Hey, over here!" Tom stood up and waved. The figure stopped moving. It came toward the window and Tom's heart sank. It was another one of them; the dead. It walked toward him slowly and Tom saw the figure was horribly burnt. With no comprehension of space, it continued coming toward Tom until it simply walked out of the window and plummeted down to the ground.

Tom watched as the figure cartwheeled around and around. Unlike the people yesterday from the Akuma tower, Tom did not see it hit the ground. Instead, it was merely swallowed up by the horde of dead below. Crammed into the plaza in their thousands, the swarming zombies were so thick that Tom wondered if the figure would even hit the ground at all. He walked over to the other side of the roof.

The sun still shone strongly, although it was behind him now and as he sat down, he felt its warmth on his back. The city was quiet; there were no sirens, no cars or traffic of any kind. There were no planes in the sky. There were no boats on the river. It was as if the city had simply ceased to exist; as if life had been extinguished practically overnight. He thought of Freddy, whose life had also been extinguished.

They knew he had been infected and had to quarantine him. There was simply no way of getting him to a hospital. Even if there was still a hospital out there operating, they had no way of calling for help. Taking him anywhere was out of the question.

He and Jackson carried Freddy down to the fifteenth floor and barricaded him in an office. They had no way of locking any of the doors from the outside, so they left him on the floor surrounded by bottles of water and a little food, and simply blocked up the doorway. They dragged desks and filing cabinets in front of the door until they were sure there was no way out. That had been over four hours ago. Explaining it to the others had been difficult.

Some, like Brad, had agreed straight away that they'd done the right thing. If he was infected, then it was too dangerous to let him back into the office where he could contaminate the others; what if he was to die and reanimate? It was too risky.

Jenny, Dina, and Caterina said they were being inhumane; it was only a rat bite and he needed taking care of, not disposing of.

Freddy was one of them. They'd argued that he should be allowed back to where they would take care of him; they would watch him carefully for any sign of infection. After all, nobody really knew what this was, did they? How could they say for sure he was infected?

When Tom had asked her, Jill refused to take sides. She said that the group must decide; the office was no longer a dictatorship. Then she retreated back into her cave. Tom wanted to shake her, to slap her, to do anything that would wake her up. He let her step back though; there was more to worry about than her.

Ultimately, they had all voted, narrowly, to keeping Freddy locked up downstairs on the proviso that on the hour, every hour, someone would go and check on him. When they had taken Freddy down, he had been slipping in and out of consciousness. He knew they were taking him someplace, but hadn't seemed concerned where or why. Tom had tried to make him drink some water but he had vomited it back up immediately.

Two hours ago, Parker came back up to the office and solemnly announced that Freddy was dead. Yes, he'd checked. Yes, he'd double checked. 'How can you be sure?' they'd asked.

"Because he's not fucking breathing!" Parker had stormed off and they'd not seen him since. After that, the office was silent again and opinions were neither sought nor offered.

Jackson and Tom had gone down to make sure that Parker had moved all the furniture back in front of the door. He had; Freddy was trapped in there. Peering in through the window, he certainly looked dead. The boils and blisters on his leg had spread up to his face and down his arms. He looked terrible. There were red tracks all over his neck and chin where he had coughed up blood and saliva. The fifteenth floor was now off limits to everyone.

Since then, Tom had come up here. He found it relatively easy getting out onto the roof. At the top of the stairwell, the door had been unlocked and he propped it open with a large brick. Discarded cigarette butts surrounded the doorway and Tom easily figured out why it had been so easy to get up here. Why would you go down twenty four floors for a smoke when you could go up just one or two?

He had no idea what the group was doing now and didn't much care. He tried to find a way out and Freddy was dead. Cindy was dead. They were facing a second night in the office and he wasn't looking forward to it. The toilets were blocked and the place was starting to smell. All of them were; they had no way of washing themselves properly. It was decided that the only working toilet, the disabled one, should be left for Caterina and emergencies only.

Rubbish from food wrappings was piling up in the kitchen, and with people being so used to having it taken away for them, they thought no more of leaving their dirty plates around for someone else to clean up.

Tempers and emotions were becoming strained. People were desperate to get home to loved ones. Thoughts had changed though. Instead of wondering if their partners missed them, they were now wondering if their partners were alive at all. Jenny had begun crying when she'd heard Freddy was dead. She hadn't stopped. He suspected there would be a lot of crying tonight.

He missed his parents mostly. His friends were his friends but they could take care of themselves and he had no girlfriend. It was beginning to look like it could be a while before he went on a date again. The last girl he'd met, he had taken to his local Chinese restaurant. Now, when he tried to picture it, all he could envisage was the restaurant smashed up and overrun by the dead.

At college, he had been a nobody; here he felt like he was a somebody. Only two days in and he felt like he had grown. Yet, he hadn't done a minutes work, hadn't switched a computer on or answered a ringing telephone. He had achieved reasonable grades and made a few friends at college, but ultimately what was the point? His tutor had asked him as much. 'What are you doing here, Tom? What do you want to achieve in life?'

A cold breeze sent a chill through Tom and he knew he was going to have to face going back downstairs. Maybe he had been too vocal; he was asked his opinion on what to do, where to go, and he gave it. Perhaps he should keep quiet from now on. He hadn't known Freddy well, but he missed him. People didn't die at work; that was only something you heard about on the news or from a friend of a friend of a friend. Even then, it was so abstract and absurd you didn't really care.

His parents let him have a pet budgie when he was young. He could remember pestering them for it for months until they finally relented. On his tenth birthday, he had been given 'Charlie' and they'd told him how to take care of it, clean the cage, change its water, and so on.

One day he had been playing with a friend and they'd taken Charlie out to let him fly around the room. Tom opened the window as it was hot, and Charlie had flown out within seconds. Tom remembered running around the garden calling for him, looking in every tree, but he never saw Charlie again. Perhaps he was happier out there, free from his cage, uninhibited, able to spread his wings? Tom knew it was more realistic that Charlie had been eaten by the neighbours' cat.

His father had scolded him, told him he was a fool. His mother simply hugged him. How he wished his mother was here now; a hug could go a long way. If humans had wings, he would fly home right now, straight to his parent's house. His mum would have a meal prepared for him in minutes, a huge smile on her face. She would smell of baking, as she always did, and most likely be wearing an apron. Rarely did he visit home and not find his mother in the kitchen, whistling along to the radio, arms buried in a bowl of pastry or cake mix.

An image of his mother fleeted across his mind; of her slack face covered in maggots, her arms gnawed off to the elbow, her eyes eaten, her hair ripped from her scalp. She was in the kitchen, the radio still playing, and his father was out in the garden in pieces. Were they both cold and dead now? Tom's legs swung freely over the side of the building and he marvelled at how easy it would be to fly; fly like Charlie through the sky, to be free, to be utterly free like he had never felt before.

A smell of death and rotting flesh wafted to him from below and he jerked back, his mouth tasting the awful smell. Tom spat and watched the globule of saliva fall. Gradually, it disappeared from sight and Tom's vision focused on where it was heading. The plaza: hundreds of square feet of prime real estate full of dead people. They were somebody's parents, too: sisters, brothers, friends, and children. Tom wondered if they thought anymore about the past, the future...were they even aware of the present? He knew the world was overpopulated, but this? If this is nature's way of thinking us out, then it's a cruel way, he thought. How many dead people were there beneath his feet; a thousand, two thousand, five?

They were human beings, people who used to come here to make money, to socialise, to work; to *do something*. Tom had to do something too, but he wasn't sure what anymore. There were no definitive answers anymore. Hell, there were no definitive questions anymore. 'To be or not to be,' he thought.

He said goodnight to the city, gave the zombies below one last cursory glance, and went back into the stairwell, leaving the door ajar. He walked down the nine flights of stairs back to the office with a heavy heart.

* * * *

Parker went over to Tom as soon as he returned. "Hey, man," Parker said.

Tom just smiled back weakly. The office was quiet and sombre. People were sat around staring into space; lethargic, and apathetic.

"What's going on?" Tom asked as he walked with Parker to the rec' room. There he found Brad, Jessica, Jackson, and Benzo sat around a bottle of wine. The new woman, Christina, was there too with Philip and Kate. They were sat further back from the group, as if purposefully keeping themselves mentally and physically distant. They all said their 'hi's' and 'hello's' as Tom walked in. Jessica poured some red wine into a white plastic cup taken from the water cooler. Tom sank into the sofa and drank.

"Hey, buddy, we've been doing some talking and want your input," said Brad.

Tom shrugged his shoulders. "Where'd you get the wine from?"

"Courtesy of yours truly," said Philip raising his glass, smiling smugly.

"We have a bar on our floor. There's plenty to go round so we thought we should share. There's white too, if you prefer," said Kate. She leant forward, keen to hear more of the conversation. Philip was happy to drink the evening away, as usual, and ignoring everyone. Kate tried not to let him irritate her.

"S'fine," said Tom.

"So we were thinking..." began Brad again. "This car park, this tunnel – it could be our ticket out of here, buddy."

"Okay?" Tom looked at Jessica who topped his cup up. She offered him a supportive smile and her brown eyes sparkled. God knows how, but she had found some makeup, washed herself and tied her hair back in a ponytail. So beautiful, Tom thought; in all this horror, she's still so beautiful.

"Staying here was a good plan, honestly, it was sound. I'm sure we coulda waited this thing out. But with what's happened to Freddy, we've realised, well, maybe we're not so safe after all."

"Freddy's not going to come back up here in the middle of the night and infect the rest of us, if that's what you're thinking," said Tom. "He's...secure."

"It was so quick," whispered Caterina. "How could it take him so quickly? My nanna got hypothermia and was in hospital for weeks before she died."

"It's not just that," said Benzo. "You know he died from the infection right, from a rat bite? Well, there are a hell of a lot of rats in this city and doors don't bother them. They can get under them, through walls, through skirting boards, up ventilation shafts and into almost anywhere. Those bastards can bite through practically anything. You see where I'm going with this?"

Tom did. He hadn't thought about it from that angle. If they sat here doing nothing, they were as good as dead. This disease wasn't just a human one. It clearly transferred between species; anything could be infected. If it affected rats, then why not mice, bugs, cockroaches... if any infected thing got up to them, then...

"And I'm starving," said Parker. "Let's be honest, we all are. We can't live on biscuits and crisps for ever and there's not an infinite amount of them either."

"So how do we do it?" asked Tom.

"We have a rough plan," said Parker.

"Rough? Ha! You can say that again," said Philip. He stood up and Kate told him quietly to sit, that he was drunk, and making a scene, *again*.

"No, I won't sit down. This is ludicrous. You should hear yourselves. Rats? Tunnels? Are you people insane? I'm going back down to the bar to wait this out. They'll send help eventually." Philip wobbled his way over to the doorway. "Come on, Kate."

"Who are 'they,' Philip? Tell me, enlighten us! There's no 'they' left, they're gone. Don't you see? The army, the government, they're gone. No. I'm staying here. These people need our help. *We* need their help, Philip."

He snickered and left his wife behind, heading back down to the bar where he could drink without having to listen to morons. Kate went red, annoyed her husband could be so flippant. She stayed put though. Philip might be able to solve everything with a corkscrew, but she had enough.

"The plan," said Christina ignoring the outburst, "is to leave; tomorrow. Our food is already running low and tomorrow will be our third day in this building. I'm not sure we can last much longer." She slipped an arm around Kate and Kate felt a lump rise in her throat. She took a sip of wine and swallowed her feelings back down. Was she wrong not to support her husband? Should she have left with him? These people seemed like good people and were at least trying.

Tom swallowed the last of his wine and felt a little better. Despite everything, he actually felt more relaxed now. Must be the wine, he thought.

"We need lights and torches if we're going into the car park. It's completely black down there; there are no lights, no emergency exit lights, nothing," he said.

"Do you think we could get in one of the cars and drive through the tunnel? It would be safer than walking, surely?" said Jessica.

"It would be, but no. I doubt the keys will be sitting in the ignition for us and I'll be fucked if we're going to waste time searching this whole building looking for them. You could be looking for a week and never find them. No, we'll have to go on foot." Tom reached for the wine and poured himself another drink.

"There are maintenance rooms on the ninth and eighteenth floors," said Reggie, who had been listening from the doorway. He had been hanging back, unsure of how to introduce himself. "I can get us some torches and lanterns, even some candles if you like."

"Thanks...er..?" said Tom.

"Reggie." He walked into the room sheepishly.

"Have a drink, Reggie," said Benzo. He handed him a mug of red wine, the plastic cups having been exhausted.

"So we can see down there," said Brad, "but what about weapons?"

"I don't think we need guns," said Christina. "Besides, we haven't got any and I doubt you've got any tucked away, eh, Reggie?" He shook his head.

"No, Brad's right," said Tom. "Guns, no; but if we get attacked, we need to defend ourselves. I don't just mean attacked by other people either. It was a rat that got Freddy. There's probably more down there. Rats, mice, who knows what. When we went down earlier, there were dogs outside too. They were infected. We need something to protect ourselves with, that's for sure."

"Well, there are plenty of knives around, although I'm not comfortable with the idea of defending myself against an onslaught of the dead with just a kitchen knife," said Benzo.

"Saucepans, pots, kettles; anything we can feasibly carry and strike with or defend ourselves with, we should take. It'll have to do," said Tom.

"You said candles, Reggie?" asked Jackson. Reggie nodded. "We could make some torches to burn; wrap some cloth around something, pour over some of your cleaning chemicals, light it, and burn any fucker that gets in our way."

"Not a bad idea, Jackson," said Benzo.

They continued talking amongst themselves, discussing how best to make the weapons they needed. Tomorrow morning they would go with Reggie and get whatever they could, bring it back to sixteen, and make as many torches to burn as they could. Jobs were divided up so as not to waste too much daylight. Troy and Michelle could go find as many backpacks or satchels as they could find. Jenny and Dina would put as much food and water as they could into them so everyone could carry supplies, and Christina would go with Tom, Parker, and Jill to the roof, so she could outline where the conference centre was and where the tunnel might come out. Beyond getting out, they could not think further than that. Some wanted to head straight home, some wanted to head to the airport, some to the police station; the only thing they could decide on for sure was that they were leaving.

"We have to know where we're going and, until we can decide otherwise, once we get out of the tunnel, we should head to the nearest building," said Christina, "which is the conference centre."

"I just want to go home," said Caterina. "I don't want to go to the ideal home show, innit."

"Okay, we've been over this a thousand times," said Tom rubbing his head. "Look, if the streets are clear and everything is peachy, then go home. Why not? I'm not going to stop you. I hope whatever this infection is has been stopped and I'd love to say that by tea time, we'll be home watching Coronation Street.

"But think about it; the reality is that the streets have been taken over. Dead people are walking around out there. Not just walking but running. It's not safe out there and if you try to get home, the chances are you're not going to make it. We need to accept that London is most likely gone. And if that is the case, we need to think bigger; not about getting home, but about getting out of the city."

"With what little food and water we've got, I'm not about to walk to Heathrow," said Benzo. "If we get to the other side of the tunnel and it's still chucking down a shit-storm out there, I say we go for the conference centre. Regroup, grab what we can, and go from there."

"But we don't know do we? I mean, we haven't been outside in three days, so who knows what it's like," said Caterina.

"I think we have a good idea. Look, there'll be food and water in there for sure," said Christina.

"Tomorrow is going to be a hell of a day," said Benzo.

"I feel like my head's going to explode," said Jackson, "there's so much to think about. Half of it I don't even *want* to think about, but I can't get it out of my head."

Caterina got up and stormed out of the office.

"Hey, Cat, come back!" said Jessica.

"It's all right, let her go," said Tom. "Things are getting tense and she should be relaxing, not stressing and getting any more upset than she has to right now."

The group sat in silence for a minute until Brad spoke.

"Kate, you said there's a bar on the tenth floor where you were, right? You think we can get some more booze and bring it up here?"

"Yeah I don't see why not."

"Then let's go. We've got tomorrow morning to get everything sorted. Let's enjoy tonight as much as we can."

"We could do with something to help us relax, that's true," said Jessica, staring at the empty wine bottle.

"I'll go down there," said Kate. "It'll give me a chance to talk to Philip. I need a couple of volunteers to help me carry back some bottles though?" said Kate.

"I'm in," said Brad. "We should ask some of the others. Everyone should feel like they're a part of this group and be involved."

"Speak to Troy," said Jackson. "He's quiet, but he's reliable. And see if you can find any more food while you're down there."

Brad and Kate left the kitchen and went into the office where they found Troy chatting to Michelle. They decided to all go down together to fetch more food and wine from the bar on the tenth floor.

"You know someone needs to go talk to Jill and someone needs to go check the foyer again," said Benzo.

"I'll go talk to Jill," said Tom.

"No, I'll go," said Jessica, getting up and straightening her hair. "You've done enough, Tom. Stay here and wait for the party to arrive. I don't know this Jill, but it seems pretty clear she's upset; she hardly comes out of her room. Maybe she'd prefer to speak to another woman."

"Thanks," said Tom watching her leave.

"I'll go check downstairs," said Benzo. "I'll sleep happier tonight knowing the door is still shut and we're not going to be eaten alive by a zillion zombies while we're up here."

He left and Reggie went back to the office to talk to Jenny; he felt more akin to her than anyone else. The group broke up and Jackson was left alone with Tom.

"You know, there's one thing I'm worried about. Jenny mentioned it last night and I dismissed her, but..."

"What is it?" asked Tom.

"Amber's missing. I'm not sure you remember her, but she went off yesterday and we haven't seen her since. I think some of the group have forgotten about her, but I'm worried. I don't understand where she could be."

"Well, I doubt she's left the building. Look, maybe she's upset about this whole thing and just wants to be alone? If she doesn't appear by tomorrow morning, we'll go look for her okay? Everyone can. We'll go floor by floor."

"Sure, I suppose so," said Jackson.

They sat in silence listening to the faint murmurs from next door. Occasionally, they would hear Reggie's booming laugh. After a while, Kate reappeared with a case of wine. Behind her came Brad, Troy, and Michelle, all carrying cases of wine. Christina walked in carrying a bag of food, mostly biscuits and junk, but at least it was something.

"No Philip?" she asked Kate whilst the others opened the wine and poured it out.

"No, he, er, wanted to be alone for a while," Kate answered, bursting into tears. Kate ran out of the room and Christina followed her.

"All right, everyone, come and get it!" shouted Brad. He emptied a bag of chocolate bars onto the table.

"Where'd you get all of them?" said Caterina grabbing a handful. She had calmed down and ripped a bar open. She stuffed it into her mouth.

"I just kicked a vending machine in," he said.

Caterina looked at him as if he were mad and mumbled something through a mouthful of satisfying chocolate.

"Well, I didn't have the right change," Brad said smiling at her.

One by one everyone filed into the kitchen. Cups and mugs of wine were handed out while crisps and chocolate bars were devoured. They drank and talked about tomorrow and the plan to escape; about what needed to be done. Jessica even managed to get Jill to come in, and she sat quietly on a chair, sipping wine for a while.

As the evening turned to night, the drinking got heavier, and the mood lighter. They had little to eat and so the alcohol affected them more. Caterina had one glass, just to calm her nerves, and people chatted and slurred as if it was a typical Saturday night in the pub. Tom found himself talking to people he had barely even met: Karl, David, Troy, Julie-Anne, Michelle. He found Michelle intriguing. She was clearly very drunk and yet she had just told him she was pregnant.

"Do you know Troy?" she had whispered to him conspiratorially, giggling.

"Yeah, just about, the blond guy, right, with the surfer hair?"

"Yeah, my Adonis," she said and laughed.

"So he's the father? Well, congratulations," said Tom.

"Yeah, right," said Michelle. The smile faded from her face and she took another gulp of wine. The music and laughter continued around them and she leant in closer to Tom. He could smell the sweet white wine on her breath.

"He told me he'd marry me. He loves me. But..." Michelle swayed in her chair, unable to focus on Tom for long. He sensed there was going to be a 'but' judging by the amount she had drunk.

"I don't want it. I'm going to have an abortion, but I haven't told him yet. I haven't told my parents either, they'd kill me."

Tom thought about what he should say, trying to come up with something reassuring. "Umm..."

"Yeah, um, indeed." Michelle looked at him and he saw through the alcohol and laughter; she was buried beneath a mountain of pain and fear. He had a fair amount to drink and was at a loss for words. He couldn't pretend to understand her issues or know how to help.

"Your parents might be more understanding than you think, you know?" began Tom.

"Maybe," said Michelle. She picked her wine glass back up. "But then again, they're probably dead so what does it matter anyway." She stood up and wobbled off to find Troy. Tom watched the party in full swing and ignored his grumbling empty belly; they all had to make do tonight. It was another reason why they had to move tomorrow, he thought: food.

Tom spied Parker and Jessica together, dancing around the office floor, and he felt a pang of jealousy. Don't be ridiculous, he thought. There was nothing to suggest they were anything more than friends, but they certainly seemed to be getting on well. If

Parker liked her, then good luck, she was undeniably hot. Tom couldn't take his eyes off her as she danced around, her long legs spinning around and her brown hair flying around her face. Her smile made everything else seem less important. All the death and destruction felt like it was in a different lifetime when he looked at her.

"Snap out of it, buddy!" shouted Brad in his ear suddenly.

Tom jerked and spilt wine over his jeans. "Shit, I was zoned out, mate," laughed Tom getting up.

"Come on, join the party. I know you're the new boy, but you're one of us now." Brad put his arm over Tom's shoulders and they both went to join the rest of the merry group.

Jackson and Reggie tried to pretend they were more civilised, refusing to get up and dance whilst they sat and got sloshed, and swapping stories. Christina came back in and talked to as many people as she could, trying to remember names and faces. Jessica danced the night away and had forgotten all about Chloe; nobody noticed that she was missing. Brad mingled and waited, watching for Kate to come back in.

When she finally did, he could tell she had been crying a lot. Her make-up was gone, washed off when she'd tried to wash away the telltale signs of crying. There were still faint streaks of mascara running down her cheeks though. Her eyes were red and tired. Now that Christina had smoothed things over, his path would be easier. Philip was clearly on the way out and an opportunity like this was not to be missed. Kate had such nice skin; he would love to try it on, he thought.

CHAPTER TEN

Benzo studied the faces pressed up against the glass. He hadn't seen the dead this close up before. The foyer was cold and he didn't want to stay down here any longer than necessary, but he was amazed. Even though it was dark outside, they were still here: people crushed up against the glass, disgusting, disfigured, faces trying to eat their way through the door and the walls to him.

There were no voices but there was sound. The zombies, the infected things outside, didn't talk, but just made short grunts and moans. Benzo felt like he was inside a bubble with a million faces staring in at him. He saw strangers. Then he saw Rob.

He was clawing at the glass. One hand had been scythed off and his eyes were distant. Benzo recognised him instantly. It was odd; he didn't feel scared. He actually felt pity. Benzo was going to leave with Rob before he stopped to help Jessica. If Rob had stopped instead of him, then it would be him out there now in the night, dead. Benzo shuddered and looked away.

Their numbers were worrying. Benzo decided to leave; if he stayed and aggravated them anymore, the pressure on the doors might start to tell. If it cracked, it would surely shatter, and then it would be over for all of them. Benzo left the foyer and went back upstairs to the party. He could hear the music and loud talking halfway down the stairwell.

Ranjit wondered if Benzo knew he was being watched. Passing by the tenth floor, Philip watched through a crack in the door as Benzo trudged upstairs. Ranjit saw Philip retreat back to the bar. The idiot would probably drink himself to death there. He had the opportunity to join the others and left! He left his wife behind. That was something Ranjit could never do. Oh, what he would give to be part of the group now, to have some human contact. The banging, the constant banging, the god-damn never-ending banging was too much. Ranjit stared at the door to the locker room, angry.

"For fuck's sake, Stu, just fucking fuck off and fucking die already!" The banging continued.

Ranjit got up and waddled over to the door. He crashed his fists down on it.

"Damn you, Stu, damn you to hell! I just want to go home and see my wife. Please." Ranjit stopped hitting the door, but Stu did not. His dead body, agitated by the sounds on the other side, crashed harder into the door but it would not budge. Ranjit sighed.

For nearly two days, he had been trapped in here with nothing but a bank of screens and Stu's relentless banging for company. He had not been too worried at first. It would be sorted out, it always was. The riots last year, the protests - they were all dealt with. The police just moved in and moved them on. But this was different. He saw the police come and go, the army too. Right now on monitor five, there were six dead soldiers hammering at the side of the building trying to get in. There were even more out there in the plaza.

Ranjit tried to contact his wife all day but the phone lines were dead. He couldn't raise anyone and he had no way out. His supplies were dwindling fast; only a few chocolate bars and a couple of cans of coke left, then he would really be in a situation.

"Come on, Ranjit." He waddled over to the furthest corner of the room where they kept the files and grimaced. The bottom drawer of the filing cabinet was now his toilet and the whole room stank of his piss and shit. What choice did he have? He pulled it open and relieved himself, kicking the drawer shut, sending a loud clang around the hollow room, which drew further attempts on breaking the door down from his dead colleague.

He went and sat back down at the console and looked at the monitors again. There they all were on floor sixteen, party central. They were immoral; amoral at best. He used to be repulsed by them, but now look at them; there was Jessica dancing around the room; there was Reggie who was talking to someone with a bottle of wine in his hand; and there was the American. How was it fair that he should be there, whilst Ranjit was stuck down here?

Ranjit flicked to eighteen; it was quiet. Nothing moved but Ranjit knew its secrets. He could see the cupboard where Blondey was and that other poor girl. How could the others not see it? How could they not notice two of their friends were missing? He leant over the desk resting his forehead on his coat. It looked like another night down here alone; another night trying to sleep whilst Stu banged on the door incessantly.

Ranjit switched the monitors off and failed to see the cupboard door on the eighteenth floor swing open. He sat there thinking about his wife and dreaming about going home.

* * * *

As the party subsided, Jill took her chance and sneaked out. It was midnight and she had endured enough torture. As the drinking carried on, someone started playing music from their phone. Jill hated it. She watched as her staff danced and drank, forgetting their troubles. Jill could not forget. She drunk a bottle of red and managed to get her hands on another when she left.

Out in the stairwell, with wine bottle in hand, she tried to decide where to go; downstairs she risked running into Philip, but she did not want company, especially that of an obnoxious City drunk. If she'd wanted that, she would've stayed married. The thought of Cindy and Freddy being down there somewhere was too hideous to think about, so she went up. On the very next floor, she paused by the door. She heard noises coming from inside. Surely the seventeenth floor was empty? The infected had not gotten into the building without them noticing had they? Cautiously, she silently pushed the door open and poked her head in. The office was dark but the fire in the Akuma Insurance building projected enough light in for her to see. Troy was sat on a chair and his head was back, his eyes closed. He groaned and his head lolled forward. He dropped an empty wine bottle and it rolled across the floor.

Jill saw a figure, a girl, knelt in front of him. As the wine bottle rolled away the light from the fire flashed across the figure and Jill saw it was Michelle. Michelle was infected and killing him! Then she saw Troy smile as he came in Michelle's mouth and Jill let the door swing shut and began climbing the stairs.

"Once a whore, always a whore," she muttered to herself. "I thought better of Troy." She climbed the stairs quietly and paused once more by the door to the eighteenth floor. There were more sounds inside; shuffling noises.

"Disgusting," she said and took a swig from the wine bottle. Ignoring the groans and noises, she carried on upward. She finally reached the twenty fifth floor and, finding the door ajar, she pushed it open. So this is where the big shot works, she thought; Christina or whatever her name is. Jill walked through the office and noticed how much more spacious it was than hers. She found herself in the boardroom and looked out at the night sky. It was dark and impossible to see much. Down below at street level, there was movement; evidently those things – she refused to call them zombies – were still there. Bar the burning building opposite, the skyscrapers visible from the boardroom were all dark and quiet.

Jill sat down in the leather chair and drank. Who would notice if she was even gone, Jackson? Not likely. Caterina might, just because she had nobody else to complain to. No, the rest of her staff wouldn't notice she was gone and wouldn't even care if they did. She was nothing to them. There was a time when they would come and talk to her. Fair enough, most of the time it had been to complain or bitch about something, but at least they knew she was there. Lately, it had become that she was invisible; as if they couldn't even be bothered to hate her anymore.

Jill took a long gulp from the wine bottle and spilt red wine down her chin, and onto her clothes. Who cares, she thought. Am I going to go home and have it washed for me? Is my boyfriend going to shout at me? Curse me? Fuck me? Well, imaginary boyfriends did very little actually. I wonder what Alan is doing now? Two years they had been together, one of those married. She could still remember vividly when she had come home to find him in bed with her ex-best friend, Suzy. She stood in the doorway to her own bedroom and watched him screwing Suzy for two whole minutes before he noticed. Even when he turned and noticed her, there was a moment's hesitation. It was as if he were daring her; come join us or fuck off and leave me to it. They had gone through the motions, the recriminations, but it had been pointless and she knew it. She didn't really care that he cheated; she expected it. And she knew that he didn't really care he had been caught in the act. He acted as though he were proud of it.

She heard from someone else that Alan and Suzy were still together, engaged even. Good luck, she thought; I hope you're both rotting together in some stinking pit, eating the brains of your unholy, unborn, children.

Looking out at the night, she saw her own reflection and noticed how tired she looked. Her face looked terrible and her hair was greasy. She had faint red marks from where she had dribbled the wine down her chin. How had she come to this?

She felt even worse than she looked. Jill stood up and walked over to the window.

"What are you looking at?" she said.

"Not much," her reflection said, "just a pathetic piece of shit that should've been flushed a long time ago."

"You repulse me," said Jill. "So high and mighty, and what have you got to show for it? Who are you to tell me what to do?"

"I'm nobody. And that's what counts here isn't it. I haven't got anything to show you, because I'm nobody, a nothing." Jill's reflection answered spitefully, spitting out the last words slowly.

"Nobody," said Jill quietly. Her reflection blurred in and out of focus.

"Nobody." Jill looked at her reflection. Her face had become her mother's. She reached up and felt the wrinkles around her eyes, the thin hair on her flaky scalp, and the sad eyes. Her mother died alone in a hospice five years ago.

"You're nobody," said her mother and Jill started weeping.

"Nobody," said Jackson.

"Nobody," said Brad and Tom in chorus.

"Nobody," said Caterina, Jenny, Jessica, and Christina. Eventually, Jill heard the whole office in her head chanting the words at her over and over.

'Nobody, nobody, nobody, nobody, nobody.'

Alan and Suzy stopped fucking and looked at Jill in the doorway and began laughing. They laughed so hard they nearly fell off the bed. As they laughed, they began fucking again, watching her as they fucked each other. Jill stood, unable to run, her feet sucking her down into the carpet.

"You're nobody," said her mother. Jill put her hands over her ears to block out the noise, the cruel words, and the laughter.

"Shut up!" Jill threw the wine bottle at her reflection and it shattered against the window. Jill fell to the floor, cutting her knees on the broken glass. Through eyes blurred by alcohol and tears, she touched her knee where it was cut. A thin trickle of blood crawled down her knee onto the floor and she looked up at the window.

Jill saw her face looking back, her real face. She did not feel the pain in her cut knees. The room was empty and she was alone as usual. She slowly picked up a piece of the wine bottle, a large sliver of jagged glass, and raised her left arm. She sliced quickly and cleanly across her wrist and then did the same with the other arm. Jill lay down on the floor and curled up in a ball.

"I'm sorry, mum, I'm sorry I wasn't there." Jill lay dying, her blood spilling out across the boardroom floor, as the night watched over her.

* * * *

Despite the hangovers and tiredness, most people were up early the next day. The sun was shining brightly again and before eight, everybody was up and making themselves busy. Caterina agreed that everyone could use her toilet, as the others were blocked and the smell was overpowering, so she had little other choice. Troy and Michelle began the search for rucksacks that people could easily carry, while leaving their hands free for weapons. Dina and Jenny were organising the kitchen, sorting out all the food and drink they could take with them. Jessica and Benzo agreed to go back to the terrace café and check what the situation was outside. Christina found Tom and Parker and headed to the roof, leaving instructions behind so whenever Jill reappeared, she could join them. Jackson and Kate organised the others into pairs to go look for Amber, whilst Brad and Reggie went to the eighteenth floor to gather the materials they would need to make the torches. Brad said he would check while they were there, just in case Amber was hiding up there. Nobody thought about Chloe.

* * * *

"Over there, see?" Christina was pointing to the west, to a large white building. "It's the one with the tower at the end, kind of like a bastard church? You see the one next to that pub? That's the Onevision centre. I think the tunnel must come out just short of it on, um, what is it, Dixon Street? Dickenson Street? Something like that."

"Yeah, I see it," said Parker. "I've been to that pub, The Fox and Hound. God, I could do with a pint right now."

"If we get out of here, mate, I'll buy you a pint of whatever you want," said Tom. He tried to figure out the tunnel's path. From the roof where they were standing, it was a straight line. The tunnel must go under the river and up almost straight away; it couldn't be more than a mile long.

"It's possible. It can't be more than a mile from start to finish," said Parker.

"Are you sure, Christina? I wouldn't want to get down there and find ourselves popping up in the middle of the plaza," Tom said.

"I'm sure as I can be. Look, I agree I think it's worth a shot." Christina looked past the conference centre to the city centre. The sun made the Thames look like a stream of shining silver.

"Right, let's convene back downstairs and see what the rest have managed to get together. No point putting it off," said Tom. "If everyone else is ready, we should just go."

"If you don't mind me asking, Tom, where are we going to?" said Christina.

"Well, that part of the plan is still a work in motion," he replied. "Everyone has their own ideas. I think we're going to play it by ear. If the streets are clear, then I think a lot of people are just going to go home. Husbands, wives, girlfriends, boyfriends; it's been days now since we had contact. I thought I'd probably try to head home if I can. How about you?"

"Yeah, home I guess." Christina said no more and looked at the city.

"You think there'll be a home to go to?" asked Parker. "I don't want to be the messenger of doom, but, like you said, we've had no contact for days. The airport over there is empty; shutdown for all we know. Can you see any traffic on the roads out there? Any boats moving down the river? I think we need to have a plan B."

"Go on." Tom sat down on the gravel roof, sheltering from the hot sun against a small ventilation shaft. Christina and Parker sat down next to him.

"Well, it looks clear over there, but for how long? As soon as we appear, then the infected will come looking for us. It might be a rat, it might be a bird, it might be a person; a dead fucking person. I don't know about the rest of the country, but I think we agreed on one thing last night; that London is a dead city. I know we want to get home and see our families. I know I do. But if we splinter off, go our own ways, we'll get picked off. We'll all be dead by sundown."

In the distance, Tom could see the arches of Wembley. He had always wanted to go there and see a cup final; he didn't even care who was playing, he just wanted to go. Would he be able to now? Were football and sport and everything else that mattered just history now? Was his home, history? Were his parents walking around with their swollen tongues hanging out as they tried to digest their neighbour?

He tried to convince himself that what was happening in the city was isolated and that outside of his world, life was going on as normal. Kids were going to school, builders were having their bacon and eggs, and the world was spinning as it had done for millennia.

"He's right," said Christina. "We have to plan further than the next five minutes or we're screwed."

"So let's talk to the others. I hear what you're saying but I'm not sure they'll go along with it. Jackson told me he hasn't spent this much time apart from his wife, Mary, in fifteen years. Caterina's worried about her baby. Benzo's worried about his dad. Trying to get everyone to stick together might be difficult." Tom picked up a loose stone and threw it over the roof.

"As you said, let's talk to them," said Parker. "They listen to you, and Brad - although I wonder why sometimes. If you two say it's a good idea we'll probably get everyone on side."

Tom nodded. They listened to him for some reason. Brad he could understand; he was physically imposing, he was confident, bold, arrogant; everything that Tom wasn't. He wondered if it might be because he was the newcomer. A strange face meant he didn't carry any baggage. Tom hadn't played any part of the office politics and had no favourites. He was impartial, whereas, Brad came with baggage. For some reason that seemed to mean people listened to him.

"I think the city is dead," said Tom. "Maybe there are one or two others out there, maybe even a small group like us, but it's over. I know in my heart that my parents are probably dead. The infection spread so quick I would be amazed if they got out in time. We have to get out of the city. That's what plan B is Parker. We get out of the tunnel and find a car, a bus, a truck, a boat; anything that moves. We get out of the city. And if we get out of the city and find the country is infected, then we get out of the country.

"You know how many people there are in this city? At last count about six point five million. If around ten per cent of those lived, and I seriously doubt those odds, then that's still over six million dead; which means there are going to be about six million fucking zombies after us."

Christina shivered. "My staff all left when this started. It seems an age ago now. I assume they got home safe and are probably laughing at me, just watching the news from their sofas, laughing at stupid Christina who stayed behind in the office. Truth is, I think they're all probably dead now.

"Quite frankly I'm amazed we're not dead yet. If the infection isn't restricted to humans, then...you said your friend Freddy got bitten by a rat? Well we're going to need to keep our wits about us. That means looking out for one another. I should've helped my staff, my friends, but I didn't. I let them go. I didn't try.

"I'm with you guys. I'll come with you. I've got money, too. I'm not bragging, but it can help and it might come in handy; who knows what's out there. Talk to your friends downstairs. I think you'll find they'll come, too."

They all stood up and Parker held out his hand to Christina. "Thanks."

"Good to have you on board. It's nice to have a level head around," said Tom. They went back down to the sixteenth floor.

* * * *

Troy and Michelle had gathered enough bags for everyone and they were being stuffed with the last pieces of food that they could find. Brad and Reggie returned with various bottles of chemicals, lighters, and torches. Caterina and Jenny had collected a pile of saucepans and pots, kitchen knives and bottles, large enough to wield against any attacker. Jackson and Reggie stuffed cloths into the empty wine bottles and doused them with chemicals that would burn.

"Don't light them until we have to though," said Jackson. "Not until the last minute when we're down in the tunnel."

Brad was on his own, filling up plastic bottles with tap water. They had gone up to the eighteenth and thankfully, Reggie's storage cupboard was on the opposite side to where he had left Amber and Chloe. He hadn't wanted to kill Reggie, but he would do what was necessary. Brad was angry with himself. He should've got rid of them straight away. He had not moved the bodies and in doing so, was leaving himself open to trouble. He was going to have to go back up there and clean up. Now there were people crawling over the building and that would be difficult. Maybe they would leave before anyone would find them. Jackson was not helping, organising his ridiculous little search parties for Amber. Maybe the old man had a crush on her. Jenny kept looking at him oddly, too. There was no way she could know, but she had asked him the other night about Amber. If she started talking, it could be trouble.

Damn it! It was just the stress of the situation. Normally, he could deal with this efficiently and cleanly. He was going to have to move things along. If he could cajole everyone into leaving now, convince them that they had to leave, then the search parties would be called off. Nobody would want to put themselves at risk just to look for that stupid blonde slut.

"Hey, Tom, good plan, buddy, I hear you. Stick together, safety in numbers and all that." Brad strode into the office and deposited the water bottles on the floor by the pile of bags.

"Well, it wasn't exactly my idea, it was a joint effort," said Tom.

"Say, did anyone find Amber yet?" said Brad loud enough for everyone to hear.

"No, we've still got a few people looking," said Jackson tying together a bundle of candles.

"Well, I hate to say it, but we should call it quits. We're ready to leave and it's time to rock and roll," said Brad.

"But what about Amber?" said Jenny. "We can't just leave her."

"Hey, nobody wants to leave the girl, but she's made her own decisions," said Brad. "She's a big girl and she has obviously decided she can take care of herself. You know I wasn't going to say anything, but I just saw a rat in the kitchen. Now it didn't bite me, I shooed it off, but, you know..."

"Shit," said Tom. "Jackson, he's right, we should get moving."

"This is bull!" said Jenny. The room was shocked into silence. "I don't know what game he's playing, but he's up to something. Brad was the last person with Amber and now she's disappeared and all of a sudden, he's in a rush to leave."

"Hey, you fat fucker, why don't you go clean the kitchen and let the rat take a chunk out of you. Maybe you'd like it. Probably be the best action you've had in years." Brad rolled his sleeves up and eyeballed Jenny.

"I'm not scared of you, *Bradley*," said Jenny looking up at him.

"So Amber disappears and it's my fault. What about Philip? Anyone know where that creep is?"

"Hey, that's true," said Troy, "we don't know anything about the man. If anything's happened to Amber, it wouldn't be because of Brad."

"What the fuck are you saying? My husband isn't perfect, but he wouldn't have touched her." Kate threw down the torch she was fitting with batteries and stood up.

"Come on, this isn't helping. We're on the same side. Everyone, just calm down, please," said Jackson. "Brad, you need to back off."

"Me back off?" Brad walked over to Jackson. "Where's Jill? Anyone? When was the last time anyone saw Jill?"

Nobody said anything.

"What are you implying?" Jackson said. He looked bewildered. "I don't know where she is."

"I'll bet you don't, you fucking perv. Last time I saw Jill was last night, and you two were thick as thieves. Then this morning, she's disappeared too?" Brad turned away and talked to the group. "All I'm saying, people, is that wild accusations are not helping. Who knows where Amber is? Or Jill? To be honest, I don't give a

117

flying fuck. All I know is, I'm not waiting to end up like Freddy. I'm getting out of here."

"All right, all right," said Tom. He slammed his hand down on a desk. "Brad, Jenny, everyone, just take a break, please. Whilst I agree it is a shitty thing to do, the facts are, we don't know where Amber and Jill are. We can't spend any more time looking for them. We do have to leave. If Brad saw a rat in there, then we need to hurry. If they're inside the building, we don't have long."

"There's only one rat in this office," said Jenny turning away and picking up a bag. She began filling it with matches and knives.

"Fifteen minutes," said Tom. "Jackson, can you get everyone back here now. I'm going to go get Benzo and Jessica. Kate, maybe you can write a message for Amber and Jill. We can pin it to the door in case they come back. We're leaving in fifteen minutes."

He left and the others resumed their jobs in silence. They were worried about Amber and Jill, but were more worried about getting out before the infection got in. Brad picked up the water bottles and grabbed a satchel from beside Jenny.

"Watch your back, *bitch*," he whispered in her ear. She turned nervously and he took the satchel away, grinning as he left.

* * * *

"It doesn't seem real, does it?" said Benzo. "On any other day, this would be perfect; just sitting out here on the terrace with a drink, deals being done, and people just chilling out in the warm sun under a blue sky. Perfect."

"Yeah, except today the tables and chairs are in the corner over there with all the shrubs, and the deals are as dead as the people making them," said Jessica. Benzo dug his hands deeper into his pockets.

"Well, I guess we're still going to try the tunnel option then," said Jessica. She looked out over the plaza at the hundreds upon hundreds of dead bodies; countless corpses crushed into the plaza, up against the buildings and towers, trying to fight past each other to the living.

"You think it's like this everywhere?" said Benzo.

"Yep."

A bang from behind surprised them and they whirled around to see Tom walking through the café. He joined them by the wall.

From the roof, the dead seemed less real and less threatening; from here he could smell them. He could smell death and decay, the rotting atoms being sucked up his nose; he could taste death in his mouth. The stench was overpowering and Tom had to fight the urge to retch.

"We're leaving," he said.

"Hey, Tom, I was wondering, if we all go down there into the foyer together, it's going to get them all...excited," said Benzo.

"Probably so," said Tom.

"Well, I'm worried that if we give them enough encouragement, then one big push might be enough for them to get in. Those glass doors have held so far, but I wouldn't want to bet my life on them."

"If you've got an idea, Benzo, spit it out," said Jessica.

"It won't take long. But if we throw some stuff off the roof here, over there to where that taxi is, then they might just be distracted enough. Let's face it, they're not reasoning, thinking, people anymore. If we throw them a decoy, it might distract enough of them to give us a better chance of getting through the foyer."

"All right, why not, it can't hurt," said Tom. He and Jessica followed him into the café and he picked up the cash register. "Two minutes, that's all, and then we need to get back. Grab what you can and chuck it."

Benzo went back onto the terrace and hurled a register over the wall, where finding a small gap in the zombies, it smashed on the road below.

Jessica picked up a laptop that had been left discarded and threw it toward an empty taxi. "Looks like I finally found a use for this thing," she said. As it crashed into the vehicle, some of the zombies turned toward the noise.

"It's working," said Benzo. They grabbed everything they could and threw it out into the crowd below. The closest of the dead began to turn toward the pile of debris by the taxi, scrabbling over it, not even knowing what they were looking for.

Tom watched Benzo lift a case of glass soda bottles over his head and throw it. It struck a fat lady below, hitting her on the head and tearing a jagged rip in her slithery skin. There was no reaction to the pain and Tom doubted if the woman could feel anything anymore.

"Okay, I think that's enough, guys," he said.

"One for the road," said Jessica. Tom couldn't help but smile as she lofted a massive glass bowl above her head and used all her strength to thrust it over the edge. He and Benzo stood by Jessica against the wall and watched as it flew through the spring air. As it struck the zombies, it burst into a million shards of glass, showering the dead with sparkling confetti. They turned away from the edge, walking back into the café. Tom and Benzo waited by the stairwell door for Jessica, who had paused for something.

The bowl had left a sharp piece of glass protruding from one female zombie. Its blood had congealed and dried so it could not bleed, but the glass stuck out of the top of her head looking like a shark's fin above water. Jessica turned and Tom noticed her face had lost its sparkle; her smile had been turned into a frown. Suddenly, it didn't seem as much fun anymore.

"What's wrong?" he asked as she got to the doorway.

"Nothing. Just someone I used to know. Let's just go," she said, and brushed past him into the stairwell, leaving Brie below. Jessica hardly recognised her girlfriend now: dead and disfigured. Maybe she would meet again soon. Hopefully not too soon, she thought.

PART TWO

CONFRONTATION

CHAPTER ELEVEN

Jill sat up and her eyes scanned the room. They didn't recognise anything. Her head tried to turn but was fixed in place, as if with a steel rod. She pried her hands off the sticky floor and stumbled to her feet. She swayed for a moment and a small rat dropped from her thigh where it had eaten a sizeable chunk from her. The rodent had been attracted by the smell of her blood and its sharp teeth had bored through her thigh to the bone. It now lost interest in her and Jill's eyes watched as the creature, missing its back legs, crawled away slowly.

Not a single thought ran through her head. She wasn't aware of Jill anymore. She wasn't aware that she was human. She wasn't aware that she was even a she. There was no conscious part of her that could even be aware of her own physical being. Jill's body was essentially controlled now by the parasite. A fungus had spread over her arms as she had lain on the floor, whilst the dead rat had burrowed inside her and eagerly eaten away half of her leg before she had reanimated.

Jill's body now bounced off the oak table and her bloodied hands prised open the door. Her body's feet remembered how to walk and they took her through to the main office. Jill stood in the middle of the room and blood spilled from her mouth. Sweet, sticky, blood trickled over her lips and down her neck. Her ears heard a faint noise and Jill's body turned toward it. Her pale arms swung loosely as she walked over to the stairwell doorway from where the noises grew louder. The dead body heard the noises. It smelt the warmth of life. Jill's hands pulled the door open and she opened her mouth wide, as if she could taste the living already. Her crooked body slipped through the door into the stairwell, and slowly began stumbling downstairs toward the noise.

* * * *

Ranjit watched monitor nine; they were leaving. He was sure of it now. Yesterday, he couldn't be sure if they were just getting more supplies to wait it out, but now there was no doubt. He watched them all pack up and the last three, Jessica, and the two men, entered floor sixteen. So that was it; they had found a way out and were going to leave. He would be alone, left to starve to death whilst Stu banged on the door, until he finally passed away in a room that smelt, literally, like shit.

He could unlock the doors now and let ten thousand zombies pour in through the foyer. Why should they be allowed to leave and not him? Ranjit's hand hovered over the button that would mean certain death for everyone in the building. If he hit the unlock button, it would open all the locked doors in the building, which included the locker room. Stu would be on him in seconds.

From the corner of his eye, he saw movement on the monitor from the camera positioned at the top of the stairwell; it was a woman. He looked closer and saw she was moving strangely. The way the woman sloped down the stairs was odd. Then he saw the huge hole in the woman's leg. He couldn't zoom in, so he pressed his face closer to the monitor and realised it was Jill.

"Jesus Christ, she's one of them," he said. He found he was rooting for floor sixteen to get out. It wasn't fair to go out like this. He took his hand away from the button. How could he warn them? There was no way. He tried to think, but with the banging on the locker room door, it was hard to concentrate.

"Shut up, Stu. You're dead. *You're dead, you're dead, you're dead!* So deal with it. Shit." Ranjit picked up the picture of his wife. "What can I do, honey, what can I do?" He sat back in his chair and watched the monitors.

All he could do was hope they got out before Jill caught up with them. If he watched them, he could see where they went and try to follow. It would mean unlocking the doors and letting Stu in, but it was his only chance. Better that, than stuck here forever. He looked at the photo again of Keti.

"I love you, honey, I'm coming home. I'm coming to see you," he said.

Ranjit put the picture down and watched the monitor as Jill made it down to the eighteenth floor.

* * * *

As the group on the sixteenth floor argued about whether they should leave now or try to look for Amber again, Jill stopped. The noises from below were getting louder, but there were noises coming from the other side of the door she had reached. It was shut. There were soft scraping noises on the door, although she sensed nothing living. Curious, Jill pushed the door open beneath the number eighteen and two more zombies stood there; splendidly naked and gloriously dead, they looked at each other for no more than a moment. Then the three of them carried on down to where the noise was coming from.

One of the dead, a girl with long blonde hair, was faster than the others and walked ahead. Chloe and Jill lurched after her, trying to keep up. Pure primal noises came from Amber as her appetite increased with each step. Her fingers scratched at the bare walls and Chloe followed her with Jill close behind.

When Amber's infected body had reactivated, it had instinctively bitten Chloe and taken a chunk out her shoulder. Chloe's body was warm when Brad had left her. Even though she was dead, Amber chewed the tissue, but had not found it satisfying and she spat it out. Amber pushed and pulled the cupboard door for several minutes before Chloe's body returned.

Awkward and stiff, Chloe had fallen against the door. Her corpse wanted out. Her feet slowly pushed her body forward and one dead hand began hammering on the door alongside Amber. One arm hung limply by her side, the bones broken, her arm now useless from when Brad had pulled it out of its socket.

It had taken the combined energy of both of them to break out of the cupboard, but they had not managed to get out of the floor. After bumbling around the deserted office for a few minutes, they sensed the noise below and stood by the exit unable to get out. Brad had shut the door to the stairwell behind him, not wanting anyone snooping around. Thankfully, it was not long before Jill's walking corpse inadvertently released them.

124

"We don't have time for this," said Tom. "Seriously, guys, come on, see sense."

"No offence, Tom, but you didn't know her. Amber was a sweet girl and we can't abandon her." Jenny was refusing to leave and had managed to stir up half the group, too, so half wanted to stay and look for her, while the other half were ready to go.

"She's right," said Troy.

"Yeah, we have to at least look for her one more time," said Michelle.

"Fuck this, I'm leaving. If anyone wants to come, now is the time. I'm not waiting any longer," said Brad. He walked toward the door to the stairwell and pulled it open. "You should know that once we're down there, they're going to figure out how we got out. We can't close the door behind us. You stay here and you will die here."

"Brad, mate..." began Parker.

"You think you're such the big man don't you?" Jenny walked over to Brad and put her hand on the door. "Close the door, Brad, you're not going anywhere."

He took a step back, letting Jenny take hold of the door. "You can..."

Jenny stood with her back to the door and watched Brad's face fall open in shock. His mouth made a perfect O shape.

Jenny's brow furrowed. "What..." Before she could move, Amber sank her teeth into the outstretched arm. Jenny screamed and Brad stepped back away from the door. Amber let go only to sink her teeth into Jenny's screaming face, ripping off her fleshy cheek and relishing in the spurting blood. Jenny turned around to fight off her attacker.

For a split second, the group was too shocked to do anything. They stood there dumbfounded, as Amber, completely naked and clearly dead, struggled with Jenny, bringing her down to the floor where she could rip her throat out and dine on the sweet, warm, blood.

Suddenly Chloe appeared in the doorway too, also naked.

"Chloe! Are you..." Jessica's voice was hidden by shouts and shrieks as Chloe ran into the room. Brad was pressed against the wall, trying to stay out of sight, and Chloe lunged at Jessica. In the panic, Kate tripped over and Chloe landed on top of her. Chloe's fingernails dug into Kate's arms as they struggled.

Jackson and Tom tried to pull Chloe off, but she had a strong hold on a screaming Kate. The others in the office were running around blindly, madly. Amber had left Jenny dying and was biting and snapping at anyone close enough. She clawed at Karl's face and he fell down at her feet.

"How do we get out? Grab the bags and run! Help me!" The words and desperate pleas got lost in the ensuing chaos and noise. Nobody knew where to turn.

Troy pulled Michelle close and told her to run through the door. "Ignore Amber and just run!" He promised he would be right behind her.

As Michelle ran, Amber leapt up from Karl's dead body and grabbed Michelle's hair. Michelle tripped and, screaming, landed on the concrete stairs, her head slamming into the wall, knocking her out cold. Amber dropped the fistful of hair she held and ignoring the unconscious body, ran to closer, living flesh.

Troy watched, as emerging from the stairwell suddenly, Jill bent down and took a chunk from Michelle's arm. With the flesh still protruding from her mouth, Jill went into the office and ran straight at the first person she saw.

Jackson tried to back away but she was too quick. He tried to dodge her, but she lunged forward and Jill's cold hands grabbed him. He grappled with her, rolling around on the floor over the bags of food. Troy ran to help Michelle but Jenny sprang up as he bounded over her and sunk her teeth into his ankle. He shouted out in pain, blood vessels bursting as she tore a vein out, a bloody strand of tissue snapping as she yanked it out of his leg.

Moving faster than she ever had in life, Jenny fell on top of Troy, her weight meaning it was nearly impossible for him to get out. He struggled, but within seconds, she had ripped the life out of him.

Jackson managed to push Jill off him and her attention was diverted long enough for him to get away. Jill clawed at Julie-Anne and they grappled with one another. Tom and Parker grabbed what few bags they could and shouted for the others to do the same.

"Reggie, light the torches!" Reggie had backed away into the kitchen and was frantically trying to light the flammable cloths. He lit the first one and handed it to Benzo, who threw the burning bottle at Amber. She lit up immediately and the fire spread over her battered naked body.

With so few weapons available, Jackson had earlier unscrewed the legs from Jill's desk, intending to use them as hefty batons with which to beat any zombies that got in their way. He picked up the four robust metal legs.

"Here!" shouted Jackson, throwing one to Benzo. Parker and Dina grabbed the other two, while Jackson held onto one.

"Go now!" shouted Tom. As Reggie ran, others tried to follow, swinging their clubs at anyone who tried to stop them.

Jill and Jenny were running through the office and Tom watched them claw a poor girl down to the floor together, where they tore her apart. Jackson struck Michelle who was standing in the doorway. Her infected dead body stumbled and fell. Amber was still burning and had tripped over the bags in the centre of the room, setting them alight. There was no way to get them now.

David and Jessica managed to pull Chloe off Kate and had pinned her back with some chairs. It only kept her at bay for seconds though. Michelle stumbled through the office, blood pouring down her head, which was hanging off her shoulders to the side. She grabbed David and bit his hands as he tried to push her away. Dina tried to help him, but only succeeded in falling over where she found Jill's snapping jaws.

Kate was crying for Philip whilst Jackson, having evaded Jill's clutches, ran to Jessica.

"Just go, now!" He practically pushed her out of the door and they sprinted out of the room.

Amber was still parading around the room whilst she burnt and the smoke from her crackling corpse was beginning to fill the room. Tom couldn't see a way past her from where he was. He grabbed a chair and was waving it in front of Jill, fending her off like a lion tamer.

Suddenly, Troy appeared in front of Tom; his eyes were wild, red, and Tom knew Troy was infected. Troy ran at Tom, forcing him to throw the chair and dive under a desk. A woman, Julie-

Anne, screamed and Troy forgot Tom, turning to the woman. She was brandishing a breadknife and slashing it through the air as Troy approached. She succeeded in cutting his face, but Tom heard her cries as Troy sunk his teeth into her skin, ferociously tearing out chunks of skin and muscle. Blood flecked Tom's face, from where he knew not, and Troy ravaged Julie-Anne, his teeth slicing through her jugular vein, spraying Tom with more blood.

Through the chaos and carnage, Tom was unable to tell who was who anymore. Under the desk, he began crawling, edging his way to the door. He kept low, making sure his head stayed down, and tried to avoid breathing in the meaty smoke. He pushed his way through a tangled mess of wires and cables, dragging himself past chair legs, bags, rubbish and extension cords; all vying for the right to ensnare him in this deadly tomb forever.

As he crawled along, he saw the exit. Suddenly, his ankle caught in a looped wire. He turned over to free himself and Chloe's hands grabbed him. She dragged herself onto his legs, her eyes locked on him and he felt a gut-wrenching fear, the likes of which he had never felt before.

Tom kicked and struggled, but he couldn't shake her off. He rolled around on the floor and bucked underneath her, but she was up to his waist now and refusing to let go. Dina crashed down beside him, her face inches away from his.

"Dina, help me!" he said, but it was too late. She was gone. Blood spilled from her mouth and her nose was gone, chewed off. The blood oozing from her neck was so thick and rich it looked black. Her once white hair was stained with dark blood. He hoped Dina would stay dead long enough for him to get away from her.

Frantically, Tom swung a punch at Chloe. He struck her over and over until dread overcame him. He weakened as Chloe's dead body continued its inexorable climb over him. His blows meant nothing to her, caused her no pain; they were nothing but an inconvenience that delayed her from being able to eat the luscious flesh before her. Finally, they were face to face, her jaws open and her breath stinking like rotten meat. Drool fell from her lips as she tried to clamp her teeth down onto his face.

Tom pushed her away, holding her head up, his hands locked around her neck, his fingers tracing the very same skin where

Brad's fingers had been last night. He could hear the sounds of his friends dying all around him, and his belief in his survival was waning. Chloe's lank hair dangled down, its limp fronds wisping across his cheeks. Her bruised breasts swung above him and he tasted burning bile in the back of his throat.

Brad had stayed hidden for as long as possible. When Amber appeared, he slunk back against the wall and watched as Jenny died, horribly. As the fighting began, he slid back further, trying to make himself small, crawling behind a filing cabinet from where he watched Amber burn and Chloe kill. Brad was confused; how had the girl he murdered, returned to kill? He watched the horror unfold, shocked and frozen with fear. As Jackson and Jessica fought their way out into the stairwell, he realised he had only one chance to get out, or he would be left behind to die in here.

From his hiding place, he took a leap of faith and jumped out. Standing in the doorway was Kate, crying. She had picked up the metal table leg that Jackson had dropped in his panic to get out.

"Kate, let me help," he said approaching her slowly. "Give me the weapon, Kate, we'll get out together," he said walking up to her.

"No. No, this is your fault. Jenny told me about you," she struggled to say through her tears. .

Brad saw Michelle advancing, her dead arms reaching out and he punched Kate, grabbing the desk leg from her as she fell into Michelle's deadly embrace. Kate screamed as Michelle's teeth scratched her neck and drew blood. Brad spat on Kate and gripped his new weapon tightly. He was about to run when he saw Chloe on top of someone beneath a desk. He coughed as the smoke in the room thickened. There was not much time left; he had to go. A hand reached out from beneath the desk next to where Dina lay, dead. It was Tom. Self-preservation was number one on the agenda but Brad decided Tom was worth saving; he was no limp dick like the rest of these dead fucks and could prove to be useful later. Michelle was occupied struggling with Kate and Brad took a chance.

"Fuck you, bitch!"

A metal desk leg struck Chloe on the side of the head as Brad swung it down on her, cursing. It tore a hole in her cheek but did not deter her. Tom held her head up and saw the metal leg strike her again and again. He felt the vibrations shudder down his arms with each violent blow.

Finally Chloe lost her grip and Tom pushed her off. He scrambled clear of the desks, as Brad continued raining blows down on Chloe, her skull finally giving in to the relentless hammering and cracking open. Brad destroyed her decaying brain, sending chunks of it flying into the air as he pounded her with the metal leg.

"Come on, Brad, let's go." Tom pulled Brad back and they ran. A man named Chris that Tom had only spoken to once, lay in the doorway. His stomach had been slit open and Tom could see the man's intestines, spilling out onto the floor. Chris was dead and Tom didn't want to stick around to see how long he would remain dead. Dina was already rolling over onto her stomach, trying to stand.

Brad and Tom followed the footsteps and screams down to the ground floor, ignoring whatever was behind them. Bursting through into the foyer, the noise from the horde outside was noticeably louder than before and the banging and clawing at the glass doors was more insistent. The grunting and moaning sounds that the dead made, the only noise they could make, was louder too. Tom looked around, bending over to his knees to catch his breath.

"Who's here?" he said wheezing. Brad was closing the door to the stairwell behind them.

"Hey, don't shut that, what if someone else is behind you?" said Parker.

"Buddy, there's no one else coming, we're the last," Brad answered. He looked around, but there was nothing to barricade the door with. He shoved it closed and hoped it would hold.

"So this is it?" said Tom. He looked around at the survivors in the foyer: himself, Brad, Parker, Jessica, Reggie, Christina, Jackson, Caterina, and Benzo.

"Jesus Christ," muttered Jackson. "Jenny, Amber, Chris, David, Jill...they're all dead. Everyone's dead." He wiped his face and unintentionally smeared blood across his forehead.

"Sort of," muttered Brad as he slumped to the floor.

"What about Karl?" said Reggie. "I thought he was right behind me...him and, shit, I forget her name...a blonde woman...I'm sure they were..."

"Save your breath, they're dead" said Brad.

"Dina too? I thought she was ahead of me?" Jessica swallowed down the feeling of nausea that was rising from her stomach.

"Trust me, they're all dead," said Brad. Nobody spoke. The only sound in the foyer came from the dead outside.

"Well, I'm not. Thanks Brad, I owe you," said Tom. He offered Brad a grim smile and was acknowledged with a slight nod of the head. Brad looked at the metal pole in his hands that used to serve as a leg for an office desk. It was covered in blood, Chloe's blood. He had killed her twice now. He looked at his shaking hands; was twice enough? How dead was dead anymore?

"So where to now, Tom?" said Benzo. "We need to get moving. I'm not waiting down here for those fucks to get in too."

Everyone looked outside. The zombies were attacking the glass doors like wild animals; pawing at it and hammering on it with their whole bodies. Tom was reminded of football crowds; people jostling and jumping up and down in their thousands, faces squashed as they crammed together and huddled in the herd.

"This way," said Tom, and he walked toward a door behind the reception desk.

"But what about Kate?" said Christina. "She might be alive, we can't just leave!"

"She's dead, or as good as, anyway. I saw her get bitten before she ran," said Brad walking away, following Tom. "Sorry, I tried to help her, but they pulled her away from me...there's nothing we can do for her anymore."

"Fuck," said Christina. She watched Jackson follow Tom and the others behind him. Their heads were bowed. Even Brad, the 'alpha male,' looked defeated, she thought. She couldn't see his smile from where she was. "And then there were nine," she said shaking her head. Christina was the last to leave the foyer, the reception door closing behind her just as Jill reached the stairwell door. Jill jumped and pushed against the door until it gave way and she tumbled out into the foyer. The reception door had barely swung shut and Jill knew where to go. She followed them, her dead legs moving slowly, her impulses taking her toward the living.

* * * *

Tom led them down corridors, past closed rooms, retracing his steps with Freddy from yesterday. There was no talking. They were too shocked, scared, and bewildered for conversation. All they wanted to do was leave. Tom couldn't understand how the plan had gone so awry. He tried to think back to the attack and how it had started. It had all been so fast it was difficult to remember it clearly. Jenny - she had been the first to die hadn't she? He remembered she had been stood in the doorway arguing with Brad and then what? All hell had broken loose. Amber had appeared, but she was naked. Why the hell was she naked? After that, it was a blur.

"What the hell is that?" said Caterina. A muffled crashing noise came from one of the rooms as they passed it.

"I don't know," said Tom. "It was the same when I was here with Freddy. I can only guess one of those things is trapped in there. As long as it stays in there away from us, I don't care." He marched on and the others tried to ignore it.

"That's the security guys' room," said Jessica quietly to Parker as they passed the door.

"So?" he said taking her hand. "What does that mean? Like Tom said, as long as they don't interfere with us, who cares." Parker pulled her past the door, reluctant to linger. He knew she worked closely with them and didn't want her getting any ideas about going in there to see if anyone needed rescuing.

"Yeah, okay," she said. She let Parker lead her onwards, but couldn't help think there was something she was missing. Why did it seem important? She felt like she was cracking up. Thank God Parker was here. Lame as it was, she felt safer with him around. He and Benzo had helped her, befriended her, and treated her like a human being. Most people treated the receptionist like shit or at least thought she'd be easy. Talking to Parker the last couple of days had been the only thing to get her through this, and the loss of Brie.

"Here," announced Tom. He stopped in front of a grey door and pulled it open. He led them down some steps and through a small passageway before opening another, larger door. When he opened it, the cold air hit them instantly and they looked out into a black underground car park.

"Jesus, you weren't kidding," said Reggie. "It's pitch black in there."

"Seriously, we have to go in there?" said Benzo.

"How many flashlights do we have?" asked Brad.

"No way, I can't do it," said Caterina. "No way I'm going in there." She began crying and turned back, heading down the passageway to the steps.

"Hey, hold on, Cat," said Jackson. He caught up with her and Brad fished around in the bags for any torches or lighters he could find whilst the others watched Jackson.

"I know this is scary, but we have to go. It's not safe in here, you know that," Jackson said putting a hand on Caterina's shoulder. He looked her in the eye whilst she wiped the tears away.

"It's not safe anywhere, is it!" she cried. "I hate the dark! I'm not going in there. I'll wait here until someone comes for us. Someone has to come!" Her shrill voice was loud in the confines of the small passageway. Jackson tried to soothe her but she was scared and panicked.

"Hey, buddy, Cat, you're going to have to calm down. If we go shouting and making too much noise, the fuckers are going to hear us."

"All right, Brad, give her a break," said Christina. "She's young, she's scared and she's pregnant. Her hormones are all over the place, so leave her be, eh?"

"I don't give a fuck where her hormones are. If she gets us killed, the first thing I'm gonna do is come back and eat the bitch." Brad continued rifling through the bags.

"Oh nice," said Christina, "such compassion."

"Look, let's just take a minute to get ourselves together," said Tom. "Christina, do you think you could talk to Cat, please?"

"Sure," she said, casting a furious glance over at Brad who ignored her.

"What have you found, Brad?" said Benzo as Brad threw one of the bags down on the floor in disgust.

"Not a lot, buddy, not a lot. We've got two flashlights, a couple of lighters and candles, some bottles of water and several crushed packets of biscuits." He picked the metal rod up and held it reassuringly. "Thankfully, I've still got this."

"I know this is not the time," said Jessica quietly, "but I'm actually hungry." Parker squeezed her hand and she put her head on his shoulder.

"What about weapons?" asked Tom. He pulled a large breadknife from one backpack.

"Well, it's not much better really; a couple of knives, two frying pans, this fucking thing," Brad said waving the leg around, "and an iron. I mean, who the fuck packed an iron?"

"Well, I do like a crisp collar," said Benzo. Tom couldn't help but laugh at the absurdness of it all, as Brad whirled the iron flex around in the air, and they all began laughing.

"Hey, guys," said Jackson returning to the others, "we can get moving soon if we're ready. She's upset, but she's calmed down a bit."

"Thanks, Jackson," said Parker. "We should get moving as soon as we can. I don't like being down here, it doesn't feel safe." Jessica slipped her arm around Parker.

"I'm over this. The thought of those things makes me sick," she said.

"Those things upstairs could attack at any time. They could be down here and we'd have no warning. I just want to get out of here now," said Reggie. Christina had her arm around Caterina and they began picking up the bags, handing out their meagre supply of weapons and lights. Suddenly, from upstairs, the door rattled.

"What's that?" said Jackson.

Christina looked up the stairs and the door rattled again, this time harder. She stood up. "We need to go, quickly." She brought Caterina with her to the group. "Can we have a torch?"

Tom and Parker looked at each other. They held the only two torches. "Well, we've only got two and..."

"Tom, Parker, let me stop you right there," said Christina. "Do you know where you're going? No, but I do. I can lead us to the conference centre. It makes sense, you know it does. Plus, it would really help Cat here."

Tom handed his torch to her.

"Tom, wait, come on, buddy," said Brad.

"No, it's all right. Christina can lead the way just as well as I can, if not better. I'll go behind her, and with my free hand, I can carry something else. Like this," he said holding the iron aloft.

Christina took the torch gratefully. "Thanks, I appreciate..."

There was a huge crash as the door to the steps swung open and into the wall. They heard shuffling noises above.

"Come on, time to move." Benzo charged through the door, followed by the rest of the group. He held a frying pan above his head, ready to smash anything in his way, hoping the dark car park was empty.

CHAPTER TWELVE

Philip jerked awake and dropped his glass of scotch on the floor. As the warm alcohol seeped into the carpet, he blinked his eyes and rubbed his head. Looking around the room, he realised it was daytime. The sun was streaming in through the windows. He scooped up the glass, and yawning, rubbed his hands over his bristly chin. What had woken him? There were noises coming from the stairwell: running footsteps, shouts, cries, and screams.

"What now?" he said and sighed. The sunlight had warmed the bar and he padded across the thick carpet to pour himself another scotch. As he did so, he heard a bang against the door to the stairwell.

"Who's there?" he said. Leaving his drink on the granite bar, he walked over to the door. "Who's there?" he said again. He listened but heard nothing. The footsteps and shouting were inaudible now. In the distance, he heard very faint noises, but nothing to worry him; the screaming had stopped.

As he stood with his hand on the door handle, a soft tapping came. It sounded like it was coming from the bottom of the door and Philip slowly pulled the door open, inch by careful inch. Kate's body fell into the room.

"Kate? Oh God, Kate!" Philip instantly dropped to his knees and took her in his arms. Her eyes were looking at him, but she had lost a lot of blood. Her clothes were covered in it and she was cold.

"Philip," she whispered. He dragged her into the room and the stairwell door closed. He lay on the floor with her, cradling his wife, holding her close.

"Kate, I'm going to get you out of here, okay?" he said.

She tried to speak, but he shushed her.

"Please, Kate, I'm sorry I was an arse before, but please, I love you. Oh, Kate, I'm sorry, I'm so sorry."

"Philip...get out...quickly." She choked and coughed up blood. Philip's tears trickled down his face, dripping onto his wife's as she died in his arms. He hugged her close to him as he felt her chest stop moving and he knew she was gone. He lay on the floor holding her for a while, as Kate's body stiffened.

"I should've stayed with you." Philip looked at his wife; she looked peaceful now. As he wiped the blood from her face, he felt her body tense. He looked down as her left arm began twitching.

"Kate? Kate?" He lay her down on the floor and stood over her as her whole body began to shudder back to life. He took a step backward as his wife opened her eyes. Her chest was still not moving.

"Kate! This isn't funny!" he shouted at her and took another step back.

With a vacant look in her eyes, Kate turned toward him and her lips parted, showing bloody teeth. Her face turned into a sneer and she pushed herself up off the floor.

"No, not you, Kate. Come on..." Philip's brain told his feet to run, and he whirled around reaching for the door as Kate charged at him.

Philip made it through the door just in time, slamming it behind him as Kate flew into it, trapped on the other side. He looked up and an old woman was staring at him. She looked like she had been in a car accident. Her white hair was covered in blood and her nose was missing. Philip knew she was dead, yet she was advancing toward him. Her arms and hands reached for him and he turned and fled downstairs.

* * * *

Christina shone her torch into the jaguar's interior, illuminating the leather seats.

"No, I can't see the keys anywhere," she said. Caterina, Benzo, Reggie, and Jackson were stood beside her, peering in.

"None over here either," shouted Parker. He was shining the other torch into a shiny black BMW. Jessica, Tom, and Brad were looking, but there were no keys anywhere.

"I didn't think we would find anything," said Tom. "Come on, we've got to get a move on." He could hear shuffling noises from the passage they had left.

Slowly they re-joined each other and formed a chain with Christina in front and Parker at the rear. In the car park, it was cold, dark, and damp. Christina kept the torch pointed down at the floor, following the road markings to try and figure out where the exit was.

"You know, there are probably thousands of tonnes of water above us right now," said Benzo quietly.

"Shut up, Benzo," said Jackson. "We don't need to know that, thank you..."

"I was just saying," said Benzo in the gloom.

There was a jangling, clinking noise, and suddenly a small light shone out from the middle of the group.

"I just remembered, I've got a little light on my key ring," said Caterina. "It was a present from my flatmates."

They kept following Christina, weapons at the ready and listening for movement. The car park was quiet and it wasn't long before the torches picked out a barrier. Christina shone the light up and down the red and white barrier.

"Be careful," she said as they filed past it. Abruptly they stopped.

"What is it?" said Tom. "Why have we stopped?" He heard Christina curse and caught up with her.

"Oh shit," he said when he saw what she was looking at.

Her light was pointed at a sign on the wall, inches in front of them. 'No admittance.' She shone her torch up and down, along the wall, looking for an exit.

"Where the hell is the exit?" she said.

"This is it," said Tom. "Damn it." The rest of the group all gathered around them.

"What's the deal?" said Brad. "Where's the tunnel? I thought you knew what you were doing?" he said to Christina.

"There's a barrier across the road blocking the exit. Basically, we're at the tunnel entrance and our way out is on the other side of this door."

"Fucking awesome," said Brad.

"It's massive," said Parker. "It must be a bloody thick door."

"I suppose it has to be," said Benzo. "It was probably built to protect the building from flooding, so it's solid. I don't think we can open it from here. The control would be back inside somewhere." They spoke in hushed voices and Tom could hear the fear in them, including his own.

Suddenly, they heard footsteps in the car park and a dragging sound on the concrete. A slither of light shone into the underground park from the passage way behind them.

"Oh fuck, something's in here with us," said Jessica. Parker put his arm around her. He held his torch up shining it into the dark, trying to find whatever, or whoever had joined them.

"Oh, God, we're going to get crucified down here," said Caterina as she stood behind Christina.

"Just keep calm, everyone," said Tom. He held a knife in one hand and the iron in the other. He felt faintly ridiculous but he was glad he had at least something to hold on to. The footsteps grew closer, but in the dark, they could not see exactly where they were coming from. Their flashlights picked out nothing but darkness.

"Keep your damn torch still!" Brad tried to grab it from Christina's hand and the light danced erratically around, flashing across the floor and high ceiling.

"Stop it!" said Caterina, and she grabbed Brad's arm. He pushed her away and she skidded across the damp concrete, falling over and dropping her small keyring. It flew out of her hands across the ground.

"Guys, for fuck's sake, stop it and listen," Tom said angrily. "Parker, shine your light on Caterina and help her, will you?"

Brad had hold of the torch now and Christina was nursing a sore wrist. Parker shone his light over at Caterina and Jackson went to help her to her feet.

"Hold on," she said, getting up, "my light." She bent down and picked up her keyring. Its pathetic beam of light picked out a pair of feet and Caterina felt goose bumps trickle down her spine. Lifting the light higher, she picked out a face. Jill stood two feet in front of Caterina.

"Argh!" Jill's arms stretched out and grabbed Caterina's coat. She screamed and Jackson joined the fight, trying to pull Jill off.

The shouts and screams echoed around the underground vault, bouncing off the damp walls, drowning out Tom's futile pleas for everyone to stay calm.

"Shine your light over there!" Parker handed his torch to Jessica and he and Tom raced to help Jackson. Tom pounded Jill's head with the iron as best he could. Parker had taken the metal desk leg from Brad and was beating on Jill, raining her head with crunching blows. Jackson tumbled away and managed to yank Caterina with him. Caterina ran off into the darkness with Jackson chasing after her, as Tom and Parker beat Jill down to the ground.

Reggie and Christina turned away, unable to watch. Brad stared, keeping his torch pointed at Jill as her body was smashed to pieces.

"Holy shit, man, that was Jill," said Benzo to Brad.

"It *was*," came Brad's reply.

With one final effort, Tom hammered the iron down onto Jill's head, embedding it in her skull, and she lay still. The flex had uncoiled and lay around her like a chalk outline.

Footsteps suddenly approached Benzo and Brad, and they whirled around. Benzo lifted a pan above his head when Jackson appeared with Caterina in hand.

"Jesus, don't creep up on us like that," Benzo said, lowering the pan.

Christina took Caterina and held her, letting the girl's tears flow, soaking her shirt.

"She bit?" Brad asked Jackson. He just shook his head. "What about you?"

Jackson grabbed Brad and pinned him back against the cool tunnel wall. His face was red and his eyes were bright. "No. Are you? No, you wouldn't be, would you, because you did nothing. You're a poor excuse for a human being, Brad."

"Whatever, old man," said Brad shoving Jackson off. "Still think we don't need a gun?"

Christina looked at Brad with hatred. "Just leave us alone."

"Hey, Tom, you all right, buddy?"

Tom was staring at Jill's body. Reggie had lit a couple of candles which helped with the light. Fortunately, or unfortunately, they also showed the mess they had made of what used to be Jill.

Tom nodded. "Yeah, I'm okay."

Exhausted, Parker went back over to Jessica. He felt sick.

"We have to get out of here," said Jessica. "If we stay here, we're dead." She kissed him on the cheek and then began waving her hands over her head. With the torch in one hand, it was like being under a strobe light.

"Open the door! Open it! Please, open the door!" she called out.

"What are you doing?" said Parker. "We need to be quiet." He tried to stop her waving, but she shrugged him off.

"He's in there, I know he is. He's watching us. Only *he* can open these doors."

"Jessica, I..."

"Parker, I *know* it. Those thumping noises we passed on the way here? That was the security team's locker room. I'm betting one of them is in there, trying to get into the control room. Which means Ranjit is still in there! He's got all the power now. He can open these doors. It was him that locked us in. I'm not going back in there. I just hope he's watching us now."

Parker watched as Jessica continued waving her arms above her head, shouting and pleading for the doors to be opened. He looked up and in the corner was a tiny blinking red light on a camera. Parker winced, ignoring the pain in his arm, and began waving for help too.

* * * *

Ranjit smashed the frame on the floor and ripped the photo of his wife out. He stuffed it into his pocket and said a small prayer. He couldn't believe what was happening. He had seen the group on sixteen practically wiped out. He had witnessed everything. He was scared.

The sixteenth floor was on fire now. Blondey had burnt away in the end to nothing, but some of the zombies had escaped and were working their way down the stairwell. If he stayed here, he would be trapped or burnt alive. There was nothing left to lose now and he had to think how to get past Stu and back to Keti.

It was a crude plan, but it was all he had. He had seen the others go down to the car park and guessed they were heading for the tunnel. Since they had gone down there, he had busied himself. If they got down the tunnel without him, he would have to go on his own and he did not like the idea of being down there alone. He spent the last three days on his own with nothing but the thumping and groaning of Stu for company. Plus, he couldn't let them leave like this; they didn't know who was in their midst or how dangerous he was.

Ranjit put his jacket on and drew in a large breath. He grabbed the top drawer of the filing cabinet and yanked it all the way out. It was full of heavy paper and he let it slam down onto the floor. Then he dragged it over to the door to the locker room and left it a foot in front of the doorway. He went back and pulled open the next drawer, pulling out the paper and files. When it was empty, he took it and put it next to the full one on the floor. The smell now was sickening; he had used the bottom drawer as a toilet for three days now.

Despite the foul stench in the air, Ranjit's stomach rumbled. He hadn't eaten at all today, having run out of food last night. If he didn't try to escape now, he may as well roll over and die. He couldn't leave Keti, he was all she had.

"I'm coming, Keti, I'm coming. Stay strong, honey," he said as he filled up his briefcase. He grabbed the first aid kit from the wall and put it in his case alongside one last can of coke he had saved. From the supply cupboard, he took four torches and some matches. There was an empty shelf where there should've been a set of Tasers. He plagued his boss for months that they should get them, but it was deemed excessive and 'not an appropriate use of resources.' He knew they were blowing him off, because they didn't want to part with the cash.

With his briefcase packed, he checked the monitors in the stairwell; the dead were getting closer. One was already down to the tenth floor and there were several behind it. Suddenly, a figure burst out into the stairwell, a man. The man looked up at the zombie and ran downstairs, heading to the foyer.

"What the hell?" said Ranjit. He turned to the other monitors and took one last look at his building. In a minute, he was going to have to unlock the system and when he did, every door's lock would be overridden. The door to the locker room would open and Stu would come in, leaving him with a chance to escape. Unfortunately, that would mean the foyer doors would open and a thousand zombies would poor in.

Ranjit watched as the strange figure from ten raced down the steps to the foyer. The man stopped unaware of where to go or what to do next. Ranjit reached to turn the monitors off when he saw a figure looking straight at the camera. The picture was faint and he could just make out two, no three, figures now, waving at him. Wherever they were, it was dark and the picture was not clear. He zoomed in and recognised Jessica. It was the car park, but why hadn't they left? Why had they...the tunnel doors! Ranjit realised why they were still underground; they were stuck there.

When the system was shut down and the building was sealed in an event such as a terrorist threat, the tunnel was sealed off too. He had forgotten about the tunnel door. Jessica was saying something but he couldn't make it out. He didn't need to hear, he knew what they wanted: out. He had to open the doors for them.

Ranjit picked up the empty drawer from the floor and held it, standing behind the door. When it swung open, he would only have a second. Stu would rush in and hopefully trip over the heavy files Ranjit had left on the floor. A swift knock to the head with the empty drawer he held, and Ranjit would run. He hadn't run in years, but today he would have to start again. He would run to the car park and catch the others up in the tunnel.

He prepared himself and leant over to the control desk, his hand hovering above the release button. There would be no going back. When he hit the button, it would all be over and his refuge would be gone. The building would be infested with the infected.

Ranjit looked at the monitors; there was Jessica shouting for him to open the tunnel door. On the other screen was Philip, standing in the foyer, in front of the huge glass doors, confronted with a never-ending sea of zombies and not knowing where to run.

"Sorry, mate," said Ranjit. He hit the release button.

CHAPTER THIRTEEN

Philip was rooted to the spot. Outside in the city plaza, on the streets where he and Kate had walked to work for the past six months, were the dead. He couldn't imagine, much less count their number. From where he was to the Akuma building, to the stock exchange on the other side and the tube station across the square, they rocked and swayed in their thousands.

He contemplated going back upstairs, but knew it was futile. They were up there. Where could he run to now? He pictured Kate coming down the stairs to kill him and tried to rub the image from his mind. He had treated her like shit lately. Now she was dead, and he couldn't take that back.

There was a clicking sound coming from the foyer doors that lasted a few seconds and then a grinding noise as the hidden motors sprang into action. Philip watched in disbelief as the huge glass doors began to part. They slid back, releasing the zombies who flooded into the foyer, running and sprinting toward him. A smell of rotting meat and decay wafted over him and Philip pissed his pants where he stood.

He ran to the nearest door to him, behind the reception desk, and pulled it open. The first zombie jumped on his back as he fell through the doorway to the floor. A man dug his nails into Philip as they struggled.

"Get off, get off!" Philip threw the man off, wiping his face where the dead man had scratched him. He tried to get up to run but another zombie pulled him down. Philip felt fingers clawing at his legs and back and in the confines of the corridor, he could not get away. He felt teeth sink into his calves and sharp fingernails gouge at his back and neck. He tried to stand, but the weight was too much for him as more and more zombies piled through the door. Philip was buried beneath the dead and before long, he was dead too, carved open by a thousand teeth. Although he became infected, there was nothing left of him to reanimate. The zombies tore him from limb to limb, pulling his insides out and devouring them, eating his alcohol soaked liver, wrenching his guts out as he drifted into painful death.

With Philip dead, the zombies continued their thirst for flesh and began scouring the building. They poured in through the foyer and soon found the stairwell. Karl, Troy, and Jenny met them on the stairs and inadvertently joined the mob. They were pushed along onto the second floor, swept out onto the terrace where they remained until their diseased bodies were burnt along with the rest of Fiscal Industries.

More zombies continued climbing upward in their ultimately pointless quest. There was to be no feeding up there today.

Michelle had taken a beating on the sixteenth floor and her body lay in the burning office where she had conceived one late drunken Friday night. Karl had sliced her throat before he too had been killed, and the living had escaped. Her body had been mutilated and beaten so badly that she had not had enough energy to move. Two more bodies had fallen on top of her and for a while, she could sense nothing.

A dog, a thick muscular Stafford, long ago infected and killed by its petrified owner with a brick to the head, found its way up to her and cast aside the meat laying over her. It pawed at her stomach. It knew she was not alive, yet something in her stirred its curiosity and it used its powerful jaws to eat its way through her belly. Michelle did not move while the dog ate though her innards. It soon found the unborn baby in her womb and consumed it almost whole. It was the nearest thing to living flesh it had found and served only to inflame its cravings. A tiny unformed hand stuck out from the dog's teeth, caught between its incisors, as it left her. Released by the dog, the weight of the dead no longer upon her, Michelle's body began to judder, and she hauled herself to her feet.

Some of the other zombies, having followed Philip, began wandering through the corridors and empty rooms. Now that they were unlocked, there was a lot to explore; both upstairs and down.

* * * *

With a scraping sound and a clang, the metal gates opened, scratching their way across the road. The exit to the tunnel appeared and they were confronted by an eerie cold blackness. A cool breeze drifted over them and Parker shivered.

"Oh, thank God," said Christina as the gates opened.

"I knew it," said Jessica smiling at Parker. She handed him the torch.

"Let's go. Whoever's got the torches, one at the front and one at the back. Reggie, stay in the middle with those candles. I doubt there's anyone down here, but there could be rats, so keep quiet and listen. Don't take any chances, okay?" Tom literally crossed his fingers, hoping they would be all right.

Brad went to the front of the group holding the torch and shining it into the black tunnel. Tom stood behind him followed by Christina and Caterina. Reggie held the flickering candles out and Jackson took one. Jessica stood between him and Parker, who was at the rear of the party.

"Hey, guys, I hate to say so already, but I hear something," Parker said.

They listened and sure enough, there were more footsteps. The noise grew louder and was heading in their direction.

"It's coming from that passage again," said Reggie, looking back at the doorway to the building.

"Oh no, it's another one of those things," said Caterina quietly. She clutched Christina's hand and she squeezed it back.

"Well, fuck this, man, let's go, let's not wait around," said Brad impatiently. He started marching off ahead, following the white lines in the middle of the road as the gates clanked back against the wall.

"Wait, please wait!"

A figure appeared in the doorway in the distance. From where Jill had come, a glimmer of weak light showed the outline of a large overweight man. He called out to them and ran into the underground darkness.

"Jesus Christ, he's alive! Who is it?" said Jackson.

"Hold on a sec, Brad," said Benzo. He jogged over to the man and returned a minute later with the strange figure. He was puffing, out of breath already, despite having only run across the car park. He wore a uniform that stretched tightly across his stomach and Tom saw the security name badge on the chest pocket.

"I'm Ranjit," said the wheezing man.

Tom shook his hand. "Thanks for opening the door."

Jessica stood beside Parker, her arms folded. "Why didn't you help before?" she said. Ranjit looked at her and then around at the group.

"We have to hurry, they're coming. Here." He unzipped his briefcase and handed out the torches.

Benzo, Tom, and Jackson, gratefully took them and Ranjit flicked one on. He walked toward Brad at the front of the group. Brad viewed the newcomer with suspicion. Ranjit was looking at him. If this guy was security, and he had seen them waving at the cameras, then what else had he seen?

"Seriously, we have to hurry, they won't be far behind," said Ranjit.

"Who is this guy?" said Brad. "People are tired and stressed and we don't need more bullshit. Poor Caterina's probably sick from a lack of decent fresh air. This dude turns up and we start listening to him without question? A complete stranger?" Brad shone his torch into Ranjit's face. "How did you get down here?"

"Look, I've been stuck in the control room since this whole bloody thing began. I've been stuck here just like you. I just had to fight my way out of there and kill my friend in the process. Although he was already dead, so figure that one out," said Ranjit. He turned away from Brad's interrogating spotlight, facing the group who were huddled together. They looked scared.

"Look, I opened the gate to let you out, but that means I had to override the security lockdown." Ranjit was nervously looking back at the passage he had come through. It was empty; for now.

"So when you opened this door, you opened *all* the doors? Shit." Tom looked at Parker.

"The foyer's open." Parker held onto Jessica's hand. She didn't have a coat and it was cold down in the car park. He wanted to tell her everything would be fine, but he knew it would be a lie.

"Let's move, as quickly and quietly as we can," said Tom and he started leading them further into the tunnel.

As they walked on in silence, it seemed to get darker. Their torches reached only so far and they were constantly spooked by their own shadows. After a couple of minutes had passed, Benzo stopped.

"Hey, stop, I hear something." He put his hand in the air and everybody stopped instantly.

"Buddy, I don't hear anything. There's no one here," said Brad.

"Shush! It's not footsteps. It's...it's like a rustling sound or something. Listen." He shone his torch at the ground, looking for the source.

"I hear it," said Jackson. There was a faint rustling sound to their left. "Over there," he said, pointing his torch down to the ground. "Rats."

Six torches aimed at once to where Jackson was pointing and they saw them. There were hundreds of rats scurrying along the side of the road, away from the building.

Caterina screamed. "They're going to get us!"

"No," said Brad. "If they were, we'd be dead already. These ones aren't infected. They're not running toward us, they're running away from us."

"I don't think it's us they're running away from," said Christina. "Listen."

"God, it's cold in here," said Reggie quietly. His fingers felt numb and he wished he were at home in bed with his wife.

Over the sound of the rats was something else, a deep thundering noise, a sort of low pitched rumble that was increasing by the second.

"Oh fuck," said Ranjit, "they're here. The dead. They're here!" Ranjit did something for the second time today he had only done once before in the last five years; he ran.

"He's right, move!" Tom started jogging, then running. They ran beside the rats in the darkness, feeling the black walls close around them. They rounded a bend and saw light. A small shaft of round light that opened up as they ran, building to a large circle of light. It was the tunnel exit. Tom turned as he ran and saw thousands of zombies tearing after them.

"Run!"

* * * *

Tom and Benzo ducked under the barrier, still holding their torches, and raced outside into the sunlight. The rats scattered in all directions looking for shelter. The road from the tunnel led upward to the street, and the conference centre loomed up ahead of them.

"Where now?" said Brad behind them.

"Don't know," said Benzo. "Just keep moving. We have to find someplace to hide." He looked back down the tunnel and saw Jackson and Reggie running past the barrier. Christina and Caterina followed them with Parker and Jessica swiftly behind. Ranjit was struggling to keep up.

"I'm not waiting for that fat fuck, he'll get us all killed," said Brad.

As Ranjit dodged around the barrier in obvious pain, clutching his briefcase to his chest, the first of the zombies appeared out of the tunnel behind him. They ran with their arms outstretched as if they thought they could catch their prey by willing it into their hands. With no depth perception or awareness of their body, they looked absurd as they ran, these deadly killing machines.

"Come on, Ranjit, you've got to run faster," shouted Tom.

They ran on and reached the top of the ramp. Tom surveyed the street and for a moment, forgot all about the dead chasing him. The street looked like a war zone. There was a taxi abandoned in the middle of the road, its doors open and the road around it stained with blood. Next to the conference centre was the pub, and next to that, a house that had caught fire. Its roof collapsed and it was just a black hollow shell now. The fire raged uninterrupted until finally, it burnt itself out.

Next to the destroyed house was a row of more houses and shops. A truck had driven into the front of a shop and been left where it had stopped. The shop windows were smashed and on the pavement in front of the shop lay bodies. Women and men scattered across the path and the road. Tom could not count nor identify all the limbs and body parts.

He looked down the road and at one end, there was a military blockade of some sort; he saw army trucks and vans, but there was no sign of life. There were no soldiers or police to help them. From the houses, doors began to open. A few doors down from the pub, a couple in pyjamas wandered out into the front yard. They were covered in hideous boils and bruises, welts and sores; the woman had vomit down her front and the man still had a knife sticking out of his chest.

On the road to his left, a small group of people were staggering in their direction. There was a pile of bodies in the road, and from behind it emerged a young boy. He had one arm and lurched toward Tom, quickly followed by more children, all dead. Tom saw the gated entrance to a school yard, the metal railings swinging loosely on their hinges.

From a side street, Tom heard a clattering and suddenly a horse appeared. Red foam was dribbling from its mouth and its mane was long and dirty. It was hauling itself along the road by its front two legs. Its back legs were broken and the horse was slowly dragging its bloated carcass across the hot tarmac toward them. A policeman was still mounted on it, his feet tangled in the stirrups, being pulled along. Tom saw that the man's legs were twisted and his body had been lopped off, or eaten away, from the waist up. Tom felt his body shaking and heaved, his guts spilling out what little food he had eaten last night.

"Holy shit," said Brad next to him, putting a hand on Tom's back.

"We have to keep going, look." Benzo pointed down into the tunnel as the rest of the group caught up with them. The zombies from the city plaza were running up the ramp, pouring out of the tunnel like a pack of animals.

"To the centre, let's go," said Christina.

"I don't want to go back inside," said Jessica looking around the streets in wonder. "We could end up trapped again."

"You want to stay out here?" said Brad. "Be my guest."

"We have to hide," said Parker. "We can't keep running like this."

Ranjit was on his knees, gasping for breath.

"We can't stay here. I'm going with her," said Reggie running after Christina. She was across the street with Caterina and almost to the entrance already.

Benzo pulled Ranjit up. "Come on, mate."

They all ran across to catch up with the others to find Christina pounding on the doors.

"It's empty. You can see inside, but the doors are locked." They peered into the dim entrance hall. There were tall posters advertising a financial investment show with the Fiscal Industries logo prominently displayed. The lights were off and the internal doors were shut. Clearly, nobody was around.

Brad swung the metal desk leg he had been carrying with him at the glass door and a small crack spread across it.

"No, stop!" said Tom. "If we break in, they'll just follow us in. We need to find a better way; something more discreet where they can't follow us. Let's check round the side, there must be a back door, a fire escape or something?"

They ran around the side of the building, and were briefly out of sight of the road. Christina pointed out the fire escape. A set of rusty metal steps led up to a door about twenty feet from the ground.

"There!" She ran and they climbed the steps quickly. At the top, she yanked on the door but it wouldn't budge. Brad looked at Tom expectantly.

"Do it," Tom said.

Brad swung the metal leg at the small window in the door and it broke immediately. Brad pushed the glass away and reached his arm inside. He managed to push down on the exit handle and the door opened.

"Okay, everyone, let's get in quick before they see us," said Tom.

Brad went into the room, and one by one, they climbed the steps into the conference centre. Ranjit, at the back of the group, closed the door behind him. As he did so, the first of the dead chasing them spilled into the yard below. He could see them looking around, wondering where the living had gone. Ranjit quietly shut the door before the zombies could see them and follow.

* * * *

"So where now?" They had entered a meeting room and there was a small horseshoe shaped table. They sank into the chairs, tired and drained.

"We should find another room," said Tom. "I don't think they saw where we went, but they'll hear us, see us, or bloody smell us through that broken window. We should find somewhere else."

"True," said Brad. "We're not safe yet. Do you want to lead the way, Christina?"

She looked at Brad holding the desk leg and bit her tongue. "I haven't been up here, only in the large hall downstairs. I can't imagine it's too hard to find our way around though."

She got up and pushed her chair back. Caterina got up and took Christina's hand.

"Just tread quietly and be careful, please," said Jackson. "We don't know for certain this place is safe yet."

Brad rolled his eyes and the weary group traipsed out of the room with Ranjit last again.

Leaving the small meeting room, they went into a sparse hallway. There was a plastic plant and a water cooler at the end, but otherwise, it was as nondescript as every other corridor back at the building they had just left. Christina pushed open doors as they progressed down the corridor, every time finding empty rooms just like the one they had left.

"I think we're above the Nelson room," she said standing at the top of a small staircase.

"Whoopee fucking do," said Brad. "And?"

Christina sighed. "It's a smaller version of the large hall. It's completely internal so there are no windows. It's big enough for us to get some rest and some space," she said taking the stairs carefully, listening out for any hint of trouble.

At the bottom of the stairs, they were confronted with a set of double doors with the words, 'Nelson Room,' above them. Christina pushed the doors open and stepped inside. She smiled and let out a small 'yes' under her breath.

The room was set up for a conference. There were no windows and only one more set of doors on the far side. In the middle of the room were tables and chairs, while at the end of the room, was a projector and screen. By the wall, another long table had been set out for lunch and was full of piles of food: pastries, sandwiches, wraps, and fruit, all covered in cellophane.

Tom closed the door and rubbed his eyes. He watched as the group dispersed once more, Ranjit plonking himself straight down on a chair, while the others took as much food as they could carry.

"Some of this is still fresh," said Benzo peeling a banana.

"Some of it isn't," said Jackson, holding up a mouldy salmon sandwich. "Careful what you eat, guys."

As the weary group sat, ate, and drank, Tom pulled a table in front of one of the doorways. Jessica grabbed one end to help him.

"Good idea," she said.

"I just think we should be extra careful," he said positioning the table directly under the door handles. "How are you doing, Jess?"

"All right, I suppose."

Jessica rummaged through the food and pulled out a bag of crisps. She offered them to Tom.

"Thanks," Tom said taking a handful. He sat down on a chair and Jessica sat down beside him. "So this Ranjit bloke, you know him very well?"

They looked over at Ranjit. He was the furthest away from them, apparently happy to keep himself distant. His face was red and he was still puffing, exhausted from the run. Tom thought he looked like he was about to have a heart attack.

"Not very well," said Jessica. "I've met him a couple of times, but I've just heard rumours really." Her voice lowered and she leant forward. As she looked at him, Tom had to force himself to concentrate on what she was saying. She was attractive, but there was clearly something between her and Parker which he didn't want to get involved in.

"He likes to pretend he's this big shot security officer, family man, whatever. He monitors the cameras. Well, monitored. I heard he got cameras put in the toilets, the changing rooms, everywhere; all under the guise of protecting us. We all knew why really. He's a creep. He sits in his office on his fat backside all day and thinks he's better than the rest of us."

"Well, he seems harmless, but I suppose you never know, right?" Tom took another handful of crisps. "If he hadn't opened the underground gate, we wouldn't have gotten out of there, you know."

"Be careful, Tom. I don't trust him." Jessica put her hand on his knee and he resisted the urge to take hold of her. Tom nodded.

"Don't worry, careful is my middle name now. It used to be danger, but, you know..."

Jessica gave a small giggle. "I'm going to talk to Christina, see how Cat's doing."

As she walked away, Tom sat back. There were hushed conversations going on around the room; Brad, Benzo, and Reggie were deep in discussion about something. Jackson was lying on the floor, stretching his back out and rubbing his feet. Parker was on his own and Tom went over to see him.

"How you doin'?" asked Parker.

"I don't know," said Tom. "I really don't."

"You know we can't stay here long. Those things out there will know we're here. Somehow, they'll find us. They'll find a way in and then..."

"What do you think we should do? Where should we go? Part of me just wants to go home and crawl into bed. Part of me doesn't give a shit if I don't see the sun come up tomorrow." Tom rolled his head on his shoulders. "I know I should eat, but I can't. I can't relax."

He opened a can of lemonade and sipped. Parker thought about how to answer.

"If anyone wants to go home, let them. As long as they know they'll be on their own out there, then there's no point stopping them." Parker let the apple he was trying to eat fall to his lap. He had only had two small bites.

"I think it's safe to assume the whole city is fucked by now though. If you ask me, we should try to get out. Get out of the city completely. The city airport's not far from here, you know. If we can get there, maybe we'll find some help; could be a way out. I don't know what else to suggest really."

"I was thinking about that," said Tom. "I don't know if the airport is still operating, but it's probably our best bet. If there's nothing there, then...shit, I don't know. We could see if we can get

154

on a boat or something?" Tom put the can of lemonade on the floor next to Parker's half-eaten apple.

Parker suddenly winced and his whole body tensed. He drew in a sharp breath.

"Are you okay, Parker? You look a little pale." Even with the lack of sleep, Parker looked visibly ill, dark patches forming under his eyes.

Parker looked around the room. "Come with me." He got up and headed to the door. Tom followed.

"Hey, where are you two going?" said Jessica, getting up.

"Just going to check around and make sure we're safe," said Parker. "Stay here, we won't be long."

Jessica sat back down next to Caterina, and Parker and Tom left. Passing the bathroom opposite them, Parker went to the next door he saw, just across the hallway, and tried the handle. It opened, and casting a glance around the room, saw it was empty; just another empty office.

"Shut the door, mate," said Parker.

Tom closed the door quietly and sat down in one of the leather chairs.

"What is it?"

Parker began rolling his sleeve up and Tom knew; he knew before he saw the bite marks and bruises. He knew without needing to look at the blisters running up the length of Parker's arm.

"Fuck. Parker, how the fuck..?"

"Jill. In the underground. It was dark and so fast I wasn't sure at first if she had even got me." Parker began rolling his sleeve down.

Tom got up and sent the chair back on its wheels so it crashed into the wall.

"This is bollocks! Parker, there must be something we can do? If we head straight to the airport now...maybe there's a cure for the infection. Maybe we can..."

Parker was shaking his head. "No. You know there's no cure. If there was, there wouldn't be a thousand zombies outside our door right now. Even if there was, it's too late for me. How long did Freddy last? An hour? Two? Three?"

Tom felt angry. This wasn't part of the plan. Why Parker? He felt guilty, but he wished it had been Ranjit, or Christina, or

Caterina; anyone but Parker. Then he felt scared. What if Parker dropped down dead right now and turned into one of those zombies.

"So when I said *we* should get to the airport, I wasn't speaking literally. I'm not going anywhere. I'm not going to be able to hide this much longer. I can feel it, Tom. I can feel the infection. My arm tingles and I feel dizzy all the time." Parker rolled down his sleeve.

"So nobody else knows?" asked Tom.

"No. I think it's best we keep it that way as long as possible. I want to tell Jess before anyone else."

Tom couldn't believe how calm Parker was. If it had been him, he would've shouted the house down and let everyone know he was sick.

"If we can get to the airport quickly though, mate, perhaps we can get you out too? We don't know for certain yet how big this thing is. It might be just the city, you know? The rest of the country might be fine..."

Parker looked at Tom with raised eyebrows. "Doubtful. Anyway, how are you going to get to the airport? It's not going to be quick by the looks of what's out there."

"I don't know," said Tom. "I just don't fucking know anything anymore." He felt frustrated. They had left one prison to find themselves in another. On top of it all, Parker was dying.

"Look, let's go back in there and talk about it. Don't put pressure on yourself to come up with all the answers." Parker swooned and grabbed the corner of the desk. "I need to sit down."

Tom took Parker and helped him back to the others. They paused before the double doors.

"Please, don't say anything just yet. I'll do it," said Parker. Tom nodded. It was only fair that Parker deal with this in his own way.

They re-entered the room and Parker made a beeline for Jessica. Benzo came over to Tom immediately.

"Hey, Tom, we've been talking and me and Jackson want to have a look around. We just want to make sure we're on our own in here. We don't want any nasty surprises."

"Yeah, of course," said Tom watching Jackson leave with Benzo. Ranjit was still propped up in a corner, looking exhausted.

"Hey, buddy, what's up?" said Brad. He approached Tom holding two cans of drink and offered him one.

"Hey, Brad, thanks. Well, I guess we need to figure out where to next." Tom was worried that once Brad found out Parker was infected, he would throw him out and feed him to the wolves. Brad had saved Tom's life, but he knew Brad was decisive and averse to risks. Parker was a liability now.

"There's no point staying here. We're no better off than before. If anything, it's worse."

"I was thinking," said Tom, "about the Tube. I was thinking it would be safer than on the streets out in broad daylight. The trains won't be running, but the tunnels could take us almost anywhere, including the airport."

Brad shook his head. "No. I see your thinking, but I think that's just too risky. It's dark and dangerous down there. You've got rats, mice, probably people too. If we ran into trouble, do you want to take them on in the dark? Like back in the car park? It's safer up top. We can see where we're going, who's who and what's what."

"But we can't take the roads," said Tom, "they're not safe. Even if we somehow got past those things out there, we could find ourselves walking down a street and end up ambushed. You know as well as I do that they can appear out of anywhere, and if we get stuck outside, there's nowhere to hide. They're relentless. They don't sleep or rest. They just keep coming. We'd be dead ducks."

"Hi, guys," said Reggie sitting down beside them. "I didn't mean to eavesdrop, but, well, it's a small room. Anyway, we're all thinking the same thing. The ladies were talking about it, too; where next?"

"Or who next," Brad muttered quietly.

Reggie ignored Brad and went on. "I had a thought. My house isn't far from here. It's only a few streets away. I can take us there and I live on my own, so there's plenty of room. You're all more than welcome to..."

Tom held up his hand. "Reggie, if you want to go home, then nobody is going to stop you. But it's not safe. You remember the thousands of zombies that chased us in here? Even if you somehow made it home, then what? This city is dead. It's overrun by the dead and this bloody infection. How long do you think you can stay at home, tucked away out of sight and sound of those things?

"The milkman's not going to come. I don't know how long you'll have power, if there's even any on now. You can't pop to Tesco's for your weekly shop. The lady who served you there last week is dead. The bus driver who went past you on the way to work every day is dead. The banks are closed because everyone who worked there is *dead*. The kids who went to school down the road and threw their chip papers in your garden are *dead*. Your neighbour who played the football too loudly is *dead*.

"Don't you see, there's nothing left, it's all gone. Whatever life this city had before, is gone now. I'm getting out. I'm going to the airport to find a way out of here. I'd be happy if you want to come along with me, but I'm not going to force anyone."

The room had gone quiet as everyone listened to Tom. Caterina let go of Christina's hand and walked over to Tom.

"I'm coming with you, if that's all right? Anyone who thinks they can just go home now must be suicidal. Sorry, Reggie, no offence. I've got to think about my baby and I need to get out of this city. I need somewhere safe to go. I'm over it."

"Amen to that. It's the airport for me," said Brad.

"I think Benzo and Jackson will come with us too," said Christina. "I'm not convinced anything is flying in or out of the city airport anymore, but we might find something. We've got to start somewhere, right? I hope you've thought of a way past those six million zombies, Tom. How about it, Reggie?"

"Well I guess if you're all going, I will too. I'm just scared you know," Reggie bit his fingernails. "I could visit my brother's family in Germany. I haven't seen him in years. Yeah, why not."

"Ranjit?" Tom knew Ranjit had been listening.

"Yeah, I'm with you." He looked nervous and frightened, like a little boy.

"Awesome, so that's the pregnant chick and the fat guy on board. What about beauty and the beast?" Brad pointed at Jessica who was holding Parker's hand. She stood up, fully aware of the conversation.

"We'll come too, even if you're going, Brad. You know, a little politeness wouldn't hurt. You don't always have to say what you're thinking. I haven't called you a damn stupid yank to your face have I?" She smiled bitterly at him.

"Parker, control her, can you?"

"Actually, Brad," said Parker getting unsteadily to his feet. "It's not her that needs controlling. You've got a mouth on you, Brad. I've tried not saying anything, but quite frankly, it's not just your mouth that troubles me. You're dangerous."

Brad laughed. "I'm dangerous? Right here, right now, with everything going on, you think *I'm* dangerous? Ha! Parker, buddy, you've lost it."

"Have I? Does anyone here remember what happened back at the office? Does anyone remember how Amber showed up naked? Now why is that? It doesn't make any sense to me."

"That's true, she was. I wondered at the time about that, but then I forgot with what happened," said Christina.

"If I remember rightly, you were the last one to be seen with her. So..." said Parker directing his eyes at Brad.

"So what? I don't know what happened to the stupid bitch."

"I suppose you don't know what happened to Chloe either?" said Parker. A wave of dizziness fell over him and he reached out for Jessica's hand to steady himself. "I've been talking to Cindy, I mean Jess, and you were the last one seen with her too. You said she'd gone back to sixteen when we saw you, but the next time we saw her, she was dead, right behind Amber."

"Shit, Parker, if you're getting your information from Cindy then you're even more fucked up than I thought." Brad laughed again. "Can you believe this guy?"

Parker fell back against the wall and Jessica held him up.

"I believe him, he's just sick, give him a break and answer the question, you dick." Jessica lowered Parker to the floor unable to hold him up. He whispered something to her.

"I know what he's getting at," said Christina. "I wouldn't put anything past you. I've got you worked out."

"Hang on, what is this?" said Tom. "What is Brad supposed to have done?"

"Dude, I don't know what her problem is, but Parker is clearly delirious. He's talking about Cindy now? I mean, how ill are you, Parker? What's going on?" Brad pointed angrily at Parker.

"Why don't we ask him?" said Caterina timidly, pointing at Ranjit.

"Yeah," said Jessica, "he has cameras all over the place. He'd know. He would know what happened to Amber and Chloe."

The room fell silent and all eyes fell on Ranjit. He looked at the faces staring at him expectantly, and his fingers felt for the picture of his wife in his pocket. He closed his eyes and prayed. 'Tell me what to do, Keti, tell me.'

"So, *buddy*, what did you see?" Ranjit looked up into Brad's glaring eyes and opened his mouth to speak.

CHAPTER FOURTEEN

"Nothing. I didn't see anything," said Ranjit. Brad smiled.

"But you must have seen *something*," said Jessica. "People don't just go missing and wind up naked and dead for no reason."

"Pipe down. I think we're missing the real point here," said Brad.

"Which is..?" asked Christina. She wasn't sure anymore. If Ranjit hadn't seen anything, then maybe Brad was all talk. Maybe she had got it wrong about him.

"Tell us, Jessica. What is wrong with Parker? Why is he sick? Why is he talking about Cindy?" Brad strode over to Parker and hauled him up to his feet. Parker was shaking and barely conscious. His face was pale and he couldn't summon up the energy to raise his head. Brad whispered into Parker's ear. "Don't worry, buddy, I'm going to take good care of your girl."

"Leave him alone!" Jessica tried to grab Brad, but Christina pulled her back.

"You know what I think? I think our old friend Parker here has, unfortunately, got himself infected. What do you think?" Brad sneered at her.

"Don't be ridiculous! He's just..."

"Jessica, it's true," said Tom.

"What? No, that's rubbish." Jessica looked at Parker's limp body and felt queasy. The group turned on Tom as one, incredulous faces looking at him.

"Is it true?" said Caterina.

"If he's one of them, we have to get him out of here" said Reggie.

Brad dropped Parker to the floor and strode over to Tom. "So you *knew*? And you let him stay in here with the rest of us? Are you a complete fucking idiot? Jesus Christ, he could turn at any time!"

"Look, Parker only told me when we got here. And we thought we'd have more time before..."

"Right, Reggie help me, let's get him out of here," said Brad grabbing Parker's legs.

"Let go of him, you fucker!" Jessica broke free of Christina's hands and jumped on Brad's back, bashing him with her fists. He threw her off and she fell painfully to the floor.

"Cool it, Brad, leave him alone. Reggie, don't move a damn muscle." Tom had suspected Brad would react this way. "Parker isn't dead yet, and we're not moving him until we have to. He's helped us get this far. He's our friend."

"I don't know, Tom. I don't think it's safe in here with Parker like this," said Caterina.

"Finally, someone with their head screwed on," said Brad standing over Parker. He reached down and took hold of Parker's ankles. "Reggie, help me out here."

"I don't know, Brad. He's sick, but he's not dead." Reggie stayed where he was, behind Tom.

"Thank you," said Jessica. She was still on the floor where Brad had thrown her. She was crying. Not from the pain, but from the realisation that Parker was going to die. First Brie, now Parker. He looked so helpless.

"Oh shut up, you little bitch. You flutter your eyelashes, flash your tits and think everyone will come to your aid. You're playing the damsel in distress real well I must say. You suckered Parker right in. How did he get infected? Did you screw him? Give him a dose of the bedtime bugs?" said Brad.

Tom lunged at Brad. He threw a punch, but Brad ducked and Tom succeeded in only scraping the side of Brad's head. The blow glanced slightly against Brad's temple. They grappled and fell backward into a stack of chairs that fell over and sent a loud crash ringing out across the room. As the two men wrestled on the floor, Jessica crawled over to Parker. Caterina screamed and Christina held onto her.

"Stop this, stop it now," Reggie shouted. He was tempted to try and break the fight up, but Tom and Brad were rolling around over the floor, refusing to let go of each other. It would be difficult to get between the two of them.

"For Christ sake, boys, stop it!" Christina let go of Caterina and tried to pull them apart. She grabbed Tom's arm and wrenched him off Brad. "Those fucking zombies are going to hear all this noise, you idiots."

Tom slipped over and Brad barged into Christina, pinning her back against the wall. "Don't tell me to shut up. I could snap your neck quite easily, little woman."

"Like you did Amber?" Tom got up and punched Brad again, this time connecting with his jaw and Brad stumbled back. Blood was pouring from Tom's nose. As Brad got up, Reggie stepped between them holding the metal desk leg above his head.

"I'm not picking sides. But if either of you move, I'm going to cave your damn skulls in. This has to end, now. I just pray that they didn't hear you." Reggie looked from Tom to Brad, and they could see the seriousness in his face.

As they regained their breath, Christina sank to the floor and Caterina ran to her.

"Oh, Parker," said Jessica ignoring the fight. She swept the hair back from his clammy forehead as she held him.

"One question, Reggie," said Brad coughing. He spat a mouthful of bloody saliva onto the floor, wiping his lips on his sleeve. "Where's Ranjit?"

They all turned to see an empty corner where Ranjit had been sitting. He had left his briefcase behind and the double doors were open.

"Oh fuck, what now?" said Tom.

* * * *

"Maybe it will be safe outside the city," said Benzo. "The only problem is, there are about ten of us, and six million zombies to get past first."

Jackson opened another door and they found themselves in the downstairs conference hall. The door creaked open and he looked up at the high ceiling where small windows were letting in the only light and air. The hall was cool and virtually empty. A stack of boxes lay at one end of the room, ready to be made into a stage. There was a lighting rig standing over them and several stacks of chairs piled up against one wall.

"Yeah, well, we have to try. I'm not staying here. Look, Benzo, we've gone around this place and it seems pretty secure. We're clearly on our own in here, but that's half the problem."

"What's the problem with that?" said Benzo following Jackson into the hall.

"If you hadn't noticed, there's not much to eat here. How long do you think we could survive cooped up in here? A few days? A week? A month? How long is this going to go on?"

"My dad used to tell me what to do if the terrorists won. You know, if they launched an attack on London, one so bad that effectively shut it down? He said it was probably only a matter of time before they managed it. One massive bomb or lots of small ones; cripple public transport, put poison in the water or destroy the communications network. He said one day a major city would be attacked and probably millions would die." Benzo sat down on one of the stage boxes.

"So did he say how the survivors would get out?" asked Jackson.

"He said a co-ordinated evacuation would be almost impossible. All the stations and airports would be closed down with instructions left for any survivors on where to head to: army barracks, triage centres, anywhere that could help. Ultimately, though, he said it would come down to the individual. If a capital city falls, then the governing body would fall with it, leaving any kind of rescue plan a long way down the list of things to get organised.

"I think what my dad was trying to drill into me, was that when it happened, not if, but *when*, then I was on my own. Find your own way, because big brother is *not* coming for you."

Jackson sat down beside Benzo. "Sounds like your father had a point. Even if the trains and planes aren't there anymore, if we head to the station, then we might at least find out what is going on and where it *is* safe. We might find directions to one of these triage centres or something." As he sat, he felt a piece of paper crinkle in his back pocket.

"What the hell are those things anyway? Zombies? That's stupid. They're people, like you and me. They were unlucky enough to get this infection and died from it. Now their bodies are moving around on their own, but they're not the same people anymore." Benzo sighed.

Jackson pulled the piece of paper from his back pocket and was reading it silently. Benzo looked at it and saw Jackson's expression.

"What is it?"

"It's the roll call I took a couple of days ago. Remember when this kicked off, and Jill made me take a list of everyone who stayed behind in the office," replied Jackson.

"Bloody health and safety bollocks," said Benzo.

"Half of these people are dead now," said Jackson sadly. He began reading the names aloud. "Amber Thorndon, Frederick Thompson, Dina Herbert, Chloe Denitz, Michelle Whittaker, Jill..."

Jackson stopped, unable to read anymore. Benzo could see Jackson's eyes were watery and said nothing, letting the names of the dead hang in the air. Freddy, Troy, Rob; most of his old mates were dead now. Benzo thought of his father and what he might be doing. Was he working with the police, still trying to help people? Was he at home? It was more likely that he was dead along with the rest of his family.

"I keep wishing I could see my Mary again, but I know it's not going to happen. It would take a miracle." Jackson folded the paper up and put it back in his pocket. He quickly wiped his face and got up.

"Come on, we'd better get back," said Benzo. No sooner had he said that, than they heard a noise like footsteps. A repetitive tapping sound that gradually increased in volume.

"Do you think someone's come looking for us?" whispered Benzo.

"No," said Jackson. "Listen."

They stood still, Benzo holding his breath for fear of being found by the dead. The footsteps reached a peak and then began to fade.

"They're coming from the other side of the hall," said Jackson. He pointed over to the stage and there, behind it, was a door, half open. "Come on, we'd better check."

"No way," said Benzo, "what if it's one of those things?"

"I don't think it is," said Jackson. "The footsteps are too regular. It's the same sound we make when we're walking. Those zombies don't walk like we do. No, I think it's someone alive. I just don't know who. If it was one of us, they would have said something."

They walked across the vast hall to the door, careful not to make any noise. The noise of the receding footsteps stopped and they heard a rattling sound coming from the adjacent corridor. Very gently, Jackson pushed the door open and poked his head around it. He couldn't see anyone, but the rattling sound was definitely coming from the end of the corridor.

"Come on," he said, and Benzo followed him into the corridor. "Whoever it is, they're making far too much noise. They're going to let the whole world know we're in here."

"Hey!" Benzo called out. "Whoever that is, for goodness sake, be quiet!"

The rattling sound stopped abruptly and Jackson and Benzo paused. A crashing sound echoed down the corridor to them as a window was smashed and glass tinkled to the ground.

"This is not good," said Jackson and he started running down the corridor. Together with Benzo, he rounded the end of the corridor and saw a man, half out of the smashed window, one leg either side of the frame.

Ranjit looked at the two men. "Get away from me. I'm leaving and you can't stop me. I need to find my wife. You lot are pathetic. Fighting at a time like this? You don't even know the half if it. If you'd seen what I'd seen...just leave me alone!"

"Ranjit stop, don't go out there!" said Jackson.

Ranjit didn't hear anything else. He clambered out of the window and fell to the ground outside. He was in the rear yard, at the foot of the fire escape they had used to get in earlier. He ran out of the yard, weaving between the scattered zombies, avoiding their clutching hands.

"Keti, I'm coming!" He screamed as he ran into the road.

Jackson watched him disappear out of sight. Alerted by the breaking glass and Ranjit's cries, the nearest zombies in the yard saw Jackson and Benzo through the open window. They rushed toward it and others followed. From the streets, more were drawn to the commotion.

"Run!" shouted Benzo.

They sprinted back down the corridor as the first zombie climbed into the conference centre. In the doorway, to the main hall, Jackson hesitated and looked back. At least a dozen dead were following them. He slammed the door shut and ran.

"We've got to get back upstairs and warn the others. It won't be long before they catch up with us," said Benzo running through the hall.

They ran back the way they had come and finally came to the 'Nelson' room. Benzo threw the door open to see Reggie holding something above his head, Tom with a bloody nose, and Brad with a cut face and a black eye. Everyone looked at Benzo, shocked by the way he had burst into the room.

"They're in," he said.

* * * *

"We can do it, I'm telling you," said Angel. "I'm not waiting anymore. We can do it."

"She's right, Don." Rosa walked over to him and took his hand, forcing him to stand up. "We've spent the last three days stuck in here and this may be our only chance to get out. You know we can do it. They're the only sign of life we've seen in days." There was a pleading in her voice that he could not ignore.

Don's bus was still in the pub car park where he had abandoned it. For the last three days, they had been trapped in the upstairs room of The Fox together. He had picked up Rosa on her way into the city and she still wore the blue uniform she had put on days ago. He had learnt a lot about Rosa. When you were stuck in a small room with someone for days on end, it was impossible not to. She had recently started working in the city plaza, front desk work for one of the big banks.

Angel, an older woman, was on her way to the same bank to take out all her money. She spent the last three days carping on about 'the system,' and how the banking institutions were bringing about the downfall of western civilisation. All he knew, was how to drive a bus, and drink, not always exclusive to each other.

"I don't know," he said running his hands through his thinning grey hair. "You saw what happened to that fat bloke when he ran from the centre. He got what, twenty feet, thirty? He's in pieces now. Can I just remind you two ladies of that?"

"Well, there's certainly not much of him left, that's true," said Angel staring out the window down into the blood-stained yard.

"But he was on foot," said Rosa. "We've got your bus. Come on, Don, think about it. With the distraction, the yard's nearly empty."

Since the outbreak, the zombies had followed the bus into the yard and surrounded it. Don, Rosa, and Angel had managed to escape it and locked themselves into the deserted pub upstairs. Some of Don's passengers hadn't been so lucky. Poor Mr Barker had gone back for his bag and vanished under a pile of animated rotting bodies. They had listened to his anguished howls before one of the zombies snapped his neck and he went silent. From a bus of nine people, only three had made it off with Don.

"Look," said Angel, "they're all going into the Onevision conference centre. There's barely a handful left down there. We can totally run past those few. I have *one vision*, Don, and it involves us getting out of here."

Bloody, Angel was right, he knew it. She was an oddball for sure, but she was usually on the money. If he hadn't found out she was forty five, he would've sworn she was thirty. She had her hair in dreadlocks and wore brightly coloured clothes as if she was Rosa's age.

"All right, fine." Don put his jacket on and took the keys out, dangling them in front of Angel. "Just remember, I'm the driver, it's my bus, and that means *I'm* in charge once we get out there."

"No problem," said Angel.

"Yay, thanks, Don!" Rosa planted a wet kiss on his cheek. He tried not to, but couldn't help a small smile escaping his wrinkled face.

"Listen, we've talked about this, so we all know what to do. Don't start messing around out there. If you start pissing about, I'm not waiting for you."

"Yes, Don, we've got it, don't worry," said Rosa gleefully. "Oh, I can't wait to get home and have a wash and put on some clean clothes."

"I'm looking forward to eating some fresh vegetables again. I'm sick of frigging dry roasted peanuts," said Angel, picking up her handbag. She looked out of the window again. Down by the bus below them, she counted the zombies. There were seven in total and four of those were small children. They were fast, but they were easier to knock over. She looked over the fence at the conference centre opposite. Hundreds of zombies were swarming over it now, and through the open window the fat man had left behind. Some of the dead milled around in the yard, unable to get into the building. Some of them had begun to climb the fire escape to find another way in.

"Hey, Rosa, come here a sec', will you?"

"What is it?" said Rosa approaching the window.

"That man wasn't alone." Angel pointed to the fire escape and Rosa's eyes traced their way up it, past the zombies, to the top. Two men were stood out on the top step, waving frantically.

Rosa waved back. "Um, Don, we might need a change of plan."

* * * *

"Quick, upstairs now!" shouted Jackson. Brad and Reggie ran after Benzo and Jackson, while the rest of the group scrambled to their feet.

"Wait, we can't leave," said Jessica. "What about Parker?"

Tom looked at his friend. He wasn't dead yet, but he certainly looked it.

"I don't think there's much we can do for him, Jess."

"We can't just leave him though. He was your friend for God's sake."

"I know, I know, but think about it, what can I do? I'm sorry, Jess but we have to go." Tom took her hand and she shrugged him away. She bent down to Parker.

"Hey, Parker, can you hear me? We have to go now. Get up, Parker, get up, please?" She pulled on his lifeless hands to no avail.

"Will you help me please, Christina?" said Tom. She nodded and together they pulled Jessica away from the unconscious Parker.

"No, leave me alone, I can't leave someone else, not again!" Jessica was crying as Tom and Christina dragged her away, leaving Parker slumped against the wall, taking in small, shallow breaths.

"Parker, please!" cried Jessica.

Christina stood in front of her and cupped her face. "Come on, Jessica, there's nothing you can do for him now. Follow me. Come on, darling."

Tom let her go and a sobbing Jessica fell into Christina's arms. Tom put an arm around Caterina but she pushed him away.

"Leave me alone," she said, and marched out of the room to follow Jackson. Tom trudged after her, whilst Christina did her best to get Jessica up the stairs. Tom shut the door behind them and took one last look at Parker. He looked like he was just sleeping, but all the colour had drained out of his face.

"Goodbye, Parker." Tom shut the door.

Jackson stood by an open door at the top of the stairs. He ushered everyone into the room where they had first entered the conference centre. He held the door open until the last of them, Tom, came through. Jackson frowned when he saw Tom's split lip.

"They're in the building. We need to get out of here before they find us," said Jackson closing the door finally.

"How the fuck did they get in?" said Brad.

"Ranjit," said Benzo. "We saw him leaving. He broke a window and ran off."

"I'll kill that fucking idiot," said Brad.

"I think you're too late for that, Brad, he's long gone," replied Benzo.

"Why didn't you try to stop him?"

"Really, Brad? Do you think we just opened the window for him? Sometimes it would be better for you not to open your god damn mouth," said Jackson. "Here's a novel idea; why don't you try thinking before you speak? I don't know what the hell is going on between you and Tom, but I can see something's happened. If you're going to start picking fights, Brad, I suggest you find out who is on your side first, because you are soon going to find yourself vastly outnumbered."

Brad sat down on the floor and looked up at Jackson. He spoke with a cocky tone. "Don't you want to know what happened to Parker?"

"No. I can see from the tears that poor girl over there is crying, that it ain't good. I can see that he is not in this room and I can put two and two together, so take my advice and shut up. Just shut up, Brad. Stop pushing it." Jackson rolled his sleeves up.

Brad chewed over Jackson's words and stayed silent. Aside from Jessica's tears, there was only one noise now; the noise of the dead. They could all hear banging noises downstairs as doors were cast open and rooms ransacked.

"Take a quick look out the window please, Tom, what do you see?" said Jackson.

Tom went to the fire escape door and peered out through the broken glass.

"Zombies. Hundreds of them. They're in the yard and they're getting into the building right beneath us. I'm guessing that's where Ranjit left. There are some on the steps, too. We can't get out this way."

"What are we going to do? I don't want to die in here. I don't want my child to die in here before she's even had a chance," said Caterina.

"Ask her," said Brad pointing at Christina. "She brought us into this death trap."

"Tom, move aside for a second, mate." Reggie went to the door and opened it, stepping out onto the top step.

"What are you doing? They'll see you!" said Caterina.

"Doesn't much matter now, Cat, they already know we're in here," said Benzo.

Reggie looked around the yard for a way out. The yard was full and the rusty fire escape was vibrating, as the zombies slowly climbed up. He scanned around as the afternoon sun shone down upon him.

"Anyone fancy a drink?" Reggie pulled Tom outside with him. "Look over there. You see the pub next door? Over the fence there's a bus. That yard is practically empty."

"Might as well be a million miles away though," said Tom despondently.

"Look up. From the bus follow the pub walls and there's a window at the top. What do you see?" Reggie pointed across the yard with one hand, shielding his eyes from the glare of the sun with the other.

"Fuck me," said Tom. He began waving, as did Reggie, hoping that the two figures in the pub window opposite would see them.

CHAPTER FIFTEEN

"You can't be serious, Rosa, I thought you had more brains than that." Don had taken off his jacket again. "No, I think we should stay here."

"And I thought you had more compassion than that, Don. We can't leave them. We just can't." Rosa picked his jacket up and held it out to him.

"With or without them, I'm leaving," said Angel. "You two coming or not?" She put her hand on Rosa's shoulder. "Leave him. If he wants to rot in here for eternity, let him. Let's go."

Rosa dropped Don's jacket on the floor and walked over to the door.

"All right, all right. Jesus, now I remember why I never got married." Don picked up his jacket. "So what do you propose? Even if we get into the bus safely, how do you suggest we pick them up? I can hardly do a U-turn and ask the zombies to wait while we go and pick them up. I mean, be realistic, it's impossible. I'm sorry for them, but they're as good as dead already."

"We get them to come to us," said Rosa. Don looked at her as if she was mad.

"How? There are several hundred infected dead between them and us." He watched as she walked back over to the window.

"I hope they understand this," she said, and opened the window.

* * * *

"Look she's waving back, she's seen us," said Reggie.

Brad got up and wandered to the door to look.

"Big deal," he said peering over Tom's shoulder. "Look, they're gone now. Why would they risk their necks to save us? We have to look after ourselves now; no one is coming to save us."

"I hate to say so, but he's right," said Benzo. "We're on our own. We should either hunker down and hide, or find something to fight with. I'm not waiting for help that isn't coming."

"Well, whatever we do has to be fast. I can hear them in the corridor outside," said Jackson, dragging the horseshoe desk in front of the door. He hoped it might just hold the zombies off and buy them valuable time.

Tom turned to face the room. "Follow me. There's a way out."

He went to a door at the end of the room. It was an adjoining door that led to another conference room.

"Where are you going? What way out?" said Reggie.

"The figures at the window? One came back. She showed me a way. It's tricky, but it's possible. Quite frankly, what choice do we have?"

The door beside Jackson started shaking violently. The horseshoe desk began quaking on rickety legs.

"Fuck it, come on then," said Benzo, and he ran after Tom. Not knowing where they were headed, they followed Tom quickly. He led them through a series of small interconnecting meeting rooms, each the same as the last, until he reached the last one. This room had balcony doors and Tom pushed them open. The roaring noise of the hungry zombies underneath them suddenly rang out loud and clear.

"I hope you know what you're doing, Tom Goode," said Jackson. He stepped out onto the balcony beside Tom and felt fear that he hadn't experienced since the day he'd been standing at the altar, waiting for Mary to show, forty years ago. Below the balcony, there was a delivery truck. It was surrounded by the dead. It had been left askew, abandoned in a hurry, so the front cab was directly beneath them and the rear was jammed up against the fence. The driver's door was open and a bloody stump sat in the driver's seat, the truck driver having long since been feasted upon by the infected.

"Nice day for a drive, Tom, but we're not going anywhere in that," said Jackson.

"Listen up," said Tom addressing the group once more, "there is a truck right beneath us. It's a bit of a jump, but we can make it.

The roof of the cab leads to the fence and it's well out of reach of those zombies. On the other side of the fence, is the pub."

"Come on, Tom, I'd love a Ploughmans," said Benzo scratching his head, "but we've hardly got time. What's the deal?"

"On the other side of that fence, is a bus. The people in that pub have the keys. If I've understood them right, then they mean to leave in that bus. *Right now*. We need to get on it."

"Are you sure? What if you're wrong?" Jessica asked. Her eyes were red, but she had stopped crying. "We'd be out there with them and with nothing to stop them from ripping us apart."

"That's true, buddy," said Brad. "How sure are you?"

Tom looked around the small room. They were all looking at him as if he had the answer to everything. All he knew, was if they stayed here, they were dead.

"This sure," he said turning back onto the balcony to face the sun. He put his legs over the balcony's edge and jumped.

* * * *

"They're going for it," said Rosa happily.

"You're mad," said Angel. "How do you feel about having a bus full of passengers again, Don?"

"Just remember to swipe on and off," he said pulling his jacket on. With the jacket on, came the grumpy demeanour and Rosa wondered if it was part of the training.

Don opened the door and crept downstairs. Rosa and Angel followed him until they reached the bar. The pub door had been taken off its hinges and all the windows had been smashed by looters. There was hardly been any booze left, but Don managed to find a stash before they locked themselves away upstairs.

They quietly walked through the empty pub toward the door. They didn't want anything or anyone to know they were there until the last minute. It was impossible though to avoid walking on the broken glass which crunched underfoot; it was all over the place.

They managed to get to the doorway before they were noticed. A small child spotted them and began shuffling its way to the pub. It was covered head to toe in boils, and the searing sun had popped many of them. Rosa saw milky, curdled pus oozing from its cracked dry skin.

"Now!" Don ran from the pub to the bus and opened the door while Rosa and Angel ran the other way. They had to give Don time to get in the bus and get it started, so they darted to the back end of the bus.

"It's working," said Rosa as she dodged the outstretched hands of the child. "The zombies' attention is on us, not Don."

"Awesome," said Angel. She ducked as a zombie tried to grab her and she doubled back with Rosa to the pub. Hearing the engine roar into life, they ran once more toward the bus.

"Quickly, quickly!" shouted Don. Rosa and Angel ran onto the bus and he closed the doors. They almost fell as he drove the bus forward and it lurched violently. A zombie threw itself against the doors, but could not get in.

"Damn that was close," said Angel sitting down. "Can we please *not* do that again?"

Rosa sat down in a seat near the front so she could see out through the large front window. Don turned the bus in the pub car park and positioned it so if anyone came over the fence from the conference centre, they would land right beside the doors. Rosa was impressed at how speedily he did it, and how he manoeuvred the bus so well in such a tight space. He left about a foot between the bus and the fence and hoped the zombies would not work out what they were doing. On the other side of the bus, more zombies had appeared and were hammering at it, slamming themselves into the side, trying to get at Don, Angel, and Rosa.

"Your friends had better hurry up," said Don revving the engine. "Two minutes and we're gone. Any longer than that and there'll be so many of these critters in the yard, we'll never get out ourselves."

"Just you be ready to open the doors," said Rosa. "They'll be here." She crossed her fingers. It wasn't just her life in the balance now - others were depending on her, not least Don and Angel. She wondered who was going to come over the wall.

* * * *

Tom landed on the truck's cab roof and could almost taste death. The smell of decay and rot, faeces and blood, and of rotting flesh, invaded his nostrils, his mouth, and his eyes. He landed on his feet and crouched down. The yard simmered with the dead.

"Come on, next one," he said hearing the engine of the bus roar into life.

He looked up and Brad's face appeared. Tom climbed onto the truck's roof out of the way and watched as Brad jumped down. He landed easily and Tom held out his hand to help him over. Brad took it, and together they stood on the truck roof.

"Sure hope you're right about this, buddy," Brad said.

"Me, too."

Tom watched as Jessica followed and they slowly made their way back across the truck to make room for the rest. One by one they dropped off the balcony onto the truck: Christina, Caterina, Benzo, Jackson, and, finally, Reggie. Tom stood at the end of the truck and could see the roof of the bus only feet away on the other side of the fence. The driver was revving the engine and Tom knew they didn't have much time.

"I'm going down first then I want Caterina to come. I'll help you, okay? After that, Jessica and Christina. Fair enough?"

Brad wanted to get off the roof but thought better of speaking out this time. Jackson was right about one thing; he had to pick his fights. He had let things get out of control back there and that was not how he usually handled things. Think it through, he thought to himself; just think it through next time. Jackson, Tom, Christina – they would be dead soon enough. When the time came, he would leave them. Jessica could be useful before he killed her. He doubted that Parker had actually stuck it to her yet. He looked at Jessica crouching down on the truck roof. She had a tight ass; if only he could get her alone, he could have a lot of fun with that.

There were no dissenting voices and Tom jumped. As he flew over the fence, dead hands and arms reached up to grab him, but he was out of reach. He fell down into the pub car park and landed painfully. There was little room to drop between the bus and the fence, and he scraped his elbows and hands when he landed.

"I'm coming, Tom," he heard Caterina shout and then he saw her heading toward him. He tried to cushion her fall, but it was difficult in the cramped space they had. As she landed, the bus doors opened behind him.

"Get in!" Tom shoved her onto the bus and hands reached for him. He looked up, surprised to see a young woman looking at him. Caterina stumbled past her.

"Hi, I'm Rosa. Are there many more?"

"Six more of us," said Tom. "I'm going to help them down. Tom, by the way."

Suddenly, Christina dropped beside him and he helped her onto the bus. Rosa stayed in the doorway helping Christina in.

"Come on, guys, hurry it up," said Tom looking down the line of the fence. At the rear of the bus, a zombie had appeared. It was a large man and he was struggling to squeeze between the fence and the bus.

Benzo swiftly appeared with Brad after him. Up on the truck roof, there was only Jackson and Reggie left.

"Go on, mate," said Reggie, "you go next."

"Thanks, Reggie," said Jackson poised to jump. He was waiting for a clear spot to land in. Brad, Benzo, and Tom were blocking the space.

"Make way, guys, I'm coming," shouted Jackson. He too had seen the dead man at the rear of the bus. The zombie had managed to get three feet at least and was inching his way toward the door slowly.

Suddenly, Reggie let out a yelp and Jackson was aware of a flapping noise behind him.

"What the hell?" Jackson saw Reggie trying to fight off a pigeon that was flapping and fluttering around his head. He pulled off a shoe and waved it around, trying to strike the bird. Reggie managed to grab the bird and threw the pigeon away. It landed on the truck roof and Jackson noticed its feathers were dark and sticky; they were covered in congealed blood.

"Fucking pigeons, I hate them," said Reggie. The pigeon flew up into the air and attacked Reggie again. Jackson tried to help and struck the pigeon's head with his shoe. It landed at his feet and Reggie stamped on it.

Jackson looked on as the pigeon tried to get to its feet. Reggie had stamped on its head, crushing its bones, and one wing was hanging off. It attempted to get to its feet and hopped over to

Reggie who kicked it again, sending it flying into the crowd of zombies, its feathers scattering in the air.

"Come on, Jackson, let's get the hell out of here," said Reggie, wiping the blood from his face. Jackson was horrified. The pigeon had nicked Reggie's face in a few places.

"Don't worry, mate, it's just a scratch," said Reggie seeing the look on Jackson's face.

"Er, yeah. Look, Reggie, pigeon's don't attack people, not normal ones anyhow."

"Oh, come on, you don't think it was infected do you? It was just scared. It was trying to get away from them."

Jackson put his shoe back on. "You know what my Mary says pigeons are? Flying rats."

"Jackson, I'm fine. Let's just go, okay? If you don't jump in a minute, I'll bloody push you off here."

Jackson smiled. Reggie was fine. "Okay, I'm going." He jumped down to Tom and clambered into the bus. Reggie followed and with him and Tom on board, Don gratefully put the bus into gear and started reversing.

"Don, what are you doing? Why are we going backwards?" said Angel.

Don watched in his mirror as the zombie that had squeezed between them and the fence was slowly crushed. Its rib cage was first to crack and Don took great delight in watching the man's eyes pop out of his head.

"Just sit tight, Angel, it's going to be a bumpy ride."

Don started the bus forward, ignoring the dead in front of him. He sped up and several fell under the bus, crushed under its huge wheels. Don turned the bus out onto the road and with most of the dead focussed on the conference centre, his path was reasonably clear. He barrelled through them, knocking over anything in his way, not hesitating. He knew if he stopped, they would be dead. Looking in his mirror, he could see the zombies in their hundreds turning away from the centre and chasing after the bus.

"Thanks for helping us out back there. Sorry to be so blunt, but where are we going?" said Tom sitting next to Rosa.

"Well, we hadn't thought about it too much. First priority was to get away from here, second was to get Angel home. That's the lady over there. She left her daughter at home with her husband."

"Where does she live?" asked Tom, as the bus careered over the road wildly.

"Canning. Don reckons he can get us there, he's a good driver. Angel said we can stay with her until whatever's happened has been sorted. It shouldn't be too long now, surely?"

Tom had to grip the seat in front of him as Don turned around a bend in the road. He was going fast, trying to evade the marauding dead behind them. He scraped the bus alongside a row of parked cars.

"Hey, Don, careful. We want to get out of here in one piece," said Angel.

"Tom, what's happening, where are we going?" Jackson leaned over to Tom, hanging onto the overhead handles as the bus swayed.

"They're still coming!" shouted Christina from the back of the bus. "We need to go faster!"

A dead soldier threw himself at the back window, making Christina and Caterina jump back.

"Where the hell are we going?" shouted Brad, as the bus lurched across the street once more. Don had to avoid a pile up in the middle of the road. An ambulance was blocking the street and he pulled the bus up the kerb to get past.

Tom staggered to the front of the bus. "Hey, mate, do you know where you're going?"

Don threw a casual glance at Tom. "Of course I do, I've been driving these streets for twenty years. I suggest you sit down, son," he said.

"Look, I know this is a fucked up situation and we can't thank you enough for helping us, but maybe you should slow down a bit, you're scaring people back here."

"Have you looked outside, son?" Don bristled. "Take a look around. We're surrounded, and if I slow down, those bastards will catch us. No, we're doing things my way for once."

Don accelerated and Tom tripped backwards, falling into an empty seat. An arm grabbed his and Tom looked up as Brad went past him.

"Hey, buddy, are you in control of this thing?" Brad clutched Don's arm as the bus lurched violently over a pile of bodies, and crashed back down onto the road with such force that Jessica and Rosa fell from their seats into the aisle.

"You're distracting me, go sit down," said Don angrily.

"Don, listen to them, please!" said Rosa. Tom helped her up and pulled her onto the seat next to him. Don swerved around an army jeep and pulled the bus into a small side street. The zombies were further away now, disappearing out of sight. Don kept the bus going hard and fast, and at the end of the street, Brad saw a low black railing fencing a park.

"Don't do what I think you're going to do," said Brad.

"I told you to sit down," said Don as he crashed the bus over the kerb, into the railings. The powerful bus smashed straight through them and bounced over the shrubs and plants before skidding onto the grass.

In the back of the bus, they went flying. Jackson managed to hold onto Angel, and Tom to Rosa, but Reggie, Christina, Caterina, and Jessica fell to the floor. Brad slammed into the bus doors and hit his head. As Don slowed the bus in the middle of the park, Brad, dazed, felt his head. There was a trickle of blood running down the side of his face.

Don slammed the brakes down and the bus slewed across the park finally coming to rest by a large beech tree. He turned the engine off.

"Do you know where we are?" he shouted getting out of his seat. "Do you?"

Brad lay on the floor. "No, I...I'm not sure exactly but..."

"Anyone else?" Don stared down the length of the bus. Nobody answered him.

"Don, come on, honey, take it easy. You're scaring everyone," said Angel.

Don looked around at the petrified eyes looking back at him. "Robin Hood Gardens. Over that wall is Cotton Street. Over in that direction is the Blackwall tunnel. Trust me, I know what I'm doing. I know how to handle this bus. She's a cantankerous old bitch at times, but unlike people, she does what she's told."

"Can we get going, please?" Christina was looking out of the rear of the bus into the park. There were figures emerging from the shadows, drawn by the noise, approaching the bus. Caterina was crying.

"Well, if I can get a bit of peace and sodding quiet." Don returned to his seat and started the engine.

"Is he usually like this?" Tom asked Rosa quietly, so Don wouldn't hear.

"He's all right really. It's just the stress, you know. Say, are you okay? Your lip's bleeding. Here," and she pulled a tissue out of her pocket, dabbing it at Tom's cut lip. He felt too ashamed to tell her he had got it fighting.

"Yeah, it's nothing. I just banged it when we stopped," he said taking the tissue from her. She gave him a kind smile and he felt doubly guilty; now he was lying, too.

The bus was inching slowly across the grass as Don let the tyre's find a grip.

"Thank God," said Jessica to Reggie, "I thought we were going to get stuck." As the bus sped up, Jessica let out an audible sigh of relief.

"Don't worry," said Reggie, "we're on our way now."

The tyres found traction on a footpath and Don increased their speed, keen to move on. Christina was trying to calm Caterina down and pleased to see the zombies getting further away now. Tom was about to ask Rosa how she'd met Don and Angel, when he saw Brad getting to his feet. Brad was looking at Don with thunder in his eyes and Tom could sense trouble.

"You don't know who you're dealing with, motherfucker." Brad punched Don on the side of the head and there was a loud crack as Don's head hit the side window. Tom could almost feel the man's jaw break. Rosa screamed and gripped Tom. Don instinctively put his hands up to protect himself and let go of the wheel. He cried out in pain and the bus lurched to the left, as Brad hit Don again.

"Who's in charge, eh? You God damn cocksucker!" Brad knocked Don out cold with his third blow and he tried to grab the wheel. The bus was travelling fast and as the wheel spun, uncontrolled, the bus began to bank. Brad tried to get both his hands around the steering wheel, but Don had slumped forward making it difficult for Brad to get hold of it.

"Brad, you idiot, look out!" Tom jumped up to help Brad steer, but it was too late. The bus ploughed over freshly dug earth, through flimsy railings and out of the park, narrowly avoiding colliding into a postal delivery van. As they mounted the pavement again, Tom was thrown to the floor. The bus careered over more grass and clattered over a gravestone. Tom heard the screams behind him. He looked up and saw a brick wall inches from the windscreen. He knew there was no way Brad would get the bus back under control in time. Tom braced himself and grabbed the nearest thing to hand, which happened to be Angel's ankle. She screamed as the bus rammed into the side of All Saints Church.

The bus came to an abrupt halt with metal being torn and twisted, as the church wall collapsed on it. Tom heard screeching metal and glass shattering before he was knocked out. The bus' occupants were thrown from their seats as the bus stopped dead. The zombies from the park staggered into the church grounds, scraping past headstones and open burial pits toward the now silent bus.

CHAPTER SIXTEEN

The air was full of dust and Caterina coughed violently. Being seated at the back of the bus meant she had been saved from the impact of the crash, the brunt of it being borne by the front of the bus. Christina had made her lie down, and so she had not fallen too hard when they'd crashed. When Caterina had finished barking out the dirt, she gingerly got up. It was lucky she hadn't fallen too hard. She rubbed her belly and instinctively knew the baby was fine. She spat out a mouthful of grime. Christina was lying on the floor and Caterina shook her awake.

"Christina! Christina!" She came to and got to her knees slowly.

"Cat, what happened? Is everyone okay?"

"I don't know." Caterina helped Christina up and she ruffled her hair, tiny shards of glass falling to the floor. The front of the bus was clouded in dust and smoke. Christina could smell burning and knew that they had to get out quickly. Between them, they helped the others. Jackson and Jessica had been knocked out, but were not seriously hurt. Just cuts and scrapes that would heal. Benzo had a deep gash on his arm and was wrapping his jumper around it to stem the bleeding. Reggie was helping him.

"It's all right, Reggie, I got it, thanks. You should take care of yourself, you look pretty bad," said Benzo.

Reggie looked at his reflection in a window - there was a large slice of glass perched on the seat beside him. His face was cut and it looked like someone had taken a cheese grater to his forehead. He felt light headed and dizzy.

"I'm okay, let's just get everyone off before *they* come," he said. He bent down to Rosa who was unconscious. She had escaped the flying glass and looked like she was sound asleep. Reggie was reminded of his younger sister; she looked so innocent when she slept. Reggie shook Rosa, but she wouldn't wake. There was a large bump on the side of her face. He scooped her up.

"The side doors are blocked, we'll have to get out through the back window," he said carrying Rosa to the back of the bus. Christina and Jackson helped him get Rosa out. Caterina clambered out with them, pleased to be off the bus. She sank to her knees and dug her fingers into the mud. The smell of the grass and flowers took her mind away from reality. The trauma subsided and she revelled in the natural smell of the earth, the cool peat in her fingers. She took in measured breaths and forcibly calmed herself down; she had to be calm, for her baby's sake.

"Where's Tom?" said Jessica.

"And Brad. He was at the front with Don," said Benzo. Jessica and Benzo clambered back into the bus. They had to tread carefully. A lot of bricks and masonry had fallen into the front area of the bus. They saw Angel first; she was slumped over the seat in front of her.

"Angel?" Benzo gently pulled her back and recoiled in horror when he saw her. She had been garrotted by a slither of glass that was still embedded in her neck. It had almost sliced her head off and her body fell back against the side of the bus.

"Oh, God," said Jessica looking at the dead woman. Angel's eyes were locked open in fright, forever staring ahead into death. They left her in her seat.

"There's nothing we can do for her now," said Benzo. Then he heard it.

"Hey, Jessica, listen, do you hear that?" he said. There was a faint groaning sound and then movement. A sole brick tumbled from the pile in front of them and came to rest at Jessica's feet. A couple more bricks moved and Benzo saw a hand.

"Tom!"

They scrabbled over the rubble, throwing bricks aside as they dug Tom out. His face was badly cut and one eye had swelled up so much it was closed.

"Thanks," was all Tom could manage as they dragged him free. His shirt was ripped and blood stained.

"Can you manage him?" Benzo asked Jessica, propping Tom up on her shoulders. "I've got to find Brad." Benzo returned to scouring the rubble, whilst Jessica helped Tom out of the bus. Jackson reached up and took him from her as they came through the rear window.

"Come on, Benzo, leave it," shouted Jessica. Smoke was beginning to drift into the bus and it was becoming difficult to see; breathing was harder, and she could hear Benzo's rasping, coughing. The smell of burning was increasing too.

"Benzo, come on, man, we can't stick around. They're coming." Jackson helped Jessica down and then clambered back into the bus to find Benzo, who was still pulling aside bricks, looking for Brad. Jackson could see the jumper wrapped around Benzo's arm, bright red, soaking up blood as it continued to escape Benzo's arteries.

"What about Brad? What about Don?" said Benzo.

Jackson looked at the twisted metal where Don had been sat. The chair was full of rubble and a stone gargoyle sat grinning in his place, as if it was going to drive the bus away into the very depths of hell. There were blood stains splattered across the dashboard and Jackson noticed that sharp protrusions of glass around the windscreen were dripping with fresh warm blood. Jackson guessed Don had not been wearing a seatbelt and was currently somewhere beneath the bus and the church.

"Benzo, we're leaving. Now." Jackson's eyes were watering from the smoke and he grabbed a weakening Benzo. They returned to the rear of the bus and Benzo almost fell to the ground, he was so weak. Jackson collapsed to the muddy earth.

"Where's Brad?" said Tom.

Jackson was curled up, coughing uncontrollably. "Couldn't...find him...don't know..."

"And Don? Angel? Where are they?" Rosa had awoken on the ground and looking around the group, was dismayed to find her friends were absent. She felt very alone. "Why aren't you getting them out? They need our help."

"Sorry, but Angel's gone," said Jessica.

"Don, too," said Jackson still coughing and rubbing his eyes.

Rosa burst into tears. Caterina bent down and put a hand on her shoulder, but Rosa shrugged her away. The throbbing on her head seemed to boom around her from all sides. Don and Angel were dead. How could they be gone? After surviving for so long, they had gone outside only to be taken so quickly. Rosa couldn't believe it.

"What the hell happened?" said Jessica. "Why did we crash?"

"Search me. I saw Brad struggling with Don, but I couldn't see what was going on," said Jackson. "It was so fast, I'm just glad we're okay."

Tom said nothing.

Christina looked at Jackson. "Not *all* of us are okay."

"Shit, they're getting close, what are we going to do now?" said Reggie. He pointed with a trembling finger across the graveyard at five zombies entering the church grounds. They were walking in the tracks the bus had made with more following behind them.

"Inside the church," said Tom.

"Do you think that's a good idea?" said Christina as Tom started looking for the church entrance. "We don't want to get trapped again."

"You got a better idea, then let's have it," said Jackson joining Tom.

They had crashed into the vestibule and the bus was deeply embedded into the wall. There was no way into the church here and Tom was looking for the main doors.

"Wait," said Rosa as others began following, "what about Don? Are you sure he's dead? He might be okay? He might need our help!"

Reggie was the only one with her now, and he helped her to her feet. "I'm sorry, but I think it's too late. If there was any way of helping your friends, Jackson would've found it. I'm sorry."

Sniffing, Rosa wiped her eyes. She bit her quivering lip. "We should've stayed in the pub. If we'd waited for help to come, then Don and Angel would still be alive. I'm such an idiot. It was me that cajoled Don into going. Oh, God."

Reggie put his arm around her and with one eye monitoring the zombies in the near distance, began ushering her toward the church.

"There's no point in talking like that, love. You don't know what's going to happen. It's not your fault. Anyway, if you hadn't come, then we'd be dead by now. We should be thanking you. Look, we need to get inside. It's not safe out here."

He led her to the others. Tom had found the church doors and was holding the huge oak door open as the others filed inside. As Rosa went past him, Reggie suddenly dropped to his knees and began coughing. He spat blood out onto the moss covered slate floor.

"You all right, Reggie?" asked Tom lifting him up.

"Yeah, I just need to rest. I don't feel so good. I think when the bus crashed, I hit my chest or something, it really hurts."

"All right, mate, just take it easy. Let's get in here and take a look at you."

Reggie passed under the arched frame of the door and Tom followed him into the quiet church, heaving the heavy door shut behind him. It shut with a clang that reverberated around the whole church. He dropped the iron latch and instantly felt safer. There was a solid barrier between them and the outside world now. He turned and looked up into the church. The sunlight was sending kaleidoscopic images through the stained glass windows, illuminating the church in an iridescent light. The tall roof meant it was cool inside, despite the warm sun outside, and Tom felt safer now than he had at any time over the last few days.

Looking around, he saw gnarled stone monsters up high, looking down on them. Gargoyles were crouching in dark corners, perched above columns, watching the intruders. There were leather-bound bibles lining the rows of pews and kneeling cushions, embroidered with religious images of old. Tom took a couple of steps forward and his footsteps echoed around the vaulted ceiling. Tom appreciated the stone walls and high windows; they meant safety. The dead couldn't get at them whilst they were here, he was sure of that.

Jackson, Christina, and Caterina, were sat on a pew in front of Tom. A few rows behind, he saw Benzo, lying down, his feet sticking out, whilst Jessica stood over him. She was wrapping his arm in a tight swathe, using a scarf she had found in the church entrance to wrap his arm and stem the bleeding.

Rosa had seated herself on a chair close to the others, but private enough that they wouldn't hear her tears. Above her, hung a huge tapestry of the last supper and around her, were wreaths and huge bouquets of flowers: Roses, Carnations, and Asiatic Lilies. They leant the air a sweet smell and Tom left her alone to grieve. There was nothing he could say or do to console her. He knew Don must be dead, there was no way he could've survived such an impact. He looked around but couldn't see Angel. He hadn't noticed outside that she was missing, but it struck him now that she was not here. Benzo would've brought her in if he could have. Tom said a quick prayer for her and Don, then he saw Reggie at the altar. He was kneeling down, hands clasped in front of him. Tom wanted to go and check on Reggie, he didn't look well, but the man seemed to need some alone time, too. Besides, Tom was feeling dizzy and his head was pounding. Reggie would have to wait.

Tom walked over to the row of wooden pews and sat down. He rolled up his shirt sleeves and examined the cuts on his arms; they were only superficial. His whole body ached, but he knew he had been lucky; he could be with Angel and Don now. Where was Brad though? Was he buried beneath the rubble?

"Hey, Tom, how are you doing?" Jackson appeared in front of Tom suddenly. "We need to make sure we're secure. Fancy doing a circuit with me? I don't really want to ask anyone else, they're in a bad way, you know."

Tom nodded and rolled his shirt sleeves back down. "Let's do it."

The doors they had entered the church through, were shut tight. Nothing was coming through those doors in a hurry, and Tom knew they would hear them before anything got in. They walked around the outer wall of the church checking for any doors or openings.

When they were out of sight, Caterina began talking to Christina. "I don't know if I trust Tom anymore. What if it's like at work? If we get surrounded, there'll be no way out."

"I don't think that's likely. Think about why all those dead people came to the city - some sort of natural instinct to go where's familiar? Thousands and thousands of people head into the city every day to work. No one goes to church anymore." Christina felt as though she could sleep for a week. Somehow, she had taken on the mother role for Caterina, which she didn't actually mind, but being a crutch for someone else meant she needed some support of her own. She felt drained.

"Maybe that's the problem," said Caterina.

"Look, I think we're safe in here for now honey," said Christina. "Jackson's gone to look around and you don't need to worry about Tom. He's doing just fine."

"But what about..?"

"Caterina, shush. The best thing you can do right now is relax. Look at the size of that door, look at these walls. We're probably safer now, than we have been for a long time. Please, Cat, just relax, okay?"

"Okay, yeah, I know I should. I just worry a lot, I..." Caterina started crying. "I miss my mum. I just want my mum and I don't know where she is, I don't even know if she's alive or..."

Christina pulled Caterina to her and let her cry. It was strange, but Christina felt good. She felt sad for Caterina; with everything going on and being pregnant, at the same time, the stress was taking its toll. It had been a long time since anyone had cried on her shoulder though. She had caught Linda crying at work a few months ago. She had gone into the toilet and heard her in one of the cubicles. When Linda had come out, she'd explained to Christina that her husband had left her. What had been Christina's advice? She had told Linda to pull herself together, or something ridiculous. She had told her that if she was too upset to work, she would have to go home and use annual leave. Now she thought about it, she could still picture Linda leaving the bathroom with such hatred in her eyes. She had looked at Linda leaving at the time and thought how pathetic she was. Linda was probably dead now. Christina felt like crying. She had turned that woman away when she needed help. It had always been work first, relationships second.

Christina pulled Caterina closer and hugged her. "It's going to be all right, honey, it's going to be all right," she whispered in her ear.

Benzo was sat up and holding his arm out.

"I've got a blinding headache," he said. "My arm doesn't really hurt anymore though. You've done a good job. Thanks, Jess."

190

"Well, it's not perfect, but it'll do. You should really get it seen to, you probably need stitches." Jessica was sat beside Benzo trying to ignore the crying she could hear from both Caterina and Rosa.

"I'll be okay. Don't think there's much point calling for an ambulance, eh? Hey, there's a thought, you still got your phone? I don't know what happened to mine. We should see if there's any signal."

Jessica fumbled through her pockets and pulled out a white tissue. "No, I must have left it behind somewhere. Shit. I'll ask the others, see if anyone else has got one."

"Yeah, but maybe wait a bit, yeah? By the sounds of it, they've got other things on their minds right now."

Jessica listened to the crying and bit her lip. She was on the brink, but refused to succumb to the relief it would bring. Everyone saw a pretty girl and assumed she would act like a princess. She was stronger than that though, stronger than most girls she knew. No, she would not cry, not now, not in front of anyone.

"I should take a look at Reggie, he's pretty cut up," she said turning to look at him. He was still kneeling, praying.

Benzo lowered his aching arm. "Damn, I don't know what happened on the bus back there. Did you see? All I heard was Brad and Don going at it and all of a sudden, I was flying through the bloody air."

"I don't know what caused the crash, but I expect Brad had something to do with it. I guess it doesn't matter now. Don and Angel are dead and we're not. It might sound selfish, but I'm fucking glad to be alive."

Benzo was surprised at her forthrightness. He had half expected her to crumble like Caterina. She was tougher than he thought.

"Me too, me too," said Benzo. "You know, there are seven of us left now. Do you know how many people worked in our office? Over a hundred. With those odds, how many people do you think are alive in this whole city? Jeez, I hope my family got out."

"Where do they live? They may have."

"Brixton. It's a hard place to live at the best of times, but with the streets full of zombies too? My mum, my dad...I can't imagine them gone, you know? It doesn't seem real, all of this. I still picture them at home watching telly."

"It seems *very* real to me," said Jessica curling her hair behind her ears. "When I think of my family, I picture them shuffling round our house, dead. I don't for one second, kid myself that they're alive. Parker's dead. My friend, Brie, she's dead, too." An image of Brie's distorted dead face flashed through Jessica's mind.

They sat in silence for a while, accompanied by the soft sound of sobbing. Benzo was unsure how to respond to Jessica and decided the safest option was to say nothing at all. His head was spinning and he needed the rest. After a short while, Jessica stood up.

"I'm going to find Tom and Jackson, see what's going on," she announced. "Maybe see if there's some water too. I'm starting to get a head ache as well."

She walked slowly through the church, admiring the colourful windows. The only other time she could remember being in a church was for her grandmother's funeral. Apart from that, there was no need to go. Her family wasn't religious and she didn't believe in God, so it felt odd being in a church now.

She noticed the ornate crosses on the walls, the paintings and the tapestries. At the altar, a set of steps led up to the pulpit and she tried to imagine the church being full of people. She couldn't hold the picture in her head though. The church was so huge and empty now, it seemed bizarre that people would come here and sit and listen to an old man telling even older stories.

She saw Reggie who was lying on some cushions near the altar, just next to the front pew. He had a lot of cuts and bruises on his face, but he appeared to be sleeping now, so she tiptoed past quietly and left him to rest.

Apart from where they had come in, she had seen no other entrances or exits. There was one open door off to one side and she glanced back; nobody was following her. She ventured into the side room and pushed the door shut behind her. The room she was in now was like a storeroom: there were chairs and books piled up, cloaks and coats hanging on hooks and candles in boxes. The room had two doors on either side, both closed. She tried one and it opened into a small kitchen. There was no sign of Tom or Jackson, so she returned to the other door.

Jessica found herself faced with uneven stone steps leading upward. There was a cold bronze handrail and she began climbing the winding staircase. The cold air pinched her cheeks and the higher she climbed, the colder she got. She decided that when she got back down, she would have to borrow one of those coats she had seen.

At the top of the staircase was a small door, and she could hear voices on the other side. She pulled the creaky door open and stooped to get through the frame. She found herself in the open air and a hand reached for hers.

"Take care, Jess, it's slippery up here," said Jackson helping her up.

Jackson and Tom were side by side on the church tower.

"Thanks, Jackson," she said, bracing herself against the cool wind.

"Hi, Jess," said Tom. "Everything okay downstairs?"

"As okay as it can be. Some crying, some praying; nothing this church hasn't seen before I expect. Wow, that's quite some view."

She looked out over the city. To the south, she could see the spires of the Dome, its yellow cranes in the air trying to touch the clouds. To the east and the west, were rows of buildings: houses, shops, and offices. To the south west, she could see the city they had come from, its skyscrapers still resolute, standing firm despite the crumbling world around it.

When she looked closer, she began to notice the details. The houses and shops were lifeless, and there was smoke pouring from several of them. The streets were empty; there was no traffic, just the odd figure walking across the road aimlessly. She could tell they were dead by the way they moved.

The sun was low in the sky and casting shadows across the rooftops. It was strange not to be surrounded by noise; the city was so busy and bustling that even at night, you wouldn't normally hear the perfect silence that she heard now. Not even the birds were singing in the twilight.

"It's like the city doesn't want us to leave," said Jessica. "Look over there, zombies. Every direction, wherever you look, they're fucking just *there*. What the hell are we going to do?"

"Look down there," said Jackson peering over the edge of the steeple, looking directly to the ground beneath them. Clamouring at the church doors were around ten dead, the ones who had followed them from the park. Scattered throughout the church grounds were several more. Some were drawn to the noise of the zombies clawing at the wooden doors, but others were shambling aimlessly through the gravestones. "If we're lucky, that group won't get much larger. If it does, we're gonna find it difficult to get out of here."

"Well, so far, they're only drawn to the main doors. Look around the side there, to the left. I think that's where we found the kitchen," said Tom. "The door was locked and it led directly outside, but they're not around that door. Why would they be? As long as they stay where they are, that'll be our way out."

Jessica saw he was correct. It looked like they had recently built an extension to the church, somewhere they could prepare for meetings and prayer groups. There was another extension around the corner from it, and it was this building the bus had crashed into. It was still there, Don and Angel's final resting place. Smoke was still pooling from the cooling engine.

"There was water in the kitchen, and I didn't look but there may be some food too," said Jessica. "We're in no condition to keep running. Where would we go to? How? Benzo needs to rest up and Reggie was already asleep when I came up here. Caterina is very fragile right now. That new girl too, Rosa? Nobody is in any condition to get back out there."

Jackson looked to Tom. "This is a good place to hold up, Tom. For now anyway. From up here we have a good lookout. We could take it in turns to watch, maybe see if there is any sign of life out there in the city."

Tom nodded. "We should stick to the plan and try to get to the airport. But for now, I agree, we should rest. All of us need it, me included." He rubbed his aching shoulders.

Jessica was still looking down at the green church grounds, leaning over the stone parapet. "It'll be dark soon. We lost everything back there: our torches, weapons, everything. Jesus, sometimes this feels hopeless, you know?"

Jackson put his hand on her back. "It'll be all right, Jess."

He crouched down and stooped in the doorway. "I'm going back down. I'll see if I can find some food and water in the kitchen, take it to the others and let them know what's going on."

"Cheers," said Tom. Jackson disappeared into the dark stairway and Tom listened as his footsteps faded. Jessica was cupping her face with her hands, elbows resting on the rough stonework while her eyes scanned the horizon.

"What's going on out there, Tom? What did we do to deserve this?"

"I don't know if it's a case of deserving it. But I guess if you're looking for a deeper answer than the one I'm about to give you, then you're in the right place."

She remained where she was and Tom leant beside her. He tried to figure out what she was looking for, or at. Her eyes were distant and not fixed on any one thing, just scanning the horizon.

"Whatever this infection is, I don't think it's divine retribution. I don't think it's the work of God, Buddha, Jesus, Mohammed, or any so-called higher power. It's a disease, a natural infection like a cancer. It's obviously not like anything else we've encountered before though. I don't think there's a cure. If there was, I don't think the city would be in the state it is now. The only cure for the infection is death, but for some reason that isn't the end of it. I've never heard of a sickness that brings a dead body back to life."

"Do you think we made this?" asked Jessica. "Some idiot in government trying to create a superman, a super-soldier? Maybe it's some experiment that ended up going wrong?"

"It's possible, but if you're asking me, then no I don't believe it. The governments of this world can't get the trains to run on time, so I certainly don't think they could create something like this. They don't have the intelligence or the organisation. This is something else."

Jessica yawned. "I feel exhausted. Not just physically, but...thinking about all this is draining. Trying to work out what's happened to my friends, my family; are they alive or dead? How do we beat this thing? Where do we go? The questions are endless. My mind reaches so far and then it just wants to give up and switch off. I passed Reggie on the way here and he was asleep, out like a light. When I close my eyes, I just see Parker, slumped in the conference centre, looking like death."

Tom idly scratched at the lime coloured lichen on the stonework. He scraped it off and threw it, watching it flutter down to the ground. He let Jessica talk.

"I had to leave. I couldn't stand the crying. I know that sounds bad, but Caterina could cry for England. Bless her but if I had to put up with that much more I would've cracked up. That other girl, what's her name again?"

"Rosa. She seemed nice." Tom looked down at the grounds and was pleased to see no more zombies seemed to be approaching.

"I guess so. She's pretty. But she's upset, she just lost her friends. And that's our fault, Tom. It's our fault they're dead."

"Look, they knew what they were doing when they rescued us, they didn't have to, they..."

Jessica looked at Tom. He knew she was right. Rosa, Don, and Angel, had come to help them and it had ended up getting two of them killed. He took his eyes away from Jessica's. He could feel her guilt burning through him and he could feel it rising in him too, swelling up from his gut.

"It wasn't a complete accident, you know?" said Tom looking down at the silent bus.

"What do you mean?" said Jessica frowning. She put a hand on his shoulder.

"It was Brad. He was fighting with Don. That's what caused the crash."

"Then maybe something good will come of it then. Brad's dead, probably buried in the bus beneath a tonne of bricks. We're better off without him. I wouldn't be surprised if he did have something to do with Amber's death."

Tom didn't want to get drawn into gossip and conjecture. "Well, he's gone now. You should get back downstairs, it's getting cold up here. Why don't you go help Jackson? I'll stay up here and keep watch for a while."

Jessica gave him a quick hug and paused in the doorway. "Any dramas, you come get me, okay? We're in this together now. We have to look out for each other."

"I will," he said as she left. Alone, Tom resumed his watch from the church tower, looking at the city as darkness began to gather once more. The zombies in the yard below were not growing in number, although they weren't leaving either. He looked beyond the park to where they had come from, the city skyscrapers now distant, a mere memory. Would they really be able to get to the airport or was he just dreaming? It was a short distance, but it felt like it was on the other side of the planet.

Tom continued to watch the city as the sun set over burning buildings and people dying. He saw the dead soldiers in the streets, the crashed cars, and empty homes. Knowing the church was secure, he paid little attention to the walls below and even less to the bus. If he had, he would've noticed the loose bricks tumbling from the front of the bus as something stirred beneath its belly. He would've noticed a hand reaching out from beneath it, an arm extending out, the fingers digging into the mud, grabbing onto the long grass as a body crawled out from underneath the silent vehicle.

CHAPTER SEVENTEEN

Jackson had found the kitchen cupboards bare of food, only a sad and lonely packet of ginger-nuts hiding in one dark corner. He had drawn the curtains across the window, so he remained out of sight of the zombies outside, and could roam throughout the room freely without worrying about being seen. If he drew them to the kitchen, then both exits out of the church would be compromised.

The door leading out of the church was shut, but not locked, and he quietly opened it to check their surroundings. Immediately behind the door were a couple of dustbins. A small paved path lead directly to another yard in the church grounds, but it was empty and useless; there were no vehicles and the house beyond it stood abandoned. He pulled the door shut, careful not to make any noise.

"God rest your soul, Mary," said Jackson resting on the bench briefly. Like a bolt of lightning to the head, it suddenly hit him he was very old. What was a man in his sixties doing running around like this? He should've gone back to his wife when he had the chance, but he had left it too late. He closed his eyes and pictured his wife as he had last seen her. He had left for work and she was sat at the table munching on toast and marmalade. Now that she was retired, she liked to take a lazy breakfast, only washing and dressing when she'd eaten. He could remember kissing her goodbye, as he had done every day for the last forty years, the only interruption being when she had spent a few nights in hospital three years ago, to have a hip replacement.

He couldn't feel her anymore. He didn't believe in ghosts or psychics or premonitions, yet somehow he knew his wife was gone. He vowed he would light a candle for her.

What of the rest of the city, the millions who lived in this great metropolis? He couldn't accept they were gone, not all of them. Surely the infection had been contained somewhere? Surely there were systems in place to contain this type of thing? He had seen the country change a lot in his lifetime: strikes, riots, political demonstrations, bombings, buildings torn down, and bigger, taller ones erected in their place, financial institutions failing only to be usurped by others. Merchants and prophets of doomsday had predicted the end every time a bomb went off in the Middle East or a plane fell out of the sky, or an economic crisis struck the west; they had all been wrong. The end would be a bug; a tiny organism infecting every living being, for which there was no cure.

Jackson wondered how he would die – would he be devoured by one of these creatures or die fighting. If living meant running from place to place, hiding and feeding on scraps, then he would look forward to seeing Mary again.

There had been a bucket beneath the sink and he'd filled it with tap water. Scooping up a cluster of plastic cups from a box on the floor, he went back into the church to find the others. Wallowing in self-pity was a fool's game, Mary had told him that many times.

'Make yourself useful, Jackson,' she'd told him. 'The past is the past and the future is yours.' He couldn't help but smile. She had told him that when he was made redundant, shortly after they wed. At a low point, she had helped him, stood by his side, and never doubted him. All he could do now was live up to her ideals. He would help these people, these friends who were scared and lost; he would die fighting if he had to.

They had gratefully taken the water, draining the bucket completely. He had to go back twice more to fetch more buckets full of water. When he returned the second time, he found Benzo standing.

"You feeling better, Benzo?" Jackson asked, filling his cup with more water.

"Yeah, thanks to Jess. My arm's sore, but it'll be fine. Let me help you." Benzo took the bucket from Jackson and they passed by Jessica who was trying to get a mobile to work.

"Any luck?" Benzo asked, topping her cup up.

"No. Caterina was the only one with a phone and there's no bloody signal. I can't get anything."

"Have you tried getting on the net?"

"Yeah, it won't connect. Battery's fine, but..." Jessica slammed the phone down on the pew beside her. "Waste of time," she sighed.

She followed Benzo and Jackson to Christina, who was talking to Rosa. She had stopped crying, but her face was red and Jessica felt guilty for not offering her more support. Rosa looked young too, certainly no older than Jessica. She had golden girlish locks that twisted around her face and Jessica had already noticed she had a curious way of twitching her nose when she was about to speak.

She took Rosa's plastic cup and scooped it through the bucket, filling it with cool fresh water.

"Here," Jessica said smiling.

Rosa took it and sipped. "Thanks."

Jessica guessed from her clothes that Rosa had been on her way to or from work. The clean cut of the dress, the simple colours, and the basic hemline, still managed to look good on her though; it showed off her slim figure.

"Rosa was just telling me how they managed to survive in the pub for so long," said Christina.

Caterina had gone to lie down and fallen asleep so Christina had decided it was a good time to talk to Rosa. She looked so young and helpless sat alone as she was. Nobody should be allowed just to sit there in the church crying, without someone at least offering her some consolation. Christina had gone over and just held her until she'd stopped. She wished she'd done the same for Linda back at the office, back when Linda had still been alive.

"It wasn't easy. We had to keep quiet all day. The rooms upstairs in the pub were locked apart from the bathroom and a storeroom. Don slept in the bathtub at night. Angel and I slept in the storeroom."

"How did you manage for food and water for so long?" asked Benzo.

"Well, we still had running water from the tap and Don found some boxes of whisky, so drink wasn't a problem. Apart from that, we survived on a diet of peanuts and pork scratching's." She offered Benzo a timid smile.

"Man I would kill for some pork scratching right now. I'm starving," he said.

"I searched the kitchen, but we've had what little there was. I'm afraid that's going to be it until whenever we get out of here," said Jackson. He put the bucket on the floor and sat down beside Christina.

"Tomorrow?" she said. "You offering to nip out to KFC for us, Jackson?"

They laughed and the sounds echoed around the hollow church, their laughter bouncing off the high ceiling. The grinning gargoyles seemed to laugh with them.

"Don't even talk about KFC," said Benzo. "My mouth is watering for that finger lickin' shit right now."

They laughed again and Jackson felt better. If they could still laugh in times like this, then it meant they hadn't all given up hope. There was still some humanity left in them.

"Well, I've been thinking about tomorrow. I was talking to Tom too. Despite how things are out there, we still think the best course of action is to aim for the airport," he said.

"I second that," said Benzo immediately. "It's not that far and if there's any way out of the city, that'll be it. The roads are clearly a no-go. I reckon when we get to the city airport, we'll find help there. My dad always said that in a time of war, the most strategic place of attack, or defence, are the arteries in and out of the country. It stands to reason that the government would keep the airport open."

"I'm not sure," said Christina. "I could see the airport from my office and I couldn't see a lot going on. I didn't notice any planes coming or going."

They thought for a moment. "Can I say something?" asked Rosa quietly.

"Absolutely," said Jackson. She spoke with such a low voice he had to lean forward to hear her.

"The airport may or may not be a way out of the city, I don't know. But I don't want to leave the city. I want to go home. I want to see my parents and know that they're okay. Are we not better to go home and wait there? It won't be long until the police or the army, or someone comes to help."

"Rosa, you could try and go home if you think you could make it through those streets," said Jessica, "but I think you'd be better off with us. We saw the police and the army. They came, they fought, and they lost. There's no one else coming."

"What do you mean? There must be."

"It's true," said Christina. "I saw an army helicopter crash. We came from the city and it was carnage."

"We saw the soldiers on the streets, Rosa," said Benzo. "Even with their guns and tanks, they couldn't stop them. The infected just kept coming and killed them all. In the end, they were overrun."

"It's been three or four days now since this started," said Jackson. "If there was any help coming, it would be here by now. We're on our own. We have to fight for ourselves and each other. Rosa, I promise you that if you want to go home, you can, nobody will stop you. But you'll be on your own."

He took her hand and grasped her small hands in his.

"Come with us. I'm sorry about your friends, but the reality is, your parents are most likely dead. They may have escaped the city, they may be fine - but they won't be at home. They won't be waiting for you there. Come with us."

Rosa didn't answer and looked around the silent group. They were looking at her expectantly, hopefully. She looked up at Jessica, into her deep brown eyes so full of hope. Jessica curled her hair around her ears as Rosa looked at her. Finally, she withdrew her hand from Jackson's and she nodded.

"I'll come with you. The airport, eh? So you lot got a plan? Is one of you a pilot?"

"No." Benzo looked at Jackson. "Actually, do we have a plan?"

"Not much of one. Look, it's nearly dark out and it would be suicidal to be out there in the dark on foot. I say we bunk here tonight. It's quite safe and secure, and apart from half a dozen zombies at the door, they don't know we're in here. I know we're hungry, but at least we have fresh water. We have heat too. We can light all those candles.

"In the morning, we'll feel better, more refreshed. Getting to the airport, well I'm not sure how best we can do that. It's not far, but it's going to feel like it's a hundred miles away once we get out on the road and we're fighting those things off."

"What if we don't go by road?" said Jessica.

"You grown wings?" Benzo said sipping his water.

"I mean we'd have to go by road initially, but the Thames goes right there. If we get to the river, then we can avoid all the zombies on the road and sail to the airport. It's quicker and safer."

"So you've grown a boat then?" Benzo looked at her like she had gone mad. "Where are we going to get a boat from?"

"Hang on, Benzo, I think it's a good idea," said Christina. "The river's not far from here at all. Provided the zombies are thinned out, we can run right through them. Five minutes of healthy cardio and we'd be at the river. There's a marina near Limehouse station. We don't need a boat or a ship. Shit, a plank of wood will do. All we need is something that floats. I'd rather do that than go by road the whole way."

"Well the bus is out of action," said Jackson. "I don't fancy looking for another vehicle. There's not much chance you'd find one out there before they'd be on you."

"Fair enough. But I'm not going out there unarmed," said Benzo.

"Me neither," said Rosa. "If something comes for me, I want to be able to defend myself."

Jackson looked around the church. "No problem," he said. "Look around. We can make plenty of weapons from here. There are some crosses on the walls - they look heavy, like they're made from oak. Those candlesticks over there are thick and solid; they'll drive through a dead body with enough weight behind them."

"These bibles aren't bad either," said Jessica picking one up, tossing it from one hand to the other. "They're leather, hard, dense, and easy to hold. Smash someone in the face with these and they're not getting up in a hurry."

"What about holy water?" said Benzo.

Everyone looked at him before bursting out in laughter.

"Kidding guys, kidding!" he said laughing.

"What's going on?" said Caterina. She had been woken by the voices and came to see what they were talking about. Jessica was holding a bible. "Not having a prayer meeting without me, are you?"

"How're you feeling?" said Christina.

"Better, thanks."

"Right, well if you guys are all right, I'm going to see Tom," said Jackson. "He's keeping a look out from the top of the steeple and he'll be getting cold. I should go and..."

"No, it's all right, I'll go," said Benzo. "Maybe you can check on Reggie, he's been out like a light since we got here."

"Sure. Just head out back and up the stairs. Be quiet though, we don't want any uninvited guests gate-crashing our party."

Benzo walked off leaving the others to prepare. Jessica and Rosa began searching for anything they could use as weapons. Christina filled Caterina in with the plan for the next day and Jackson strolled over to Reggie to check on him.

* * * *

"Benzo!" Tom was surprised when the door opened. He had been expecting Jackson, if anyone, to come back up. "Good to see you, mate."

They embraced and Benzo took in the scene. The fires above the rooftops mingled with the dying embers of the sunlight and the city was bathed in orange.

"Anything to report?" Benzo asked Tom.

"Not much. Nothing else has come this way. I haven't seen anything; no planes, no helicopters, no cars, nothing - just the dead."

"Can't see much," said Benzo looking over the parapet. "Are there many of them down there?"

"Not too many. The few that followed us from the park and a few more that were drawn by the crash. They're all gathered by the main doors or the bus though. There are some in the church grounds dotted around, but nothing major. Nothing like before."

"Well that's something I suppose."

"Benzo I was meaning to ask you. On the bus, did you see Angel? Was she..?"

"She didn't make it, mate. Look, what's done is done, we need to forget about it and focus on tomorrow. I'm kind of looking forward to it in a way."

"Oh, yeah?" asked Tom.

"Well, just getting out of here. I'm sick of living on scraps. I'm sick of stinking and wearing these dirty clothes I've been wearing for the last three days. I just want to sleep in a bed. I'm sick of not being in control of my own life. You know what I mean?"

"Yeah, I do. These clothes could walk around on their own."

"You are pretty ripe, mate."

Tom laughed, but Benzo could tell it was out of politeness. "Tom, there's water downstairs, you need to relax. It's safe here, okay? It's safe. You don't need to worry about it."

"I guess. It's just hard to switch off. If Rosa hadn't rescued us, then her friends would still be alive and I keep thinking..."

"That's your problem, Tom, you keep thinking! Listen, everything is taken care of. Tomorrow, we're going to get to the airport, the girls are gathering weapons and there's nothing else to do, so stop beating yourself up. You're not responsible for us. Shit, a few days ago, you didn't even know us."

"I could do with some water. I'm parched. Maybe I'll go down for a bit." Tom rubbed his eyes. He was sure that if he put his head down, he would sleep like a rock.

"I'll stay up here until it's too dark to see anything and then I'll come down. There's not much point being up here if we can't see anything anyway," said Benzo.

Tom walked toward the door. "Don't stay too long, mate. Say, you said the girls were getting weapons?"

"Yeah, Jessica, and Rosa, the new chick."

"Did they say anything about me?" asked Tom.

"Like what?"

"Oh, I don't know, I just wondered if Jessica had said, like, um..."

"Oh, I see," said Benzo. "Yeah, man, I get it. She's cute. Look, she hasn't said anything about you to me. Sorry to disappoint you."

"It's nothing," said Tom, thankful the dark was hiding his blushing cheeks. "See you soon, mate."

Tom went into the stairwell closing the door behind him.

* * * *

"Feel this," said Jessica, handing Rosa a golden candelabra. Its base was so thick Rosa struggled to hold it in her hands. She admired the ornate carvings that had been etched into it from the base to the tip.

"You could do some damage with this," said Rosa handing it back to Jessica.

"I intend to." Jessica kept hold of it as they continued walking around the western side of the church. The stained glass windows were dark now and the church was mostly lit from the candles burning near the nave. Rosa took a cross down from the wall.

"No good," said Jessica.

"Why not?"

"It's too small. By the time you've stuck someone with it, they'll be all over you. No, put it back, we'll find something bigger and better."

Rosa replaced the cross on the wall carefully. "Well, they do say that bigger is better."

Jessica looked curiously at Rosa but couldn't see her expression in the dim light. "Some do."

"You believe in all this?" asked Rosa as they came across another painting. There were angels surrounding a baby in a crib. Tumultuous clouds blossomed in the sky and the sleeping child was bathed in a light from above, so bright it was almost white.

"No. You?"

"Nah, my mum and dad do. Did. Not me though, always seemed a bit like fantasy to me."

"It's the rules I couldn't abide. You shouldn't live your life by a doctrine, especially a man made one. I don't just mean Christianity, but all of them. They're just invented by humans to control us if you ask me."

Suddenly Jessica realised Rosa was weeping. "Hey, what's wrong?" Jessica embraced her.

"I'm sorry, it's just the whole church thing. It reminds me of my parents. I began thinking about how they must've died. How my dad probably died trying to protect my mum. He would do anything for her."

Jessica took hold of Rosa by the shoulders. "Well, stop. Thinking like that won't help you."

Jessica rummaged in her pockets for a tissue but found none. She pulled her sleeve down and used the end to wipe Rosa's tears.

"I don't know how you stay so...*together*," said Rosa as they embraced once more. Jessica held onto her. She hadn't realised how much she craved physical touch, the reassurance of another human being, the compassion and empathy borne out of being so close to another person.

"I have to," Jessica whispered in Rosa's ear. They drew apart slowly, and Jessica let her hair brush Rosa's cheek. She felt Rosa's hand caress the back of her neck and Jessica didn't want to let go. It had been so long.

In the flickering candlelight, Jessica kissed Rosa on the cheek. She drew breath and kissed her on the lips, at first gently, then more passionately. Jessica pulled Rosa toward her, feeling Rosa's slender frame pressed against hers. At first, Rosa reciprocated the kiss, sweet, yet salty, tainted by her tears. When Jessica began kissing her more insistently, she pushed her away.

"No, no, it's not right," Rosa said.

"I'm sorry," said Jessica. Shadows danced across her frowning face and she thought of Brie. What was she doing? "You're right, I was just...I thought..."

"You thought wrong. I was just caught up in the moment. You shouldn't take advantage of me," Rosa turned away to face the three angels.

Jessica's heart was racing. "Sorry, I'll leave you alone. I didn't mean anything. I should check on Reggie anyway."

Rosa heard Jessica walk away. She clutched the bible she was carrying to her chest. Thoughts raced through her mind blocking out reality, until she heard Jessica call out.

"Rosa, I'm sorry, but can you come here. I can't find Reggie."

* * * *

Reggie had been lying on the cushions near the altar, sleeping, until Jackson had knelt down beside him. Reggie's face was cut badly and the wounds were not healing. Blood still seeped from the gashes on his forehead and cheeks. Jackson put his fingers to Reggie's neck; his pulse was fine.

"Reggie." Jackson gently shook him but he didn't wake. Jackson frowned. Maybe Reggie had been hurt in the crash worse than he had let on.

"Reggie, mate, wake up," he said shaking him rougher. Reggie could not be woken and as Jackson shook him, he rolled over, his shirt opening at the neck exposing his neck. Jackson saw the white fungal growth on Reggie's chest that was spreading up his neck and recoiled.

"How the hell..?" Then Jackson remembered the bird. They had been attacked when they'd left the conference centre and Jackson had been persuaded it was nothing. Reggie had convinced him it was just scared. It wasn't. The pigeon had been infected, just like the rat that had bitten Freddy.

Jackson took a step back. If he told the others, they would panic. They needed the rest and the sanctuary the church offered, at least for tonight. But if he did nothing, how long would it be before Reggie turned? He couldn't risk that. He looked around the church and caught Jessica's eye. She gave him a wave and a smile and he smiled back. She and Rosa were stood by a huge painting and Jessica was clutching a huge candelabra.

Jackson decided he would move Reggie to the kitchen. If he dragged him in there quietly, he could barricade the door. If he turned in the night, he would hear nothing and hopefully stay quiet. If he was lucky, he wouldn't turn for a while and they could escape safely.

Making sure nobody was watching, Jackson took hold of Reggie's arms and slowly pulled him off the cushions onto the hard stone floor. Bending low, he dragged the unconscious Reggie into the storeroom. Once he had gotten him over the threshold, he closed the door behind him and breathed a sigh of relief. He had gotten Reggie out unnoticed. It would be easier to explain to the others what was going on without Reggie being there. His presence would be unwelcome now. Any infection would be very unwelcome when they thought they had finally found a place to rest.

Jackson opened the door to the kitchen. It was dark in there now, the faint sunlight unable to penetrate through the curtains. A figure was slumped, resting against the cupboards, a gun in its hands.

"Hey, buddy," said the figure, raising the gun and pointing it straight at Jackson. A shiver ran down Jackson's spine and he froze.

"Brad?"

CHAPTER EIGHTEEN

Jessica jumped, startled as the vestry door burst open and Jackson walked through with his hands on his head.

"Shit you made me jump, Jackson. Hey is Reggie with you? I was..."

Jessica stopped as Jackson said nothing and was followed out of the doorway by a man holding a gun to Jackson's head. Jessica's jaw dropped open as she recognised Brad.

"Holy shit." She put her hand to her mouth. Brad's hair was matted with blood and he was caked with dirt. He grinned as he pushed Jackson forward.

"Jessica, good to see you, I thought my fucking days were over. Man, I am glad to see you."

He waved the gun at her and motioned for her to sit. She sat on the nearest pew and Jackson sat down beside her. He dropped his hands to his lap.

"Tut, tut, Jackson. Back on your head, please, where I can see 'em. You too, Jess."

"What the hell is going on, Brad?" She stood up to confront him and he slapped her.

"Sit the fuck down, bitch! Hands on your head! I won't tell you again."

She retook her seat with the sting of Brad's hand still fresh on her cheek.

"You, out of the shadows. Get over here." Brad was pointing the gun at Rosa who stepped out from behind a column. She obeyed the stranger and sat next to Jessica. She followed suit and put her hands on her head. Rosa looked at Jessica questioningly, but Jessica just shook her head.

"Christina, Cat, don't think I can't see you back there. Move it up here, now."

Christina stepped into the aisle. "Brad, whatever you're doing, you don't need to do this. We thought you were dead."

Brad sighed. "Bitch, I don't give a fuck what you think or what you thought. You and Cat get up here now, or I'll shoot you in the face. Understand? It really makes no difference to me whether you're alive or dead. I *would* prefer to save the ammo if possible though."

"Come on, Cat, it'll be okay." Christina and Caterina slowly walked to the front of the church and sat opposite the others. Brad stood in the middle as if facing the congregation.

"Dearly beloved, we are gathered here today...hang on, we're missing one at least. Where's Tommy boy?"

The door creaked behind him and Brad whirled around. Tom strode into the church, surprised to see everyone sat on the front row with their hands on their heads. He was even more surprised to see Brad holding a gun over them.

"Hi, buddy, perfect timing, take a seat would you?"

Tom was so shocked he didn't move. Brad had died in the bus. He had been at the front with Don. This couldn't be him.

The figure that looked and sounded so remarkably like Brad, walked over to Tom and he brought the butt of the gun down on Tom's face, smashing his nose. Tom fell to the floor, blood gushing out over the stone floor.

"Stop it!" screamed Jessica. Jackson stood up.

Brad kept the gun trained on them whilst he dragged Tom over to the altar.

"I swear, Jackson, you make one more move, I will put a fucking bullet in your brain."

Brad dropped Tom who rolled over onto his stomach. He cradled his face in his hands, blood pouring from his broken nose.

"Anyone else here, or is this it? Benzo? That old hag? That fucking moron bus driver? Anyone?"

"No," said Christina solemnly. "No one else made it. We're all that's left. Brad, we thought you were dead, I don't understand."

"Sorry to disappoint, but I'm not dead yet. No thanks to you. Sincerely, I would like to thank every last one of you motherfuckers for leaving me for dead. If you hadn't, I wouldn't have this gun and I wouldn't be in charge. So thank you."

"Brad? Is that you?" Tom grunted and got to his knees. He had managed to stem the bleeding from his nose, but he looked a mess. His shirt was covered in blood.

"Tom, buddy, you are a little slow on the uptake today. Yes, it's me, your old friend, Brad. The one who saved your pathetic life, remember? And how did you repay me? You picked a fight with me back at the conference centre and then you leave me to die in that God damn bus. Wow, good thing you're not my enemy, eh, Tom?"

Brad kicked Tom in the groin and Tom shouted out in pain. He curled up on the floor as Brad kicked him again and again in the stomach, the ribs, anywhere he could.

"Brad, please, stop it!" Jessica pleaded with him to stop, but Brad ignored her. He ignored their cries, relishing in Tom's pain. Finally, he stopped. He hauled Tom up onto his knees and Tom stayed there dazed, his face bruised, his mouth bleeding and his eyes swelling.

"Now, if you'll just stay on your knees like that, that would help me out a lot."

Brad walked around so Tom was facing away from him and he put the gun against Tom's head. He cocked the trigger and braced his feet on the floor, ready to execute Tom.

Jackson stood up again. "If you pull that trigger, Brad, you're a dead man."

"Really? Who's going to stop me from doing whatever the hell I want now? You, old man?"

"And me," said Christina standing.

"Me too, Brad. You're pathetic." Caterina took Christina's hand and stood. Finally, Jessica stood too and took Rosa's hand. Together they stood beside Jackson.

"Us too," said Jessica. "How many bullets you got in that gun, Brad? Enough for everyone?"

Brad hesitated and looked at Jessica. She stared back at him. He was used to women being submissive to him, but Jessica was different, stronger; Christina too. He could see they weren't afraid of him. How strange, he thought; unarmed, women were always intimidated by him, yet, here he was waving a gun around and suddenly they weren't afraid of him anymore.

He un-cocked the gun, flipped it around, and smashed the butt against the back of Tom's head, knocking him out cold. Tom fell to the floor unconscious.

"Ah, I was just kidding," said Brad. "I wouldn't waste a bullet on Tom. Now sit down, my dears, because I do have six locked and loaded and I *will* use them if I have to."

Reluctantly, they sat down. Brad waited for them to be seated and told them to put their hands back on their heads.

"Why are you doing this? You don't even know me. We tried to help you." said Rosa.

"Help me? That faggot driving the bus was a maniac. It's his damn fault we crashed. Yeah, you were a great help."

"Save your breath, dear, he's not on the same page as us. Hell, he's not even reading the same book," said Christina.

Brad picked up a bible as he paced the floor. "If this is what you're reading, then damn straight we're not on the same page."

He took the bible to one of the candles and held it over the flame before the pages began to singe. As the fire swept through the book, he dropped it and let it burn.

"You're right though, I don't know you. What was your name again?"

"Rosa." As she spoke she slipped her hand into Jessica's. Their fingers entwined and Rosa felt reassured by the strong grip on her hand.

"Rosa. Nice name. You remind me of someone I used to know with that blonde hair of yours. She was a sweet girl too. Amber."

Jessica squeezed Rosa's hand tighter.

"Brad you can't do this," said Jackson.

"Oh, pipe down, I ain't doing anything. She'll keep for later, pops." Brad blew a kiss at Rosa who turned her face away from him. Jessica stared at Brad, wishing he were dead.

"No, this is the part where I tell you how it is. Think of me as a villain in a James Bond movie. I am your Scaramanga - although sadly, my gun isn't golden. So anyway, this is where I tell you my evil plan and you listen. Unlike those stupid movies though, the baddie does not die at the end after revealing his plans to the hero."

Brad looked at Tom, still unconscious on the floor and cackled. Jackson cast a furtive glance at Christina. They both knew that Benzo was still up in the steeple and instinctively they knew what the other was thinking. If they kept Brad talking long enough, maybe Benzo would realise something was wrong. It was their only opportunity; they *had* to buy Benzo some time.

"How did you get out, Brad?" asked Christina.

"Weren't you buried beneath the bus, beneath the rubble?" asked Jackson.

"How'd you get that gun?" asked Christina.

Brad continued pacing up and down in front of the altar, rubbing his temples, restless.

"One thing at a time. Jesus Christ. You fuckers can be really irritating you know that?"

They waited, sensing Brad wanted to speak, to tell his story.

"When I came to, I thought I was dead. I mean I actually thought I was dead, literally. It was pitch black, I couldn't move, I couldn't hear anything. It was like being back in the womb, man. After a few minutes, I guess my senses got attuned and I figured it out.

"When we'd crashed, I was thrown back into the doors. I remember hitting them hard and falling into the footwell. I can remember seeing Don flying through the windscreen and I thought my number was up. The doors must've buckled, as when I woke up, I was under the bus. I was wedged under the doors, a pile of bricks by my head and a ten tonne fucking bus above me."

Brad continued pacing back and forth, from one side of the church to the other, all the time waving the gun around.

"There must've been an inch between me and that thing above me, so I had to crawl out. It took me a while, but finally I threw some stones and bricks aside and I was free. None of you fuckers were around, but I didn't expect you to be quite frankly. I had barely hauled my ass outta there when something grabbed me. It was some diseased old woman; fleshy hands all over me, trying to frigging eat me. Her face was just, like, covered in blisters and shit. It looked like someone had thrown acid over her.

"I pushed her off, grabbed a brick, and pounded her fucking skull in until she stopped moving. Next second though, they were all around me. I couldn't see clearly, but there were shapes moving in the dark; vague things, dead things, just shifting and moaning and coming toward me. One of them reached for me as I tried to run, and it turned out to be a soldier.

"He was stronger than the woman, but not strong enough. I pulled this gun out of his belt and battered his face to a mushy pulp. I just ran blind and found the door back there. Fate must've been on my side. I didn't know you lot would be here, that was just a bonus. I'd only been in there a few minutes when I saw Jackson walk in on me. I was as shocked as you were."

"So did those things follow you here?" said Jackson. If they had, then they were in a fix; both exits would be swarming with zombies.

"How the fuck should I know, buddy? I didn't stop to ask directions. Yeah, probably they did. Whatever, that's irrelevant right now."

"Brad, that's our way out of here," said Jackson. "We can't get out past the main doors, the kitchen is our exit."

"What's all this talk of 'our'?" said Brad. "Stop interrupting me, Jackson, I hadn't finished."

"So what's your plan, Brad?" said Christina. "I can understand that you're pissed, but if you think logically, we can help each other out here. This situation doesn't have to get any worse than it already is. We didn't leave you behind intentionally - we thought you had died with Don and Angel in the bus.

"Look, we're going to stay here tonight. Rest up, get going tomorrow. We're going to the airport and..."

"Christina, you might have been the boss back in the city, doing whatever it is rich snobs do, making your millions, but you're not boss anymore. See this? This is a gun, and that puts me in charge. So stop fucking talking!"

Brad strode over to her and put the gun to her head. She looked at him as he pointed the barrel at her forehead.

"Cat, take your socks off," he said, fuming, not taking his eyes off Christina's.

Confused, Caterina slipped off her shoes and rolled down her white socks. Shivers spread all over her body as her bare feet touched the stone cold floor.

"Shove them in her mouth. If she speaks one more word, you're going to be scooping up bits of her brain for weeks."

Caterina gritted her teeth and balled up her socks.

"I'm sorry," she said to Christina. She slowly pushed the soiled socks into Christina's mouth. Brad sneered as Christina gagged.

"Guess they're not the freshest, eh, buddy? Sit down, Cat, and stop..." He was about to tell her to stop crying when he noticed she wasn't. She was looking at him defiantly. She had obviously been learning a thing or two from her mentor.

Brad returned to Tom and sat cross-legged on the floor.

"Right, this is what's going to happen. First of all, sleeping here tonight? No. Your pyjama party is finished. In about ten minutes, we are going back out that door. You're right, Jackson, they did follow me here, so I'm guessing there must be at least a dozen of those things by the back door already. If we wait until tomorrow, or any longer, there'll be a hundred of them, maybe more. It'll be worse than the city, as we've no way out. I'd say there's no secret tunnel out of here."

"So how then?" said Jackson. He was hoping that Benzo would come down soon. They didn't have long left.

"It's pretty simple really. It's a trick I learnt from my father. He served in Iraq, the first time around. You see, Saddam used to create these human shields by surrounding himself with people; women and children in particular. That way, you're hidden and protected from the enemy. My father taught me a lot."

"So we're going to be a human shield for you? Are you crazy?" said Jessica. "No way, that's ridiculous. Where are we even going? What do you plan on doing when you get out of this church?"

"Well, for starters, no, I'm not crazy. I think it'll work pretty well actually. For me at least. Any of those zombies come for us, they'll take you lot first. Don't worry, you can have weapons to defend yourself. I don't want you dropping dead before I even get out of the church yard. Secondly, I want to go home. That's the grand old U S of A for any of you imbeciles who weren't sure. So I guess the airport, it is."

"And if I refuse to help you?" said Jessica.

"Then I may as well put a bullet in your head right now, darling. If you come with me, then you've got a fighting chance. It's a slim one, admittedly, but it's all you've got right now."

Brad smiled as he lowered the gun at Jessica.

"All right, fine. Like you said, what choice do we have?" Jessica realised she had been gripping Rosa's hand tightly all the time Brad had been talking and let go.

"Right," said Brad getting up. "I think about ten minutes is enough. Go find something to defend yourself with. Oh, everyone except for you, Christina. You're going to keep me company. When you're all ready, meet me back here. I'll be watching you. It goes without saying, don't try anything stupid or Christina and Tom here will be sucking bullets."

Jessica, Rosa, and Jackson, took Caterina and they gathered together what they could lay their hands on. As they walked out of earshot of Brad, Jackson told them that they had to try and delay him.

"Benzo will surely come down soon. When he does, be ready. It'll take Brad off guard and we may only get one chance at this."

"And if it doesn't work? What will we do out there in the dark? How will we know where to go?" said Rosa taking Jessica's hand again.

"Once we're outside, we abandon him," said Caterina. "He might try and shoot us, but if we all run at once in different directions, he won't know what to do. There'll be so many of those zombie things, he won't have time trying to get us, he'll be too busy fighting them off. Plus, it's dark, so he won't be able to see clearly. The second we're outside, we split."

"But where to?" said Jackson. "I wouldn't know one street from another round here."

Caterina pulled her mobile phone out.

"Follow me, I know where to head. I know what Christina was talking about. I can get us to Limehouse station and from there down to the marina. As long as there's a boat, or something we can get down the river on, we're home free.

"My phone has got a torch on it. I'll turn it on as soon as we're outside and you just follow the light."

"Won't the zombies follow it, too?" said Jackson.

"I think they'll be too busy trying to eat Brad, don't you? I don't think they have the intelligence to figure out what we're doing. If they follow the light, well...I guess we just have to take that chance."

"When you can, Cat, tell Christina, Tom too if you get a chance," said Jackson. "The second we're outside, we split up and run. Anywhere you can. Run for it and follow Cat's light. It's the best idea we have at this stage."

"Fuck, we'd better get ready for this," said Jessica.

They broke off into pairs, Caterina and Jackson taking the west wing, whilst Rosa and Jessica took the east.

"I'm sorry about before," said Rosa as they searched through a bookshelf.

"What about?" said Jessica.

Rosa pulled Jessica quickly into the shadows and kissed her. Jessica briefly kissed her back before withdrawing. Rosa's hands reluctantly left Jessica's waist.

"You're messed up, you know that?" said Jessica pushing her away.

"What's the problem?" hissed Rosa. "I thought that's what you wanted?"

"Yeah, no, I don't know. Not now, anyway. You were right before when you said it's not right. We've a madman waving a gun around and you want to make out? Just keep looking for something we can use, Rosa."

Rosa sulked back to the corner to look for a weapon or a picture, anything to distract her from her thoughts. The way Jessica looked at her, she had thought there was something there, some connection between the two of them. She had been wrong before though, and wondered if she had got it wrong again. It was probably just the stress of the situation.

Jessica shook her head and pulled a large figure of Jesus from the wall. He was cast in solid iron, arms and legs spread eagled as if on the cross. It felt heavy, meaty, and she weighed it up in her hands. It would suffice. She thought about Tom up there at the nave, at Brad's feet. He had taken a beating and Christina had a gun to her head. Yet, all she could think about was how Rosa tasted. Was she as selfish as people thought? Maybe.

"Five minutes," shouted Brad. He saw the others skulking in the shadows and knew they were plotting against him. He also knew they wouldn't do jack shit, not whilst he had a gun over their friends.

"Take that shit out of your mouth," he said to Christina. She pulled the balled up socks out and threw them on the floor. She choked and spat a glob of disgusting saliva onto the floor.

"You know we should put that mouth of yours to good use," said Brad. He sat on the floor opposite her. He had made her sit beside him and the unconscious Tom.

Christina closed her eyes and her body went stiff as Brad trailed the gun up her body. The gun pressed against her stomach before Brad drew it up between her breasts, its cold nuzzle sending shivers over her as he brought it up around her neck and left it hovering over her lips.

"Open your mouth," he whispered.

She shook her head. Her eyes were still closed and the taste of metal on her lips made her want to vomit.

"You're not going to do this for me?" said Brad, pushing the gun against her closed mouth.

"No." She opened her eyes and looked at him. Finally, he could see what he wanted; the fear in her eyes, etched across her face as clearly as the striations a plane leaves across a crisp blue sky. He took the gun away and unzipped his trousers.

"Then you had better do this instead," he said motioning with his gun from her to his crotch.

"Please, Brad, I don't..."

He cocked the trigger and motioned to her once again. She could see he had an erection and she felt sick.

"In case you hadn't noticed, I'm a little stressed right now. It's been quite a day, what with nearly being killed and all. So let me put it another way. If you don't, I'll just blow you away and say you were trying to escape. So quit complaining and just do it. Don't act precious. Like you haven't sucked a cock before. If I feel teeth, I'll blow your brains out, simple as that. Then Tom's. So what's it to be, Christina? You gonna blow me, or am I gonna blow you?"

Christina crossed herself and crawled forwards to him. She put her hands either side of Brad's waist on the cold stone floor. She could feel the gun again, this time pressed against her temple. Fighting back the urge to cry, not wanting to give him the satisfaction, she lowered herself down and with one hand took his erect penis out. She closed her eyes once more and he pushed her head down. She nearly gagged as he thrust himself inside her mouth.

"Thank you, Jesus," said Brad quietly as he held the gun to Christina's temple. He looked up at the wooden carving that towered over him, the Son of God watching as Christina was forced to perform fellatio on Brad.

CHAPTER NINETEEN

Benzo looked through the crack in the door, incredulous. Brad was alive, and he was pissed. Benzo had come down from the steeple, casually winding his way down the staircase until he'd heard strange noises coming from the church. Fearing the zombies had broken in, he quietly slipped into the vestibule and opened the door, just a crack, enough to see through. He had seen Brad giving Tom a good beating. Brad was waving a gun around and the others were sat with their hands on their heads. What was happening?

Benzo had listened as Brad explained how he had survived the crash and what they were going to do next.

"He's mad," said Benzo under his breath. When Brad sent the others to search for weapons, Benzo realised there was precious little time left to do anything. He knew he had to do something though; if Brad took them outside, they would all wind up dead. There were thumping noises now coming from the kitchen. So Brad had been right, the dead had followed him. Maybe it was better they leave now. If they stayed, how many would be at the door by morning?

In the dark storeroom, Benzo crouched down. What could he do? If he rushed out there into the church, Brad would be surprised, but then what? Would he shoot him? Would he tie him up, leave him here to die? Benzo had always gotten on well with Brad, but he'd flipped. This wasn't the same Brad he had worked with and shared a pint with. This Brad was nasty, cruel: sadistic. And what was that comment about Amber about? Benzo was finding it difficult to accept the new order, but he had to; his friends' lives were depending on him.

"What would dad do?" he said. In the darkness of the storeroom, he looked around for help. Boxes, books, chairs, nothing of use; surprise was his only weapon. Benzo returned to the door. Brad held a gun to Christina's head. He couldn't hear what was being said, but he knew the scene and how it would play out. He watched as Brad forced Christina's head down and Benzo turned away, sickened and shaking with anger. How could Brad do this? Benzo was so angry and frustrated that he wanted to charge in there and kill him.

'Control it,' he thought. If I charge in there like an elephant, Brad will probably shoot me in surprise. Or Christina. Or maybe everyone.

Benzo felt hopeless. What could he do? If he went into the kitchen and opened the door, the dead would rush in and cause Brad a major problem, but it would jeopardise his friends too. He couldn't retreat back up the steeple and do nothing. He may as well slit his friends' throats now himself if he did that. He decided that the best course of action was to surprise Brad. He would hide in the kitchen and when Brad came in, jump him. Brad had the gun, but Benzo had the element of surprise and he *had* to make it count. He could hide behind the door and pounce as soon as he saw Brad coming.

Benzo opened the door to the kitchen quietly. To his shock, the thumps he had heard were not coming from outside but inside. Reggie threw himself upon Benzo and grabbed his neck.

"Get off, what the hell are you doing?" Benzo tried to push Reggie off but he was heavy. They rolled around on the kitchen floor. As they fought, they clattered into the shelves and benches, knocking jars over and a bottle fell to the floor, smashing into pieces. Reggie tore a chunk from Benzo's cheek and he screamed.

* * * *

"What was that?" said Brad. He pushed Christina off and zipped his trousers back up. Christina spat once more onto the dusty floor and grabbed Tom.

"Please, Tom, wake up," she said. Tom murmured incoherently as Christina shook his shoulders.

"Who the fuck is in there?" shouted Brad.

Jackson, Caterina, Jessica, and Rosa all came running. Tom was stirring and Caterina bent down over him.

"Is he all right?" asked Jessica.

"Yes, just help me get him to his feet," said Christina. As they picked Tom up, Caterina whispered to Christina the plan to escape.

Brad pointed the gun squarely at Christina as Tom sagged over her shoulder. "What the hell is going on in there? You said this was it, there was nobody else. Who haven't you told me about?"

"Nobody," said Jackson, "it must be Reggie, he must have woken up." Jackson took a few steps casually toward Christina, trying to put himself between her and the gun.

"You said he was infected. If he's woken up, then who's doing the screaming?" Brad was shouting loudly, the gun trembling in his unsteady hands.

"Reggie's infected? What?" said Christina.

"Oh God, Benzo," said Jessica.

More crashing and banging came from behind the door and then it stopped.

"I'm going to see," said Jackson.

"No, you stay here," said Brad. Jackson thought about trying to grab the gun. He was only a few feet away from Brad but it was risky. The gun could go off with Brad so out of control like this.

"You," Brad said to Rosa. "You go. If you don't come back in one minute I'll shoot Christina."

"Brad, let me go, it's not safe." Jackson took another step toward Brad.

"Please, Brad," said Jessica.

Brad pointed the gun to the ceiling and fired. The blast drew a curtain of dust down upon them and the shot pierced the silence like a pin bursting a balloon.

"Last chance," said Brad.

"It's all right, Jess, I'll go," said Rosa. She approached the door and took a look back over her shoulder.

"I'm waiting," said Brad.

Rosa pushed the door open and stepped into the dark storeroom. The candlelight from the church lit the gloom and she could see the room was empty; boxes and chairs, but no Benzo.

223

"There's no one here, I'm going into the kitchen," she called out.

Rosa pushed the kitchen door open and saw two figures on the floor. Reggie was face down with Benzo sat on his back. Reggie's face was mushed into the stone floor, blood curdling around his broken skull. Benzo still gripped Reggie's head, his fingers entwined in Reggie's matted hair.

"Benzo?"

Rosa walked to him slowly, quietly: carefully. Benzo got up and leant on the worktop.

"I had to, he was...he was infected. He just attacked me. I couldn't get him off and then..." Benzo reached up to his face and touched the wound on his face.

"He bit me. He fucking bit me!"

From the church, they heard Brad calling out, asking what was happening.

"Benzo, he's got a gun. If we don't go in there, he's going to shoot Christina. Probably everyone." Rosa spoke in a hushed whisper.

"Right, then, let's not keep him waiting," said Benzo.

Rosa finally reappeared with Benzo and Jessica gasped.

"Benzo, you're hurt, what happened?"

"Never mind that," said Brad. "What about Reggie? You finish him off?"

Benzo walked directly toward Brad as Rosa returned to Jessica's side. Brad raised the gun at Benzo.

"Hold it, buddy, that's close enough."

Benzo stopped when the gun was inches away from his face.

"Brad, you shit, what are you doing? There's no need for all this. I wish you had died back there on the bus. I went back to look for you, you know?"

"Shit happens, buddy." Brad looked at Benzo's bleeding cheek. "Looks like Reggie got a chunk out of you."

Benzo nodded and sighed. "Looks like the end of the road for me, eh, Brad?"

He said it with such a cool level tone, that Brad was caught off guard. How could he be so calm knowing he was dying?

"Well, you're not done yet. In fact, we were just leaving. You can come with us for now. When you're done, I won't let you turn, I'll put you down."

Tom was conscious now and Christina was quietly filling him in: Reggie, the escape plan, Benzo, and Brad's growing psychosis.

Benzo shook his head. "No, Brad." He took a step forward so he was within touching distance of him.

"Benzo, we're leaving. Your wrestling match with Reggie will have brought more of those things. We can't stay here," said Brad.

"He's right," said Tom. "We have to leave."

Benzo shook his head again. "Not all of us have to leave. You see, Brad, I'm infected, which means in a few hours I'll be dead. It's a pisser, it really is, but I'm not going down without a fight. I've got nothing to lose now."

A smile spread across Benzo's face. Jackson realised what Benzo was planning. He'd lost the element of surprise, but he had another weapon now; the infection. Jackson looked at Christina and nodded.

Benzo and Brad stared at each other. Suddenly, Benzo jumped forward and grabbed Brad's arm. The gun fired and a bullet whistled past Benzo's ear, ricocheting off a stone gargoyle and embedding itself in the cross above the altar.

Benzo and Brad tussled on the floor. Brad was trying to get the gun back to face Benzo, who was busy trying to bite Brad anywhere he could.

"Let's go, now!" shouted Jackson. "Those gunshots will alert more of the dead to our location. Cat, your light?"

She flicked on her phone. Jackson, Christina, Caterina, and Rosa, ran to the storeroom.

"We need to take the weapons!" said Jessica. She frantically grabbed some of the crosses and candle sticks they had gathered up earlier. She quickly tossed them to Rosa who handed them around.

"Benzo!" said Tom, looking for an angle at which he could join the fight and help. Benzo was still struggling with Brad on the floor. Suddenly the gun went off again and the bullet shattered the tall arched window above them. As pieces of glass fell around them, Tom saw his chance.

He lunged and grabbed Brad's arm. Brad was unable to hold off both Benzo and Tom, and finally relinquished his hold of the gun. Brad rolled away and the gun skidded across the floor. They all stood up. Benzo was panting and coughing.

"Unlucky, buddy, you didn't get me," said Brad wearing a wicked smile. Benzo hadn't been able to bite him, but had managed to end up nearer the gun. He bent down and picked it up. He raised it at Brad.

"Oh, come on, you're not going to shoot me, Benzo," said Brad, sweating and dirty.

Benzo stared at him and kept the gun pointed at Brad's head.

"Why shouldn't I?"

The smile faded from Brad's face as he realised Benzo might just do it. "I can help you. I...I can help you fight those things out there. Come on, buddy, don't do this."

"Is that what Amber said to you, when you killed her?" he said. "Or Chloe? Who else, Brad? I saw what you did to Christina."

"What does he mean?" said Caterina.

"Nothing." Christina gripped the heavy golden candelabra in her hands and looked at the floor. She pressed her teeth together and pursed her lips.

"Let's go, Benzo. It's going to be swarming with zombies in here a minute," said Tom. Benzo lowered the gun and then passed it to Tom.

"I shouldn't come with you, I'm infected. I'm a liability now."

"Fuck that. You're coming with us for as long as you can. We'd be dead if it wasn't for you. Go to the others. We're getting out of here, together."

Tom took the gun and Benzo joined the others at the storeroom. They were watching from the doorway, waiting for Benzo and Tom. They had one item each to defend themselves; Christina and Caterina held solid candle sticks whilst Jackson and Jessica held thick crosses. Jackson told Rosa about the dustbins by the back door. They were metal and had solid lids with handles; they would make perfect shields, and once outside, she was to grab both. Jackson was praying the zombies outside wouldn't have converged too closely to the church door.

"Ain't that sweet," said Brad getting to his feet and walking toward Tom. "You're gonna take Benzo with you, even though he's infected? What about me, you gonna leave me here?"

"No, I'm not gonna leave you here, *buddy*," said Tom. He pulled the trigger and shot Brad in the left leg, just above the knee. Brad screamed and fell to the floor clutching his leg as blood spurted out.

"You fucker, Tom, you dirty fucker!" Brad shouted through gritted teeth. The pain soared through his body as he sat on the floor holding his bleeding leg.

"I'd say there are two bullets left, wouldn't you, Brad?" said Tom pointing the gun at him.

"Please, Tom, don't." Brad looked at him with pleading eyes. "Don't kill me, I'm sorry, I'll help you. Please, buddy, please."

Brad began crying and his tears splashed onto the stone church floor. Snot ran from his nose and at that point, Tom thought Brad looked no older than a ten year old boy.

"Pathetic," said Christina under her breath.

"Oh, I'm not going to kill you," said Tom. "Why would I waste the last two bullets we've got on you?"

Tom lowered the gun and tucking it into his belt, walked to the storeroom. He turned to give Brad one last withering look. The others had opened the kitchen door and were waiting to leave. Christina had waited for Tom. She looked at Brad sitting on the floor. He had shuffled back against the wall, leaving a trail of blood behind him. He was pale and weak, nothing like the confident man she had met twenty four hours earlier.

"We probably won't have time to shut the door on our way out. You might want to try saying a prayer. Sorry, *buddy*," said Tom. He took Christina into the kitchen as Brad howled and moaned, alone in the church.

"Right, we ready for this?" said Tom.

"I'll go out first," said Jackson nodding. "Head down, barrel right through them like a bowling ball. Rosa next, she's going to grab the bin lids, use them as shields, then Cat with the light. After that, it's everyone for themselves."

"You good with this, Cat?" said Tom.

"Just make sure," she said smiling, "that the last one out leaves the door open."

Tom winked at her and Jackson pulled the door open.

"Go!"

Jackson rushed headlong into the night and true to his word, kept his head down. The cluster of zombies tried to grab him, but his momentum carried him through until he was clear. Hands tore at his clothing but could not get enough grip to slow him. With Jackson outside, the zombies' attention were drawn to him and away from the door.

Rosa sprinted out and saw the bins. She snapped up the metal lids quickly and instantly put them to use, smashing into an approaching figure. As they darted outside, Cat kept firm hold on her phone. If she dropped it, they would be separated and lost with no idea where to go.

Tom followed the light as it bounced up and down in the dark. Jessica and Christina managed to stick close to him as they ran. The pack of dead by the church sensed the living were close and turned to follow them. Tom jabbed at gnarled grabbing fingers, trying to dodge the figures in the graveyard.

Jackson had fallen on the ground and jumped up. He saw Caterina's light heading away from him and ran. A dead child suddenly loomed out at him from behind a gravestone and Jackson slashed at its face. The silver cross he held left a gash across the child's face and it fell back out of his way. As it fell, another attacked. Red, raw fingers reached up from a freshly dug grave and grabbed Jackson's ankles. He tripped and fell into the muddy ground. The fingers pulled at his feet and he kicked out. The hands disappeared as the dead body was unable to get enough purchase on Jackson to pull him down, or to haul itself up out of the grave. Jumping up, Jackson ran, following the light.

Rosa continued to batter and beat at anything that came close. A dead postman, the skin hanging off his face in tatters, jumped at her and she swung the metal lid at him, cleaving his frail skull in half. Caterina's light bounced off the metal lids, illuminating dead bodies and grotesque faces, feet away, inches away, desperately reaching for them.

Jessica stabbed the cross into a man's face, green slime slithering down her hands as she burst his eyeballs. A recently deceased housewife tried to grab her. More blood splattered over Jessica as she skewered the woman's neck, ramming the cross up to the hilt, only Jesus' head protruding.

They kept running, down the road, past the crashed cars and vans as the zombies gradually thinned out. A lone street light stood casting a yellow-orangey glow over the junction ahead and Caterina stopped beneath it. She was trying to suck in air, finding running difficult whilst being four months pregnant.

Christina, Rosa, and Jessica, soon joined her. They looked down the road and saw two figures running toward them. Benzo and Tom appeared, the church receding behind them.

"How far?" said Tom.

"Not too far," said Caterina wheezing. "It's just..."

There was an almighty bang as Rosa swung her metal shield low over the pavement, the shield striking the dog's head full on. It only had three legs and she sent the dog flying backwards, the terrier crashing into a car and sliding down to the tarmac. It appeared dazed, but not dead. It dragged its carcass slowly across the road, sharp teeth bared, putrid eyes covered in a grey fungal growth. There was no way it could see, but it could smell them.

Christina took her candelabra, walked over to the advancing dog, and pulverised the terrier with the weighted base. She cracked the dogs skull open and it lay on the road, twitching, until she had crushed its head completely.

"Where's Jackson?" said Benzo. The darkness of the road offered no sight of him. Shapes moved in the dark, the infected dead following the light and the noise of the living.

"There!" said Jessica, pointing to the footpath on the other side of the road.

Jackson was fighting with another man. They saw Jackson disappear behind the car as a dead man fell on top of him.

"Jackson!" exclaimed Christina.

Benzo and Tom rushed over to help him. Tom beat at the zombies head as Benzo pulled it off. Jackson got to his feet.

"Thanks," he said as Benzo pushed the creature away. It staggered for a few seconds before resuming its attack. As the walking corpse shambled towards Tom, he shot it at point blank range. Its head flung back and the body fell to the ground.

"Only one bullet left, Tom. Save it, you don't know when we're going to need it," said Benzo.

They rejoined the others under the street light.

"You okay to keep going, Cat?" said Jessica.

"Yep."

"Benzo?" asked Jessica.

"I'm not dead yet. We can't hang around here anyway."

"I hope Brad isn't following us," said Rosa.

"No way. I saw the zombies flooding into the church when we ran," said Tom smiling. "He's a dead man."

Caterina took off and they followed. The streets away from the church were mostly empty. They easily dodged the few dead that were present. As they ran past the houses and homes, the shops and garages, Tom saw no evidence of life. A few lights had been left on, but the curtains were open and the rooms were empty.

The only noise was the sound of their own feet pounding the road and their laborious breathing. They ran straight down the middle of the road, preferring to be in the open where they could see their attackers. The pavements were dangerous, enclosed by fences and cars from which an assailant could easily spring out at the last moment.

Tom's head was spinning. His whole body hurt from the kicking Brad had given him and his head felt like it had been hit by a ten tonne hammer. As he ran, it began to sink in that Benzo was not going to make it. Like Parker before him, he had unwittingly fallen to the infection. How easy it was to succumb, so difficult to avoid. Tom wondered how long Benzo had. Freddy and Parker hadn't lasted more than a few hours.

He focused on the light in Caterina's hand, bobbing up and down as she ran at the front of the group. She led them across a larger road where two ambulances had been left abandoned in the middle of the road. The back doors were open and Tom saw trails of blood glistening inside.

He slipped in a bloody pile of entrails and fell to the ground. Hands felt their way under his arms, lifting him up.

"Come on, mate, nearly there," said Benzo.

They ran, aching limbs crying out for rest. On this larger road, the houses had given way to shops, warehouses, florists, and butchers. There was still no sign of life in any of them. Up ahead, Caterina had stopped.

"This...is...the...station," she said between short gasps.

Tom looked up at the station: monolithic, derelict, destroyed. The gates had been pulled down and there were bodies piled up in front of them. Dozens and dozens of dead stacked up ten feet high. There were six police cars in front of the station, three of them mounted on the pavement, but all of them with their doors open. The road was covered in dark pools of blood. Caterina was shocked to see the station looking so desolate and deserted, shocked at the carnage on its steps where she had walked so many times.

"Can you find your way to the river?" asked Christina. She could hear the moaning and shuffling sounds in the distance. They were alone, but not for long.

"I...I think so. Down there, under the railway bridge, there's a path. It leads down to the Thames," said Caterina composing herself.

"Can we have two minutes, I'm shattered," said Rosa. The metal lids weighed heavy on her arms and she put one down on the ground slowly, careful not to drop it in case the clattering noise drew attention to them.

Jackson picked it up. "No, we have to keep going. We can rest later. Right now, there's an army after us and it's growing. We can't afford to stop now."

"He's right," said Tom. He was on his knees, drawing in long breaths of fresh air. "Keep going," he said getting to his feet.

Caterina jogged off toward the bridge. The road continued up over the bridge, but they took a small set of steps leading down next to it. Tom felt the icy cold bricks as he brushed past them. Their solidity and familiarity somehow reassured him. On the other side of the steps was a chain link fence. Nothing moved in the yard beyond and they reached the bottom of the steps safely.

Caterina led them along a footpath that flanked the river. They could smell the Thames now, its polluted churning water both enticing and repulsive at the same time. Tom watched as she switched her light off. There was no need for it now. The glowing moon gave them enough light to see by. The path ahead was clear and he could see a small pier jutting out into the river. The moon illuminated tall buildings on the southern side of the river, giant and foreboding, enormous repositories and gigantic depots standing guard over the river as they had done for years.

"There," said Caterina pointing to the boats.

The footpath opened out and she slowed to a walking pace. There was a ticket office where you could buy day-tripper tickets and an advertising board outside offering river tours. There were only two boats still moored up. They swayed gently in the night, the water lapping at their hulls.

"What now?" she said.

Almost in a perfect row, the group of desperate survivors stood beside her looking at the boats. One was a public ferry, an open topped shuttle that could seat a hundred people; the other was a small sailing yacht, its mast tall and its sail down.

"Search me," said Jackson. "Anyone know how to sail?"

There was a pitter patter of feet behind them and Tom saw movement in the shadows by the bridge.

"They're coming. So we're going to have to learn, fast," he said, and strode toward the yacht.

CHAPTER TWENTY

"This is impossible," said Tom. "I have no idea what to do."

He was stood at the yacht's controls, staring blankly at the buttons and levers in front of him.

"You're right, this is impossible," said Jackson. "We need the keys."

"Fuck."

Tom and Jackson left the yacht and hopped back up onto the pier.

"Any joy?" said Benzo, shivering.

"No. We can't start it," said Jackson.

"What about the other one then?" said Jessica. "We can't stand here. I can hear something. There's definitely something, or someone, coming this way."

"This isn't going to work," said Tom.

"So we came all this way for nothing? We can't give up now," said Jessica.

"That's not what I mean. I'm not giving up. I thought the river would be the best way, the safest way, to the airport, but let's face it, we don't have a boat. We can't swim."

"So you think we should go back to the road?"

"Yeah, we made it this far, why not?"

"That's why not," said Benzo. He pointed up at the bridge to a herd of the dead. Hundreds of dead faces were looking at them, hundreds of dead bodies clamouring over one another to find a way down. A few had found the steps and were only minutes away.

"Any ideas, now's the time," said Tom feeling deflated. To have come so far, only to be stopped here, was more than frustrating; all that fighting and effort to meet a dead end.

"Who says we need a big boat," said Christina.

"We don't. As long as it floats, it'll do," said Tom.

"There you go then." She pointed to the passenger ferry where a lifeboat hung from the starboard side. The interior of the ferry was dark and the moonlight showed a hundred empty seats. It felt like they were looking at a spooky ghost ship.

They ran onto the ferry and Jackson was first to the lifeboat. He jostled the chain that tethered it to the ferry. He rang his hands along the ropes and ties that bound it until he found the latch. He slipped the ropes out and the boat dangled above the water but refused to drop.

"It's hooked here, I can't free it," he said. Jackson pulled on the chain but it wouldn't budge. "I can't see what's stopping it," he grunted as he continued to pull on the chain.

"Guys, they're getting close," said Rosa. The smell of death wafted over the water to her.

"Caterina, get your light out will you?" said Tom.

She took her phone out and turned the torch mode on, shining it on the small lifeboat.

"Hold it here can you, on the hook?" asked Jackson.

Tom steadied her hand and pinpointed the small arc of light onto the large hook that held the lifeboat to the ferry.

"I'm going to shoot it," Tom said. He aimed the gun at the crucial point where the jib met the chains that were holding the boat in the air.

"Be careful, Tom," said Jackson. "We've only one chance at this."

Tom aimed, held his breath, and squeezed the trigger. With their final bullet, he shot the hook and it sheared straight through. There was a flash of light as the bullet exploded, a cracking noise that whipped across the water and rebounded off the buildings, before the boat suddenly fell into the river below with a splash.

"Everyone in, quick," said Christina.

Tom threw the gun into the black water. It was useless now. The gunshot seemed to alert the zombies to exactly where they should go, and Rosa saw the first few appear on the pier.

"Hurry," she said scrambling to the others. Benzo and Jessica were in the boat already. There was a rope ladder on the ferry's deck, which Jackson had lowered over the side. Christina was lowering herself down the short distance into the lifeboat whilst Jessica helped her.

"Go on, Rosa," said Tom helping her over the side. She lay the bin lids down on the deck and swiftly slid down the rope ladder to take a position in the boat beside Jessica. Tom picked up the bin lids and tossed them down to Benzo.

"We're going to need them as paddles," he said.

Tom lowered himself down as the first zombie got up onto the ferry.

"Hurry up, Jackson!" shouted Christina. He scrambled down and lowered himself over the side. As soon as he was in the lifeboat, Tom handed him one of the bin lids.

"Use this as a paddle. Now let's get the hell out of dodge."

Jackson took it and put his hand through the clasp. He looked up at the ferry and a zombie threw itself over the side toward them.

"Look out!"

Rosa screamed as Jackson raised the shield above his head. The zombie struck it and cartwheeled off into the water. Tom was trying to get them away from the ferry, which was now swarming with the dead. Jackson plunged the lid into the water and began pushing too. The lifeboat slowly crept away from the ferry, but it initially took them closer to the pier. They were sandwiched between the large ferry and the pier full of zombies.

The zombies, unaware they could not walk on water, fell into the Thames, splashing the lifeboat as they fell in, and sank beneath the waves. The boat rocked from side to side as dozens of them fell in, making it difficult to navigate a way out of the tiny marina.

Caterina shone her light up at the pier, revealing the horde above. Faces, twisted in agony, stared back at them. Hands and arms reached out uselessly, unable to reach Tom and the others. Without warning, a mangy cat sprang off the pier. The mobile phone's light bounced off the cat's eyes and it let out a hiss as it extended its claws. Caterina screamed and dropped her phone. It plopped into the water and sank immediately.

As she recoiled from the flying feline, Benzo pushed her down and the cat landed on him, digging its talons into his bleeding arm. The cat scratched and tore at him as he tried to grab it. Its teeth ripped his fingers, nipping him as he tried to shove it away. Jessica and Rosa were cowering in the back of the craft, scared that should Benzo drop it, it would attack them next.

"Benzo, get rid of it!" screamed Caterina.

He held it over the side of the boat, but its claws were digging into him and he couldn't shake it loose.

"Hold it still, Benzo," said Christina. She raised the candelabra once again and smashed the cat's head in. Its skull broke in half and it whimpered, its tiny bones broken, yet still it clutched onto Benzo. Christina raised her arms again and smashed the candelabra down onto the cat until its face was nothing but a bloody pulp.

Benzo pulled the cat's claws out and let the body slide off the side of the boat into the water. It floated away on the current under the bridge. Caterina let out an audible sigh of relief as the dead cat disappeared.

Tom and Jackson had steered them out into the middle of the river, away from the marina. They stopped paddling when they were clear of the ferry.

"You all right, mate?" said Tom to Benzo.

Benzo shrugged. Caterina sidled next to him and put her arms around him.

"Thank you, Benzo, thank you," she said. She took his quivering hands in hers and he lay back exhausted.

Tom looked at Jackson and they ploughed on. Benzo knew what he was doing and there was nothing they could do to help him now. He had put himself in front of Caterina to save her. Tom was proud of his friend. He was a brave man he had known for only a few days. Jackson said nothing, but thought of the list in his back pocket. The names were dwindling. How many would be alive when the sun came up in the morning?

The dustbin lids were not easy to lift in and out of the water. The lifeboat slewed through the Thames as though the river were full of tar and honey. The lids were heavy and Tom and Jackson did not have much strength left. They tried to keep the lifeboat in the middle of the Thames as much as possible, away from the river banks where anything might be hiding, lurking, or waiting. If they capsized, Tom doubted they would be able to get the boat back up again, much less survive the ice cold water.

They pushed on as the river turned a corner and they came to another bridge. The river was so wide at this point that the bridge had a buttress in the middle and there was a small island, a concrete circle no more than six feet across where the buttress was reinforced.

"We need to stop for a minute," said Jackson to Tom. "Over there, see that island, stop there."

They splashed on until they reached the base of the bridge and the boat slopped against it, the rusty hull squeaking against the damp walls of the island as they drew up slowly.

When the boat stopped, nobody spoke. The water lapped against the hull quietly until Rosa spoke.

"What are we doing?" she said. Jessica put an arm around her. "We can't stop."

"I know," said Tom leaning back, "but we're exhausted. I can't go on. Not to mention it's bloody dark and we don't know where we're heading."

"We could carry on a little farther, but we might miss the airport. I doubt if there'll be a big sign in the water saying 'Airport this way,'" said Jackson.

"We need to wait for daylight. That was the original plan. Splashing around out here in the darkness is crazy," said Tom.

"Do you think it's safe here?" said Christina. "I mean, surely we're not going to spend the night here under this bridge are we?"

"I suppose not, but what else can we do? You want to risk going ashore? Or finding another boat?" said Jackson.

"I can get us to the airport," said Caterina. "If I remember rightly, there's one more bridge after this, then it'll come up on our left hand side. Once we get to the airport, we'll be okay. We can rest there and find a way out of the city. Maybe there'll be rescue planes, doctors, police...I don't want to spend the night in this boat when we're so close."

"Fine, we'll keep going. But when we get there, don't expect them to roll out the red carpet. We're going to have to take things slowly," said Jackson plunging the bin lid back into the freezing water of the Thames.

"Let me help," said Jessica. She carefully clambered to the front of the boat and took the lid from Tom. "I'm not a helpless princess," she said. "We can take it in turns if you like."

He looked at her, surprised.

"Move out the way then." Jessica gave him a prod and smiled. He snaked his way to the back next to Rosa.

"She's quite something," Tom said to Rosa as Jessica plunged the lid into the water and began to sync her strokes with Jackson.

"Yeah, she is," said Rosa admiring Jessica in the moonlight.

The small lifeboat was cramped but it felt safe. Out on the water, nothing could touch them; nothing could reach them. Sure enough, as Caterina had said, they eventually came to another bridge. Jackson was tiring and Christina took over from him as they passed beneath its arches.

"How're you doing, Benzo?" said Jackson sitting down beside him.

"Cold," came Benzo's weak reply.

Jackson could hear Benzo's teeth chattering. He took Benzo's hand in his, grateful he could not see how pale and sickly his friend looked.

"Just you hang in there, mate, you hear me? We'll be at the airport soon. What do you say to a warm bed?"

Benzo gripped Jackson's hand. "I guess I'll be with my family soon, eh? Shit, I didn't think it would end like this."

Jackson could feel Benzo shivering and shaking but had nothing to offer him for warmth. Tom, Rosa, and Caterina, listened to the conversation.

"Fuck, Benzo, it's not going to end like this," said Jackson. "We're a team. Who's to say at the airport, we're not going to find an army compound full of doctors and nurses with a cure for this thing?"

"Nurses, eh? Sounds good to me." Benzo coughed and spluttered out the last few words.

Jackson laughed and let his tears fall silently. The blackness of the night hid his wet face from Benzo and they sat on the swaying boat in silence for a while. Jackson knew it was unlikely they were going to find help, but he couldn't let Benzo slip away like this.

"Shit!" exclaimed Jessica suddenly. She splashed her numb hands around in the water. "I dropped it!"

Tom jumped up and fished around in the cold water, but knew it was too late.

"Sorry, I should've helped you out. You're tired," he said.

"Shit, I'm sorry. Damn it!" Jessica struck the side of the boat.

"Hey," said Tom, "it's fine. We're almost there. Don't worry. Go back to Rosa and Cat, I'm fine, I'll carry on."

"But how? Without the paddle..?"

"Jess," he said taking her arm, "just let it go. Don't worry."

She smacked the side of the boat in frustration once more and crawled back, past Benzo and Jackson, to Rosa. She felt Rosa reach for her hand in the darkness and pushed her away.

"Leave me be," Jessica said in a hushed voice.

Rosa crossed her arms. She turned her back on Jessica and stretched out. The stars and moon shone above the buildings on the water's edge. Rosa thought about Don and Angel. She wondered if Angel's husband was still at home with their daughter, or if they were dead too. What of her own family? She tried to think where they might be now. Even if they were alive, surely they wouldn't be at home. If the city was overrun by the infected, they would have been evacuated wouldn't they? She mused where they might have been taken to: Oxford, Birmingham, another city somewhere further north perhaps? Scotland even?

It took them another hour before they reached the turning point. Caterina pointed it out to them.

"We would have missed it," said Christina wiping the sweat from her brow.

Tom took his aching arms from the river. His hands were so cold that his fingers had gone numb. He tried pushing the boat along through the water along with Christina, but it had been difficult and she frequently had to pause so they didn't just turn in circles.

"Through there, that inlet leads to the airport, I'm sure of it," said Caterina. "See that long stretch of flat land over there, that's the runway."

"One last push," said Christina to Tom.

He just nodded and put his arms back into the water. They swept the lifeboat swiftly to the shore and they landed on a muddy bank. The lifeboat lodged itself in the silt and Christina jumped out.

"Be careful," said Tom.

"You lot stay here. Keep quiet or whistle out if you see anything. I'm just going up the bank to see what's what. Won't be long."

Christina disappeared into the night, slopping her way through the mud and water, up through reeds and grasses, until she was over the crest and out of sight.

"Man, I'm beat," said Tom.

"Me too," said Jackson.

They heard a rustling from above and Jessica tensed. She felt around in the boat and found a candle stick. She grabbed it as they all looked up at the reeds. Something was coming. Tom grabbed their solitary bin lid and held it out in front of him like a gladiator.

The rustling stopped and suddenly Christina sprang out of the grasses.

"Shit," said Tom, dropping the shield back into the boat.

"The airport looks quiet. There are no lights on that I can see. It looks like we're on the wrong side of the runway though. There's an electrified fence running around it. It runs down the road at the top of the bank here. To get into the airport, we're going to have to go around it, and that means back in the boat."

"Oh, God, I can't face it, I'm exhausted," said Jackson.

"Well, I reckon there can only be a couple of hours until dawn. There's a shed up by the road there, it looked like it was just used for storage. I couldn't see anyone around. Why don't we crash there until the sun comes up? I'm beat too," said Christina.

"Benzo, can you walk?" said Jackson.

Benzo propped himself up and slowly stood. "I'm not done for yet, Jackson."

"Will we all fit in there?" said Caterina.

"Do you want to stay out here?" Christina raised her eyebrows. "Yes, Cat, we'll be fine, let's go. That all right with you girls?"

Rosa just murmured in agreement.

"Lead on," said Jessica getting up. "I don't care if I have to use a can of lead-based paint for a pillow, I'm dead on my feet."

She looked at Benzo standing unsteadily and instantly regretted her choice of words. If anyone had noticed her faux pas, they chose to ignore it. Nobody spoke. They filed out of the boat, leaving it lodged on the mud bank, and dragged their tired bodies up the hill, through the path that Christina had already walked for them.

The top of the bank led to a small road beside the runway, as Christina had said. Tom saw the airport in the distance. He could make out a few planes on the ground and outside of the terminal building, but Christina was right, there were no lights on. Twenty feet away stood the shed. They walked to it and Jackson tried the door.

"It's locked," said Jackson heaving on the door. There was a tiny window above the handle, but Jackson couldn't see any other way in.

"Watch out, Jackson," said Jessica.

He stood aside and she smashed the window with the cross she held. As the ground was sprinkled with broken glass, she put her arm through the opening to unlatch the door. She fumbled for the lock until she found it and finally was able to open the door.

As it swung in, the smell hit her. The shed was used purely for storing paint and chemicals. She wafted the air in front of her face and stepped inside. Feeling around on the wall she found a switch and bathed the shed in light.

"Come on, it's clear," she said as she ventured inside, looking around the small brick building.

Caterina rubbed her tired grainy eyes and picked up a dirty mop. "Not exactly the Ritz."

"It'll do for tonight," said Tom. He began dragging pots of paint to the side. They cleared the floor quickly and one by one, lay down on the hard floor. Jessica found a blanket on a shelf and handed it to Benzo.

"Here, you take it."

"Thanks. Jess, look, would you mind sleeping next to me for a while?"

She looked at him puzzled.

"You're the only one with a weapon and quite frankly, I don't know if I go to sleep if I'll wake up again. If I do, I might not be myself, you know, so..."

"Sure, I'll stick close," she said as he lay down. "But you're a fighter, Benzo. You hang in there, okay?"

He smiled weakly and pulled the blanket over him.

"We'd better turn this light out, we don't want to let anyone know we're here," said Tom. "Not yet anyway."

Everyone had found a small spot on the floor on which to rest. The room smelt of sickly paint and body odour. Jackson gave Tom the nod and he flicked the light off. Rosa was already asleep and Benzo looked like he was seconds away from nodding off too.

"I'm going to sleep in front of the door," said Tom. "If anything drops by and tries to get in, it'll buy us time."

"Hope you don't sleep walk, Tom," said Christina.

Tom checked the door was shut and lay down in front of it. His feet touched some shelving and his head was squashed up against the door, but he didn't care. He had been going on pure adrenalin. He couldn't remember the last time he had eaten or drunk anything. When the sun came up, they had to get to the airport. There could be food, water, and shelter. Anything more than that, he would consider a bonus.

Gradually they fell into a deep slumber. In five minutes, they were all fast asleep. The river was quiet and the runway was deserted. The airport terminal appeared to be devoid of life.

* * * *

The man watched as the light in the storage shed flicked off. Someone was out there. He would have to check it out in the morning. He didn't do running around in the dark, that was a sure fire way to end up dead. Zombies didn't use light switches, which meant someone was definitely out there. He pulled the shutter down and reclined back in the business class seat. The aeroplane made for a useful temporary base. Passers-by, alive or dead, assumed it was empty and ignored him. He was off the ground, up where the dead couldn't reach him. It was peaceful too. Since he had been abandoned, it hadn't taken him long to realise this was as good a place as anywhere to stay. Why fight your way into the city when there was nowhere to go?

He had dealt with intruders before and he could do it again. As he lay back to sleep, he felt for his semi-automatic. As always, he slept with it by his side. Not that anything could get to him up here, but it still made sense. Always sleep with your best friend at your side.

Private Dean Ferrera knew he shared the airport with one other, but they kept apart. The other man stayed in a lounge inside the terminal. He could get out to the runways, but the terminal building itself was off limits. Going in there was suicidal; around a hundred zombies were stuck in there and he didn't have enough bullets to clear it, so there they stayed. Ferrera knew he had enough food to at least last a couple more weeks. With only one mouth to feed, he could scavenge from the other planes. The other man was armed and he could survive on whatever rations had been left behind in the lounge. If he ran out, tough. This is the way the world is now. Kill or get killed; eat or get eaten.

There wasn't enough to share with anyone else. He would have to check out the intruders tomorrow. If they came into the airport, he would make sure they didn't interfere with his private new home; a round of shells would soon see to that.

Ferrera slept soundly, looking forward to the next day. It had been a few days since he had been able to shoot someone. It looked like he would be getting some target practise after all. Got to stay sharp, he thought, as he drifted back to sleep.

CHAPTER TWENTY ONE

Two military jets scorched past overhead and woke Tom with a startle. They flew low over the building and the walls rattled. Pots of paints jittered and jostled across the hard concrete of the storeroom. Tom jumped up, opened the door, and raced outside as the others woke.

"What is it?" said Christina joining him.

The jets had left vapour trails in the early morning sky and the planes were now just distant specks on the horizon.

"Military, travelling south I think. The speed they were going, they didn't come from this airport, but it's a good sign, right? It means someone is taking action. It means someone is organising things. It means we still have a chance."

Jackson appeared beside Tom and yawned. "Was that what I thought it was?"

"Yep," said Tom. Whilst his body ached, he felt invigorated by the sight of the jets. "Military. Two of them."

The sky was a light blue and Jackson yawned again. It had been several days now since he had gotten a good sleep. He looked over to the airport. "I don't see any military camp."

"Maybe they're not based here?" said Christina.

"They would've left help though," said Tom. "Directions at least. Come on, let's rouse everyone and get going."

He went back excitedly into the shed as Jackson walked over to Christina.

"What do you think?" she said.

"Well, I'm not sure. The jets are a damn good sign, that's for sure. It could just be that Tom's right. We've made it this far. We have to check it out and hope for the best."

Rosa and Jessica stumbled out, blinking as the sun beamed down upon their faces. Jackson saw they looked tired, still. Jessica especially looked as though she had the weight of the world on her shoulders. From the low angle of the sun, he guessed they had slept for three hours, no more than that. Tom came out with Benzo.

"Christ Almighty," said Jackson rushing to help him. The skin on Benzo's face was stretched taught and his capillaries had broken. His face was etched with pain and sickly brown algae grew from the wound where Reggie had bitten him. It trailed down his cheek to his neck where it almost reached a line of blisters that arced their way around his jawbone.

"You should leave me here," said Benzo quietly. "Just leave me be. I just want to sleep."

"No," said Jackson firmly, helping Tom take Benzo's weight. "You're coming with us."

They all wandered over the crest of the hill and looked down the river bank. Tom and Jackson held Benzo up between them.

"Christina, um, where's the boat?" said Jessica. "This is the right place, isn't it? I'm sure we left it about here."

"Oh shit." Christina scanned up and down the bank, but it was nowhere to be seen.

"It must've drifted off. I guess the tide came up. We had nothing to anchor it with. It's gone."

"Oh give me a break," said Tom wearily.

"Fine, then we'll walk," said Rosa twitching her nose. "There might be a gap in the fence somewhere."

"We can't, Rosa, it's too far." Jackson and Tom lowered Benzo to the ground. He lay on the grass and closed his eyes. "Benzo can't walk all that way," said Jackson.

"Well I hate to say it, but..."

"Then don't say it, Rosa," said Jessica. "Just don't." She glared at Rosa who stormed off back to the shed.

"Just leave me," slurred Benzo quietly. "I don't mind, truly. It's okay."

Jackson lifted him up. He put his arms underneath Benzo and dragged him to his feet. "Tom help me, we'll carry him."

"All the way to the airport?"

"Tom Goode, so help me God, you help me pick him up or..."

He was interrupted by an odd trundling sound. Rosa was pushing a cleaning cart along the road to them from the shed. She had thrown the chemicals and bottles onto the ground and she pushed it over the grass to Jackson.

"Thank you, Rosa," Jackson said as he and Tom helped Benzo onto it. Benzo sat on the cart, his legs dangling off the front. He held onto the sides.

"Jessica, come here," said Benzo. He struggled to sit upright and he swayed as he spoke. Jessica came to him and took his hand.

"Remember what I said," he whispered to her. "If I fall asleep again..."

Benzo grabbed her other hand that was holding the cross and she understood. She knew what he was asking. He let her go and Jackson began pushing the cart back to the road.

"Let's go then. It's probably about a half mile or so I would reckon to the airport. Keep your eyes open for any gaps in the fence, anything at all. Watch out for trouble too and if you see anything, shout," said Tom.

As they left, Jessica looked up Rosa. "I'm sorry, I..."

"You never gave me a chance. You thought I was going to suggest we just leave him here to die alone, didn't you? Die alone out here? Thanks for the faith, Jess. Whatever."

Rosa turned away and walked beside Jackson. Christina and Caterina walked behind them, while Tom led the way on his own, alert for any path or gate through the fence to the runway.

Jessica rubbed the cross in her hands. The silver glistened in the morning sunshine. She was so quick tongued she knew she often spoke before she thought. She felt like hurling the cross into the river and held it aloft. The breeze brought the salty smell of the river to her and she brought her arm back down. This was not the time to give up.

Jessica trudged after the others feeling ashamed. She liked to think she was tough, streetwise, but that was only part of her makeup. She had dropped the paddle back there last night and compromised all their safety. She had berated Rosa in front of everyone. When the time came, she would use the cross; use it to kill anything that endangered them again. All she could hope to offer was some protection. Benzo had saved her in the Fiscal

Industries building and taken her back to his friends. They had accepted her and protected her, and like it or not, she was part of this group now. She didn't have time to feel sorry for herself. Benzo was dying and she owed him her life. If necessary, she would do what she had to do when the time came; for the benefit of everyone.

As they walked, Tom noticed the warning signs on the fence. Every hundred yards there was a notice, pinned to a pillar, advising them that the fence was electrified and monitored twenty four hours a day. A red jagged lightning bolt accompanied the warning sign. They kept walking. There were no zombies around that they could see. Water flanked either side of the runway and the airport began to take shape as they got closer.

There were still planes surrounding the terminal and vehicles of varying size: loaders, vans, and cars. As they got closer, Tom saw military vehicles. He counted three jeeps and a truck. There was even a small helicopter perched at the edge of the runway. He couldn't see any soldiers or barriers though. There seemed to be no activity of any sort.

"If we go much further, we're going to end up heading away from the airport," he said stopping.

The road began to curve away from the runway, toward a parking barrier. From there, Tom could see a car park and then just more buildings.

"So what do you reckon?" said Christina.

Tom was looking at the fence with interest. "I think we have to climb over the fence."

"Climb over an electric fence? What?" she answered.

Tom strode over to the fence and grabbed it. Jessica and Rosa screamed. Tom let go of the fence and stepped back. He pointed back at the fence, a few feet behind them. A seagull was perched on top of it, watching nothing in particular.

"Shit, Tom, you could have said," said Jessica.

"You know Tom, everything has to be dramatic," chuckled Benzo.

"I only just noticed it," said Tom. "The power must be out. Looks like we finally caught a break."

He put his fingers through the wires and climbed up. The fence was shaky, but not too difficult. When he reached the top, he sat astride one of the posts, legs both side of the fence, and reached a hand down.

"Next?"

Christina climbed up and he helped her over. When she had dropped down the other side, onto the grass verge beside the runway, Caterina began climbing too. Rosa and Jessica followed. When they were all safely over, Jackson wheeled Benzo right up to the fence.

"You hold onto me, mate, Tom will help you over."

Benzo tried to smile, but his face was covered in blotches and mould, and his gums were bleeding so his smile seemed more like an evil grimace. Jackson lifted Benzo onto his back and climbed up the fence. When he was halfway up, Tom leant down and pulled Benzo up. He hoisted him over the fence and on the other side Christina took hold of Benzo's legs.

"Got him," she said. Tom let go and Benzo sank into Christina's arms. She knelt on the ground cradling him as Tom and Jackson came over.

"It's not far now, Benzo," she said.

He coughed and bloody saliva trickled out of his mouth. His eyelids fluttered, but he stayed conscious. "Thanks, mum," he said.

Jackson picked him up and threw Benzo onto his back again. Benzo draped his arms over Jackson's shoulders and they continued on. They were inside the airport perimeter now. If they could just find a way into the terminal, they might find help. Jackson ignored the pain in his back. The weight of Benzo's body slumped over him made Jackson feel like he was walking through quicksand. Every step sent jarring pain searing into his brain.

A piece of paper flitted around Caterina's feet and she stepped on it. She picked it up and read it.

"Wait!" she said.

"What is it?" asked Christina.

"I don't know. It's some kind of evacuation notice. Here, look." Caterina handed the paper to Christina.

"This is an enforced evacuation of the Greater London area," she read. "All residents are advised to meet at their local community centre or nearest police station. Do not bring any belongings or bags with you. Anyone doing so will be turned away or forced to leave them behind."

Christina stopped reading aloud and muttered something inaudible. To Caterina it sounded a lot like 'we're fucked.'

"Go on," said Tom. "What else?"

"All train, underground, and bus stations, airports and ports, will be sealed as at 01.00 hours on the sixteenth. Any attempt to leave after this time will be met with deadly force. The infection must be contained. There will be a zero tolerance for any signs of infection. All healthy citizens are urged to evacuate as instructed or, we repeat, face deadly force. There's a signature on the bottom and it's printed on government paper. There's some sort of insignia at the bottom from the Department of Defence."

"The sixteenth? That was two days ago wasn't it?" said Jessica.

"Are you fucking kidding? You mean we've been left behind? There's no help coming?" said Rosa.

"I don't care what that bullshit says," said Jackson. "I'm not stopping now." He turned and carried on walking toward the terminal with Benzo on his shoulders.

"Jackson, they said deadly force. What if..?" Jessica caught up with him.

"Do you see anything, Jess? The only deadly force around here is this stinking infection and the millions of dead it's left behind. The military? Don't make me laugh. They're long gone."

"I agree," said Caterina, "I don't see anyone around. I say let's keep going. Even if there's nobody here we need a decent rest, some food. I'm so hungry and tired."

"Medical supplies," said Jackson determinedly. "We need medical supplies for Benzo."

They walked on, following Jackson. If the whole city had been evacuated, thought Tom, they were going to struggle to get out. Would they be able to find another boat? Would the roads be blocked? Surely if they got to the city edge and could prove they weren't infected, the army would have to help them? Getting to the city's edge would be a tall order though. The anxious group walked on with similar thoughts; sullen, worried thoughts. They had been abandoned.

They didn't notice the aeroplane's door open. A lone figure walked down the steps onto the runway and watched the group approach down the runway. The figure took up a position behind one of the deserted army jeeps, crouched down out of sight, and trained his scope on the advancing party. When they were close, he fired a warning shot that whistled just above their heads.

"That's far enough!" shouted Private Ferrera.

They dropped to the ground, Caterina and Rosa screaming.

"Don't shoot!" shouted Tom. Jackson continued walking.

"I said that's far enough. That was a warning shot. Any closer and I am authorised to use deadly force. Stop!"

Jackson continued walking toward the vehicles. He wasn't sure where the shot had come from, but he knew it was a lone shot. If the army had left a post here to guard the airport, they would have had a bigger welcoming party than one man with a gun.

"We're unarmed civilians," shouted Jackson. "You are not at war with us soldier, so stand down. The enemy is the other side of that fence. I have an injured man here who needs urgent medical assistance. I demand..."

"You demand? You demand?" Ferrera stood up, staying behind the jeep and keeping the gun trained on Jackson.

"God damn it," said Ferrera quietly as he decided what to do next. This old man was not taking him seriously. Ferrera couldn't risk getting infected.

Another bullet shattered the tarmac in front of Jackson as Ferrera fired again, his shot missing Jackson by millimetres. It spat up gravel and dirt from the runway and Jackson finally stopped walking. He slumped to the ground and lowered Benzo down gently off his shoulders.

"You're too late for help. You need to turn around and keep walking. My next shot will *not* miss," shouted Ferrera.

Jackson knelt over Benzo, his head blocking the sun, shielding it from Benzo's red tired eyes.

"It's okay, Benzo, I'm going to find help," Jackson said.

Another figure walked out from the terminal behind the soldiers. Tom watched as the other man slipped out of a door quietly. He didn't appear to be with the military; he wore black trousers and shoes with a white shirt. He was, however, holding a gun too. The man was sneaking up on the soldier stealthily.

"What the hell is this?" whispered Tom quietly to Christina. She slowly shook her head, too scared to speak in case the soldier fired again and decided to take someone's head off. Jackson stood up and took a step forward. He was now about fifteen feet from the soldier.

"Back off. I gave you a chance to leave," shouted Ferrera. "You've run out of warnings, old timer."

Jackson watched as Ferrera aimed his gun carefully at him.

"Jesus, we shouldn't have come here," whispered Jessica.

"We need help, that's all," said Jackson holding his hands up. He had faced bigger boys with bigger toys over his lifetime. "Then we'll leave, okay?"

Jackson took another step forward. Tom braced himself, expecting the soldier to fire, to shoot Jackson dead before their very eyes. The other man suddenly appeared from behind a truck and startled them all.

"Ferrera, leave them," barked the lone man.

"Back off, I'm dealing with this," said Ferrera surprised. He whirled round and the two men pointed their guns at one another.

"Not any more, these people need our help," said the man.

"We've got a good thing going here, mate. You've got yours and I've got mine. I thought we were clear on that?" said Ferrera. "Don't go spoiling things now. You know full well these people are probably infected. We can't risk letting them in. I won't risk it. You..."

A gunshot rang out and they all ducked; Tom, Christina, Caterina, Jessica, and Rosa, dropped to the ground instantly. Jackson stayed on his feet and watched as the soldier crumpled. Ferrera let out a scream and fired his gun, but the bullets missed wildly and tore through the truck by the lone man. Jackson watched as the man who had shot the soldier raced out from behind the truck, apparently unharmed, and kicked Ferrera's gun away. It skidded over the tarmac and came to rest underneath a car, well out of reach of the soldier.

Jackson strode over to help, as Ferrera continued to scream. Blood was pouring from his gut. The lone man handed his gun to Jackson.

"Here, hold this. If he moves, shoot him again."

Jackson took the weapon and shook the stranger's hand vigorously.

"Thank you, thank you. Can you help us? Do you know what's going on? We've an injured man here who's sick, we..."

"Slow down," said the man. "I'll help you best I can."

The stranger had begun tying Ferrera's hands and feet, although Jackson suspected it would prove to be redundant; from the look of the pale soldier, he didn't have long left. Ferrera's screaming had stopped and he was shaking and shivering, holding his stomach.

"It's all right guys, we're safe," called Jackson to the others. Rosa sank to her knees sobbing and Jessica put an arm around her. She was so relieved she let her tears flow too, trying to wash away the tension from her head.

"Who's injured?" asked the man as he finished tying Ferrera up. He took the gun back from Jackson. "That man you brought here, is he infected?"

"Yes, is there a cure? Is there anything you can do?"

"What's your name?" asked the man putting the gun back in his belt.

"Jackson."

"Well, Jackson, if your friend is infected, then unfortunately there's nothing we can do. The best thing you can do for your friend now, is to put him out of his misery and put a bullet between his eyes."

Jackson looked downcast. He looked back toward Benzo still lying on the ground. Tom and Christina were kneeling over Benzo and obscured him from Jackson's vision. They knew the end was near and were trying to comfort him. Jessica and Rosa were still a little way off, holding each other as the harsh sun dried their tears.

"We don't have a gun," said Jackson forlornly. "We thought maybe...will you...can you..?"

The stranger nodded and looked down at Ferrera who was quiet now. They had propped the soldier up against the tyre of a truck and his face was almost white. Ferrera's clothes were soaked in blood and he knew he was dying. Jackson led the strange man across the tarmac.

"Sorry about the welcoming party, I should've taken care of him earlier," said the stranger.

"What's your name?" Jackson asked him as they walked.

"Enrique, Enrique Benzema. But call me Harry. I'm a DI in the Met'. Was..."

Jackson only half took in the man's words. He was thinking about Benzo. His friend was dying and there was nothing they could do. He had thought they might find help here at the airport: a way out, a cure, something to give them hope. Now he felt none. Jackson felt empty. All they had found was a psychotic soldier and an abandoned airport. As they neared the others, Jackson suddenly stopped.

"Wait. Your name again, Benzema. Did you say DI Benzema?"

"Yeah?" The man saw that Jackson recognised his name and felt for his gun. In this new world, you couldn't be too careful. Surprises now were rarely good ones.

"Harry, I don't suppose you're the same DI Benzema that would have a son, Marin Benzema? Benzo, we call him. We worked together at Fiscal Industries? Is that..."

"Yes," said the man clearly shocked. "How do you know? Do you know where he is? I've been trying to..."

DI Benzema trailed off when he saw Jackson's face drop. He turned to the group and they parted. After searching and waiting for days, Harry finally saw his son. His little boy, Marin, lay on the tarmac. Benzo looked dead already.

"Marin!"

As Harry crouched over Benzo, Tom went over to Jackson.

"Who is he? What's going on?"

"That's Benzo's father, Harry."

Jackson left as Tom watched Harry cradling Benzo. Tom knew that Benzo was barely holding onto life. He was surprised he had made it this far. Tom motioned for Christina, Jessica, and Caterina to follow him.

"We need to give them some space," said Tom explaining to the others who the stranger was.

Tom found Jackson with the soldier. He was holding him up by his shirt collar and the soldier's arms hung limply at his side. Jackson was forcing Ferrera back against the truck.

"What the hell is wrong with you? What the hell is going on? Answer me, God damn it!"

"You know what's going on, don't bullshit me. What, have you been living under a rock?" Ferrera coughed and a thin trickle of blood spilled from his mouth.

"Where is everyone? Where's the army, the survivors, the police?" Jackson said, shaking Ferrera.

Tom and Christina looked on, unwilling to step in. Quite frankly, they were content to let Jackson interrogate this soldier. Caterina was quiet and eager to hear the story too.

"You really don't know? Ha!" Ferrera laughed but the attempt to smile only brought more pain. "The country is under quarantine. You should've left with the evacuation. You're as good as dead now. Like me."

Jackson let go of Ferrera and he fell to the ground. He curled up into a ball. Jackson stormed off shaking his head. Tom bent down and took Ferrera's hand.

"Tell me."

"Some infection," said Ferrera. "Something crazy. It happened quickly, spread out like wildfire. Reckoned it started near Westminster Bridge. London was gone within twenty four hours."

"What do you mean, 'gone'? You're telling me some superbug killed millions of people that quickly? It doesn't exist," said Tom.

"Superbug? You could call it that. We had orders not to let it get into the public domain, but I guess it's too late for that now. It was some sort of *alien* infection. That's why we couldn't stop it. There was just no way of containing it. Last I heard, they were working on a cure, but..."

"What's the survival rate?" asked Tom.

"Zero. You get infected, you die. Simple. At first, we tried to quarantine the city, but it spread too fast. I was stationed here to guard the airport. Our orders were relayed to us remotely until finally they stopped coming. My platoon split not long after, went their own way. Some tried for home, some said they were going to try to get a boat or a plane."

"And did they? I mean there must be a way out?"

Ferrera shrugged. "What do you think? We didn't get many out of the city before it was closed down. Based on the numbers they worked out, how many died and how many lived. In round numbers...barely one per cent. You lot must've been shit lucky to keep out of it for so long."

Only one per cent, thought Tom. If that were so, then in a city of about six million there could be fifty to sixty thousand left alive, if that. Of those, how many had survived the last few days on the streets without weapons, aid, water, and food?

"So when you closed down the city, what happened to the rest of the country?" said Christina. She was stood behind Tom, arms folded.

Ferrera looked up at her and then back down to Tom. "That got fucked too. I heard of outbreaks in all the cities, all the way up to Scotland."

Ferrera winced and drew in a sharp breath. "Shit, are you going to help me or what?"

Tom let go of his hand and stood. "What do you say, Christina?"

"Leave him to rot," she said. Christina took Tom's hand and they left Ferrera in the shadow of the truck. "Tom, he said 'alien.' Do you think he was telling the truth? Sounds a bit..."

"Far-fetched? Yeah, but I believe him. He's got nothing to gain by lying to us now. Whatever is happening to us doesn't seem like anything I've ever heard of or seen before. I guess it's as likely as anything else." Tom could see Caterina walking toward them. "Look, Christina, I don't think there's anything to gain by letting the others know what he said, about the alien thing. Keep it between us for now."

Christina nodded as Caterina joined them. They surveyed the scene in front of them. Jessica and Rosa were still sat on the tarmac, tired, scared, and drained.

"If what he says is true, Tom," said Christina, "then we don't just need to get out of the city, we need to get out of the country. And quick. If so few people survived this thing, then there might be a quarter of a million people left in the whole of the country, if we're lucky."

"And it's not the six million zombies in London we have to worry about either," said Tom. "If it's taken this country, then there are around seventy million zombies trying to sniff us out."

"Jesus Christ guys, look," said Caterina.

Benzo was getting to his feet. Harry was only a few feet away from him, watching. Benzo stood and seemed to wobble. His neck was leaning to one side and his arms were stiff. They heard Benzo emit a low growl before Harry pulled his gun out and shot him in the head. Benzo's body crashed to the ground and Harry fell to his knees.

CHAPTER TWENTY TWO

Freddy banged on the door unable to escape. The office had become a cell from which he would never escape. The financial ties that bound him to Fiscal Industries would never break, never let him go now. He would spend the rest of his days in the world his living body had longed for.

Rob wandered through the underground car park. His rotting body had followed the crowds underneath the building when the others had escaped, but in the darkness, his infected brain had lost track of the living, lost track of what it was supposed to be doing, and left his body to shamble the damp darkness and the dark dampness endlessly.

Cindy's body was perfectly preserved. Save for the bullet hole where her eye should be, she looked as beautiful as the day she was born. To the inquisitive rodents who scampered across the frigid floor, it looked like she was sleeping soundly in the cold locker she had been left in. She had died cleanly, uninfected, and this huge fridge would hold her until the building fell.

Chloe and Amber finally found peace on the sixteenth floor. Chloe's body lay where Brad and Tom had left it, her skull crushed, her arms and hands tangled in the mess of wires beneath her desk where she had sat for months on end giving out useless advice. Amber's charred remains hid the abuse that Brad had dispensed upon her. Her burning body had bounced around the office until it finally gave into nature, accepting it was dead, and collapsed. Her corpse was next to Troy, who in turn was spread-eagled over Dina. Her bloated carcass had been unable to get out from under a pile of bodies and it still twitched now, unable to muster enough energy from its torn useless limbs to stand.

Ranjit had no resting place. Once he had been ripped apart, he had been devoured, only his belt buckle and gold wedding ring not ingested by the cannibalistic zombies. Mrs Conway from Greenwich had eaten his legs, a young girl who used to be called Sally, shared his face with a recently deceased stockbroker, and Ranjit's ample belly had provided several schoolchildren with enough fresh meat to keep them going for weeks.

Parker had not moved from the spot he had died in the conference centre. That is to say, his infected corpse had indeed awoken, but had found itself trapped in a small room with nothing but a table of mouldy sandwiches for company. Parker's body had stumbled around the room for thirty seven hours before it succumbed to a strange apathy and slumped back down on the very spot it had expired. The infected body listened, smelt the air and tried to *sense* the living; it could not. Parker would stay there for several days before a passing survivor would rouse his body into the big bad outside world.

Reggie was in the church, his stiff body still prostrate on the cold stones where Benzo had smashed his brains in. Michelle's baby had been eaten, but she had ventured further than most. With her body in tatters, she had still managed to haul herself down the stairs and out of the Fiscal Industries building into the courtyard. Leaving a trail of rotting guts and intestines behind her, Michelle's body had walked out of the plaza, across the bridge and for no apparent reason, onto the A13. At one point, a group of the living, survivors, had raced past her, but she had been unable to catch them before they passed her. She followed in their wake, along with several thousand other dead, but the group had frustratingly escaped by a small boat on the Thames. Once her dead eyes watched them float out of sight, she had resumed hunting the living on land, day and night, the hunger that could never be satisfied never leaving her.

Jackson held the list in his hands and stared at it. He stared at it, memorising the names on it. The roll call of the dead was a long one. Other than himself, only Tom and Caterina had survived from the office. Everyone else was dead. He was thankful for Christina,

Jessica, and Rosa too, but he felt lonely. His wife, Mary, was dead. His friends were dead. His sister, her children, their pets, their friends, their teachers, their doctors and dentists: all dead.

"Drink?" Tom offered Jackson a glass and sat down beside him. Jackson took it and drank. He folded the paper up and put it back in his pocket.

"What's that?" said Tom.

"Nothing," said Jackson. He reclined in the sofa, feeling guilty that he should be here, sitting in this comfortable chair drinking wine as if he didn't have a care in the world.

The airport lounge was homely, warm and most of all, secure. Harry had warned them that the terminal, the rest of the building entirely however, was off limits; the dead still roamed the corridors, rooms and gates. Within the lounge though, they could do as they wished and, after Benzo had died, they had all found their way inside.

Christina and Caterina had washed up, showering in icy cold water, not caring how cold it was, just relishing in its freshness, thankful to feel clean once again. They had found a couple of discarded coats and left their dirty clothes to dry, having rinsed them in the same shower. Jessica had coaxed Rosa into the building eventually, but she had withdrawn into herself. Jessica had given Rosa food and water, but she'd refused to speak. Finally, Jessica had lain Rosa down on a couch, covered her with a blanket, and left her alone. Rosa succumbed to a light sleep, utterly exhausted, leaving Jessica to herself.

Tom had wanted to talk to her, but the shock of seeing Benzo die had been too much for all of them. They were malnourished, weak, scared: they had taken this refuge, this bizarre home, and crashed. They had all found their own place to hunker down and think, letting their minds and bodies crash until they could think clearly again. The dead were always close.

Tom had left Harry alone outside with his dead son, and like sinking into a pit of tar, let sleep pull his aching body onto the nearest seat in the lounge. He had slept for five hours and when he'd awoken, he was hungry. The bar was well stocked and he devoured crisps, shortbread, and biscuits, before downing two pints of water.

"Is that right?" asked Jackson looking at the ticking clock above the bar.

"I think so," said Tom. "Feels right."

They both turned to look out of the window at the runway. The sun was still high, yet it was mid-afternoon. The clouds had skittered away and left an untarnished deep blue sky. Tom thought about the jets they had seen earlier. Before he could say anything Jackson spoke.

"How's he doing?"

"As well as can be expected I suppose," said Tom. Harry was still outside, sat on the tarmac. About an hour ago, Jackson watched him pick up Benzo's body and take it somewhere out of sight. After a few minutes, Harry returned and sat on the tarmac ever since.

"And how are you doing?" said Jackson.

"Yeah, fine I suppose. I...I guess, I don't know really. I'm alive. We're here. That's all. You?"

"I'm here, but I don't know why. So many younger, healthier people should be here instead of me. Benzo should be sat here now talking to you, not me."

"Don't beat yourself up, Jackson, it's nobody's fault. We all did our best and we all knew the risks out here. It's just..."

"...Shit," said Jackson finishing Tom's sentence.

"Yeah, it's shit."

Tom got up and grabbed two bottles of beer from the bar.

"I'm going out to see him."

Jackson watched as Tom went back outside, feeling the afternoon warmth temporarily invading the cool lounge as the door swung open.

Tom sat down beside Harry on the tarmac. They said nothing and Harry took the beer from Tom. They sat on the runway, past the army trucks and jeeps, away from Ferrera's body, looking out at the city through the chain link fence that surrounded them.

It was quiet. After the past few days, Tom felt it more so; the quietness and stillness unnervingly unusual. He knew that a few feet away, the other side of the lounge, there were a hundred zombies. Yet, out here, the only movement came as a seagull flew overhead, wheeling away silently. Nothing approached the fence, no more jets flew overhead and no traffic noise reached them. The sun's heat rebounded from the tarmac and Tom began sweating after only a few minutes. He wondered how Benzo's father could stand it out here all day.

"Did you know him well?" said Harry.

"Quite well, but not for long. We've been together the last few days, ever since this thing started," said Tom. "Jackson knows him better than anyone. Benzo saved my life, all our lives."

"He was a good son," said Harry. "I knew he'd come here. He was a thinker, was my boy. He was going to make something of himself. When he was five, we thought about having another kid, giving him a brother or sister you know, but we couldn't. I'm glad now."

Tom didn't respond but sipped on the cold beer, beads of sweat trickling down his neck.

"So tell me, how did you get here, why the airport?"

"How we got here is a long story. Why? Well, we just figured it made sense; it's the closest place to the city where we thought we might be able to find help and get out of here."

"Good idea," said Harry. "I was banking on it. I tried to get to your office, to reach Benzo, but it was impossible. They're everywhere. The whole city is infested. I managed to get home, but my wife was already gone. One of the neighbours had broken in and...well, anyway, there was no point waiting at home. I knew Benzo had more sense than to try too.

"It was a long shot, but I eventually made it here and just kept my fingers crossed Benzo would make it too. I'm glad you came today - I was going to give up tomorrow. There's only so much food in there and with Ferrera taking half of it, things were...tense."

"I'm sorry about Benzo," said Tom.

Harry chugged on his beer until half of it was gone. "So tell me, how *did* you get here? How did Benzo end up like that? We've plenty of time now," he said, smiling at Tom.

They talked for a couple of hours with just the sun, the sky, and cold beer for company. When the sun finally sank behind the nearby buildings and the cool shade crept up on them, they went back inside.

Once inside the lounge, Jackson made a beeline for Harry.

"Sorry for your loss, Harry, Benzo was a good man. He was my friend," he said shaking hands.

"Appreciate that," said Harry. Jackson saw a different man to that he had met earlier. He had looked into the eyes of a man earlier who had looked desperate, a man who had killed to survive, who hadn't found what he was looking for. Now he saw something stronger.

Harry went to the bar and pulled a cold bottle of water out.

"I'm sorry we met like this everyone, but I'd like to talk to all of you, if that's okay?"

His self-assured posture and resonant voice brought instant attention and focus in the room. Jessica and Rosa got up from the couch and ventured over to him, Caterina and Christina too, finding large plush chairs to sit in nearby, whilst Tom and Jackson leant against the bar. With the small group of six sat around him expectantly, Harry began.

"I'm Harry, for those of you who haven't met me. There are a few things we should talk about. First of all, I want to thank you for bringing my son here. I know things didn't turn out the way I'd hoped, but I'm thankful that I was able to see him again one last time before he died. For that I am indebted to all of you."

"To Benzo and all our friends, past and present," said Jackson holding up a glass. There were small murmurs toasting Benzo and their dead friends. Harry continued.

"Secondly, I assume, and hope, that you will stay here tonight? There is plenty of room for all of us. If you want some privacy, then Private Ferrera was staying in the aeroplane out there, you can stay there if you like. Within the fence, we're safe. The plane is safe too. I don't think Ferrera will be using it anymore."

"Speaking of which," said Christina, "I don't mean to be blunt, but I think we should do something about him. I mean we can't just leave him out there, what if his body attracts...them?"

"Agreed. When we're through, Tom and I are going to take care of him. We'll dispose of the body in the river. Anyone object?"

Nobody said anything and Harry went on.

"I should add, before I go on, that I am *not* in charge. I am simply taking the floor as I've been talking to Tom, and it sounds like I know a bit more about our situation than the rest of you. I'll fill you all in as best I can, but then any decisions we make will be made by *us*. By you.

"This thing, this infection; once it gets hold of you, there is no way back. There is no cure. By rights, as soon as Marin, I mean Benzo, was infected, you should've taken care of him. That means if any one of us gets infected, we have to expect the same. And that also means, be careful. You're safe within the airport perimeter, but don't go attracting unnecessary attention. Make too much noise and they'll be on us in a heartbeat. These walls are not that thick, and I don't need to tell you what is on the other side."

"What happened to everyone?" said Caterina. "Is there any chance my parents might still be...?"

"No," said Harry. "The authorities tried to enforce a curfew, they tried to evacuate, but it was too late. From the city only a few hundred got out."

"Out of millions, you're saying only a few hundred got away?" Christina felt Caterina's hand tighten around hers.

"I'm afraid the chances of finding a loved one alive are worse than winning the lottery. Actually, that brings me on to my next point."

"How to find your loved ones," said Jackson quietly.

"Exactly." Harry poured himself a glass of water. "Nobody is coming for us. There will be no rescue missions, no flotilla of boats to take us away, and the SAS is not going to parachute in and whisk us away in a tank or a helicopter or anything else you might have dreamed about. I'm only telling you this so you are aware of all the facts.

"Speaking from experience, I can tell you that we were reliant on technology that ultimately proved pointless: guns, bombs, satellites and fast cars. Nothing could save us. The city, the whole country in fact, was so bloody over crowded that when one got infected, it spread to the next like an unstoppable chain reaction. It was dog eat dog.

"There is no police anymore. There is no government. There are no doctors and nurses, no hospitals, no schools. What's left of the British army is dying out there on the tarmac with its guts hanging out, ready to be the next meal for whatever zombie stumbles this way. We are on our own. Completely on our own."

"Don't hold back, eh?" said Jessica. "So what are you saying, we might as well have one last big alcohol-fuelled orgy and then slit our wrists?"

"No, he's not saying that," said Tom.

"If I thought that, then I wouldn't be stood here now," said Harry. "Neither would you. You're here because you're a fighter; a survivor. You didn't make it this far with an apathetic attitude, so please don't grow one now. No, what I'm saying is we need a plan; a concrete plan that will get us out of the country safely, all of us, and all in one piece."

"But how, where?" said Rosa. "We haven't got further than three miles yet and you think we can leave the country? Do you know how to fly a plane, because I can't see how else we're getting out of here?"

"What about a boat?" said Jackson. "We got this far with a tiny piece of shit boat no bigger than this sofa - if we find something bigger, maybe we can get across the channel?"

Harry was shaking his head. "Any of you know how to steer a boat? Any of you even know the difference between starboard and port? Between a rudder and mast?"

"I'd give it a try. Better than staying here and waiting to die," said Jessica.

Harry smiled. "I hear you on that one, Jess. But if we flew a plane out of here, we would almost certainly be shot down in two minutes. If we tried to sail a ship, no matter how big or small, we'd be blown out of the water."

"Why?" said Tom. "They'd have to know we weren't infected. Zombies don't fly planes."

"Doesn't matter," said Harry. "When you contain and isolate an incident that's exactly what you do. This whole country is, effectively, isolated now. Britain has been contained, like a specimen in a jar. You think the Americans or the Russians are going to risk the end of their country, the end of the world, just to save half a dozen Brits? There's too much at stake, too much money at stake for that. For all they know, we've got something on board that could be infected and that's a threat to them. In times of war, threats are dealt with as they only know how."

"Deadly force, right?" said Jackson.

"You got anything stronger than water, Harry?" said Christina. He plucked a beer from the fridge and tossed it to her. As she opened it, Caterina grabbed it and stole a quick mouthful.

"I think I'm forgiven, under the circumstances," she said winking, passing the bottle back to Christina.

"So what then?" said Tom.

Harry sighed. "In the force I had some good contacts and I was party to a lot of information that, shall we say, is not common knowledge. My boss, a friend, a good friend that I trust, knew I wouldn't leave without my son. I talked to him before he got out and he told me that if I made it, there would be only one way out of the country. They would leave the door open as long as possible, but that door closes tomorrow.

"We have to get to France. Not by air or sea, but underground. It's the only way."

"The tunnel?" said Christina. "Shit, really?"

"Back underground again?" said Jessica. "No way, we tried that once and it cost us a friend. Parker was bitten down there in the dark and we nearly didn't make it out."

"It might work," said Tom. "You know for sure it's safe?"

"Pretty sure," said Harry. "As soon as the infection broke out, the tunnel was closed off at both ends. It's not sealed though, there's still a way in. The Super' told me it would only be sealed seven days after it began. It won't be sealed this end, there's no one here to do it."

"So our fate is in the hands of the French?" said Jackson. "Then we really are fucked."

"Think on it," said Harry. "Getting to the tunnel entrance is the hard part. If we can do that, the tunnel will be deserted. There's no reason for the dead to go down there, nothing to attract them. It's a long walk, but I think it's our best shot."

"Why don't we just stay here?" said Jessica. "Find a deserted part of the country, an old house or something and stay there. They can't leave Britain forever, surely?"

"True, not forever," said Harry. "There's a lot of land here that's valuable to the right people. Someone will come back eventually. Of course, it's contaminated by seventy million infected dead bodies, so it would have to be purified first."

"Purified?" said Jessica nervously. "You mean wiped clean, like..?"

"Probably not nuclear," said Harry. "That would ruin the land for generations. My guess is a firestorm. Burn the country from top to bottom. They'd burn everything of course, leave nothing to chance. I'm not telling you that you can't stay, Jessica, maybe I'm wrong. But I would strongly urge you to come with me."

There was silence in the room as they thought. Tom already knew his decision.

"Tom, can you help me with Ferrera? I think I'd like to shift him and have a wash. Then maybe we can talk some more?"

Harry left with Tom and the room stayed silent. It took the two of them just over half an hour to get rid of Ferrera's body. They carried him down the runway as far as possible and then threw him into a small channel of water than ran between the two runways. Ferrera's body bobbed up and down in the water as the tide gradually took him away from the airport.

"I'm coming with you," said Tom as they walked back.

"Pleased to hear it, son," said Harry. Tom welled up on hearing those words. He was remembering the day he told his father he was going to college, when his own father had used the exact same words.

They walked back to the lounge and found a greeting party when they returned. In the coolness of the lounge, Christina, Caterina, Jackson, Jessica, and Rosa stood before them.

"We're in," said Jackson.

"All of us," said Jess. She gave Tom a smile and he marvelled at how beautiful she looked, even after all that had happened.

"We'd better get some rest then," said Harry. "We'll gather up some food and water, as much as we can carry. There are guns out there too. I know Ferrera had a stash on the plane. This time tomorrow, with a little luck, we'll be out of here. If we make good time, who knows, we could be in Paris."

Could it be true, could it be real? Tom barely dared to hope. He knew he would never go home again, that was a dream that would stay just that: a dream. His parents and his friends were gone, but, looking around the room, there were clear emotions displayed on everyone's face. Where he had seen fear, there was now strength;

where he had seen despondency, he now saw optimism. This was his family now. He felt pride when he looked at them all.

Tom scratched at the itchy scab on his elbow, flecks of dead skin burying themselves beneath his fingernails. He made his way over to Jackson and the others to talk, to relax, and to laugh; to plan for the future. If there was one...

THE END

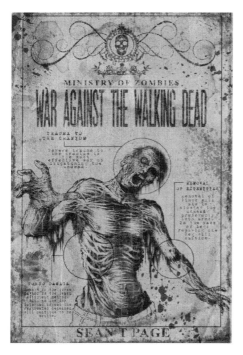

More than 63% of people now believe that there will be a global zombie apocalypse before 2050...

So, you've got your survival guide, you've lived through the first chaotic months of the crisis, what next?
Employing real science and pioneering field work, War against the Walking Dead provides a complete blueprint for taking back your country from the rotting clutches of the dead after a zombie apocalypse.

* A glimpse inside the mind of the zombie using a team of top psychics - what do the walking dead think about? What lessons can we learn to help us defeat this pervading menace?
* Detailed guidelines on how to galvanise a band of scared survivors into a fighting force capable of defeating the zombies and dealing with emerging groups such as end of the world cults, raiders and even cannibals!
* Features insights from real zombie fighting organisations across the world, from America to the Philippines, Australia to China - the experts offer advice in every aspect of fighting the walking dead.
Packed with crucial zombie war information and advice, from how to build a city of the living in a land of the dead to tactics on how to use a survivor army to liberate your country from the zombies - War against the Walking Dead may be humanity's last chance.

Remember, dying is not an option!

Available at www.severedpress.com, Amazon and most online bookstores

RESURRECTION

By Tim Curran

www.corpseking.com

The rain is falling and the dead are rising. It began at an ultra-secret government laboratory. Experiments in limb regeneration-an unspeakable union of Medieval alchemy and cutting edge genetics result in the very germ of horror itself: a gene trigger that will reanimate dead tissue...any dead tissue. Now it's loose. It's gone viral. It's in the rain. And the rain has not stopped falling for weeks. As the country floods and corpses float in the streets, as cities are submerged, the evil dead are rising. And they are hungry.

"I REALLY love this book...Curran is a wonderful storyteller who really should be unleashed upon the general horror reading public sooner rather than leter." – *DREAD CENTRAL*

Dead Bait

DEMONMACHY
Brant Danay

As the universe slowly dies, all demonkind is at war in a tournament of genocide. The prize? Nirvana. The Necrodelic, a death addict who smokes the flesh of his victims as a drug, is determined to win this afterlife for himself. His quest has taken him to the planet Grystiawa, and into a duel with a dream-devouring snake demon who is more than he seems. Grystiawa has also been chosen as the final battleground in the ancient spider-serpent wars. As armies of arachnid monstrosities and ophidian gladiators converge upon the planet, the Necrodelic is forced to choose sides in a cataclysmic combat that could well prove his demise. Beyond Grystiawa, a Siamese twin incubus and succubus, a brain-raping nightmare fetishist, a gargantuan insect queen, and an entire universe of genocidal demons are forming battle plans of their own. Observing the apocalyptic carnage all the while is Satan himself, watching voyeuristically from the very Hell in which all those who fail will be damned to eternal torment. Who will emerge victorious from this cosmic armageddon? And what awaits the victor beyond the blood-drenched end of time? The battle begins in Demonmachy. Twisting Satanic mythologies and Eastern religions into an ultraviolent grotesque nightmare, the Messiah of Death Saga will rip your eyeballs right out of your skull. Addicted to its psychedelic darkness, you'll immediately sew and screw and staple and weld them back into their sockets so you can read more. It's an intergalactic, interdimensional harrowing that you'll never forget...and may never recover from.

Available at www.severedpress.com, Amazon and most online bookstores

Zombie Zoology
Unnatural History:

Severed Press has assembled a truly original anthology of never before published stories of living dead beasts. Inside you will find tales of prehistoric creatures rising from the Bog, a survivalist taking on a troop of rotting baboons, a NASA experiment going Ape, A hunter going a Moose too far and many more undead creatures from Hell. The crawling, buzzing, flying abominations of mother nature have risen and they are hungry.

"Clever and engaging a reanimated rarity"
FANGORIA

"I loved this very unique anthology and highly recommend it"
Monster Librarian

Available at www.severedpress.com, Amazon and most online bookstores

BIOHAZARD
Tim Curran

The day after tomorrow: Nuclear fallout. Mutations. Deadly pandemics. Corpse wagons. Body pits. Empty cities. The human race trembling on the edge of extinction. Only the desperate survive. One of them is Rick Nash. But there is a price for survival: communion with a ravenous evil born from the furnace of radioactive waste. It demands sacrifice. Only it can keep Nash one step ahead of the nightmare that stalks him-a sentient, seething plague-entity that stalks its chosen prey: the last of the human race. To accept it is a living death. To defy it, a hell beyond imagining

"kick back and enjoy some the most violent and genuinely scary apocalyptic horror written by one of the finest dark fiction authors plying his trade today" HORRORWORLD

Printed in Great Britain
by Amazon.co.uk, Ltd.,
Marston Gate.